Have You Met the Hawkes?

Cc Sumner

ISBN 978-1-7750703-3-7

Text design/layout, print production: Beth Crane, WeMakeBooks.ca
Cover illustration: msonick, iStockPhoto.com

Printed and bound in Canada

I dedicate this book to my friend and partner, Carol, who can spell.
Also, for those living with Dyslexia with all its gifts
and all the challenges it creates.

CHAPTER 1

Up until the age of ten I had no memory of my life and what I was about. Life as I know it now, began the day I came to live at Hawkes Manor in the Lake District of England

I was born in New Jersey, U.S.A.; both my parents were from England and met when attending Princeton University. My mother gave birth to me and graduated with full honors all in the same week. They were pleased with the fact that their child would have dual British—US citizenship as this would give me more opportunities in life. We returned home to the Lake District and eventually became a family of five. Our principal home was in the Lake District with another house in Scotland and a flat in London.

The small plane that my family and I were in, crashed as we neared our home in Scotland. All were killed but me. The thinking at the time was I might have been pushed from the plane as I was found in another field. In my mind's eye as I lay there on the ground, I saw my parents, sister and brother walking away from the crashed plane. "Wait for me, please wait," I called out. My mother replied "not now dear" turned and never looked back. Was it a trick of the mind, a memory, or a dream? When you have nothing to remember what difference does it make?

My name is Natasha Taylor Bennett. My parents Peter and Jane Bennett were very close friends with Harry and Susan Hawkes. Both men knew each other professionally plus were childhood friends attending the same school and University. Both families gave each other legal guardianship, to their under-age children until age twenty-one.

After my recovery in hospital, I joined my new family at Hawkes Manor.

It became my home just as the Hawkes became my family; Harry, Susan and son Max plus three other children who were away at private school, so I would not get to meet them until Christmas. I grew to love them all as they loved me. Girls, identical triplets Max said they were the naughtiest sisters he ever had. As there were only a couple of years between Max and I we became constant companions.

CHAPTER 2

Often after dinner, everyone would sit around the fireplace and tell me delightful stories about their family history, well not all the tales were full of delight, but in the telling we would laugh always seeing the humor of times past. Sometimes, one by one, other times all talking at once, each one having different perceptions of the same story. Harry and Susan when first married wanted to travel before starting a family. Susan was barely twenty, so they had plenty of time to see the world. Six months later Susan was pregnant, and they had only been on one trip to see Hurry's twin sister in Australia. It was nearly Christmas on a Sunday morning when Susan delivered a daughter then another daughter, guess what the third baby was a girl. The doctor had to sit down as he was in shock. Three identical little girls!

They had been so quiet and little, nobody knew, and why not. There had been multiple births in Harry's family going back generations. Susan and babies had to stay in the hospital for a while. Harry went home and worried what were they going to do with three little girls.

The whole village helped, and it still was not enough. Whole families came together, and I can assure you they left together. Susan and Harry's mothers came to help. After a while Susan's mum went home for week's rest and returned, then Harry's mum had to go home for a rest and feed her husband. She explained "He wants me to go back home, it's best that I go now, I will be back. It is ok when they are young, full of piss and vinegar, then they start ageing and before you know it, you are running a bloody Nursing Home. Soon as I get home, your father will start complaining that his boils on his bum have flared up and are hurting."

Continuing the story Harry said, "Mum why do you stay?"

"I stay because I have been programmed to stay. Times are changing now, and my granddaughters will give themselves a freedom about which I can only dream."

"Don't go mum, there is plenty of room here."

"Harry you now have a wife and three beautiful daughters."

"I know Mum, but many men have had lots of wives and children but only one mother."

"I love your dad."

"So, do I Mum."

"Harry it's just sometimes in the evenings when he is down the pub, I get lonely. He is from a different generation back then when we were first married, and your dad was young, he and his mates thought they were the bee's knees. The young wives gave too much, and the young husbands' expectations were too high."

"Ok, this is how I feel, Mum, the freedom that you seek for my daughters will be found if my son, that I hope we will have one day, will stand with his sisters, and together will remove the yoke of oppression that has been placed on men and woman throughout history. A few men that have never known love, never felt the power to love they live in darkness, so dark they never make a shadow. I say a few men, Mum, but as we all know history is a lie. Show me the history book that gives a lot of credit to women even when the truth be told there is nothing wickeder then a wicked woman because she will do nothing, say nothing when told she is to blame for the way his life unfolds. Sometimes she smiles, as she waits… waiting for him to get old."

"Oh Harry, where do you get your stories from?"

I rang my sister, Terri, in Australia late that night and told her about our dad, and his boils on the bum, and that our mum was lonely as our dad spent his evenings down at the pub telling anybody that would listen about his boils, well that's what our mum think he says! When the truth be told according to our dad he has bullet holes in his bum from fighting in the second world war. "He was not born then said Terri laughing I am coming home, Harry., I have been away far too long. The Land of OZ is a lovely country, but I miss my mother and dad. I miss you, and I miss England's rainy days and damp nights. Harry, I have met someone, he is Scottish and twenty-four years old. His two-year work contract is up, and he does not want to renew it. He wants to return to the UK, so we can marry there. I love him so much."

My mum, dad and I were so happy she had met someone, and she was coming home to get married here in England.

■

By the time, the girls were three years old they had exhausted both sides of the family. So many nannies had been hired and if they stayed two weeks Harry and Susan were lucky, very lucky. Some of them called a taxicab to come right now, some of them couldn't wait to get out of the house so they ran down the driveway! It was not unusual for Harry to come home to find Susan and one of the girls at the doctors. The Doctor's suggestion, after seeing each of the girls over a two weeks period, was that they wear crash helmets and kneepads. "Once they start school, meeting new friends, teachers, things to learn, a new world, they should grow out of this obsession they each have about doing away with the other two," the doctor said smiling. A tear ran down Hurry's face as he remembered them as little children. "They looked like little angels; when not fighting they would cuddle and kiss each other then, come to us and cuddle and kiss and tell us how much we were loved by them. They were Susan's daughters; Susan was a wooer and for sure so were her girls. The trouble was they all wanted to be leader of the pack."

Harry was so proud the way they all turned out. They didn't know until they were grown and wanted their own birth certificates, which was born first.

Susan had written and phoned all the boarding schools for young ladies in the area. The responses were the same "NO Madam. Your first letter stated they were your children. The reply was NO, too young. Your second letter now states they are three Chinese orphans with nowhere to live. The answer is still NO. We do not take in four-year-old orphaned children." Then the local school would not take the girls for another two terms. By this time, Susan no longer referred to the triplets as the girls and only in the privacy of their bedroom they were called… well you don't have to know that! Susan now saw herself as a complete failure as a mother. Harry was always saying, "Let's go away on holiday just a few weeks. Your mother and my mother have said over and over again they would look after the girls."

"NO, Harry, NO! What if the girls killed each other, then what would we do?" Sometimes Susan could be such a Drama Queen.

CHAPTER 3

On Tuesdays, Mrs. Lovelock would arrive early in the morning to make a good breakfast. Tuesdays and Fridays were the days she cooked meat pies, cakes and 'what have you'. Harry heard a car door close and thought, that's funny Mrs. Lovelock always walks up from the village. He half expected to see the Lovelock's car outside but no it was a car he had never seen before. As he watched it drive off, Mrs. Lovelock was at the door.

"Oh, Sir Harry just the person I want to see, that was my sister, Maude, in her car. She lost her husband last year; she looked for days, never found him and it took the police two months before they found him in a ditch two fields from their home. He had fallen and hit his head. My sister said it was just as well, as he fell and broke his hip the year before and had trouble getting around. Maude is feeling lonely so she is going to stay with Arthur and me awhile. My husband says Maude can stay as long as she wants to because Maude treats him with respect and dignity. My Arthur must have heard them words on the BBC radio, as I have never heard him use words like that before now. Anyway, I was telling Maude about the triplets and youse being such a young couple; it is far too much work with three babies all at once and no experience. So, Maude asked if she could be of any help. My sister has all her certificates in childcare and has nannied a few times, and she is much more educated than I am, always going to evening classes and day courses. She won top marks in how to drive and fix an army jeep and she was not even in the army! Saved three people from drowning off the Isle of Wight where she was a lifeguard, plus my sister lived in America for a few years and did modeling for a very posh firm that made knickers and things…. Fred's Intimates No that is not right…I remember now it was FREDERICK OF HOLLYWOOD."

It was agreed Mrs. Maude Bickles would come the next day at 11:00 a.m. Harry decided not to mention this to Susan until the next morning just before 11:00 a.m. in case she got her hopes up for nothing; maybe Mrs. Bickles would not like the girls or us! The cuckoo clock struck 11:00 and Mrs. Bickles was at the door.

"My name is Susan Hawkes. Please come in". Then Susan brought Mrs. B. into the kitchen where Harry was having cup of tea. He stood to greet her; she was of average height and of normal build, nothing extraordinary about her until she looked up. It was her eyes, such green eyes. It was then he realized what a beautiful woman she was.

Susan asked about where Mrs. B. had worked and for how long and that's when she mentioned she had lived in America for a few years, "Oooooooh" said Susan "that's nice." It was at this point Harry thought, good God, she's going to tell her about modeling knickers. Mrs. Lovelock, her sister, knows. Now if Susan knows, before long the whole county will know. Well that just did not happen as Mrs. B. told us she had a baby and had left her with the father in America, who at the time could give the baby a much better life and opportunities. "Is this something I regret now? I still do not know," said Mrs. B.

She was straightforward; it would have been one thing to leave a baby behind, but to model knickers in America that would have been too much for the locals to take in.

Mrs. Bickles asked if she might see the children. Mrs. Bickles looked at the girls, looked at Harry, then looked at Susan, then she looked back at the girls.

"Who gave these girls their ridiculous haircuts"?

"We…I did said Harry. Sometimes when they were playing outside or fighting and it was too far to see which one was the lead hitter. I decided if they each had different, hairstyles it would be…Well you know." It was just a few days before Mrs. B. first came to the house. Susan had just returned from lunch with a friend in town and saw the girls playing outside Susan look stunned, "did you girls cut each other hair?" "No daddy did.

"OK dears go away and play now."

Harry had never seen Susan this mad, she came into the kitchen closed the door behind her and just stood there, with a large long stick in her hand. "What have you done to my beautiful daughters Harry?"

"Now listen here Susan," … she wacked the kitchen table with the stick.

"Shut up Harry! They now look like clowns. If we had only one daughter, it would not look so bad. Just one bad haircut, but the three of them; one has a crew cut, the next had one side of her hair cut so short it is sitting on top of her ear while the other side was hanging long, and the operative word Harry is hanging, two inches below the ear. Where did you dream up the third hairstyle? Pigtails Harry! Bloody PIGTAILS with a half inch fringe on top of her forehead. When did you see any child around here with pigtails? They look like two poodles and a dog's dinner walking along together. They will be the laughing stock of the county."

"The girls do not care," said Harry.

"Maybe not Harry, but I do." Then she wacked kitchen table again. "At school, they will be ridiculed and people will say, have you seen the triplet's hair?" "My husband thinks she did it." "Why would the mother cut their hair like that? She had been drinking I bet that's is …she was drunk and Sir Harry being such a nice man. And that, Harry," said Susan," is the way life is. It is always the mother's fault. I can hear it now. "Have you ever met the mother, well…no, but have you seen her husband he is sooo good looking and loves those little girls so much? Oh! Well somebody has to with a mother like that. To sum it all up, mothers have been blamed since the beginning of time, and by the way Harry, what is it that you do exactly? Besides having to walk a few more yards to see what your daughters are up to and checking to see if the local pub is still there. The local hairdressers are closed for the week, gone on holidays, and for sure, the girls are not going into town looking like that. You will have to wait a week before you take them to the local hairdresser for their hair to be restyled if it is possible! The only reason you are allowed to stay here in my house with my daughters is that you have more money than I do. Therefore, you had better pull your socks up Harry or I will have all the money."

Harry said, "It was true. All I did was pay the bills and left everything else for Susan to do. She was the mother of the triplets (and later a fourth, Max). She has given this old house a soul and light that shines through every window. When we first were married, Susan was so full of life all she wanted to do was travel, meet new people and have fun. Then the triplets came along and she was like a frightened little sparrow looking for support from a partner. At our age, I had no idea about the responsibility of three babies born all at the same time. Because of the hair business, I saw Susan not as a girl anymore but a woman that had to take control. She was raising three little girls and a baby husband. I came and went as I pleased. I got up in the morning when I pleased; I took the love of my wife and children and showed very little in return. I had become a lodger, a boarder, in my own home. "

∎

"Up until I was twenty-six years old I had taken shortcuts, all my life, shortcuts. When you do that, somebody else has to pick up the slack; in my case, it was Susan.

One night after Harry had been down at the pub he came home to an empty house. No children, no wife or help, just a note on the kitchen table.

The note said, "The girls and I are at my parents then we are all going up to Scotland to see my sister. My mother is so happy about the girls and I are coming for a visit without you, as you always looked bored, now we can stay for as long as we want to. When I told the girls, we are going to see Auntie Liz, Timmy and Sarah they were over the moon. I have spoken with the ladies from the village and told them there was no need for them to come to the manor while we are away. I also paid them a month wages as I was giving them such short notice and they may have been relying on the money. Harry, while we are away please make yourself useful. Maybe you can learn to use a lawn mower, wash your own clothes, and feed yourself. The larder is the third door down from the window that looks out over the pond. If you are not here when we get back, I will presume you are at your mother's."

Harry's mother was as mad as a hatter and so was his dad who said "You big lump, you can't expect her to do all the parenting and run a house. Just one of your daughters is enough to handle. I have never once heard you discipline them. They would take over the house; sometimes it was like a battlefield and you would sit there as if you were brain dead, while that poor wee wife of yours looked like she was going to have a nervous breakdown. You big lump, what happened to you? Oh, well it takes two to make a marriage."

"You are not coming back here Harry," his mother chirped in.

Susan and the girls stayed away four weeks. That was the lowest point in Harry's life. He hardly bathed, never shaved, lost over twenty pounds, and for the first time in his life, he knew his self-interest paled beside the love for his wife and daughters. All the 'she's' came home; Susan and Harry never looked back. God was in his heaven and all was right with the world.

It had been awhile since Harry and Susan had heard or seen Mrs. Bickles. Apparently, after the interview she left her sister's to return home, as someone was interested in buying her house.

They told Mrs. Lovelock that they would like to see her sister again when she returns and does she (Mrs. Lovelock) think her sister would be interested working full time as a live in.

As a result, Mrs. B. was given one of the best bedrooms in the house, plenty of sunlight and windows with a view of the village, TV, radio, double bed, toaster, small fridge and her own bathroom, and on top of all this; wages and car expenses. They even had to buy another double bed. The big event for the girls for years was a sleep over with Mrs. B. watching the tele until they fell asleep or the tele went off the air. As the girls grew, Mrs. B. was getting fed up with being kicked out of bed in the night so the girls got a new bed to themselves, then they would fight over which one would sleep in Mrs. B's bed. They saw this as un-fair that three sleeps in one bed and only one in another. It never crossed their minds that Mrs. B. should have the deciding vote—her room, her rules!

"Mrs. B's. cooking, well she can make boiling water an art form; I have never tasted food like Mrs. B. cooked. On special occasions, she would go to family friends' homes and cook a meal for their guests. Mrs. B. has gained herself quite a reputation in this part of the Lake District. She had a small list of clients that paid well, but as Mrs. B. said, "the girls come first and I will stay until Hawkes Manor no longer needs me, then maybe I will have my own business." Mrs. B. had quite lot of male admirers. When Harry saw the same car coming and going he began to worry. What if she got married again and we would lose her.

How did Mrs. B. win over the girls, it was with her cooking? When the girls gave the family a lot of trouble in the day, Mrs. B. was unavailable in the evening to cook. If the girls complained to Susan, she would say Mrs. B. was not hired to be a cook. They soon' cottoned on' if they wanted good food they had to be good, sometimes.

When I first arrived at Hawkes Manor to live, the triplets were away at school, so it was Christmas before I first met them. Mrs. B. said they had been the naughtiest children she had ever known, just looking for trouble all the time, but now they have grown to be such nice young ladies. They still like a lot of fun but it is fun now we can all share.

I was in the village getting groceries when the triplets (the girls, as everyone called them) arrived home. When I got to the manor the whole family was in the kitchen waiting for me so Mrs. B. could dish up the dinner. The three girls rushed over to meet me. Three identical faces with three identical mouths talking at the same time. Typical Sagittarians with big white teeth like a horse, tall, hippy, not bad look-ing. Two of the girls, Jennie and Claire let their hair hang loose; 'Crewe' had her hair in a ponytail. Her real name was Sara but after the haircut business when Sir Harry gave all three young girls silly haircuts, Sara's cut was a Crew cut and the name stuck. Nobody ever called her Sara again. Mrs. B. served dinner in the kitchen as she said it's a family night, which everyone loved. The girls one by one entertained us over dinner and they were for sure Susan's daughters, wooers and so charming. The whole evening, I sat there mesmerized by all three, with their stories of school life and what happened behind closed doors. Mrs. B. who seemed to know all things worth knowing said the reason the girls are so charming, delightful, funny and so clever at wooing and making you feel that you are the only one they are interested in is because of her influence over the years and all three girls had moon in Libra.

CHAPTER 4

In the following years Max and I married, Jennie married Mick and set up her own business, Claire was studying to be a physician and Crewe moved down to London and as far as I knew was doing artsy things. Jennie came by all the time, as she lived not that far way. Claire was back and forth from hospital to university and with home studies. When Harry went down to London on business, he saw Crewe and reported she looked fine. Susan and Crewe often would talk on the phone but as Susan put it was not as if she could see or touch her daughter. Go on Skype the whole family would tell her. The answer was always the same. Twice when on Skype with Crewe the screen went blank and made funny banging sounds so Susan thought that London had blown up and that was the end of Crewe. You know what they say about the third time lucky, who will be the lucky one, Crewe or the bomb? Every night as they were getting into bed, Harry heard the same story. "I am worried about Crewe, Harry. It's been two months since she has been home. Are you sure she looked ok when you saw her last time?"

One morning Susan woke up to the happiest of e-mails saying Crewe would like to come home for the long week-end, she met someone she cares about very much and, would it be Ok for the two of them to come together!

"Just the Manor family mum, please, you, dad, the kids, my sisters and Mick, and Mrs. B."

Susan showed the e-mail to Harry.

"Thank God, now Susan what does Crewe say?"

"I know, I know, Harry."

"Well, say the words Susan."

"Just family"

"What else?"

"Just family please mum."

"And who are they Susan, say their names please?"

"You, me, the kids, Jennie, Mick, Claire and Mrs. B."

"You are not going to mess this up thinking you know better than anyone else does. You know what Crewe means, not half the village or my sister and kids, your sister, their kids, the Aunties, my parents, your parents and cousins. All she wants is you and me, Nat and Max, her sisters, Mick and Mrs. B, that's it. If you invite just one extra family member all hell will break loose and the rest will find out as they have done in the past that when you have been asked not to do 'whatever' and you have gone ahead and done it anyway. Are you listening Susan?"

"I am Harry. The last thing I want to do is upset Crewe."

The weekend arrived and Susan and the girls were running around like chickens with their heads cut off. Mrs. B. had an engagement made weeks prior to cater a luncheon so would not be home until late afternoon. She went away very upset about the whole hullaballoo that was going to happen because she was not there to take charge, but Susan was. Mrs. B. had done most of the cooking the day before and set the table in the dining room. However, one small wrong thing could send the household into disarray. It would be best if she didn't return until the next day or so. Well the 'small thing' turned out to be Susan dropping a heavy frying pan on her foot, which hurt and she had to spend most of the day resting, off her foot.

Both Susan and Mrs. B. had tried in the past to show the girls how to cook and run a kitchen, but all three girls said, in one voice, "NO." When asked "what about your husband 'to be', or when you leave home." They ANSWERED, "'Take Out' and as far as 'to be husbands we are not marrying to come home from work to cook a meal for some bloke. If he wants to eat, let him do the cooking."

Mrs. B. would get so mad her face would turn red. "You three are so bright you are stupid. Sure, lots of men love to cook, but how long is that going to last? His mother cooked for him and so did his grandmother. History has cooked for him…he hunts you cook. After a couple of years of married bliss and the sex is becoming mundane, what are you going to come up with then? You had better become the best cook there is and he will never leave home or better still earn a lot more money than he does. I know it's not the same for everyone but having sex with the same person for forty odd years is like having sex with the same person for forty odd years. So, you had better come up with something else you silly, silly girls. If you can't cook or are no good in bed, your problems are over before they begin, as no man will ask you to marry him."

Susan then looked at Mrs. B. and said, "This has to be your finest hour and your best performance."

CHAPTER 5

Harry went to the pub and Max was in a tennis match. Susan and the girls were resting in the back porch. Harry was just coming in the front door when the phone rang. "It is for you Nat, it's Max."

"What!"

"I have seen them they are on the side of the driveway at the corner kissing; they didn't see me I was lying in the long grass having a rest, when they stopped."

"Ok so Max they will be here now, are you coming home?"

"You bet I am not going to miss this for anything. Hold on they have stopped the car again."

"So what Max, why are making such a big deal of this so they kiss so what, so they stop the car again."

"Ok Nat, Crewe is with another woman."

"There are three of them?"

"NO Nat, there is Crewe plus another woman."

"Oh, Max, are you sure?"

"Yes, they are in an open sports car. The woman took off her cap, her hair is long and what a looker she is. I am sure I have seen her before."

"What will your mother do or better still say? Oh, Max let's go to the pictures or something. First, she will yell at your father blaming him. She will say, "It's all your fault. It was that haircut you gave them years ago, a crew cut for the most sensitive of the three girls you gave a boy's haircut, it turned her. I knew then it would, you turned her Harry. She would not get her hair cut for five years after that, no matter what I said. I hope you are happy now you big lump."

We both laughed at my rendition of Susan. "Maybe this will be fun. Hurry home Max and come in the back way so we can watch from the kitchen. More will be said if 'us kids' are not there."

I was sitting in the front room which had wall to wall and ceiling to floor windows that looked out to the driveway lined with a canopy of trees so any car or person could be seen for a good distance and could park right outside the front window.

"Here they are" I called out. Susan and Harry came in and sat down, the girls stood by the window looking out. Crewe had parked back a bit under the shade of the trees. I went back into the kitchen where you can see and hear all that is going on in front. Max was already there. He came across the fields by the footpath where he would ride his bike. Susan knew nothing of the path so Max came and went without being seen by Susan in the house.

"Well, Susan said, what does he look like?"

"They are just getting out of car. Ok, he is tall, very thin, has a cap on so it's hard to see his face. He is now bending down taking the cap off and shaking his hair…Good God …"

"What does Good God mean?" Susan said.

"Well, who would have thought," said Jennie looking at her sister laughing.

"Good God, who would have thought what, what's happening girls?" said Susan her voice by now reaching fever pitch. "Ok I know he has white hair, he is an old man and no teeth. I know he has a white stick. Go and look Harry."

"I don't want to Susan, please don't make me."

"What the hell is going on out there?"

"Please mum, don't get up, the shock may kill you."

"Is he so funny looking that both of you are laughing?"

"Claire look, look! It's…you know… how can it be… yes, it is, it's that cop on the telly." "Oh, Jennie," said Claire. "This has to be best day ever!"

"Help me up Harry."

"Girls help your mother. Now I am getting out of here." Harry walking very fast through the French doors and went into the garden looking to hide.

There was a knock on the door and in came Crewe with Elizabeth Michaels, actor, star of her own TV show (Detective Molly Rafferty, top shooter who can outshoot any man on the police force) theatre actor and TV screen star. The girls (Jennie and Claire) ran over to meet her, leaving Susan still sitting alone and speechless. Meanwhile 'us kids' were still in the kitchen with hankies stuffed in our mouths to stop ourselves from laughing out loud.

"Mum, I would like you to meet Elizabeth Michaels."

Susan's eyes hooked on to her daughter's 'what have you'. "So, what do you want me to call you?" Susan spat at her.

"My friends call me Liz, but you may call me Elizabeth."

We will see 'miss movie star silly pants', Susan thought. Susan looked up into Elizabeth's eyes expecting to see trouble, instead she saw Mrs. B.'s green eyes looking back at her, younger but still Mrs. B.'s eyes. She was the right age and American. Susan had seen many photos of Mrs. B. when she was Liz's age and Susan was looking at a double of a younger Mrs. B. Susan had no idea what to think or say she just looked ahead. A few tears rolled down her face, tears of happiness for Mrs. B. she hoped. Susan took Liz's hand, "I am so pleased to meet you Liz."

"Oh mum, I love you," Crewe bending down to kiss her mother.

"Help me up girls we all need a drink, a large one." The head hen and her four chicks went in to the kitchen and found Nat and Max still laughing about the day's events.

"Close your mouth Max," one of the girls called out, "we are here looking for the booze." Mrs. B. had setup a bar near a window with gin, whiskey, rum, brandy, soda, cipolles, water, sliced lemons, olives, all kinds of wines, dry crackers and cheeses plus beer and a note that cold beers and wine were in the fridge. Still in the garden, Harry was beginning to hear sounds, loud sounds, happy sounds, laughing coming from the house. Susan was standing up and walking a little, she saw Harry walking along the path towards her.

"What's happening, it sounds like a big booze up?"

"It's a woman Harry ..."

"I thought as much, did you hit her?"

"Nearly but I looked into her eyes, Harry her eyes are green she is the double of Mrs. B. when she was this girl's age. I think she is Mrs. B.'s daughter, she is an American and the right age." Harry looked at Susan as if she had gone nuts.

"Come on Susan you hurt your foot not your head."

"Harry just go and meet her, say nothing and come and tell me what you think, I will be sitting over by the pond." Half an hour later Harry returned. "I think you may be right Susan. What a lovely girl. Crewe could have done a lot worse, man or woman, and she looks so happy."

"I know, I have never seen her so happy so I will just have to accept it Harry. No grandbabies." Harry walked with Susan who hopped back through the French doors to a family that had a power of love, and a few drinks. Crewe ran up to her parents thanking them for their love and that they gave her the freedom to love whomever she chose.

Mick, Jennie's husband had arrived late, as he had to work this Saturday. "Hi Harry," he called out. Harry liked Mick. They always found something or someone to amuse them in the local pub. "Harry I would have given anything to have been here when Crewe and the girlfriend drove up. I would have booked in sick at work if I had known, just to see Susan's face." "Sure, Mick and I would have given anything not to be here."

CHAPTER 6

Meanwhile Mrs. B. was so tired after preparing the catered lunch that when she went to her sister's she fell asleep in her chair and did not wake until after seven that evening. "Good heavens look at the time, why did you not wake me before now?"

"You needed the sleep," her sister said. "Mrs. Hawkes rang a while ago in case you were here. I told her you were asleep and she said that was fine and to tell you that you were missed, but they were having a wonderful time. They are all drunk. The food was yum, yum. She dropped a frying pan on her foot and had to sit most of the day. Oh, Maude listen to this, I am still laughing at the way Mrs. Hawkes tells her human-interest stories (gossip) like it's an everyday occurrence. Anyway, the story is… tell your sister to come home soon, as Crewe came home with what we thought was her boyfriend, only now it is a girlfriend, to meet the family and she dying to meet you."

"I knew it, I knew, it was that haircut that Sir Harry gave her years ago, the crew cut. It 'turned' her. No cup of tea for me, I am off, talk to you when I know more."

When Mrs. B. arrived, the whole family was singing and dancing an old pub song 'Knees up Mother Brown under the table you must go…' Crewe saw Mrs. B. first and ran over to her.

"Why are you all dressed up Mrs. B.? Makeup, no glasses, you look so nice." It was as if Crewe was seeing Mrs. B. for the first time and was stunned at what a good-looking woman she was. No, it was more than that. Crewe turned to look for Liz and saw both parents standing nearby looking at her, softly shaking their heads.

"Go over to them Harry, I think Crewe has seen it too."

"I will talk to Mrs. B. outside and send Crewe over to you Susan."

"Hi Mrs. B., I need to talk you about something that happened years ago and please excuse us Crewe, your mother needs you," said Harry. Harry took Mrs. B.'s arm and guided her through the French doors into the Garden and to Harry's secret place.

"What is it Sir Harry, am I being fired, you do not need me anymore, because today went ok without me?"

"Oh! No, no, oh please I did not mean to upset you I just wanted you all to myself. Good, here comes Susan."

"Have you said anything yet Harry?"

"Not yet but I think I have scared her." Susan sat down on the other side of Mrs. B. and held her hand.

"Good God, you two, will you tell me what the hell is going on!"

Susan started, "Well Crewe's 'boyfriend' who she was bringing home for all us to meet has turned out to be a woman, Elizabeth Michaels. She is in her twenties, an American, an actor, has her own TV show (Molly Rafferty). Have you seen the show? No. Well, we are just going to have to come out with what we think. Liz is your double going by the photos you showed us when you were her age. Your eye coloring is very unusual, the same as Crewe's friend Elizabeth Michaels. She may be your daughter."

"Don't talk so ridiculous, why would my daughter turn up after all these years? She and I are not the only ones in this world who have the same shade of green eyes." Mrs. B. was beginning to get upset now.

"Ok Mrs. B. calm down," said Harry. The three sat in silence thinking what to say next. Susan said, "Harry, get Crewe."

"Maybe I should Susan."

Five minutes later Harry was back with Crewe in hand.

"Crewe did you see what we saw," Susan said.

"I think so mum. I have never noticed before as Mrs. B. always wore glasses so I have never seen the color of her eyes really."

"What do you know about Liz's background?" Harry asked.

"Liz lived with her father until she was about ten, when he died. He was the only son in a family of one son and six sisters. They were very close and all wanted Liz to live with them but she ended up living with one aunt. All her aunties were very good and loving to her, and they all lived near Los Angeles. Although he had a daughter (Liz), her father never married. There were women, but none lived with them. Liz loved him very much but although she wished she had her own mother she felt very lucky in some ways with six aunties. She knew it was not the same." At this point in Crewe's story, Mrs. B. was sobbing her heart out.

"It's too late now she will hate me. I have to leave Hawkes Manor."

"Don't talk so daft, you are not going anywhere" said Harry. Susan put her arms around her old friend saying "We will work this out. Anyway, who said Liz is your daughter?"

"My daughter's father's name was Michaels."

"How do you think she will take it Crewe?"

"Well she has been looking for years. Her father told her very little about her mother just something like 'she went over to England on holiday and never came back.' After he died, Liz later found some old letters from her mother. It looked like he had only replied to one. In it, he said 'With my wealth you will never be able to have your daughter back.' Also, with the letter was a photo of her mother. "Do you remember this Mrs. B.?" Harry asked "I remember the photo I sent to my daughter. That's all. I was in my mid-twenties."

"Crewe, does Liz still have the photo?"

"Oh yes, it's in her handbag."

"Well we can do nothing until Crewe gets the photo then we can compare it to Mrs. B's collection of photos". It was the next afternoon that Crewe went looking for the photo when Liz was busy. She took it to Mrs. B. She looked at it. "That's me. Where is Liz now?" She is in our room I will go and see her now," said Mrs. B. "Coming," Liz called out in response to the knock on the door. "Come in Mrs. B. what can I do for you?" Mrs. B. handed the photo to Liz, "I sent you this photo of me many years ago." She looked at Liz smiling "You are my daughter, my only child. I have dreamed of this day for so long." Nothing was said for the longest time, then Liz touched her mother's face. "Yes, I have your eyes." All this time, Liz was crying as she tried wiping away her mother's tears. Mrs. B. explained, "I am so sorry, I was so young, I had to go back to England, as my mother was very ill. She and I were very close. He would not let me have you, he was a lawyer with money I was a young girl that knew nothing."

CHAPTER 7

When my husband Max and I separated, I got the condominium in New York City overlooking Central Park, which he owned before we married. A great uncle of his left it to him. Max disliked the condominium and wanted to sell it, but I didn't. I had done such a good job fixing it up. Max is a wonderful man; we just did not want the same things. Silly things, like children and he wanted me not to work. We were so young when we married I had not thought about if or when I wanted children. I had a career…I knew after a year that I had made a mistake. Max went to the best schools Britain had to offer. When he was with his classmates, you knew by the way they talked and what they talked about they had advanced their education. When he was having a drink at the local pub, he would talk as if he had never left the Lake District as a local boy. I have never heard him talk at people. Max would make a comment on anything that he saw or heard.

'Why Nat do you thinks that man's right eye is bigger than the other, Nat you would think that woman would get herself false teeth, look that guy has on a good suit and wearing white socks and he has got himself girlfriend, I wonder why Fred is not working at the butcher's today it's not his day off?'

Some of this silly chatter he has outgrown now, but not all. That is his nature, a chatterer, and people like him. To give Susan credit she raised Max knowing he was no better than anyone else was and no one was better than he was. Thank God she did. People, both women and men, turned around in the street just to look at him, as he is so handsome.

I have heard this story so many times; it still had not lost its magic no matter how many times it was told. Max was about seven years old when he found, at the end of their driveway a very dirty man. Max thought, with the wisdom that seven-year-old boys have, I will take him home.

"Oh! No dear, your father would not like that! You know how funny he gets if someone else uses all the hot water." Max then took Ben (dirty man) over to the head gardener's home and asked him to give Ben a bath as his mother was unable to in case his father came home to find

Susan washing a strange man in the bath tub with his Dad's hot water! Thus, began this very unusual friendship. For nearly two decades, Ben came back every few years to help the gardener in the summer and charm the family with tales of his adventures across land and sea. When Ben was there the whole family, cousins, old aunties, Sir Harry's sister and her lot, Susan's sister and kids, Susan and Sir Harry's parents spent part of the summer at the family Manor. They all liked Ben and his stories and it gave everyone a reason for getting together maybe! However, they all also had a great interest in visiting the local pub twice a day, telling themselves it is was because they were on holiday. One evening Ben was telling one of his tales and he looked at one of the two old aunties and smiled. Ben had black hair, big blue eyes and white teeth and spoke perfect English with an Irish lilt. One auntie stood up, fainted and fell on top of her older sister and knocked her out. The story from then on was Ben's smile made both aunties faint from lust.

I asked Harry once if he minded Ben coming here, he gave me such a funny look. "Why would I mind?"

I shrugged my shoulders "oh I don't know! Just maybe Susan is the calling card so to speak."

Looking away, Harry laughed. "You think that I do not know that Ben would love me to go away and never come back. I can't meet all Susan's needs. That is asking too much from anyone, and I don't expect that from Susan, some she will have to meet herself. Before the girls were born all Susan would talk about were the countries she wanted to tour. Well, that never happened, instead she made a house into a home. Susan gave four children plus one, a happy childhood and me her love with so many happy memories, even the girl's haircut days we look back at with humour. Ben is a story teller, he has a gift, he can paint pictures of places that few would every dream to visit, which he paints with words. They shared a time together and through Ben's sculpting of words gave vision to Susan's dreams as he shared his adventures. Susan in return gave Ben a place at our table and made room for him in her heart. Is this love? Of course, it is, what else can it be?"

CHAPTER 8

"From the day I met Susan," said Harry, "she was as she is now; very flirtatious, loved to woo people, and what she loved to woo the most were babies. I have seen her show such love to such ugly babies, the mothers they just adored Susan. Women wore Susan's friendship as a medal of honor to show other women in a lower social group, that their great leader the Grand Rooster had shown favor to them by wooing them and their babies.

Susan never forgot a name or a face. The more attention Susan gave them the more people grew to understand this woman with the eccentric personality. Born in the year of the Rooster, when this big bird crows, the entire flock of little hens comes running. Susan loves to be praised, hates to be criticized, and will not share the limelight. A perfectionist, and because she believed in her convictions strongly, her mind was closed to anyone else's opinions.

There is another side to Susan; her power of love. After the haircuts, as I said before, Susan and I never looked back. Our love for each other and family has just grown and grown. Some people that do not know us well, think that Susan is too much and is rude to me and belittling by calling me 'big lump'. Well I know differently. When my sister and I were babies my mum told me and my twin sister that our Dad would look at my sister Terri and say what a beautiful princess you are, then look at me and smile and laugh saying are you my big lump, my big baby boy. I was twice the size of Terri. My mum, dad, Terri and I would laugh and laugh. As babies my dad loved to play and tease us and even as I was growing up my dad would hug me and say I love you 'big lump'. To me, it was the way he said it. I could feel the love he had for me and I know he was proud that I was his son. He loved me no matter what and he made me feel good about myself. He took the time to come to school to see the teachers about us, he came to nearly every game, match and play that Terri and I were in and so did our mum. When Susan and I were dating and young she heard my dad say my big lump or you big lump to me a few times one day, well she found that description of me so funny. "

When I was taking her home that night, Susan said, " You and your dad love one another very much."

Yes, we do and my mum too."

"Good, because one day you will be my husband and my children's father and I will call you big lump because I will love you as much as your parents."

"That is ok with me," I said. Susan is just as kind to animals as she is to babies, although I think it is because they don't talk back to her. She gives money, clothes, and furniture to the older people in the village that don't have as much as others do. She rents and sets up the church hall once a month for the old people to meet and socialize with tea in the afternoon followed by a dinner in the evening for which Mrs. B. cooks. Now nearly the whole village comes, over sixty-five years old must show their pension book and the dinner is free, anyone else must pay for the dinner. Oh, yes between fifty and sixty-five if you volunteer to help serve and wash dishes you get a free dinner. Mrs. B. told me people in their thirties and forties put grey wigs on and walked with canes trying to get in the church without paying with false pension books. They had to post guards at the church gate and doors. They had an army of old girls with walkers and canes hiding in the bushes, praying for a 'grey wig' to walk by. The vicar of the church gave a sermon one Sunday on stealing from the church. Those with grey wigs were abusing the church by taking the food out of the mouths of the elderly, as sometimes they ate the meals set aside as free meals. They would even block the road to the church at the bottom of the hill with cars so the old people could not ride up the hill on their scooters. The next Sunday the vicar did the same thing with the army of old girls with walkers. This time his sermon was on abuse of underage 'grey wigs' causing physical injuries by running walkers into the thieves."

CHAPTER 9

It had been over a year since the family had heard from Ben and two years since he was last at Hawkes Manor. Then, at last a letter from Ben. His mail was usually addressed to the Hawkes family; this one was to Susan Hawkes only. It was a love and farewell letter. He was dying in a hospital in the UK and only had week or so. He said how happy the last part of his life had been because of her and her loving family.

It took Susan two days to find the hospital where Ben was. She stayed by his bed for two weeks giving herself rest only when the family came, that is Harry, Max, the girls, Harry's sister, Mrs. B. Dave the head gardener and friend, many more and myself. Oh, yes and one of the Aunties, the young one. Ben was buried at a local church on a corner field of the Hawkes Manor Estate. The gravesite backed right onto the field. Susan would walk across the field along the footpath to Ben's grave every few months, as she did not want anyone to think that Ben had no one to mourn him.

A month or so later a letter came from a firm of lawyers in Hong Kong who had offices in London, New York, Paris, and Rome etc. etc. It was addressed to Sir Harry Andrew Hawkes and Susan Cox Mac-Nab Hawkes. The letter read more or less that Ben had remembered us in his will. Representatives of the law firm would like to make an appointment to visit Hawkes Manor to settle this matter as soon as possible as it had taken some time to document and locate Ben's assets due to his extensive world travels. Now they wanted closure and to get this part of the will off the books, so to speak. Harry and Susan really did not give Ben's will much thought as to its having any monetary value but rather odds and ends, and small treasures that were peculiar to the country he was in at that time.

The following month two lawyers from the London office came to Hawkes Manor. Harry was quite taken by surprise by the royal treatment given to them by the lawyers from London given that Harry thought that Ben's will was just 'odds and ends'. The older of the two men began by stating that their law firm had already followed Ben's wishes by taking care of all other legal matters except what had been left to the two of them in a separate will. At that point, Susan and Harry were given an estimate of the amount they would receive. Neither Harry nor Susan said a word and just had a look of shock on their faces. "Well," said the number one lawyer, "I can see that neither of you knew of Ben's vast estate. I have been Ben's lawyer and friend for many, many years. As a young man Ben walked away from his family and untold wealth, to a life as he saw it, of freedom. He never looked back. I personally felt that his father made his only child Ben beneficiary just to one up Ben and have the last word. 'One day you will learn about the responsibility of being born into this family.' These were the last words spoken by father to son. Ben's father lived to be an old man, which I am sad to say my friend did not. Both you and your family gave love to Ben, something he had been short of most of his life. We have a lot to discuss. The law firm and I have done very well handling Ben's affairs and we in turn have given the very best possible legal advice in making this will as airtight as we can. We are going to have to spend some time, that is, you Susan, Harry and I, plus the firm, figuring out how to disburse the monies from the will.

Susan and Harry were handed two letters, one letter from Ben in which he sang the praises of his lawyer Colin Thomas and it was ok for Harry to check out that his friend and lawyer was on the up and up. He stated that Colin had been his friend and ear for so many years. The second letter was also from Ben.

"My dear friends, only I know how you enriched my life. My own father never spoke of me or to me again after I left England. I lost contact with any distant relatives and my mother died long ago when I was very young. That had to be the luckiest day of my life when Max and I met, and he took me to the manor. The very rich are different from you and me… this is so true, I lived in their world once. There are different rules for people with untold wealth from money handed down from one generation to the next. Wealth is expected and with that, expectation comes 'privilege' that the common person knows nothing about. When you have that kind of wealth and power to whom are you accountable? Very few! Each generation is a guardian of the family name and wealth, whatever it may be; real estate, art, land and with this also comes a responsibility that you will invest well and your estate becomes bigger than the one you inherited. Maybe the word miser would be most fitting describing someone who is terrified they will be the one that loses the family estate and ruins the family name. Well my family name is still intact and worth a lot, more than my father's estate was, due to my trusted friend and lawyer Colin's guidance and investment savvy. My estate including new holdings will, as it should, remain where it belongs with the Bentley family, whoever they may be.

This is for the many summers I have been part of a family that showed me what love is about, you filled my heart with happy memories. As you can see, I have left you a fair amount of money, enough for you both to have a very comfortable life. All I ask from you is tell no one the amount, with the exception of Natasha. She can be trusted to be your spokesperson if something should happen to you both, so your children will hopefully understand why they were never told the amount of the will. Natasha's needs are not for more money, but for self-forgiveness and to be free of guilt for living when the rest of her family died. Please trust that what I am saying may happen because it happens all the time. Once again, tell no one the amount of money you received.

Always someone wants more. They may justify their greed by thinking you both are getting older and don't need that much money now. They will call it a loan but they will never ever think of paying you back, I promise you. Some will say there are only the two of you and 'I have four children to feed and need a bigger house…'. There will be few not happy with what they received from you via me and they never will, and it will more likely be your children with help from their spouses. You may say 'No! Not my kids and I will say Yes, Yes! Your kids! Colin practices Family Law and if you think you know better than I do, ask Colin. He has seen loving, giving families turn on each other when suddenly money arrives. Of course, you will share with your family. It is there for you and all your family to enjoy and have more freedom to do what you want to do. All this is so hard for me to write down as it looks like I'm telling you what to do and being too bossy but I am just thinking of you both and your family. The money may become more of a hindrance to the way your family develops. They are not used to this kind of money and they are young and know very little of the working world of scam artists and highly unethical financial crooks. One more thing to do then you will never hear from me again! Please take care of Mrs. B., the two aunties and my friend Dave the gardener.

Signed
Benjamin Forbes Bentley III'

It was beginning to rain and there was lightening crackling in the sky. It was getting dark far too early so Susan excused herself and went to the kitchen to listen to the radio about the weather. Just as she thought, a bad storm was coming. Returning to the library Susan found the three men standing by the French windows looking out. "Ah, Susan," Harry acknowledging his wife's return, "Looks like our guests will be here for dinner and overnight too."

Numbers one and two lawyers stayed at Hawkes Manor two days due to the weather. The will was sorted out as to the proximity of and access to the monies until all, Susan, Harry and one and two were satisfied. Lawyers number one and two spent hours entertaining Susan and Harry with tales of horror. 'Too much too soon'. Anyway, we will see what happens… At this point, you the reader are wondering if this is supposed to be such a big secret and how come you are writing about it! The answer is simple, because it's my book… and I can do what I want to.

CHAPTER 10

After Max and I married, we decided to go to New York City for one year and live at the condominium in Central Park. British Intelligence transferred me from their London to their New York office for one year and Max was doing some of his studies in linguistics and translation here in New York due to the many cultural differences and languages in the city. When we arrived at LaGuardia airport, we gave the cabdriver our new address and told him to take his time driving around New York City. Three extra-large hotdogs, three large coffees, three hours later, plus one Riccardo taxi company owner's son, we arrived at our new home. We had so much luggage, we sent it ahead of us. We promised Riccardo that the next cab we called for would be his.

All we knew about the condo was it had been just cleaned and minor repairs done by the condo management. It had some pieces of furniture, some needed to be replaced. We just stood there looking at the door to our new home. Then Max with a written code on the palm of his hand programmed the numbers into a box on the side of door. We walked into a lobby that I thought was of gigantic proportions. To the left of us was a set of double doors and in front of us were two sets of double doors. When we opened the doors, I saw nothing but the view. Neither Max nor I said a word as we walked across the floor of our penthouse to windows covering most of the wall overlooking Central Park and beyond. I felt humbled by how mankind could create a view so breathtaking.

The old man (Max's great uncle) had done some renovation. It was mostly an open concept, as it appears some walls had been taken down so the living room area, dining room and kitchen were open. It still needed a lot of work if we were going to stay here in New York in the future or sell; either way work had to be done. The windows in the living area were floor to ceiling, and where once had been plaster now there was exposed brick with slightly different red tones and shades of blue and grey. The brickwork ran the length of the windows at the bottom just wide enough to sit on. There were old wooden beams running across the ceiling with big lights hanging down, the floor was old barn wood. I very much liked the renovation that had been done so far. The furniture, I could not find another word for it, awful!

Not a morning went by that I did not sit with my coffee enjoying the panoramic view of After a while, I began to realize that not only did I have an unbelievable view I now was beginning to feel the unyielding power this city had, and I wanted to be part of it. In addition, I would be forever grateful I had 'A Room with a View.'

It had been Sir Harry's idea I apply for a job with British Intelligence. He had a few ex-marine mates working there and was always bragging about my IQ. It was the highest Harry had ever seen, and according to Harry, in a previous life I had been Sherlock Holmes. Of course, anyone hearing Harry making this statement about Sherlock Holmes all came to the same conclusion that Harry did not have much of an IQ.

I did very well in the British Intelligence so when I told them I was thinking of going to the States they reluctantly asked would I take a transfer for a year at the New York office. Yes, yes, I jumped at the chance. After nine months on the job and loving it, I was approached by a non-British agency that must have heard that I was 'Sherlock Holmes' in a previous life! I was offered a position in a newly created Homeland Security division within the government. Well this really was a life changer. Not just for me but Max too.

I knew within three months that Max wanted very much to go back home; he never said it but I knew. It was then I realized what a big mistake it was for both of us to marry, he did not want this life but I did. Max has always loved children and would like to have one now and I wanted to wait a few years if not longer.

We had not talked about when we would have children before marrying and I never thought I would be keen on a career. Oh, dear I have always loved Max and always will, but not as a husband. There is no passion in our love. I knew that and I think he did too now. That evening I told Max about the new job offer. I asked what he thought about living here in New York after his first year of studying was over.

"Nat I just want to go home. I know you love it here. When we lived in North London while you worked for British Intelligence, I found the noise and crowds a bit much. New York to me is crazy making and

I cannot tune in to it. What I want now is what you and I should have discussed before we married and that is children, where we are going to live and whether you would be happy to stay at home with my help raising the children."

I could not look at Max because I knew what I had to say was not what he wanted to hear, no matter how I said it. If we had children now that to me would be a commitment of about 18 years for each child and if we had several kids, more years for me to stay home and raise our children as we had been. Let us face it that is what we would want. "Dear Max, I am still looking for 'me', I have only known this 'me' for a few years. After university, I never thought about living overseas or a career, only that we were going to get married. Now, I want to wait a few years to have children. Now, at this moment, and at this age I would like to live here in New York City, but England will always be my home!"

"Ok Nat, I will have to sleep on all this, good night."

Two months later Max left and went back home to Hawkes Manor. We had separated and we both cried as we said farewell at the airport. I left it up to Max as to what to say to Sir Harry and Susan. I returned home to an empty condo. The freedom and joy I expected never happened. It was replaced with such guilt and depression there were days I was unable to get up from my bed. I was to start my new job the next month. My friends from British Intelligence (B.I.) would often come around to cheer me up me. They also phoned they were thinking of going to so-so bar that night, and would I join them. I had a most enjoyable time, after that I felt the cloud lifting, and by the time I was starting my new job maybe I would be ok with life again.

I had been in close contact with Harry and Susan since Max had left New York. They both kept threatening to come over to see me but I asked them to give to me time, please. The day of reckoning: Susan rang me when Harry was at the local pub.

"You know you can't do any wrong in Harry's eyes. He would be so mad if he heard me say this, but you are his favorite child Natasha. Harry loves his girls very much but the time Harry was overseas with the British Royal Marine Commandos fighting he can't separate them, he can't see them as individuals. In some way I blame myself for this, some war in which he nearly got killed he came back a hero, the most decorated officer of the British Armed Forces. He was given a knighthood but when he came back home he was a different man. Then you came along and he started to get better. You gave Harry reason to restore what I had always loved so much about him, his power to love. It got lost when he and so many other soldiers came home living with sights and sounds of man's inhumanity to man. You needed him but he needed you more.

We all called Harry 'Sir Harry' as a fun name not because we all saw him as an SIR the name just cottoned on and the village loved having a 'Sir' living in the Manor. Harry would tell me about young boys fighting in the war who had never seen anything like a finger cut off in their lives before the war now they were part of such horror. Even if you lived and came home, many left their minds over there!

Harry had no time for Max who was too much like himself at that age. Max had trouble understanding other people's needs and was too overly sensitive to his own. Harry knows Max has the making of a fine young man but like his Dad, it is going to take time for him to mature. When you and Max wanted to marry, we were so happy for the two of you, and your children my love, would be my grandchildren. Harry and I see it differently now. Max was always a happy child and teenager it took very little to please him. He is one of these rare beings that are happy with their lot in life so Max could not understand why you wanted to live in New York; it was beyond his way of thinking. I believe each one of us born with a map encoded which rules our destiny, not that everything you do is predicted or a foregone conclusion. 'There are many paths to heaven.' Maybe it's part of our DNA influencing our choices about what paths we take at different stages of life. We are all given just so many roads and turns to make and as we travel we meet people along the way, some stay to the end some don't, they have other roads to travel, other people to be with.

I hope you understand Nat what I am trying to say, your life needs are not the same as Max and there is nothing wrong with that.

The way Harry fusses over you I am sure you feel the love he has for you. However, you may not know how much I love you, in every way, you are my daughter and I pray that one day you will know inner peace and be free from guilt. Free from guilt not just over Max but even bigger the guilt over why you lived and your family did not!"

I cried tears, tears I should have cried years ago.

"Nat you hardly ever talk about how you feel about those times. You are living in the U.S. A. now, so do what the Americans do; they break a nail and they are off to therapy. I think therapy will do you a world of good, there is nothing like telling a stranger your troubles. I know at the time many of us tried to help, but we were all colored by what happened. The anger, pain and scars are now part of you but with fresh eyes to help you the anger can turn to compassion, the pain to empathy and the scars well maybe they never go away but as we age, they change shape. Will the scars always be there to remind you of the horror of that day? That is up to you Nat. I knew and remember your mother you do not?"

"You know of Harry's gift. So really, this is for Harry to tell, not me but I think the time for telling is now. I would never want Harry to know I have broken his trust, so 'mum's the word' Natasha. Harry feels and 'sees' your mother, the rest of your family have moved on and are waiting for her, they moved on so she will have the strength to stay with you. Harry will not tell you this in case it upsets you, but I will. Nat, she stays hoping, praying and giving her strength to you so you will not make one day of horror the cushion for the rest of your life." Susan was now crying. "Let them go, Natasha, please let them go and let my boy go too. You were both too young to know it was not meant to be, he is in pain too. Natasha this is what you are going to do; you are going to find yourself the best counselor on grief within the next three weeks. If I feel in three weeks you have done very little about this and are covering up with your little stories, I will come over to stay with you until we find someone, without Harry to protect you and I will be carrying my big long stick. Then when you are beginning to feel better, you will to write to Max and show him forgiveness so he can forgive himself. Don't think for a moment Harry is going to worm his way to come over with my stick and me... Harry is getting too harsh with Max. He needs to stay here and show a boy how to be a man, do you understand Natasha?"

"Yes Susan."

"Your way is no longer working; we will find another way my love, and we will travel this path together until you find yourself, the good side and the dark. All God, life, the universe expects from you is to be the best person you can be and to know and accept yourself. It is so simple when you know how and so hard when you don't."

"Hold on a sec. Susan I may not be hearing you right. What you are saying is when I am beginning to feel better I am to write to your son and show forgiveness and show him how he can forgive himself for abandoning me? I will never forgive him Susan, and I never will give him permission to forgive himself. He left his young wife on her own in New York City knowing few people; he could have waited until I was settled in this new job instead he left me in a dark and lonely space in my mind. We knew we had to part. What did he do when he came running back to you Susan? He spent night after night in the pub crying in his beer. What he did was not the act of an immature thoughtless boy it was one of some arsehole that had to punish me. When all I asked was for time… for time …so I could find inner happiness, all mine to share or not. You have no idea what it is like to remember nothing Susan. This whole telephone call has been about you fixing me up so I can forgive Max and he can be happy again. If these are the conditions of your love Susan, you know what you can do with that." Then I hung up and took the phone off the hook.

I had not felt that good in months. Sometimes hating and, I mean really hating someone is just as rewarding, if not more so, as loving them. How many times and ways can you describe why you love your lover. It's his hair, the way he looks at you or the way he does it. It is boring, oh so bloody boring. Just think about it. How many ways can you hate your lover and what you would love to do to them? You would never run out of ideas. I went to bed that night and slept like a baby.

CHAPTER 11

Iwoke up the next morning with a start. Someone else was there and I could smell coffee. The bedroom door opened, he looked so thin standing there. Long gone was the boy from our childhood whose face always looked so happy with life.

"Nat I am not an arsehole, I am a fucking arsehole, who never once considered that your dreams were not mine to dream for you, never once did I think you needed to make your own dreams to build your future. One day you will forgive Hawkes Manor and me. Our family, friends and I will become such happy memories for your tomorrow, but my mother needs your forgiveness now for you to love her unconditionally, as she does you. My mother rang you up out of love for you and me, she felt helpless and maybe just maybe she was looking to you for the answers because she had no idea what to do. I will be staying awhile. I will put my bags in one of the other bedrooms, maybe travel around New England a bit then the west coast. Anyway, I will not be in your way."

Max spent a few days here in New York then went up to the Boston and looked around. The day after Max got back from his New England trip; he asked if I would like to go out for dinner with him. We had a wonderful time and over the next few weeks, we went to the theatre, jazz clubs, ballet and coffee bars. Max stayed about a month.

The day before he left for the UK I told him; "You know Max, you are so handsome. Do you know how many women look at you when we were out together?

"Yes, I have noticed American women appear to like my looks, Natasha. I pushed and pushed you into getting married. My Dad suggested a few times to wait 'let her find herself first'. He never said anything to Mum because he didn't want to upset her. All Susan looked forward to was having grandbabies."

"Max, I tried so hard, so please, forgive me."

"I know Nat; it does not hurt as much when I know it's not something personal about me. I am going to put this condo under your name, remember I said this to you a few months."

"No, Max. I can buy it from you or get a smaller place."

"Please Nat, this way when I come back to New York and I may, depending on the work situation in the UK. I need a place to stay."

"Stop Max, no matter where I live you will always have a room in my heart and my home; we have found a power to love through forgiveness. Max, I wish it had been different, Oh God, how I wish I could go back with you, have babies and be the woman I would like to be for you, but she does not exist and one day you will want more from me only to discover I have nothing more to give to you. As long as you are single, you will have room here."

"What do you mean as long as I am single?"

"Well you don't think you are coming over here to stay with a wife and half a dozen kids. Once she sees the place after I have fixed it up she will never leave. That's a thought. You had better sell it to me now because, if you meet someone soon before our divorce is final and she see this place she will fight tooth and nail for it."

Max started laughing; "Have you have gone mad Natasha? What wife, what kids? I will speak to my lawyer about the buy and sell agreement, have it appraised and send you the money. Bye, the way Nat how much money did your parents leave you! After our US adventure, we were going to see one of Dad's lawyer friends about the best way to handle our finances for the future, including taxes."

"I have no idea who is coming into your life and what part they will be playing, so I am not telling you. Your parents do not even know. I am much smarter than you are, so nothing more will be said about me buying this apartment and other monies. I know when you get home you will be mad at me thinking I am the boss and telling you that you should be happy that you have me in your life. Also, I have transferred money to your bank and removed my name from our account, I hope."

Leslie Faggot, the lawyer, sent someone around to have the condo. appraised, set up the written agreement which was sent to Max. Max e-mailed he was returning next week with the agreement.

It took me a while to find him; he was sitting on a bench in Central Park feeding the birds. He was dressed all in black with a small yarmulke on his head. He had well-spoken America accent. It was the way he phrased his sentences a few words rearranged but still implying the same. So delightful, so Jewish. He came out of the war camps. In 1945, he was sent to an uncle in Queens, New York. He had lost everyone, his parents, two sisters, a brother, four cousins, and many more. His uncle and family gave him time to mourn and no more. "You cannot cry for what is no longer yours, what will be yours is yet to come. Why this happened to you and me?" he shrugged his shoulders, "No idea. When you look for the truth in life, go with love Natasha, as I did. It may hurt more but it will set you free, to love and be loved by whomever you choose. When you look back to the horrors of that day also think about what it gave you, not only what it took away. A rare family that already had four children, one boy and three devils and they all had such love for you; They asked nothing in return you had freedom, love and knew happiness. this was and is your destiny, how it came about, is how it came about." He and I have fed many birds together over time and still to this day we meet now and then in Central Park, same park bench just different birds.

CHAPTER 12

It was the first day at the office and already I was going out to lunch with the girls, as it was someone's birthday. We went to a little Italian place about block away; the food was out of this world. If they ate like this every day I could see why all six of the office ladies were such whoppers. I know anything goes in New York so maybe there is a Whoppers club and that's where they all met first!

"We were supposed to take you downstairs for lunch and show you around and explain the seating arrangements but we already made plans plus we usually don't eat downstairs as all of us can't sit at one table."

"So where are you from Gladys?" No one spoke, I looked up and all eyes were on me "Are you talking to me?"

"Yes Gladys."

"Well my name is not Gladys."

"Are you not the girl from the temp. agency?"

"NO!"

"Then, who are you and what the hell are you doing eating with us?"

"I am a quality employment analyst. That means, if an employer feels that there is a problem with employees in the work place the company that I work for will send a job analyst for a few days, even a few months, to observe the work area and workers, and make a report back to the person or persons who felt there was a problem."

"Good God look at the time, we had better get back to work," one of the ladies called out. I was beginning to wonder if this was a usual lunch break as we had been at the restaurant an hour and a half and nobody was making any moves to leave. Have you ever had a moment in time which has been embedded in your memory? I saw six x-large women flying down one of the avenues of New York City with their knock-off handbags in one-hand and brown paper bags full of Italian takeout food in the other. Some of the crowds of people walking a long started running with them, I think just for the fun of it.

Eventually I found the correct floor and department of my new job. I had to phone to find out the right floor as it appears there had been a typo in the e-mail sent to me which should have read floor 5 not 6. My new boss George Johnston was a-buzz when I arrived. I told him what happened earlier, that I landed on the wrong floor and the staff there were planning to go for lunch and invited me to join them. I think they had to ask me, as they didn't know what to do with me. All the phones were already put through to the answering service. When I got to the part about the made-up story of me telling the ladies I was a quality employment analyst, the new boss had to sit down he was laughing so much. "Do you know them?" I asked. "Do we know them? We have lawsuits pending against them… I wish," the boss said jokingly. "Come on, I will introduce you to the rest of the gang." George pressed the buzzer on the door and we walked through to a large room with lots of noise. There were phones, computers, cables and desks plus people sitting around. "Listen up 'peeps' this is Natasha Bennett, our new hero. She has already taken on the Big six upstairs." Still to this day, I am not sure why floors 5 & 6 had this feud going on. The following day an ad for Mario's Italian Restaurant appeared in one of New York's daily newspapers with a color cartoon picture of the Big Six flying back to work with a crowd of New Yorkers plus their dogs running behind them. Each of the big girls was carrying an enlarged cartoon copy of a brown paper bag with the words Takeout Food from Mario's Italian Restaurant.

CHAPTER 13

George showed me around including where I was going to work. The next day we went downstairs for lunch. On leaving the elevator, we turned right and stood on top of an equestrian staircase, looking down on the most bizarre setup.

Maybe it was because I came from England where in comparison everything was so much smaller, but this room ' took the biscuit'. It was a large, full basement to a very large skyscraper. There were big round picnic tables covered with canopies. Long poles sat in the middle of the tables poking up through the canopies like fairground flags flying so high with names of every hobby you can think of… woodwork, spelling, cooking, painting, drawing, sewing, all the arts, history, genealogy, geography, general chitchat, and many more. Above the flags a sign that read 'IF NO OFFENCE WAS MEANT, NO OFFENCE WILL BE TAKEN, them's the rules.'

Beyond this room was an outside terrace with beds of flowers set along paths running beside lawns of well-kept grass, where people sat and ate at picnic tables. Inside the restaurant along one side was an open kitchen, you could help yourself; only the hot meals/dinner were served up by kitchen staff in case a greedy person took too much food as the plates were already priced by the cook. So that means if you took two potatoes instead one at the end of the day when the head chef finds out that three potatoes are missing, all hell breaks out in the kitchen. As we all know kitchens that serve the public are on the FBI top ten most dangerous places to work.

Many branches of the government have offices within this building. There were also banks, dentists, doctors, hairstylist and cosmeticians, travel agents, child care, pet care facilities, hotels for the rich and poor, donut cafes, bars that opened after five o'clock, supermarkets, cleaners, department stores and massage parlors and more. Because of the many secrets that this building lends itself to, some wise owl that worked here many years ago, claimed it was dark corners were trouble and gossip grew, boring lunches with nothing to do. This building can be very isolating for many workers, if you have a small work staff, seeing the same old faces every day, listening to the same old stories people get fed up. The time it takes to go outside for lunch was not worth it. Not all rewards for good work are found in a paycheck.

■

It is found in the smiles of workmates from all walks of life, from meeting new friends or 'to-be' lovers, wives and husbands. Everyone that works in this building can come to this social area to learn and share with each other, the possibilities were endless. If you wanted to know about India or some remote island in the Bering Sea, you could find the answers there. Staff runs the show from 7am to 9 p.m., five days a week, full security 24/7. In return, the company gets undying loyalty from its staff. With this loyalty in mind, secrets can be kept and ideas shared. Moreover, what is loved and shared by all is our local newspaper, printed weekly. Human interest stories, parties, weddings, weight watchers and weight losses, all kinds of clubs you could join…teams, winter sports, bicycling, swimming, summer games, dates and places where games were played, a list of evening classes from October to May. There were cooking competitions, indoor games, and discussion groups with rules. To join a social club, you must work for a firm in the building. The most important item in the newspaper was a map of the whole building with every company listed on every floor, stair, elevators and bathrooms. In case you have not guessed it, the staff turnover is very small. Because many people in New York wanted to work here, only the best were hired. When new companies move in it is part of the lease that so many hours must be given to employees with pay when it is their turn to run a social function.

CHAPTER 14

As soon as we arrived, George had to go back to the office for a phone call. I grabbed some food and found a table with no one there, a knitting table. After a few minutes I hear, "Hello, may I join you? "I looked up to see the most beautiful woman I had ever seen. She and I didn't stop talking for an hour. "Oh!" I said, "Look at the time I must go."

"Until next time?" She looked at me smiling.

Yes, and your name it is?"

"Ann, Ann Gilbert."

Over the months, Ann and I became good friends over lunch, dining out, bars, off-street car racing, ballet and theatre, etc. When I got back to the office, I was met with clapping, fists banging on desks cheering and booing.

"Well it didn't take long for Ann to zero in on you. Good luck," one of the guys said.

One of the girls, Kate, stood up, "Take no notice, Natasha every one of these boys has asked Ann out. Go on boys, tell Natasha more or less what kind of response you got from Ann. "Well," said Kate. "It appears you have all forgotten," she went on to say. "Ann looks them up and down as they stand there with mouths open, baggy pants, soft old shoes and un-ironed white shirts, looking like they have slept in them for twenty-four hours."

"No!" Ann would reply. "When asking a woman out first thing you do is dress like a man that's looking for a lady, not a tramp and, in my case, the answer may have been the same, but I would treat you with respect and gone to great length to spare your feelings." Not one guy said a word, the woman stood up cheering and clapping. My God, I thought, how someone as beautiful as Ann could have balls too.

I know now I had made the right decision to stay here in New York and to be at the beginning of such an intriguing career. You will not find records or references within the halls, corridors, or houses of this government nor public mention of the office that was created after the first world war, when so many never returned home. Souls left to wander lost and buried beneath unmarked land. I am an agent for a satellite company of the above. We. are called 'The Lost Souls'.

Today George called me in to his office. "It is time for you to go on a field trip. How do you feel about this?" If I had the right knickers on that day, I would have done summersaults. I thought it would be another six months! "You are fast learner." George said. "Joe is going day after tomorrow, maybe a month. Can you go with him? "I liked Joe, so another imaginary summersault was in order.

"Ok."

"Go and see Joe to make arrangements. You need not come to work tomorrow. Rest, pack. Oh yeah, Joe has a passport for you and don't take yours. Joe will tell you what you will need. Good luck Nat."

Well dear readers, this is as far as I can take you. On my journey overseas, you will have to wait until I return or of course, there is always the possibility one day I may not.

CHAPTER 15

I had been working so much the past few months that I took a few weeks off, just laid around my apartment, had a few dinner parties, went to a few parties and visited friends. I liked to visit the Park just across the way, Central Park.

I was well rested by the time I got back to work, and planed on returning to England a few days early so I could visit my family in the Lake District UK. Then on to France to help finish up a case that was of upmost important to the department and Homeland. The agent in charge in France was very good at his job, "The Big Boys" just wanted me to dot the I's and cross the tees.

A few days before I was leaving to overseas a good friend of mine from the *New York Times* phoned. "Natasha, I need a very small favor, remember that time a few years when I saved" I cut him off and asked…"Ok. Ok, what is it Tom?"

"When you go overseas looking for lost people Nat would you take this new reporter with you? She is an excellent writer, one of the best, but she needs a story to write and I need a rest from her asking me when she can do that."

I laughed." No Tom, you think that little, little favor from a few years ago, that only you remember or better still made up, of which I have no recall, is going to get me to take one of your prodigies with me so you can have a rest. Even if you gave up your grandmother's life for me, the answer is still 'no.' Tom, I go alone as it is not an easy job and there are risks involved, having somebody along who doesn't know the ropes would not be fair to me. Tom, I hope you understand."

"What if I told you her name, would that make a difference?"

"Tom… no! Why would knowing her name make a difference to me! God Tom, the woman must be a beauty for you to go to all this trouble. Goodnight Tom."

"Her name is Ann Gilbert, goodnight Nat."

Tom hung up. I was not that shocked that Tom phoned. Ann could make men do anything. Ann and I had not seen each other in over year since we had a row. Words were said that I wish I had never even thought. A casual affair had turned into a commitment for life, well that was the way I saw it then. My marriage had ended, ended before it began. I was left feeling guilty at the time for not loving him the way I had promise to when marrying him. Now in a relationship with a woman, I read Ann's way of expressing herself the wrong way.

She and I got on so well, and we had fun together, she was happy. We both were happy with our relationship. All Ann said was that as things were going so well with us she did not want to mess it up by seeing others and she hoped I felt the same. Under normal light that makes a lot of sense, why would you think of looking elsewhere when you already have what you want. I never thought for one minute about playing the field, it never entered my head that either of us would. Maybe the moon was full, or Mercury was retrograde but all of a sudden, I felt trapped and that dirty word 'commitment' sprang into my mind. Then I said the silliest of words; "what else Ann, accountability too?" No more was said by either of us. My phone rang, and Ann left It was my boss phoning to say one of the other agents had suddenly become ill and was in hospital would I please, please cover for him by to going Rome? The flight was leaving the next morning and I was the one who knew most of what the other agent had been working on as he and I had discussed the case many times together. "Please Nat."

"Ok, ok" I said.

"Thank you Nat I will not forget this I will fax over everything you need. This will be a long one so I am sorry, as it will take a few months to finish."

"Goodbye George."

I phoned Ann, no answer I left a message to for her to call me. I phoned Fadil at the front desk to tell him I would be way a month or two and maybe my 'still husband' would be coming over from the UK to stay while I was away. In my haste to tie up all my affairs for the next two months, I forgot to ring Ann again. I did not bother with details about having to fill in for a co-worker in hospital. Once I got to Rome, I called Ann a few more times, nothing. I checked to see if there were any messages on my phone in New York, there was none. I thought, by the time I returned from the job she would have met someone else and moved in with her. This was breaking my heart.

After I finished up in Rome, I phoned George and told him I was too tired and depressed to come back to the US and work. I told him I would give my report over closed circuit.

"I don't know Nat," George said, "we are busy right now, maybe in a few months."

"Well then, George it is 3:00 p.m. Rome time please accept my resignation effective now. I will fax a written statement that I no longer wish to work for a company whose motto must be WORK TILL YOU DROP. George I will not change my mind. Goodbye."

The next day I went to our Rome office, made the closed-circuit video, and gave a copy to a clerk plus a copy of my resignation sealed and locked under 'classified' to be taken to the airport to be flown to the States. Sometimes if I thought, my reports were of extra importance I would send one copy by pigeon, the other by closed circuit. I like to do this in case somehow unauthorized editing was done on either one.

I caught the next plane to England. I had phoned Crewe when I was still in Rome and told her how down I was and asked her to meet me at Heathrow airport.

"I hope you do not mind," said Crewe, "Liz is with me and we were just leaving to go to Hawkes Manor when you phoned so we hung around for your plane to land then you can come with us. What's wrong Nat you look awful?" I told them what happened with Ann and that it was all my fault, I had been wrong. I had sent e-mails and made phone calls but still no reply. I told her how much I loved her, still no reply. I gave my resignation to my boss before I left Rome.

"You what?" said Crewe. "You loved that job! Oh Nat, you are really in a mess. Well, in a few days we will have it all figured out." We stopped about halfway to have tea. Crewe rang Susan to say they were half way there and a very unhappy and sad Natasha was with them.

"What happened, Crewe, tell me? Tell me now is she sick?"

"No Mum, it is over some woman I have never met. Crewe tell me the 'some woman's' name now".

"Ann Gilbert."

"Oh dear, she phoned from New York a month or so ago to see if Natasha was here, and I told her no she is on an assignment. She thanked me and hung up. And she has resigned her job."

"She has resigned? She loved that job, it is her life."

Why Susan forgot or decided not to tell is a good question. In Susan's mind she may have thought if this woman can hurt me so much she did not belong in my life. I stayed at Hawkes Manor about two months, my family made sure I had no contact with my ex-work place. If anything came up Harry took care of it. I found myself in a much better space. During that time, Max was in New York waiting for me to come back from Rome. When he found out I had been at Hawkes Manor all this time he was mad as a hatter at Susan for not telling him, which was okay with me, as he would have fussed so much with my weight loss and sadness. Harry was in shock when he saw me; it's one thing to break up with someone you care about, but to go away on business for weeks with no one to talk to about it plus the pressure of the job where decisions are made about peoples' lives was just too much for anyone.

Unbeknownst to me Harry had taken photos of me and written a letter to the biggest cheeses that he knew personally in State Security, James Noitall. "Dear Jim…and if my girl said she is too ill to work at this time, she is too ill to work. Her personal data is under 'highly classified' but you can see she has become one of the wealthiest women in the UK & USA., so it is not the paycheck that keeps her working for you. Natasha's records must show she is one of your best field agents. Best wishes Jim. Thanks for taking the time to read the above. Harry Hawkes."

Well it turned out that Harry knew more than I thought. That following week Max and I made our way back to New York.

"Susan, I am going back just to see what I am going to do with my life. If nothing is there for me, I will come back home to England, please do not worry. I have Max with me, we are both wiser and maybe we can help one another, and Max is ok, Susan. He is showing a lot of interest in other women and I am not leading him on. I told him to do all his dreaming with other women and if I think differently, I will send him home to Mamma."

Well what fan-fare was waiting when I got back to New York? The phone had long stopped taking messages and tons of snail mail had piled up. I stopped looking at my e-mail a few months ago and they were there waiting to be read. We showered, ordered brunch in and lay down in our own bedrooms. It was dark outside when I woke to Max standing over me with a mug of coffee. "Maybe we can go out for a drink later."

"That sounds nice," I said.

"The phone rang a few times Nat. I did not pick up and I think it has stopped recording and I am unsure how to fix it over here in the big city, without losing your old messages."

"That is fine Max I will fix it tomorrow, after all, tomorrow is another day!"

The list is too long to tell who wrote, e -mailed and phoned, the bottom line is my old job had now been filled but would I be interested in a position as a field boss within the next six months in Manhattan. I must phone George, poor George, he sounded so upset in the phone recordings, feeling he was instrumental in me leaving and not understanding how down I was. It happened so quickly, of course, he would be upset. I did not give him time to think, he acted, as a boss should, company first.

"George, YES, it is me."

"Who is me?"

"It's Hillary," I said.

"Hillary who?"

"Hillary, Hillary Clinton," I said, with my newfound Illinois accent...I was that good that he had to think for a few seconds.

"How are you feeling Nat?"

"Good, thanks George."

"Do you know how many times I have phoned you, e-mailed, went to your condo expecting to find a body, your body? When are you coming in Nat, just so we can talk?" "Day after tomorrow, about 10 am, just to talk George. Is that time ok with you?"

"Ok, Thursday at 10 am. By the way Nat, thank you for writing in to the bosses exonerating me from playing any part in your resignation. Apparently, the powers that be were so pleased with the job you did and finding out the true reality of the situation, it was a gold flag for our department. The awful thing is no one recognized you. If you had not said your name etc. we would still be looking for the person on the video. I am so sorry Nat you looked so thin."

The phone was ringing, ringing, I was so deep in thought it took me a few moments to understand what was making the noise. Without thinking, I picked up the phone. Damn it was her, damn!

"Hello Nat."

"I am sorry, I think you have the wrong number, this is a new listing." She rang a few more times that evening but I did not pick the calls up. Next morning the same thing happened. Ann would not give up. That damn phone. "Nat, pick up, please. It was Max calling out to me. Okay I picked it up. "What do you want Ann?" At first a lot of small talk. "Please Ann, stop and listen. I am never letting you back into my life." Then I heard the silliest story. I was just going to ask her to repeat it, as I did not understand what the hell she was talking about, but now why would I want to know? "Give it a rest Ann."

Now when I look back I realize Ann consistently manipulated people even when there was no reason to manipulate. It was her way of having fun. Then Ann dropped the ball that she had met my boss a few times, and he said it was OK with him if she were to join me on my next trip. "What boss? What are you talking about Ann? You know I work for the Department of Lost Souls. You only know my co-workers and my secretary. How many times have you been up to my office when we go for lunch, and when have you ever known or seen a big boss? There is no big boss sitting in the office that you would know. You went behind my back, as Tom must have told you. I said no. Who is my boss Ann?"

"Well, you know Natasha do not be silly."

"You are not coming with me, you silly, silly cow…OH, NO! You don't mean little Freddie the office manager, do you? He would not get into that with you; tiny Fred is the office manager not a field boss. What is it you do not understand about the word no, Ann."

"Natasha, Nat! Are you still there…it's…? I am talking about George, George Johnston, you do know that don't you?"

"No Ann I did not. I am going away soon on business and have a few things to do. By the way, Ann you do know that I will have to report this about a George Johnston implying he is my boss to you. You have nothing to do with where I work or whom I work for, so why would this George Johnston imply he is my boss to you, a civilian. There is something very wrong here. I hope your George can help you out. I have a good mind to have you arrested for interfering in government matters."

How had Ann found out about George Johnston and how much did she know? Did she know that where I worked is just a front! I only had to wait an hour before my boss George phoned me. He yelled at me, "Ann has gone 'ding-dong', she thinks she will be charged with high treason and that I, George, am a spy that she shared secrets with, about you…"

"Good heavens, George. It is obvious Ann had two plans in operation. She asked Tom for help and if that did not work, she went on to woo you. Yes, she did George. Ann is a very attractive woman and you are a middle-aged man, it happens all the time. George, this is the first and last time that you will professionally embarrass, undermine and minimize me over a piece of skirt, you dirty old man."

CHAPTER 16

I had just finished eating when the lobby Desk Manager buzzed, "Good evening Miss Bennett, it is Fadil, and a George Johnston would like to come up."

Okay. Another shock, George had been or was still crying! "Natasha, my wife is dying." Men do funny things and…. Then I held him while he cried. I was very fond of George. He had helped me a great deal with my career and had asked nothing in return.

I made us a drink and asked where his wife June was and what was wrong with her. Was he ok with the hospital and doctors? Was our health coverage from work enough to cover if she had better treatment? I knew he would be short of money now with two children in college and a third going next year, plus two not in high school yet. I already knew the answers by the look on his face. "Ok George, do you have a family member or a good friend that you can trust completely with your wife's life?"

"Yes, my wife's brother, Larry."

"Good, is he brighter than you are?"

"Yes."

"Good. I have no idea what more can be done for June, all I know is I will find and provide the very best health care for her in the city, including the best doctors and hospitals. Ask for a leave of absence to look after your wife. Say nothing about Ann, it may all blow over. I am going to e-mail my New York lawyer about your wife and tomorrow he or an associate who knows all the legalities of the heath system in New York will come here. I will contact you to let you know what time you and your brother-in-law are to be here tomorrow. Having somebody else you can trust with you for support will be a great help. The lawyer will need all your wife's medical records, your Government health card, Social Security and birth certificate. I will give him your personal and business phone and cell numbers and my e-mail, in case there is a need to contact you before meeting here. Did you hear what I said George, George, do you understand what I am saying?"

"Some, who's going to pay for this, you?" "Yes."

"OK, how Natasha?"

"George, just do as you are told."

"Just one thing Nat, is this money coming from your savings account or piggy bank?" George was smiling now.

"Both my parents left me a very wealthy woman so paying June's hospital bill will make little difference to my wealth George, so please say no more."

I explained that Ann and I were friends, but never once did we talk business. I said we had a lot in common and were very interested in one another's lives but that was all. Suddenly George made a noise; I looked up to see he had his hand over his month as he was crying. No, he wasn't, he was trying to hide a smile and muffle a laugh. "Are you ok George?"

"Yes, yes I am fine please go on with what you were saying."

"Okay then," I just told him. "I knew she loves to write and described what she wanted to do with her writing skills. The articles Ann wrote for the *New York Times* had such depth, Ann made you feel she was right there when the story was happening. Why this sudden need for her to meet my boss so she can go with me overseas on a job? Funny, I never noticed until now how little interest she had in what I did career wise. It was as if Ann didn't want to draw attention to the fact that she would like to know more. Ok George are you laughing again to not to cry over your wife?"

"No, that's not it."

"Ok George what is it?"

"Oh nothing, Nat. It is just the words you use; maybe it is the way you English use different words to mean something else." I just sat there and looked at him. What words? I tried to remember what words would be so funny, as all I talked about was Ann being in the picture and how interested we were in each other.

"You know George you really are a dirty old man. Do you want me to draw pictures or just talk about it?" At that point George was laughing so much he could hardly say the words, "Yes please, both."

Nine o'clock the next morning my lawyer, Mr. Lesley Faggot, arrived with another lawyer well informed of NY city's health systems, Margo Roth. George and brother-in-law Larry were already there. Introductions were made. Coffee, tea, juice, and a continental breakfast were served. After an hour, Margo had all the necessary papers and signatures she needed to spend the rest of the day taking care of business. Larry was a young man just out of law school unsure of his next move. Lesley Faggot was one of New York's top lawyers in financial law plus a senior partner in a successful law practice. Chances are Lesley Faggot and Larry would never have met but they did. Larry became one of the best lawyers at Faggot, Faggot and Faggot. Lesley Faggot, my father and Sir Harry all attended the same school, Windermere in the Lake District.

By 6 p.m., Margo returned with three Doctors' names who felt they had more to offer to June. Lesley Faggot had already left so it was just the four of us to decide which doctor had more to offer. George and Larry chose the same doctor and Margo agreed it was her choice too. We all decided that drinkiepoos were in order. We sat by the fireplace in silence, finding comfort knowing today was well spent.

Margo got up to leave, she turned and looked at the three of us and said, "This day has made me proud to be a lawyer, thank you. Goodbye men my prayers will be for you, so very glad to have met you Natasha. Good night."

She was half way down hall before I ran after her calling out, "You have dropped something Margo."

No, I have not Natasha; he would fire me if I took it." She walked away laughing.

"Now that's clout and boy do you have that Nat," piped up George.

"No, I do not George; it's my money that has clout. Come and sit with me for a few more minutes before you go. George, helping you and June is one thing, my finances are nobody's business but mine. I do not want every Tom, Dick and Harry in the office hitting on me for money or treating me any differently than before. George, you have been more than kind to me, helping me at work more than you needed to and most of all you asked for nothing, never touched my bottom once, never told me those boring dirty jokes going around the office."

"Larry, it appears Lesley Faggot has taken an interest in you because of the way you handled yourself today. Lesley knew George's wife is your sister. After your mother died, June raised you so maybe the family tie is stronger, anyway very impressive how you maintained an air of professionalism under very trying circumstances. He left his card for you to phone him after George is not in need of your help anymore. Larry, what I told George the same thing applies to you: 'mum's the word.'

CHAPTER 17

As soon as they left, I phoned down to the lobby to Fadil. "Yes Miss Bennett?"

"Do you know anything about scooters for women to ride around the city on?"

"Yes, my uncle has a motorbike shop."

"Ok I want red, top of the line for a woman with all the bells and whistles but easy to ride. Oh, and waterproof. The woman's height is 5' 7" and weighs about 120 lbs. She is in her mid-twenties, so not a kids' scooter. Have it delivered tomorrow evening? Ok call me back with good, or bad news, thank you."

Three hours later Fadil had a scooter in the lobby. "Good for you Fadil. Oh, Fadil this is like a piece of art! Is it one of kind? I may just keep this for myself!"

"Just what I was thinking Miss Bennett. I get off at ten and you and I can drive around to see if you want it for yourself or for a friend."

"Good idea Fadil. You buzz me when you are ready to go." It was electric, key or coded to start the scooter. We had such fun with it. "Remember Fadil, this is mine, not yours. Let me drive now."

"No, you do not have a license for a scooter."

"No, neither do you, Fadil." I had to punch him before he would get off the front seat. I was unsure if I needed a scooter license. I think Fadil just made that up about the license. "Fadil, because of what it is I am going to pay by cheque plus taxes made out to your uncle's company. How much of this amount is your commission? Just a little tip Fadil, one lie to me and you will be off my dance card." I expected him, just because he was young, to laugh and say, 'who me' and give a lot of silly talk about how honest he was. His mother who he loved more than his own life would cry if she thought he lied.

Well was I wrong. He did not smile, laugh, or talk just looked right into my eyes.

"Did you hear me Fadil?"

"Yes? Then stop playing this silly game or I will shut this door right now do you understand?"

"XXX dollars," he said.

"What, XXX dollars? On top of the amount for the bike?" I said. "Yes," Fadil said.

"Please arrange for this to be returned to your uncle and thank him for me."

"Miss Bennett, I told you the truth." "I know you did Fadil but it was such a big truth, next time we will not be so greedy."

CHAPTER 18

Next evening George phoned. His wife had already been transferred to the new hospital and met with her new doctors. "No promises, but they do appear to be a lot more hopeful with their more advanced ideas in medicine."

"Oh, I am pleased. George I am leaving tomorrow or the next day for the UK a few days with my family then over to France. You have the Hawkes Manor and my cell phone and telephone numbers. I have spoken with Lesley Faggot and he has agreed to let me hire Margo Roth as the liaison between you and the hospital if needed. She will check with you every day.

June will need you and Larry more now if she feels there is hope so you do not need any outside problems. Please do not tell Margo if Ann acts up. Margo, at the moment, is very pleased with herself and rightly so as she helped find the right hospital and doctors. She now sees you and Larry as her chicks; she is the mother hen, and if she feels any threat to your well-being, she will peck it (Ann) to death or worse lay charges of some kind with the police."

"Oh, no! Do you think so? Nat"

"Maybe," I said laughing.

Twenty-four hours later George phoned and asked, "Why and how did you get involved with this woman? She is not just ding-dong she is crazy, really crazy Natasha, in some ways you are so bright, brighter than anyone I have ever met so why would you get hooked up with this lulu bird?"

"Maybe George, for the same reason you wanted to get hooked up with her."

"Oooooooh," said George.

"She is playing a game with you, George. Would you have called me by now if Ann had been phoning you every few hours asking you very nicely for what she wants to know? The answer is no. By acting crazy, she knows you will give in sooner or later. You know what George, Ann in some ways is brighter than anyone I have ever met. Love you George. I will phone her and tell her she can come with me."

"Ann, I was thinking of leaving tomorrow or the next for the UK to visit with my family for a few days. You can come with me."

"I can come with you, is that what you saying? I CAN COME WITH YOU, NATASHA? Thank you, thank you, I am so sorry I upset you."

"Now don't get too excited Ann, I am thinking about having you done in, I am just waiting to hear from the Public Guard that you have been deemed a dangerous person, a danger to the wellbeing of humanity."

"Oh, you are so funny Nat."

"I will ring you when my assistant books our air tickets."

"Natasha, you are joking. I have never heard of the Public Guard!"

"Well you soon will. Do not play this game with me Ann, making out you are such a simple soul," and I hung up.

We flew first class to London and got a taxi to my St. John woods apartment to drop off our bags and freshen up. We were thinking of going to London's west end, to look and maybe buy a few odds and ends at the big stores along Regent Street etc. We planned to eat at one of the better restaurants we could find, and then afterwards I would walk ahead and leave Ann to pay.

At the apartment, the door would not open. I turned the key again and still no 'do-ey'. What the hell, someone was in my apartment. "Phone the police," Ann said.

"No, I will ring first." A man answered, a man answered my phone in my apartment!

"WHO ARE YOU? OPEN THIS DOOR!" I shouted. I heard the sound of a bolt being pulled back and the door slowly opened. At that point I was so mad I kicked the door open to find Harry standing there laughing.

"Oh Harry," I said. "It's been too long." We hugged. "Harry I would like you to meet a colleague of mine, Ann Gilbert, Ann this is my Harry. I have told you all about him. I did not ring Susan to tell her I was coming home for few days because she would make such a fuss."

Harry started laughing. "Make a fuss you say? Susan will be mad at you for not telling her you were bringing Ann along with you. You know what she's like, the more good looking she thinks someone is, the more Susan feels a need to dress up not to be out done by the person. Wait until Susan sees Ann and Susan is dressed in baggy trousers and an old jumper. She will take you outside and shoot you if you do not ring her and tell her you are both coming up."

"No Harry I will not. Oh, let's have some fun! You are not to tell her!" Ann just stood there not knowing what was going on. She was in one of her dreams.

"Well," Harry said. "I am going back tomorrow by train after a meeting with So & So. Law firm."

"Good, we also are going tomorrow, no idea what time."

After having a coffee and a chat with Harry, Ann and I carried out our plans to shop and do lunch. We left the apartment the following morning. We had been driving awhile and I was thinking Ann was up to something, but what? Nothing was making any sense, maybe I never did know her, and maybe it was a big joke to her. I went over the moments we shared, the times past when all I could do was think about her. Well, that was yesterday. I looked at Ann, she was asleep, head resting on the car door window with a smile on her face, just like the Cheshire cat from Alice. A story I disliked. I saw the smile disappear and tears ran down her beautiful face. I stopped the car and I pulled her to me, we held each other until the tears stopped. Suddenly the sun came out, just like in the movies, as we drove off into the sunset, well not quite sunset.

Maybe walking ahead after we had eaten and leaving her to pay the bill had upset her too much. It was a very expensive restaurant. "Ann, I will reimburse you for the meal, it was my idea to eat there."

"That's ok Nat, I put it on your credit card including the tip, and I also signed your name."

"No, you did not; I have my credit card in my handbag."

"Don't you remember you gave me a second credit card so I could pick up those dresses you bought at Lord and Taylor?"

"Anything else, Ann?"

"Yes, a house…you know better then ask that Natasha."

CHAPTER 19

It was late afternoon when we arrived and there was Susan outside, gardening, clad in an old 1940s brown and cream striped skirt of her late grandmother's and one of Harry's old shirts. Harry was looking out of an upstairs window laughing his head off, miming with his hands and tie that there was going to be hanging and a bloodletting.

Susan was just about to call out to me when she saw Ann getting out of the car, she turned around and began running back to the house. She shouted, "Hello Natasha… I will get Madam for you." Within fifteen seconds, Susan was at the top of the stairs, shouting at Harry who had arrived home twenty minutes earlier… "You knew Nat was coming with a friend, yes you did."

The window closed. Ann and I were sitting in the lounge having a cup of tea when Susan came in wearing a navy suit with a pencil line skirt, the jacket opened showing a scarlet red lining which matched her high-heel shoes. What set off this attire of how to dress to impress, was the sensuous camisole top that could be seen under her jacket. It just needed Susan to put all this together. Her hair was styled and makeup was perfect. Harry walked in a minute later shaking his head with pride. I had to laugh to myself. I knew until we left Susan would spend her time and energy wooing Ann, and Ann would just love it. A good time was had by all, well nearly all. Susan was at her best, in love again. Both Susan and Ann are the 'Jack of Clubs', both loved to debate, progressive in their thinking, nothing is right or wrong just another way of looking at things, but oh so crafty.

That evening I told Harry I had to go outside to make a personal phone call. "You want me to keep Ann inside?"

"Yes."

"No good will come out of this love you have for each other."

"Is this what you see Harry?"

"Ann will manipulate you with her vulnerabilities that she has only shown to you. How you handle this situation will show you what destiny lies ahead for both of you. Please let me make the phone call."

"No Harry, it is not your call to make."

Harry has a gift, a 'second sight' or 'what have you'. He cannot make it happen; it suddenly appears, a dream, a sudden thought that will not go away, a feeling that is here to stay. Harry is a barrister and because of his service in the British Marines, he has an association with both the British and USA governments.

I went outside into the dark. It was the same view that I had seen so many times before. I knew it to be so true when often said,

There is something eerie about the English countryside.

I would never walk alone across the fields at night, even when the moon shines bright. The earth that glows with such beauty in the sun light, turns to dread at night. When the bones of our ancestors rise by the thousands, to see if the land that they died for is still free, and the flag of St. George still flies in defense of this England, this crown, that belongs to you and me. Cc.

My fingers found the buttons on my phone. When it was answered, I pressed the numbers of my code and I then was asked for one word, a word that changed daily. At last, I was put through. It rang five times but no answer. Then I heard the phone change lines.

"Hello, is that you Dolly?"

Silence… then, "Is this you, Natasha? We have had another baby."

Good God, they are like rabbits. How many babies can this woman carry? I was not about to ask how many children he had now, scared he would tell me their names and weight at birth. Dolly was five feet three inches tall and five feet around and lived somewhere in the world.

"What can I do for you, Nat?"

I told him what I wanted and that he personally was to take of care of it.

"Dolly, this is personal. Just lay the person up for a month or so, one leg, nothing permanent and nothing else."

"HOW MUCH…WHAT… OK…OK. I will have the money wired to you after it is done. Mess it up Dolly and I will personally ensure that your wife will never have another baby by you again."

"Natasha! Oh, Natasha. You speak so bad of me you scare me sometimes," Dolly said laughing in his thick whatever country he came from accent.

"I will send photos and identify where she will be. Starting from tomorrow noon GMT until the third day at noon, that is three days. "Any changes, I will contact you. Goodnight Dolly, thank you. And best wishes to your wife and baby."

> I turned once again and looked out over the manor fields. Rain was coming; I could smell the sea air as the wind and tall trees were dancing then reaching out as to embrace the moon's fullness now near hidden by clouds. These British Isles where many come to visit and none are asked to stay. The countryside of my parents and their parents, now forgotten lost to the industrial needs of others. Fields that once were alive and breathing now lay choking from decay. Building after building, that's all you see when driving on the motor way. Remember she will come one day and stay. Goddess of Divine Retribution Nemesis, Cc

The second day there Harry, Susan, Ann and I went walking in the woods nearby when Ann got her toes caught in an old trap! Do not ask me how it happened, I do not know. However, money can buy you anything. With a smile and a show of respect, you can get the very best. Susan and I struggled with Ann getting her back to the manor and into a car so we could drive to the Hospital in town.

Harry had to run back home as he was expecting an overseas phone call on the hour and his client was not a man to be fooled with. Harry needed to speak from the manor library where sometimes his clients liked to take shots of Harry with the time and date showing on his screen. It would not look good if Harry's backdrop was the woods with Ann jumping around on one-foot crying, Susan, and me trying to grab her and shouting at her to be quiet.

Ann had her foot x-rayed although it took forever for the doctor to show up. When he arrived, I swear I heard trumpets as he walked into the cubical with an entourage of second year interns, followed by nurses in waiting. He looked down at the x-ray, feeling Ann's foot and toes. "You can't walk on this foot with these toes for one month. In ten days, you are to come back to the hospital to see me, understand?"

It was then that Susan sprang forward and said, "How can she come here to see you if she is not allowed to walk?"

Hop. He then looked at Ann, his eyes widened. "My, aren't you the pretty one" and he smiled. He then asked one of the nurses in waiting for the Out Patients' form, read it, then had a think, then said to Ann, "Do you live here?"

"No" said Ann, I am visiting with Mrs. Susan?" Ann then looked at me.

I whispered "Hawkes"

"I am staying at Hawkes Manor, a guest of Susan Hawkes."

The doctor swung to face Susan. "Tell me how he does it, the three best-looking women I have seen in this hospital in years." He then turned to his entourage of second year interns and nurses in waiting and said, "That old bastard out at Hawkes Manor is living a life that I would die for. How does he do it? He has a harem of these three beautiful creatures," and at that point, he bowed to each one of us in turn as he walked out of the cubicle. "I will come out to examine your foot and toes at Hawkes Manor in ten days—that will be the 25th at 5:30 p.m. Somebody from the hospital will phone to confirm the date and time with you, and please tell Harry to have the right whiskey this time, not that cheap stuff he pours into the good bottles. Yeah tell him to get Irish Redbreast Single Pot Still. The three of us stood there with our mouths open as the doctor with his entourage floated down the corridors laughing. We arrived home all fired up to tell Harry about the very strange experiences we had at the hospital!

Harry was so spellbound by what happened at the hospital, we had to repeat the whole story twice.

"And none of you knew his name or what this doctor specialized in" Harry said. "I am puzzled who this can be and you said he had a name-tag but none of you could see to read it. Well I hope you 'Three Blind Mice' are not planning a trip together. You will be getting on different trains arriving only to find the three of you staying in different cities. Now tell me again what he looked like."

"Well, he kind of looked like the opera singer Luciano Pavarotti when he was younger," Susan said. Harry just sat there. Nothing rang a bell. Ann's foot and toes were beginning to hurt her now as the meds where wearing off. We kicked Harry off the sofa so Ann could lay out with her foot up. That evening I wired the money to an account number. No name, just numbers that Dolly gave me, and where did the money come from, to pay Dolly? Who knows and for sure, if I don't know you the reader will never know.

That evening Harry carried Ann upstairs, nearly dropping her. Harry yelled out "I know who it is, Peter Cartwright. He and I played rugby together at Windermere."

"That's nice," said Susan and nothing more was mentioned about the matter again that night. Susan and I managed to get Ann in the bathtub so she could have a shower with a plastic bag up to her knee to keep her foot dry. Harry found an old pair of crutches that belonged to Max, which Ann could hop around on upstairs? Susan and I saw Ann to her room and joined Harry downstairs in the library where we very much enjoyed a bottle of brandy among us. I sat opposite Harry and Susan, and just looked. "Ann will have to stay here," said Susan smiling," until she can walk and we do not mind at all. It will be fun."

"So, Nat, what are your thoughts and plans?" asked Harry. At that point, Susan threw back the last of her brandy and stood up (well kind of). "I am going to bed. Goodnight, kiss, kiss."

"I have put too much time into this case to turn it over to another agent," I said. "It will take far too long for me to convey my findings without compromising the case. The next agent will have to start all over again to come to an honest impartial opinion and if that happens, the case would fall apart as it may take too long. I will leave tomorrow morning and try to wrap it up as soon as I can and only if I can. If Ann is still here, I will come back. If not, I may still come back to join you for Christmas. Also, it depends on the agency if they want me back before Christmas to make a report in person, or will they be happy to see, talk and ask questions of me on closed circuit." As I came out of the bathroom from having a hot bath to remove the odor of the hospital, Ann was wandering around the landing upstairs looking for a glass of water. Susan and I had left Ann in bed with only the meds and nothing to drink or drink from.

"Oh, Ann I am so sorry I will get some right now. Anything else, hot milk?" I returned with a glass of water, a cup of hot milk and a chocolate bar and put them on the bedside table.

All of sudden Ann yells out, "YOU HAVE BEEN DRINKING! The three of you sitting down having a booze up and nice little chat with me upstairs with nothing. What did you drink?"

Then I told her we killed one bottle of brandy. "You cow, I hope you have nightmares and get fat." I was laughing as I made my way to the door. Ann called to me, "Stay the night." "Why?" I didn't wait for the answer before the tears began to flow I closed the door.

I caught the train to London the next day leaving the car that I had rented in London with Harry who would take it to the local same company rent-a-car in town. I stayed at my St John's Woods flat making plans and thinking what to do. The flat at one time belonged to my parents and Sir Harry had kept it for me. The case turned out to be uneventful so I tied it up within a month and flew back to London where I made my report to the Head office via closed circuit. Then I took the train home to Hawkes Manor.

If I can and have time, I love to travel by train. You can take a snooze, smile and nod to the other travelers sitting near you or get up and walk a little. Better still, go to the bar and you will be sure to find someone to talk to you. Harry met me at the station with all his news.

Ann had left Hawkes Manor a few days after Harry's long-lost friend Doctor Peter Cartwright came to examine Ann's toes; all three toes were doing well. Doctor Peter stayed two nights. He and Harry drank their way to happiness with Susan cooking away with Ann's help, trying to keep up with these huge men. "Ann appeared worried that she had not heard from you. I told her and that you were Ok, no problems and you did not want to ring in case you and she got upset because you both were not together and that you could not wait to see her."

"YOU SAID WHAT HARRY? Ann's not going to believe that silly story. What world are you living on? Harry I am so mad at you." As soon as we were at the manor, I was out of the car. "SUSAN,

SUSAN!" Susan came running out. "What is wrong" "Do you know what your husband said to Ann? What did I tell you Harry?"

Harry was sitting in his car with his head down. "Natasha has just been through a separation, and in her mind, she feels she has failed. When women hear words like 'being so upset they are not together' they see this as a commitment. That is the last thing Natasha wants to do, commit herself to another at this moment. Nat needs to find herself on her own. Nearly half her life other people have had to tell her who she is. Nat is no longer the ten-year old child we took in. We did a wonderful job, and now is time for her to tie up her own shoes laces. Let us hope that Ann has been around the block, a few more times than you Harry."

CHAPTER 20

As much as I have told myself, it was over it wasn't and it never would be, I prayed and hoped Ann would still be at Hawkes Manor upon my return. Why she went to all the trouble to come with me I may never know. It was then I realized how pointless my life was. I always saw myself as strong. Oh, sure I needed people and loved my family and friends, but this love when Ann and I were together filled that dark, empty space I kept for my parents, brother and sister. I sat down at the kitchen table and cried. Then I felt the comfort of Susan's arms around me and I felt her power to love. I told Susan how I felt, that I still loved, needed, wanted Ann and that goddess Nemesis had done her job well. Don't talk silly why the goddess of divine retribution would be after you!

"That is, it. She comes after people that have too much."

"You think that is you, is it Natasha?"

"Yes, I have too much money."

"Well give it to me then," said Susan. Then we both started laughing.

"Oh look, there is Harry standing over there listening. Come here Harry," Susan said. "It will work itself out in time Nat. You will just have to get on with life now. It is neither your time nor Ann's to be a couple. If the love you have for each other is meant to be, you will come together again. However, there is another that I 'see'; it will be a love like no other. Have fun now, as if you do get together, it will be a long time."

"Is that what you see Harry?"

"Enough already, no more. Good night Natasha, Susan" he replied. Susan made some hot milk, and we sat by the window looking out at the trees painted against the dark sky. "You know Nat," Susan said, "Sometimes when I look out at night across the fields I am so glad I am inside and not out. There something not quit right with the English countryside when it's this late at night."

We had a wonderful Christmas. The whole family was there; the 'Girls' (the triplets), Mick, Max, Mrs. B, Liz, Mrs. B.'s sister and family. Also present were Harry's sister Terri and her lot, Susan's sister, both sets of parents and a collection of aunties who were still alive. It really was an open house for all we knew and cared for.

"I am going back to New York on the twenty-eighth," I told Max. "So, I will see you when I see you."

"Are you sure you do not mind me coming and going all the time Nat?"

"The condo is so big, maybe too big for one person, so having you come and go, I like that Max. Our relationship is so different from many other couples that have broken up. We have gone back to being like brother and sister, both sharing the same parents and we are the best of friends. I have told you already my home is your home while you are single."

"So, I can't bring my wife and six kids then," Max said laughing.

"I hope you know you can bring a girl or friends with you."

Why I thought the condo was too big was a bit funny as there was always some of the family there. Harry's sister loved it there. I think she goes to get away from her lot. Frequent guests also included the triplets and mates, a few friends of both Max and I, such as good friends from university. I love it when Mrs. B. and her sister are there as after they leave the condo is spotless and the freezer is full of Mrs. B's. Cooking Sometimes I am there; sometimes I may be traveling and working overseas. All know that guests are to look after themselves. It is easier to get into Fort Knox's than my condo. When I am not, there the front desk has passport numbers and photos for overseas visitors. Local visitors need a photo and ID. If they get past the front desk, guests are given a temporary key number for their length of stay.

"Max, would you like to come back now with me?"

"Oh God, I thought you would never ask. Yes please Nat."

"Good, I will get two first class tickets. I love being out with you traveling or going places in New York. You are so handsome the women and young men give you the old 'come on' look, which is just amazing. From now on, I will hold your arm or you may hold my hand."

"Why?"

"I like showing you off. I do not know why and I do not care. Maybe I am more like Susan than I know. That is why I came to live at Hawkes Manor. I am the hen and you are my chick, so to speak. Please allow me the freedom Max to show you how much I care for you without reading anything more into it. You may see a few women visiting me there but never another man."

"As time goes by the memory of Ann will fade and you will meet someone else," Max said.

"Maybe Max, remember I am 'Scorpio rising' and we never forget, our emotions they are buried so deep."

Susan and her sister and Harry are coming here to the condo in the spring.

Ooops, I never told you, the reader, about the layout of my condo. There are two floors with a second floor having five large bedrooms, bathrooms and a common area; the ground floor has two sitting areas, library, media room, storage room very big pantry, one dining room which will sit twenty at the table and a kitchen with more of an informal dining area.

We landed on the twenty-eighth and I was back to work the next day.

"Well," said George, "We expected you back sometime in November."

"The plane was delayed. I did write and tell the personal department I would not be back until after Christmas, so what do you say about that Georgie. In addition, how much have you missed me, I bet you want to kiss me to death." Well, that made the whole department laugh. Afraid to ask I made myself say "How is June, George"?

He smiled. "The doctors are very hopeful; one doctor on the QT told me she's going to make it."

"So, when can I come and visit"?

"You can't. June will not let you yet but when she is in full recovery and looks good you can come and see her. (He then lowered his voice so no one could hear). "She just wants to show you what your act of kindness and love has done for her and for us. Whether the treatment had worked or not your power of love has shown my children how one act of caring can give hope to a whole family. They in return will move on with or without their mother to help others. Nat, my children can see what a difference someone's gift of giving has made to their mother. She is getting the very best of care, it has given her peace of mind, and she believes that no matter what happens our children will be ok."

The day before New Year Eve, Max and I sat down with my New Year eve parties invites to see where we should go. Max was beside himself with excitement over all the cards. Look at this one; my God, I never knew you knew these people, look at this a Royal seal on the back from the British embassy even. We best get going now or we will never make it to all of them.

We were home by five thirty a.m. and were as drunk as lords and that was after turning up at only three parties. The next morning, I awoke in Max's bed… with Max. As I slowly remembered all, I had to laugh. Hadn't I been telling Max he is welcome here as my best friend, a brother and sister relationship, but as soon as we got drunk I am following him in to his bed. I hoped he could not remember or thought he had dreamt it.

A few hours later Max was up reading his e-mail and drinking coffee. "Nat, look at this. I have been offered a job in London and they are asking can I come for an interview on this Thursday.

Thank God, I thought. "Are you going to go?"

"You know Nat, I may just do that, get an idea what kinds of jobs are open in my field."

Thank God again. Max will never remember sex at 6 am with all this on his mind. Max left the next day for London hoping to land a new job. Though I will miss him, he will be back as early as Saturday and I will have to listen to him go on and on about this job for the rest of Saturday. Thank God, I was going out Sunday with a new friend. I know Max does not remember anything about sex at 6am. Now I am remembering as we walked home from the last party horror upon horror; we went in to a laneway and did it. Now I do not know what is upsetting me more, doing it twice or that I am I so sexually boring that Max remembers nothing. Max was still looking at his computer, e-mailing his mother and father about the job interview. I walked by, gave him such a kick, and walked on. "Oops I am so sorry Max. Did I hurt you?"

"Yes, you did, but it was so worth it… three times we did it," Max said, "three times! It took us nearly two hours to walk what usually takes thirty-five minutes."

"For goodness sake, do not tell your mother." We were both laughing more now seeing this image of Max telling his mother, "Mum, we did it three times. Mum, three times!"

"And what would Susan say?" I asked.

"I know," I said, she would say, "count yourselves lucky, when the time comes you reach your father's age you will be lucky if you do it once." We both rolled on the floor laughing so much and with that cheeky smile of his he rolled over and said let's see how many more times we can do it today!"

I had a real good time with my friend on Sunday. We went to the zoo of all things then out to dinner.

Max left Monday evening for another interview scheduled for Wednesday. I called him and said, "Now Max sometimes with these interviews there are three stages so there may be another one after Wednesday. If you come back, will they know you are in New York? If they e-mail you at nine a.m. GMT, which is four a.m. EST, and they are unaware of you being here in New York plus the five hours difference, they may think you are just taking your time to reply and not that interested. It's ok to ask at the end of the second interview if is there going to be third. If so, and it's within the next few days you can stay in England instead of flying back and forth to New York. Tell them this Max. If they are interested in you they will tell you something then because they will know you are a planner and do not like to waste your time!"

"Jolly good Nat, thank you I will phone or e-mail you."

Max e-mailed to say, "The next and last interview is Friday morning and they are putting me on the list. I will stay in London, wish me luck, love, Max."

Hmm so, he is interested in the job, good. Can you imagine being so excited about getting a job in linguistics, well neither can I. Well he got it. I was so happy for Max, "When do you start Max?"

"The day after tomorrow, two months at head office here in London; after that I am not sure."

"Oh! Max I am so happy for you, "but there is always a personal price that you have to pay for someone else's happiness. For forty-five minutes, I had to listen on the phone to Max's blow-by-blow description of his new job. Thank God, he was in London and I am in New York. I know Max, every week he will phone his mother and father his three sisters and of course, me in turn to tell us every working moment on the job, until we all dread that phone call from London.

"Max, Max can you hear me, yes, I am going to hang up do you know why?" I said.

"Because, you're bored?"

"Yes. What happened to all those classmates of yours from University that you studied with whom you were so madly in love? Did they die from boredom?"

"Now that's a good one" Max said.

"Yes, one of my best" and then we both laughed. "I am going to miss you Max."

"You know Nat, I would look for job in New York if I thought for a minute we would be doing it three times a day."

"Max, some days I could feel your sadness and wish I was the one to take it away but that's not going to happen". Goodnight Max."

"Goodnight Nat."

CHAPTER 21

"**W**ell, how are you feeling today Natasha?"

"I feel a little better today thank you, so what do my reports say doctor?"

He smiled, "You are healthy and pregnant."

"I am what?"

"Pregnant, my dear. "You and your husband are having a baby."

"My husband is now living in New Zealand."

"Oh," said the doctor.

"Oh, it's his child" I said. "The job he is on means the world to him, plus we have parted."

"Well at least it appears to have been a very friendly parting."

I had to laugh at his humor.

"You're a few months along, so come in soon and we can have a look at the baby." When I returned I was in for a big surprise as a nurse conducted the sonogram.

"Babies! Twins! I am having twins?"

"Yes, but I cannot tell for sure, but one is a boy and the other a girl I think. You said you and your husband have parted. "Would he help you in any way?"

"Max adores children just loves them."

Then next the birth "Three, three beautiful babies, two boys and one girl, three healthy babies". If this Nurse said 'three' one more time, I would have to kick her, kick her hard. I think at that point, when 'three' was on the end of her tongue she read my mind and backed away making room for the doctor.

"Good afternoon, my dear."

"Hello Doctor," I said as he entered the room. He explained the second boy was hidden behind the other boy so we had been unable to see him.

"If I may say so, after two, one more baby is not that much different as far as all the trouble they are going to cause you as they grow up. It's the girl you have to watch out for she came out fighting first; her brothers were just pushed out of the way."

I knew right then this was my daughter and I hoped and prayed the boys would be like their father. It's foolish to think the human race could be happy. Our history has never shown that we are a happy contented, loving and forgiving species. Then there's Max. He is forever the boy that's learning to be a man. When I found out I was pregnant I buried my head in the sand and it stayed there until now. What am I going to do? My family, Susan and Harry are on a six-month boat tour. Max is still in New Zealand and I cannot ask Max's sisters to drop everything and come over here to New York without some notice. So, I told the family the condo was being renovated so no one in the family could see I was pregnant. Why I did this is beyond my thinking now. I had no idea what to do with my life, what country to live in, what to do about my job. How can I by myself look after three babies? What about Max and his girlfriend, he has rights to his children. We would have to share but no way is she raising my children when they are with Max.

I did not tell Max because he would have just up and left his job, and his plans and hopes for a career in the job he loves may be over. I realize now that was not my decision to make, it was Max's to decide where his responsibilities lie. The person who I needed, of course, was Mrs. B., level-headed Mrs. B, of all the family. I could lean on her. Now I have support from women co-workers and old friends from the British Intelligence office, working in shifts.

I phoned Mrs. B., reminding her that I had cancelled their trip (Mrs. B. and her sister) from the UK to New York a few months ago because of the condo fix-up. That was one of my many silly lies to cover up when I was first pregnant. I asked if she would like to visit now as I had some free time to spend with her and her sister.

"That would be fine," said Mrs. B. "Yes, very good."

"I will see you then. Let me know the airline, flight number, day, time, and a car will be waiting for you." I told my friends help was on its way from England and how grateful I was to all my friends here. I thought they would feel relieved Mrs. B. was coming but no, they just loved coming here to mind the babies. One said it was the best job ever.

Mrs. B. and Mrs. Lovelock arrived Saturday and we all enjoyed a lunch catered by Mario's take out restaurant. All my friends joined the two sisters; we decided that, and in the future, I would call the group of friends 'the aunties'. We celebrated with wine and beer and although we were getting loud, the babies slept on. I had put them in the next room so they would get used to people laughing and making some noise. I never wanted me or anyone else to feel they had to creep around while the children were in bed. Well that turned out to be a joke, as the kids, when older, would make more noise than the New York subway at rush hour. I knew nothing about babies so I hired a nurse who had worked with children to cover the lunch party hours. As there usually was beer and wine served, I thought it would be a good idea just to have a sober eye on them.

When they first arrived, Mrs. B. and her sister had no idea what to make of this loud group of women. "Hi Mrs. B., Hi Mrs. Lovelock" the aunties all called out. Now Mrs. B. looked scared. "Natasha, she said, "This is not one of those all girls' parties is it?"

"All girls' party, what do you mean Mrs. B?" I said.

"You know damn well what I mean. Natasha I am too old for this nonsense."

"Mrs. B., I need you. Of all the family you are the most level headed and I need you to tell me what I am to do."

"About what" she asked?

"Well, surprise Mrs. B.! It's about my three babies." I took them into the next room and showed them, they both screamed, "Where did you get these babies from?"

"The internet" Mrs. Lovelock whispered. "The internet's black market."

"Honest to God, you are getting sillier each day." Mrs. B. said to her sister "I gave birth to them, so what do I do now?"

"Does anyone "else know back home?"

"Max? No, no!"

"Why not?"

I don't know," I said.

How come someone as daft as you have such beautiful babies," Mrs. B. said looking down and smiling at them. "Well, maybe not so daft. That was smart. Putting them in a room close to the girls laughing so they can hear and having the nurse keeping an eye on them just to see if they are coping alright was wise."

"I tell you, I am not sharing my babies with Max so his girlfriend can raise my children when they are with him. That will never happen. I think that's why I told no one at home before. There will be no six here and six month there. Plus, I wanted them born in the USA so there will have the same opportunities that had afforded me, having dual citizenship.

That would not have happened if I had been made to go back to England by a well-meaning family. So, Mrs. B. and Mrs. Lovelock, what do you suggest?

"First, we have time and while it matters little, where they spend their days now, the three of us can easily look after the babies. Later we can start taking them outside, maybe in separate prams to central Park, to get used to other people around them, that's if it is alright with you."

Mrs. B. said looking at her sister, "Are you kidding, I would love that as long as we can hire other baby sitters sometimes so we can go out and have fun too."

"That's no problem, all the 'aunties' who are in the kitchen eating would love to baby sit with a gourmet meal and a view. You had better phone your Arthur (husband) then," said Mrs. B. to her sister.

The phone rang. "Shall I pick it up?" asked Mrs. B., standing by the phone.

"Please tell me who it is before you say I am here."

"Hello (silence), hello (silence). May I ask to whom I am speaking? No, oh! I think you have the wrong number. Thank you" and Mrs. B hung up. "That was Susan."

The phone rang again. "Give it to me please," I said laughing.

"Hello, is that you Natasha?" Susan asked.

"Yes, is this you Susan?" We both laughed. Susan went on to say, "We left the boat as it was very nice but too long for us. We went to New Zealand to visit Max as he has broken up with his girlfriend Joan."

"Why?"

"She did not want children and made that very clear."

"Was he upset Susan?"

"Not really, he was thinking she would not be the kind of mother he would want for his children. Max said Joan has a sister with children and Joan showed very little interest in the children never gave them anything and showed no interest in taking them out with them. Other than that, Max said she is very nice person."

"Oh! Max is such a funny person let's hope I pass the test."

"What does that mean Natasha?"

Well I have just said the wrong thing. "Oh, nothing Susan, I meant if we had stayed together would I have passed Max's exam and would I have to take the test every year."

"Yes, you would" Susan said. "Max had a perfect mother and every year I had to take the exam to be his mother. Max has some very funny ways that you can only laugh at. You know Harry has some very odd ways too, must run in their family. Anyway, my dear we are at the airport, tired and hungry, so we are going to find ourselves an A-1 hotel to spend the night and we will be out tomorrow to see you and visit for a few days' maybe even weeks. We will see how it goes."

I could hear Harry and someone else laughing in the background when Susan said, 'maybe weeks'.

"Susan, what airport are you at now?"

"You know the one with the funny name. La G something."

"In New York?"

"Yes dear."

"Well that's so funny, guess who popped over today. Mrs. B. and Mrs. Lovelock"

"Mrs. B. and her sister popped over from England today? Are they there now?"

"Oh, no they are staying at a hotel tonight and coming here tomorrow for a holiday."

"Natasha, I am so tired, I cannot think anymore. The three of us will be there tomorrow."

"What, three of you?"

"Harry, Max and I. Goodnight Nat."

"They are at the airport here in New York. The three, Harry, Susan and Max will be here tomorrow because the three are tired and hungry so will stay at an A-1 hotel overnight. Max has broken up with his girlfriend as he thinks she will not make a good mum. So, I had to tell Susan, you both were here and staying at an A-1 hotel in New York and that you are coming here for a holiday tomorrow. I had to lie in case Susan decided to come now to make sure you did not choose the bedroom she wants."

The look on the faces of Mrs. B. and her sister was as if they just heard the story of the 'sister they thought dead was alive and just run off with all their parents money'. I stood there waiting for Mrs. B to tell me what a strange bird Susan was and she did.

"You know Susan is a strange bird and you know she will not sleep all night worrying in case we get here first and get the bedroom with the view."

Oh no, I thought, Susan will be here at five a.m. knowing Mrs. B. does not like to get up early. Susan and Mrs. B. really care about each other and are the best of friends, then all of a sudden, a big disagreement would take place. Maybe it's the full moon. Reader you may laugh or not believe in universal forces beyond our understanding, but I remember when I lived at Hawkes Manor as a child, if Sir Harry saw a troubling full moon which would affect Mrs. B. and Susan, he would say "watch out for the kitchen… full moon tomorrow." On this day Max, Sir Harry and I would not go anywhere near the kitchen and the girls never came to visit. I can remember a time when each of us, the girls being older then Max and I, laughed at Sir Harry and this silliness about the moon. No more, not after the kitchen was flooded and the next month the oven was on fire. One-time Susan hit Mrs. B.'s bottom with a frying pan as she bent down. She told Mrs. B. it was her fault as she had such a big bum and Susan could not help herself.

Hawkes Manor had many house pets, loved by all. With my own eyes I have seen them all leave together, to spend the day far away in the next field and come home when other members of the family had returned on those fateful days.

The phone rang again. This time it was Harry. "Are Mrs. B. and her sister there now?"

"Yes."

"I thought so. You were wise to tell Susan they were at a hotel, which would make no sense to anyone else but her. Why would two parties of people be visiting and staying with family in New York stay in a hotel near by the day before? It's a full moon tomorrow," Harry said.

"Well, Susan is not coming here Harry, not tomorrow no way, no sir, take her to the zoo. What about a cruise around Manhattan?"

"She's just got off a cruise."

"Well take her on another."

"Listen Nat. Mrs. B. and her sister will not mind going out for the day, I will pay for everything and they can stay at the best hotel in New York while we visit, all on me" said Harry in a silly boyish way.

"That's fine Harry, you ask her." "Mrs. B." I called out.

"No, no Nat. Please, you ask, not me."

"Why Harry, why me? Why should I have to ask invited guests to move out for a day and pretend she has never been here over night but staying at a hotel so Susan can turn-up out of the blue. Your plan is to take what is Mrs. B. and her sister's room for their stay here while they are on holidays. Dear Harry, I know you must be at your wits end, locked up on a boat for months with Susan. We all love her dearly but why would you put yourself in harm's way like that. Did you hear your own death rattle and think this was your last farewell to Susan? I know once I get off the phone with you that I am going to cry, because I am hurting you, and I love you so much, but what about Mrs. B. and sister, who I invited over here. You want me to ask them to move out and pretend they were never going to stay in hotel room. Susan turns up out of the blue and has to have the room Mrs. B. was in. If I were Mrs. B., I would pack up my bags, give you and Susan the finger, get on the first plane out of here and go back to Hawkes Manor. Now I am upset Harry that you would ask this of me. It's ok for me to hurt Mrs. B but not you. Harry please take Susan home. I do not want to see either of you right now. You know Harry, can you not see how nutty this is. All I can think is you were on the boat too long with Susan. Bye."

Mrs. B. and sister sat there with their mouths open wide and said, "Harry is not going to keep Susan away."

"If we did not have the babies to think about we could just take off for the day, so you better tell the desk not to let your Harry and Susan up until you tell them otherwise, and do not open the door in case Susan outfoxes the desk. Where there's a will there is a way. One more thing Nat, Mrs. B. said, tell Susan one way or another that they're your babies and they are not hers or she will take over completely. If Susan takes no notice of you, you might as well 'do her in' now rather than later." "Thank you for doing the right thing and keeping me from doing something I would have come to regret by taking the first plane out of here. I know if Harry had his way I would have done."

At 10:00 p.m., Max phoned and said of his parents, "They have just gone to bed. Am I on the no-visit list or may I come over now?"

"Don't be silly; of course, you can visit. Max are they going back home?"

"What do you think Nat? That's right they are going to stay until you give in, and, as we both know my mum and Mrs. B., after a few days, will fall into each other arms and wonder what all the fuss was about. "

"How long will you be Max?"

"About half an hour."

Ok. The sisters had long gone to bed as their bodies were still on British time. The three of us had taken the babies upstairs to my room with extra milk. I flew into the bedroom, woke and changed the babies, got the milk ready for Max to bottle-feed the boys and I would breast-fed my girl. I could hear Max running up the stairs.

"Nat, Natasha."

"I am in my bedroom, Max."

He walked over to me but never took his eyes off the bed with babies on it. "Whose are these babies Nat?"

"They are the woman's in the next condo," I said.

"Where is she now Nat?"

"Outside, walking her dog."

All the time he is talking his eyes never left the babies. "That's it, the mother is outside walking her dog and you are babysitting these little babies you know nothing about Nat?"

"Ok Max, they are my babies and they are your babies too."

Max cried, laughed and cried some more. It was then I knew I had four babies, three would grow up and one would be forever Peter Pan. Max just sat on the bed looking at them. "I love them already are you ok about them?"

"Oh Max! I love them so much!"

"I have so many questions to ask Nat. Is it because we 'did it' so many times? When did you know it was triplets?"

"The day of the delivery. It was a C-section because the boy was so big, which turned out to be two boys."

"Any names yet?"

"No, that's for the both of us to decided Max. I do like the name Bradley and no names for the living if that is ok. I mean like Max Junior. It's too confusing and it would not be right for the other twin boy." Max agreed.

"Would the twins look alike? Did the doctor say there are twin boys with a girl thrown in?"

"Max, the doctor said she came first, pushing the boys aside. I was to watch her, as she may be trouble, so no showing favarites with the boys."

Are you kidding, you know of all people how I love butch girls. Look Nat, Nat look, she is the only one awake and she is smiling at me". Max took my hand and said, "Is this happiness Nat"

"Yes, it is Max."

The next morning Max and his babies were in the kitchen waiting for Mrs. B. and her sister. Where are they, I thought. It is 7:35 am. I knocked on their bedroom. No answer, I knocked again. Still no answers so I opened the door and saw they were both still fast asleep. I called out" Mrs. B. it's me Susan!" Mrs. B. was out of her bed in two seconds and looked at me.

"That was not funny Natasha. I could have had a heart attack. Oh! The babies of course, the babies! You poor girl, what help have we been! You must be so tired."

"It is ok, Max has been with me. He is sitting in the kitchen with his babies waiting for you both to get up. He will not leave them alone with just me in case I drop, lose, not feed or not change all three." Have I ever lucked out with Max being the father? He fed, changed and chatted them to sleep, and if it had been possible Max would have breast fed them himself.

Fifteen minutes later both sisters and Max sat around the table, each holding a baby. Thank God, I thought, that Susan and Harry can't see this very happy family picture. It would really hurt them so much not to be included. I was upset that we all could not be together, but not today, not on a full moon, with Mrs. B. and Susan. (You may laugh dear reader, but if you just had three of the most beautiful babies in the world, would you not cover all the bases? You bet your sweet arse you would.) It was another three days before we heard from Susan.

"Hi Nat. I was wondering if I could come and see you before I leave as I am going back to the UK the day after tomorrow. Harry has gone down to Key West, Florida as he has an old army chum living there."

I could hear the sadness her voice. "What happened, Susan?"

"He is mad at me and fed up. He said that you did not want to see us at all because Mrs. B. was there with her sister, I would fight with her over the bedroom, and because Mrs. B. was invited by you I had no business causing trouble just turning up."

"Oh Susan, that's not true." I told Susan what happened. Well, not all of it, "Harry wanted Mrs. B. and her sister to stay away the next day after your arrival and he would pay the expenses. I said fine, you ask her, no, he wanted me to ask so I would be the one that would hurt Mrs. B.'s feelings. I was mad at him about that so I told him not to come and you could both go home. You come over here right now Susan."

"Thank you, Nat.," I told Max and the sisters what happened, and that Harry had gone to Key West.

"How long has he been gone?"

"I do not know but Susan sounded very sad on the phone."

Max was mad. "So, he just left my mother alone in a hotel suite not knowing what's going on. I should have phoned her."

"Max, we were all wrong. We thought they had gone back home."

"I was with them. I came with them from New Zealand. I am her son. I have three children now and I cannot look after my own mother. Not a very good son."

"Stop it Max. We all got caught up with the babies, you cannot blame yourself."

"You better phone the desk and tell them it is ok for Susan to come up" said Mrs. B. It was an hour before Susan arrived. There was no other word for it, she looked awful, her eyes were bloodshot and she looked thinner than when I last saw her. I just stood at the door looking at her and cried, asking her to forgive me for being so cruel. "When did Harry leave?"

"Two days ago," Susan cried.

I held her as along as Mrs. B. would let me, knocking me out of the way to give comfort to her best friend. Then there was Max.

"I was so happy Mum. I did not want to phone and hear about the full moon and who was going to sleep in what room. I was upset about Dad telling Nat she should be the one to tell Mrs. B. and her sister to stay in a hotel. We were all so happy we just wanted to keep it that way." Susan would be the first to tell you sometimes she is a drama queen but not today. She looked like life had just beaten her up. She had not even wondered why we had all been happy. Good God she just fainted. Max and Mrs. B. took care of her as Mrs. Lovelock was calling me to help with the babies. Susan could not remember when she had last eaten.

"Ok Max, you stay with her and I will cook this silly woman something to eat." Max sat there holding and sweet talking his mother while Susan's best friend cooked her meal. I sat with our babies so Mrs. Lovelock could join her sister to have a good gossip.

Mrs. B. fed Susan, gave her one of her magic pills, and sent her off to 'noddyland' until the next morning.

"Good morning everyone', said Susan walking into the kitchen. "Boy did I have a good sleep."

"Hi Susan, do you feel better? You look it," I said.

"Oh, Mum you look a lot better than yesterday," said Max, coming over to kiss her with a baby in his arms.

"Who is this baby, who is that baby?" looking over to me also holding a second baby. "And what the hell is Mrs. B. doing with yet another one? Ok Mrs. Lovelock, why do you not have a baby and if everyone has a baby where is mine?"

Well that was good for a laugh. "They are your grandchildren Susan," I said.

Susan's reaction was nothing like I expected. She just stood there looking down, never saying a word. One minute passed and Mrs. B. could not contain herself any longer.

"You really are a strange bird Susan. You are just mad because there's not more so you can take one home."

"Don't be silly Mrs. B. I am taking them all home with me. I was just thinking how. Nat, when you came to live with us my three daughters had left or were about to leave for a boarding school so there is no way I am comparing them with you or you with them. You became my pride and joy. You were so easy to raise, bright and clever, and because you needed Harry and me, so much we needed you. I would have given my life for the darkness of your past losses to leave you, for you to have the power to love yourself as we did. Natasha, you may never find the past you long to know. The only past your children will know or care about as far as you are concerned is the day you came to Hawkes Manor into this family and all at Hawkes Manor. I hope we all can show and share with these babies what the power of love is all about.

As it appears, I am your main speaker for today so a few more things to say. This may upset me, I feel ill over it, about Harry and this full moon business. It has been setup that Mrs. B. and I are the main villains and everybody else are innocent bystanders. Sometimes at the full moon, Mrs. B. and I do go potty, but my husband, son and you Nat also go potty. My daughters, if I were dying, would not come to see me if they know the animals have also left home. At the full moon, Mrs. B. and I have such power we can move heaven and earth. It is a story that my husband told you and if you believe the full moon or just any moon can move tides then why is it only Mrs. B. and I are the ones that are swept out to sea? Enough of that, Natasha and Max, you have made me the happiest grandmother in the world."

Well I had to tell the whole history of the babies to Susan now. Max listened as if it was the first time he had heard it.

"Look at him he is beginning to walk like an old hen hopping from one baby to the other. Look out Nat, Max does not need you now."

"I know he is going to run the show for about six months, then he is going to wonder what the hell do I do around here as he has been made to feed, change, bathe, play, chatter, and take them out. I hope he can laugh about this as much you and I are, Susan."

"Well Mum, I think we had better go to your hotel, get your suitcases and come back here. You will need to change your clothes soon."

Susan and I fell over laughing at Max. He really was becoming an old hen.

"He will be pecking you clean soon if you do not bathe and change. Now Susan, do not ask Mrs. B. and her sister to move to another bedroom."

"As if I would," said Susan, smiling at me.

"Have you and Max made any plans or know what you are going to do or is it too soon to think?"

"Well, one thing I know. Max would never let me raise them on my own and I would never allow another woman to raise my children if Max wanted to live with someone else. This happened over New Year's Susan, we were drunk from all the parties and we had a lovely time. When Max took the job in UK then New Zealand, he said he would look for a job in New York. If I thought for minute…However, that's not going to happen. Susan, I love Max, we get on very well, we have fun together, we laugh at the same things and we will make good parents, He and I are going to have to change roles. If I stayed home with the children I can see it now…he would be trying to control from wherever he was: why do the children have those good clothes on today; they went to the park yesterday so why again today; do not let the girl boss the boys too much; do not let them wear dirty clothes. I know he would not raise them like that if he stayed home with them, but Max being Max needs to have more say in how the children are raised. And coming home from work after the children's day is nearly done would not be enough for Max."

"I agree," said Susan. "What a wise and cunning woman you are."

"I know Susan, it takes one to know one. Yes, and I still want to work. You know Susan, he supervises me when I pump my milk he is such an old woman."

"Don't look now Nat, he is coming towards us, pushing all three babies in a pram, with three bottles of milk under his armpits and he is wearing a hair net."

"Shut up Susan."

The three of us sat down and fed the babies then Max informed us we might have a problem. "Mrs. B. and her sister have gone for a nap as they are both tired, so if I go with Mum to get her suitcases that will leave you, Nat, on your own with the babies. Mum, we will have to wait until Mrs. B. gets up.

"I have a better idea Max. Why don't I go with Susan? We can get a porter to help us down with the bags."

"Are you sure Nat?"

"Yes. I need some air." Twenty minutes later Susan and I hopped into a cab.

"When he was a little boy and I asked him to do something, Max would say as long as it's not a girly thing that you make my sisters do."

"You know what I think, too many females, that is, you, the girls, me, have played a big part in his young life."

"Don't talk daft Natasha, what about Harry?"

"He is the biggest old woman there is" Susan said. "That's where Max gets it from. I bet our babies are as good as gold, and Max will think it's nothing to be with them all day, so he is the best one to be with them and that mothers complain too much. He and I are going have a talk about his plans when we get back, that is if Mrs. B. and her sister are up and ready to take the babies."

"You know Natasha, I once did have triplets, I could manage."

"Oh, I am sorry Susan. Are you sure, you are up to it with what you have been through the last few weeks?

"I am going to smack you in a minute if you don't stop Natasha."

CHAPTER 22

We arrived home to find Max on the floor with his three babies circled around his head. All were smiling and blowing bubbles, and this time I had a camera with me. Susan looked at me. You are so lucky Nat. Make all your plans now before they turn two years old."

I was nearly crying. What a lovely scene to come home to. I bent down looking at my girl smiling away at me. As I went to pick her up Max hit my hand then my leg hard. "No!" He said.

I went to the phone. "Hi Fadil."

"Yes Miss Bennett?"

"Is Riccardo with you? Yes, well then, would you please both come up here and escort my husband out of my home."

"Yes Miss Bennett."

Max was standing up now and was white as a sheet. I went over to him and said "I carried those babies around for months, all three. I felt my back was going to break when all you cared about was getting it up."

The boys arrived and Max walked out with them.

"I am sorry you had to see that Susan, but Max will never lay a finger on me again or come between my babies and me."

"Well I guess you told him! Come here my dear." It appears Mrs. B. and her sister were also witness to the who-ha between Max and I and were shocked at Max's behavior; even triple shocked that I found the nerve to have Max removed.

"Well that is what happens when you try to take cubs from a mother bear. I think you best check with your Arthur to see if he is ok. It appears men are going a bit funny," Mrs. B. said to her sister. The next morning at breakfast, only Mrs. B. found the words we were thinking. Well nobody phoned, not Sir Harry or Max.

"If the phone rings Nat may I answer the phone in case it's Max? He may want to check out the situation with me first."

"Of course, Susan" I said. As we said it, the phone rang.

"Hello, hello Max." Susan got up from the table moved over to a comfortable chair and sat there listening. "Max, this is the second time you have hurt Nat in such a cruel way. She is not yours and she never will be, which is neither her fault, nor is it yours. It's not fair I know. Nat was happy, so very happy the way you loved the babies and what did you do Max? What's wrong with you? You know I am the only one in this family that does not have a dark and cruel side." Mrs. B., Mrs. Lovelock and I looked at each other wondering if Susan really believed what she was saying.

Mrs. B. whispered, "If this was not such sad and difficult moment for Susan and Max, and Nat and Max, Susan should win a best performance award."

"I have no idea what she will do" Susan continued. "I don't know Max. Max that's something you will have to ask Nat. yourself. You will have to give her some time to think all this out."

Oh dear, Susan began to cry, really cry, and this was not an act. "Max where did I go wrong, I tried so hard with you as a child. Maybe you were loved by too many women and it was so easy for you. You did not have to work for anything; life just gave it to you. You did not even have to go looking for a wife. Nat was handed to you on a silver platter but when she wanted something different from what you wanted, she was punished and now you have done it again. Max you have no idea what Natasha is about. I love you Max. I am not going to say anymore. I may have said too much already." Susan looked at me and asked if I wanted to talk to Max. I shook my head. "Give it a few more days Max" Susan said and hung up.

"He thinks and rightly, so you don't trust him and will not trust him again. Well he has a point there, so let's forget Max, for now," Susan said. "Susan if he ever hit me again or took my babies I would have him 'done in' and there would never be any proof it was me in any way. I understand Max is your son and maybe your loyalty lies with him. If that is the case, you cannot stay with me."

"Like hell I am leaving. Max has his father and sisters. Who do you have?"

"She has me Susan," Mrs. B. said," and I will stay here as long as Nat needs me."

"That's just what I said, whom does Nat have?"

"What the hell does that mean?" said Mrs. B., getting red in the face.

Susan backtracked saying, "That means, well that means you and I are in this together."

The phone rang. This time Mrs. B. got the phone.

"Oh, hello Sir Harry, how are you and where are you?"

"I am at home at the manor. Have you seen Susan by chance?"

"Hang on, I will get her."

"Hi Harry, did you have a good time in Key west?"

"It was ok. Susan, when are you coming home?"

"Not at the moment, maybe in a while. Maybe Mrs. B. and I are staying with Natasha."

"Why, Susan?"

"Because I did not care how you treated me and left me. Is that good enough answer for you Harry? I will see you when I see you. Now, I am staying here. Harry, I do not want you coming over here or phoning again right now. It's taken you all this time you to contact me to see how I am doing."

"I have been sick Susan."

"What do you mean sick?"

"I got knocked down by a bus."

"When and where?"

"Well I did not go down to Key West. I hung around N.Y. a few days then I came back to the hotel. The desk clerk said you had already checked out so I flew home. Well at least I flew to Heathrow and found a very good hotel, phoned you hoping you would come down to London and have some fun, a little honeymoon, but there was no answer. I phoned each of the girls and they had not seen you but were not concerned. They thought we should still be on the boat. Jennie and Mick invited me for dinner so I stopped off at the store to get a bottle of wine. When I came out and crossed the road, I was hit by the number 102 bus."

"So how hurt were you Harry?"

"I had one broken arm and was in a coma for one week."

"Are you ok now?"

"Yes, why didn't the girls, the triplets, phone Natasha or Mrs. B. or Max in New Zealand?"

"They did but his company said he was on holiday."

"Say no more Harry. Can you fly? Harry, we need you so much! Are you sure you are ok now?"

"Yes, yes. What's happening?"

Well there's one thing you are going be so happy about, the other Max has been very hurtful to Nat again. Anyway, Nat said if he does this one more time she is going to have him done in and nobody will ever know it was her."

"Nat said she is going to have Max done in?" exclaimed Harry. "I find that a little hard to believe. She is having you on. I will try to get a hold of Mick or Jennie and tell them of my plans to go to N.Y. I love you Susan, I am so sorry I hurt you and left you like that."

"Oh, Harry I love you too."

"What's going on?" Mrs. B. and Nat said together.

"Harry never went to Key West and he stayed here a few days, then flew to London. He tried to phone Hawkes Manor for me to come down to London to make up. He came home and was going to Jennie and Mick's for dinner. He got knocked down by the number 102 bus, which resulted in a broken arm and he was in a coma for one week. He will be here soon as he can."

The next day Mrs. B. said, "You had better tell the desk it is ok for Harry come up." Before his arrival, we left Susan alone to answer the door to Harry.

Susan opened to a knock. "Oh Harry, you look so thin, come here dear one." After a few minutes Susan called out, "Look who's here, it's Harry."

We all asked Harry about his health. He insisted he was fine.

"Come on, out with it. Tell me all that's been going on," he said.

"Well," Susan said. "There would not be a story to tell if Natasha does not show you our family's pride and joy."

Harry could not believe his eyes. "Triplets, my God triplets! I thought you were getting a little heavier Mrs. B."

"They're not mine, you silly old man, they're Natasha and Max's babies."

"Why did we not know? Oh, they are so beautiful."

I know Harry wanted to pick them up but then Susan piped up," Wait until they are a wake Harry then you can hold them."

"Okay now Nat; tell me all that's happened between you and Max."

"Well, the usual things. New Year's Eve Max and I went to a few parties and got drunk, so one thing led to another."

"Very funny Nat. Now tell me, when did the trouble begin? I would have thought Max would be over the moon about the triplets."

"He was, and what happened is he began to think they were his and his alone. When I showed Max the babies, he was laughing and crying. He held my hand and asked me "Is this happiness, Nat."

I said, "Yes Max, this is happiness." By now, tears were rolling down Harry's face. "Then it took three of us to wash, change and feed the babies, whereas Max could do it alone in the same time." I told Harry the rest of the drama and I showed him black and blue marks still visible on my leg from Max grabbing me.

"Where is he now?" Harry asked.

"Staying around here somewhere," Susan replied, "and when Natasha does not come to the park with us and the babies he appears from nowhere."

"Why didn't you tell me this?"

I said, "What good would that have done? Just upset you. Next thing you would be scared that he would run off with the babies. Harry, I never discussed my hopes and dreams of what could be with Max. It was all too new and exciting for Max. I just wanted him just to get to know and love the babies. I was thinking Max and I could come to some arrangement. Oh, just forget it Harry, it's not going to happen and I have no idea what to do. All I know is Max will not be any part of my life now. We could have shared some parts of each other's lives with our babies but he had to have it all now but he has nothing. Anyway, these are my problems, not yours."

Susan jumped up, mad as a hatter saying "Even when you were a child I felt like giving you a slap with yourself centered poor-me attitudes. Those children are just as much Harry's and mine plus Mrs. B.'s, as they are yours. As for my son, have you ever seen anything about him until your marriage broke up that would make you think he was

not kind and loving? Have you ever seen him hurt another child or an-
imal? We'll have you? You two were always together. No, my son saved
you from that dark hole you so wanted to live in, my son gave you the
power to love, please, please give it back to him."

Susan was right, in the end, she was always right. I had three new
babies, a family and a man that loved me and all I thought about were
the ones that got away, living in times I am unable to remember.

"Thank you, Susan, I can always rely on you to show me and tell
me all my imperfections. I am taking the babies to the park now. This
will give you more time Susan to hang me out to dry."

Macy's had sent us six cots'; three up, three down, three separate
prams and one big pram for triplets. I put all three in their big pram
and took off to the park and a few moments of freedom. I had been
walking awhile before I saw him sitting on a bench. It was then I knew
how much I blamed myself for his unhappiness. If only, if only I were
different, I started to push the pram to him. I had to stop as I was crying
so much. He saw me and ran over to us holding on to me and trying to
kiss his babies. We sat down and just talked. I looked at my watch, I had
been gone nearly an hour. I said "We have to talk more Max. I will phone
home to see if one of them will come and get the babies. Hi Harry, Max
and I met in the park and we need to stay and talk on our own."

"I'll come to park entrance."

"Thank you, Harry, it's the 85th. St. Entrance. "We will be on the
park side."

Max had told me when we were teenagers how he felt about his father going overseas to fight. All the time he was away, he thought Harry
was never coming home and when he did, he was a changed man. It
took Max a long time to bond again with his father. While Harry was
gone Susan sent him to a doctor for therapy to deal with abandonment
and security issues. As of today, Harry knows nothing of Max's therapy.
We went to a cafe for a bun and coffee Max kept saying how sorry he
was." I have no idea why I did that, please forgive me Natasha."

"Okay Max, please stop now. I have been thinking what happened
when Harry was overseas and how you must have felt. I have asked you
to understand how I felt; we were both abandoned as children. God
knows how it has affected us and what our issues will be as parents. I

am not telling you what to do Max but I know I am still angry over my losses. I still see my dear Jewish friend in the park who has helped me a great deal and recommended a doctor for grief and loss and anger. I have been three times Max. It's painful but that's seems to be the only way we humans grow."

"Would you like me to see a therapist Nat?"

I did not say anything for minute then I said, "I only want for you what you want. Max, I confess when I was lying down on the floor with the babies and you came over, looked at our little girl, tried to pick her up—the look on your face, and in your eyes showed such love. I wanted you look at me that way too, and then you pulled away."

I did not hear anything else Max was saying I was crying once again. "Max, what you saw was me, a mother, looking at her babies, it was only then I knew what true happiness was, as we hugged each other with new understanding. Max, do you remember me telling you once that I was smarter than you, and maybe I should take on the role of being the boss and that you should be happy that you have me in your life?"

"Yes, I remember that Nat, Max said laughing, and the point is?"

"Well I do not feel as smart as I once did; I do not have all the answers to how we will raise our children. I cannot just stay home all the time. I may be smarter Max but that does not make me mother of the year.

"Let me first tell you what I want to do with my life. I do not like working for other people or companies, I would like to be a freelance writer, as I love to be involved at the beginning, middle and end of a product. I would like to see how far I could take an idea and working for somebody else would be a waste of time. I know you would help me if you believed in me."

I looked at him smiling, "I like them their dreams of yours."

"Nat, do you understand where I am coming from, that I could do something with my life?" "Yes. Max, I am so glad you have found yourself at last. It often happens that people with exceptional IQ's drift through life. I am talking about you Max."

He was smiling now. When I went up to Oxford, for fun some friends and I wanted to take IQ tests to see who was the brightest of us all, Well I never got my results back so, my friends joked it was so low that it did not register. What happened was the school got hold of them and sent them to our parents. Well my dad showed up at Oxford and told me if I wanted to live my own life, "Never, never show these to your mother or your life as you know it will be over, as she will never leave you alone. By the time, you are thirty she will expect you to be a doctor, surgeon, practice law, be chair of a bank, dress designer or famous architect. So please Max, find yourself a woman with a high IQ, get married and let Susan worry about her smart grandchildren." Thank God, I took notice of Harry as I see my mum a little differently now. "So, what cunning thing did you do to out fox me and know all about me Nat.?"

"Well the letter that you refer to came in the post. I saw it was addressed to Mr. and Mrs. H. Hawkes. Harry took it, put in his desk, and locked the drawer. I knew he didn't

Show it to Susan. Three days later, I saw Harry driving off. I went to the desk it was open. I read the letter. I locked the desk, took the key, and told Harry I found the key on floor. Harry said did you lock it, yes I replied, and nothing else was said."

"You cheeky monkey," Max said.

"One thing Max, if you and I had been on our own when you grabbed my leg I could have had you on the floor in 5 seconds you know."

"Oh, that's nice and what makes you think that?"

"My black belt." We got up to walk back home and I just threw him on the grass; he was so shocked but laughed.

He said, "You know how I love butch women." We were in time for dinner, one of Mrs. B.'s specials. At dinner, we told them of our plans that I had decided that we will stay here in N.Y. for year or so until the kids can walk and get around on their own. I could see how far I was going with my career.

"I hope my new job does not include traveling now so I can work from home and office and Max will be here with the kids plus working from home. After that, we would like to come back to Hawkes Manor for the children to be raised arount the family. As far as Max and I are concerned we are open to what or who comes a long, but the children will come first. We were hoping, Harry and Susan, that we could buy some land from you so we could build a house nearby, within walking distance" I said laughing. "We know we may have trouble ahead because we are both young and have our own personal needs, but with your support, we may have a chance." Well Susan started crying, everyone was so happy that we were coming back to Hawkes Manor and the family. "Was that ok Max, saying all that?"

"You bet. I am so happy the children will grow up where we did."

Harry and Susan came up with a better idea for where we should live at Hawkes Manor. "Because of your somewhat unusual relationship and not knowing what your future may hold, it may change it may not. What do you both think about adding another wing or so onto the house? While the children are growing up they will always have a sense of family. There will be grandparents, the girls coming and going, both our sisters and children, and their children and even great grandparents. They would still have Mrs. B.'s food, and with anybody else coming to visit the manor, your kids would get to know them, avoiding any feelings of isolation that they might have and you would feel by not being under the same roof. Of course, we would all be in the same plans. Anyway, I am not sure if the village council has to be involved."

There was no question that Max and I would love this idea. Everyone loved the idea.

I felt good. I told Max we were having a party this weekend and we did, all my mates from "missing US persons" came, old friends from British Intelligence, Lester Faggott's family and some co-workers that including George Johnston's brother Larry and Margo Roth.

Larry and Margo came together. I am not sure as a couple though. Margo struck me as having a fondness for men that looked like crooks with big bellies, pockets with lots of cash, no credit cards, wearing white shirts with collars that are far too small for their neck, like a bull. Yes, just like a Taurus, the sign of the Bull. Now I did not say they were crooks, they just looked like ones. My George came with his wife June and their older children. June looked better and better each time I saw her. It will be six months before she needs to be checked again. You know, money does sometime buy you happiness. When all hope was gone, I had the good fortune to have the money to give June a second chance at life. I did not work for it, it was my parent's legacy to me. In turn with that legacy, a gift was given to a friend.

It was one of the best parties I have ever been to or gave. Harry met some people he knew that worked at British Intelligence. Susan somehow found this second-hand dress shop and found herself a dress designed by an English designer, Elizabeth Pompa, one of England top dress designers in her day. Accompanying the dress was a hat designed by her sister Louisa Sumner. Both sisters have stopped designing now, as they are dead. Never have I seen Susan look as stunning as she did that night, turning heads as she walked by. Mrs. B. and her sister were dressed to kill. One of girls from B.I. made up Mrs. B.'s green eyes. I decided that evening I liked Margo Roth for her humor. It was so dry you never knew if she was joking. In the distance, I saw Max coming over to where Margo and I were standing. Max was wearing dusty rose pants, an old boat jacket (whatever an old boat coat is) pale grey with navy blue strips, navy boat shoes and a rose-colored bow tie. "Hello ladies."

"Max, this is Margo Roth, Margo, this is my husband Max Hawkes. Max said hello again. Margo looked at Max and said, "You look ridiculous." "I know," he said laughing. Someone called out to Max. "Have to run, bye."

"If you think by introducing me to your husband has put me off, you are mistaken." She, Margo, was hitting on me.

"Would you like to see the rest of the condo?"

"Yes Natasha, I would," which made the party even more enjoyable for me and I think for Margo too.

Next day Margo phoned, thanked me for a party to remember. "Next time maybe there will be just the two of us, that is, if there was going to be a next time."

"I hope so" I said. "What about Wednesday? I like it in the afternoon."

Harry left Monday for Hawkes Manor to check with the council and to look for an architect. Max would follow later if needed. Mrs. B. and Susan wanted to stay on, Mrs. Lovelock stayed one more week and went home to tell her Arthur about the triplets and of course, the party. I saw Margo quite a few times over the next month or so, then the time came for me to see the Big Boys at work to discuss what if any future did they had to offer me, now a mother with three children. I knew straight away by who attended, they were looking to accommodate me. I am not going to name names as to who was there as it was not important.

I asked if I might begin first.

"I think I am going to repeat some of what you already know. My husband and I ended our marriage on very friendly terms, in fact so friendly he went to New Zealand and I gave birth to triplets. The irony of this breakup was that my husband wanted children now, but I wanted to wait. I have to work, it is who I am and I have a lot to give. Max, my husband, does not have to prove who he is by going to work for others. I had to laugh when I said "He is just like his mother and she is one big mother hen so he is staying home to be with our children here in New York for the next one or two years. I wanted our children to be raised in a family environment back in England where we hope the Family Manor will be greatly enlarged. What happens here influences where I work.

"Well you will not hear any complaints here as you have been more than we were expecting. Where do want to start?"

Field Boss, I believe I was offered this position a while ago. Are you sure we were thinking maybe number three? It's higher you know!"

"No thank you, I will go higher when I know more. I do believe I was going to work with George Johnston to show me the ropes so to speak, the first month or so. Is that still standing? I learn quicker that way. I would like a few more days before I come back to show my husband how to wash dishes and make beds."

"Will a week Monday be all right with you?"

"Thank you, Good afternoon Gentlemen."

My phone vibrated. "Hi, where are you?" "Well I was thinking of making my way home, and you, I was thinking of … forty-five minutes, yes." I gave her one hour and in five minutes I was in her bed.

"Next week I start back to work full time. Margo, I do not know where I will find the time and I know I am not the only one, so I am not breaking your heart." Margo looked at me and said it's awful, my middle name should have been "excuse me, I see another coming "

"It's all because you are the three of hearts" I said. "You love to keep your options open, and you have trouble with commitment."

"What's wrong with that?"

"Nothing. You are far from boring and lot of fun, Margo." We bid our farewells, with Margo saying, "Call me anytime."

Now what did I just say, the three hearts love to keep their options open.

Later back home Harry said on leaving he would not call until he had everything arranged, so it was the following Monday before he phoned, we used Skype, so we could all see one another. "Harry sees no problem with the council but we do have to show the plans before we start building. He has found a wonderful architect." He knew it was up to not only me but all the women have to approve the plans as well. The architect's plans were well received by all. Harry stayed on at Hawkes Manor.

Susan and Mrs. B wanted very much to stay on in New York. Max needed to be with his babies. The babies were in their cots and Max was asleep in a rocking chair. I looked down on him. God, he was so handsome, blond hair, blue eyes and perfect white teeth, a Greek God. You know if we needed money, I could raffle Max off for the evenings to older women that had plenty of money. Or just for the summer he could get a job as a waiter maybe at those five or more-star resorts and high roller hotels all over the world where the older gals go hunting. Neither of us knows what the future holds. Today we are family.

CHAPTER 23

Somehow, the girls found out about the triplets. Must have been from Mrs. Lovelock, Mrs. B.'s sister. As soon as Harry was home all three arrived together at Hawkes Manor demanding to know why they had not been told about the triplets before and why did it have to come from Mrs. B's sister. Harry tried to explain that he told no one in the family. He explained "Nat buried her head in the sand, plus she wanted the children to be born in the U.S.A. and all this while Max had a girl-friend. I am beginning to believe that silly story all you kids thought was true years ago that Natasha was really Susan's birth daughter and that Susan gave Nat away at birth to the Bennet family and when they were all killed Natasha came back to 'real' mother. Why I am beginning to wonder about this now is Natasha is as nutty as Susan is. Nobody else thinks like Susan or is as cunning as Susan is. Who else do you know that would think they could raise triplets on their own and no one in the family would know, only Susan. Susan was the only one that did not find this whole scene odd. Thank God Natasha came to her senses and asked Mrs. B. for help."

All four had lunch together. Harry told them he had a lot to do and soon the family should get together as they had a lot to talk about. That is fine, said the girls and left. Claire went to her part time bedroom at the manor to pack her bags. Crewe already had her suitcase with her as she was up from London. All went back to Jennie's home. Then Jennie called and told her husband she would be back in a few back days, as she needed to go to N.Y. Crewe likewise rang Liz in London and left a message: "Be back in a few days. Gone to see the triplets with my sisters in N.Y."

As Liz had no knowledge of the triplets being born, she thought Crewe and her sisters had gone to N.Y. Central Park to hear a new rock group 'The Triplets' play. When Liz told me this later, I laughed and asked, "How on earth did you come to that conclusion? There is no such rock group called The Triplets. Maybe you should not spend too much time around Susan, Liz."

As the girls had not told Harry of their plans, we were not fore-warned of our latest guests. While still in bed, I could hear screaming, laughing and crying. Max was yelling "Get out of bed Nat, we have company."

Before I could think to get out of bed, the girls came running in and jumped on me. To tell the truth I was so happy to see them.

"What are you doing still sleeping, and where are they?" they demanded.

"We take it in turns to be with them. It is Mrs. B. and Susan's turn today, ask them."

They turned around to find Max, Susan and Mrs. B. each holding a baby, then more yelling screaming and laughing. They may have had wind but to all of us it looked like the babies were laughing too. It was then I realized, because the girls did not have children that they expect to be asked to be the Godmothers. This will be trouble, big trouble when Mrs. B. and Susan hear of this. Max and I had decided to wait until we returned to UK to have the children christened at our local church.

The few days turned into weeks, Mick and Liz came over some weekends and we had another party, mostly with the same people as before plus a few others, just to freshen the pot so to speak. Also, with Crewe and Liz here we now had a calling card besides the triplets; we had Elizabeth Michaels, TV star. Her TV show was so poplar it was shown in the UK and the USA as well as in some parts of Europe.

For the past few years the show had been filmed in London and it looks like it is going to stay that way. Liz's character is an American (USA) cop assigned to New Scotland Yard.

Of course, Margo Roth was a guest.

"Look at all the people you have staying with you, no wonder you do not have the time."

I smiled at her knowing she was not expecting my reply. "I like it in the afternoons, shall we say Wednesday, or, oh let's make it Monday." Monday came and I turned off my cell phone as I walked into Margo's apartment and turned it back on only when I was leaving. I called back over my shoulder, "So we will leave it as me calling again one day."

"Yes. That is fine Natasha."

I walked out of the lobby into sun light, opened my handbag, took out the phone. "Hi, Wednesday afternoon good for you?"

"Yes Nat, yes." It may not last forever, but for now we can sure make such memories and when we do remember each other, it will be with such sweet delight" " Margo, while we are making memories, it is just you and me."

"Nat, there has been no one since you."

"Oh, I did not know that. Am I to think you feel the same way as I feel, Margo?"

"Every waking hour you are in my thoughts, Nat."

"The whole family is having dinner here at the condo tonight, Mario's takeout. I would like you to come, sit next to me and play footsie with me all evening."

As always when we are all together with the exception of Harry, who was away in England, we have such a lot fun and oh, how we love to tease each other about times past. This evening Susan was showing more of an interest in Claire who by now was a Doctor of Medicine and was very interested in what was happening at Hawkes Manor regarding the building project. She asked if Harry and Susan would be interested in having a doctor's office built onto Hawkes Manor. If only the town /county council would change zoning for this, for we are greatly in need of medical health centers. We all thought this was a marvelous idea. "Where," Susan said, "would Claire sleep?"

"In my own bedroom," Claire replied.

"I see," said Susan. "Would you be bringing a partner of some kind with you?"

"No," said Claire.

"Oh, surely there must have been somebody, sometime, somewhere that you at some point would have liked to bring home for your dear old mother to meet."

"No, Mum!"

Oh boy, are we in for a good laugh, maybe not tonight but in the retelling of what is going to happen next. I looked around the table at the rest of the family. Here we go, Max is pushing his chair away from the table, and he knows Susan is going to blow any moment. Max does not like to watch his mother lose control but afterwards I will have to repeat to him everything that was said by whom and in what order, including what was the expression on their faces, were they still sitting or standing. He even asks what his mother was doing when others were talking. Then an hour later, "Nat, tell me again what happened."

Anyway, back to the rest of the family, Liz sat with a sweet smile listening but not sure what was happening. Crewe who knew from previous scenes turned to Liz saying, "Now do not say a word until it is over." Mick, Jennie's husband, gets out his glasses, puts them on, empties the rest of a bottle of wine into Jennie's glass and his, sits back with arms crossed and waits. Jennie then and there decided she better go to the bathroom and runs. As for Mrs. B. who was sitting on one side of me, said, "Here we go again." On the other side, Margo who had her foot on mine until this minute, suddenly realized there was more fun going on with Claire and Susan than with my foot.

Susan carried on at Claire. "…and why not, did you ever have a partner while you were at university or since then?"

"Yes, Mum."

"So why is it such a big secret?" Susan whispered.

"Because it is my secret and if I had told you it would have no longer been my love to keep inside of me, the whole family would know, you would have made me out a silly girl instead of being so proud of me for becoming a doctor. You have a big mouth Mum and everybody here knows it."

No one was laughing at what was just said. Mrs. B. grabbed my hand and said, "My poor Susan."

I stood up and said "Claire, there is…"

"It's ok Nat, I have it."

Appearing from nowhere, Max strides over to Claire. "Do you remember when Dad was away fighting with the Marines I honestly thought he would never come home as he was going to be killed. It was so bad and Mum was so upset for me. She knew I needed more help than she could give me. You three never gave her a break, always trying to get the better of her. My mother asked me if I would go with her to see a doctor. She asked me, she did not tell me, I had to go for help. She did not have to tell me she could not cope with dad away. Did you three try to help her or me, no sir you did not, so I went to therapy for the four of us. I saw our Mum learning to cope, as I got better. One more thing Claire, Mum said to me this would be our little secret, no one will ever know, unless you tell them. And as far as I know, my dad still does not know."

There was not one dry eye in the house. Max put on some soft music and asked his mother for a dance. "Come on Mick, girls." Mrs. B. got up and said she was going to dance with Claire, hoping she and Max would change partners so she could dance with Susan, and Max with Claire, so all could calm down. She also looked at me and Margo saying, "Please you two, do not get up and dance with each other. Susan can only take so much, put on your shoes. Do not sit there looking at one another either, Susan misses nothing."

Well if that was not good for a laugh, nothing was.

Margo commented, "You have the most delightful family, do you know that? One's as mad as a hatter, the rest follow suit."

"I know, but I would not have it any other way. Can you see Mrs. B., she is watching us like a hawk? "I bet if we got up and danced she would fly over here and make it a threesome," said Margo. "Come on I said, let's get my babies instead."

They were in their own prams so we could wheel them from room to room. We had a ramp put in the condo and a lift to the bedrooms so it was very easy to get around. Still, it was not easy for two people to push three prams so we sat by the windows looking onto Central Park.

"I am thinking of taking a week off and going over to the UK to see what is doing with Harry and the Manor. Would you like to come with me Margo?"

"Good God Nat you have just started back to work and you are taking week off already."

"I have told you before Margo I am special."

"You know Nat sometimes I think that you really believe this rubbish you tell yourself. You got this special bit from Susan."

"I only said that just to get a reaction out of you. I agree, how can I take a week off from my babies, plus I would not want to. I wish Max would go over. He needs a change and I need a rest from his chatter. He never stops chattering away to the babies and you know, sometimes Margo I have nightmares that I will be chattered to death by all four."

"Oh Nat, you have to be the silliest cow I have ever met." We both were laughing and rocking the babies under the watchful eye of Mrs. B.

Margo stood up and touched the window overlooking central park.

"I love New York, my family is here, I know lots of people, I have many good friends and I have a very good job. New York is part of me. My memories of you will become part of me because we happened. Everyone is made up of 'happenings'. Everything that happens to us makes us who we are. Look at this evening with your family, you all believe and think that family love is unconditional and that there is no other way to love. Susan, with all her faults, and there are many, has shown you all what the power of love is and above all is the only thing that really matters. Tonight, one family member started trouble and one family member ended it, look at them dancing, laughing, and drinking."

"Well, do not give them too much credit Margo, we have had so many family punch-ups over the years with Susan and the girls, and actually with Susan and anyone that gave her a funny look. Let's face it, many people give Susan ' the look' on first meeting her; Susan and the town council, Susan on a windy night when noise from the local pub blew our way."

"That may be Nat, but do you know how much you are all like her, and you are more like her then she is."

"I know," I said.

"And one more thing then I have to go, because you are part of it you may not notice, when you are all together, I can feel the love. I bet Mrs. B. would have long gone if it was not for this love that embraces you all as a family, and you have added three more little love buckets that will always be loved and molded by that wicked witch. I am off now Nat, very busy day tomorrow."

"Good night Margo. I know you had a wonderful time, now watch me throw Mrs. B. off course. Max, Max, Margo is leaving come and show her the door."

"Very funny Nat, I still am going to kiss and hug you. Good night everyone."

"Bye Margo." Three prams, Margo with Max's arms around her and me all going down to the lobby to put Margo in a cab. I turned and looked back and said to Max, "Can you feel it?"

He looked at me in surprise, "You mean the love? Yes."

He looked at the babies. "And they are the glue that will hold it together tomorrow."

There was nothing funny to recall about last night so we will leave it at that. The girls and Mick were going back home tomorrow. Crewe would be very busy with an art collection she was showing. Liz asked would I mind if she stayed on a bit so she could be with her mum. Liz did not have to work for another week or so, that sounded like a great idea. I was so pleased Liz wanted to stay and spend time with her mum, and I could see it made Mrs. B. happy. Liz went back to London after a few weeks, and once again became Molly Rafferty, her character.

■

I met with my assistant Sally the next day. She is twenty-one years old, lives at home with her parents and four younger siblings. She has a steady boyfriend and when they can afford their own home, they will marry and have children. Sally is self-taught, born and lived in Queens, New York, but because of her father's job they moved many times around Queens. He loved to fix up and sell houses. The Borough of Queens is known for its diversity with people from many different countries and many languages spoken. Sally can speak and read five languages as well as English, has friends from many cultures, is streetwise, and she knows and understands peoples' motives just from growing up on the streets. She went to college for two years just to have it on her résumé. I was very lucky to find her working in a typing pool on the fourth floor. It just happened that I was on the fourth floor looking for a typist for the day. You could do that if the work was classified non-secret. I showed her what I wanted her to do. By mistake, I had given her piles of paper written in non-English.

She asked, "What languages would you like me to translate to?"

"Sorry, I gave them to you by mistake." and I left her and went back to the fourth floor to find her boss.

"What gives with this typist I have for the day?" I asked.

"Don't worry about her send her back when you are finished with her."

I laughed, oh she's that good.

Sally is so smart although a little unsure of herself. I have told nobody about her in case she leaves the pool. "It was my day off and my assistant booked Sally in to type for you today but that's not fair to her. Do you want her?"

"Let me go back and talk to her and see what goals she has if any." Sally told me that her boss was wrong and it was not her that was booked to work with me today. Sally gave the typist who was supposed to come fifty dollars so she could come instead. Sally had heard of me and that I was going places.

Then the cheeky little cow said to herself, well I bet she does not know what I know.

She may be right as she is a New Yorker and knows the culture of New York more than I do. Well, that's how Sally got the job. One day Sally and I went to lunch at a new cafe she had found. We needed a quiet place to talk shop. After we ate I told Sally I was not going back to work but was going home.

"I would like you to come with me. They are some videos, papers and tapes I have in a box in a safe. If something happens to me you are to go to my home and open the safe with the code I give you. Give the box to George Johnston and if something has happened to him give it to Sir Harry Hawkes, my Guardian and father-in-law."

"Oh boy," said Sally, "This is big time."

"You will tell no one of this, not your boyfriend or parents. You are still new on the job so what I tell you will be on a 'need to know' basis. You will meet my family and babies and have dinner with us so phone your mum." I phoned Mrs. B. to tell her there would be an extra for dinner.

"When you have lunch with your friends at work what gossip to tell!"

Sally looked shocked that I would think she might talk about me to her friends.

"Am I that boring Sally?" I joked.

"When I got my job, I was told to get myself an assistant but nobody thought for one moment I would go looking on the fourth floor in the typing pool. I had to fight for you because you did not have the skills listed for this job, but you will succeed because you are the type of person that will watch me, and I mean watch everything I do and come up with the right answer. I believe in time you will come up with a better answer than I do."

Natasha that's what I think, I think I will out smart you one day."

"Come up with a better answer maybe, outsmart me, never. What you gossip about to your workmates is of little concern to me but my job is not gossip and neither is yours; other people's lives depend on us."

Fadil was on duty standing behind the lobby desk, looking very pleased with himself, "Miss Roth came by to get her scooter today," he said.

"What scooter Fadil?"

"The one you told me to take back to my uncle's place. He refused it, he told me too bad and that I had to buy it now. I sold to it Miss Roth."

"You think you are pretty clever don't you Fadil?"

"Yes, I do," and we both laughed. Just then, we all heard the sound of the scooter as Margo drove up.

"Oh boy, that's a nice set of wheels," Sally said.

"Are you with Natasha?" Margo asked, smiling at me.

"Yes, have you had it long," Sally asked?

"My first day. Glad you like it did you want to go for a ride?"

Sally looked at me, please...

"OK," I am going up Fadil, "Let them both in when they come back." Half an hour later, there was no sign of them and I was jealous, mad but more jealous. I am going to kick Margo when she gets back. It was just under an hour before they returned. I pushed Margo into the media room. "You are one cruel bitch Margo, you knew I would be jealous of you going off with her."

Margo smiled, "I know, that's why I did it. Come here Nat and tell me why you felt like that." Her lips found my mine then the door bursts open, and there stood Susan and Sally looking for God knows what.

"Anything I can do for you Susan"? I asked.

Margo had to sit down she was laughing so much, and the response that Susan gave was priceless. She held Sally close to her and said, "And in front of the child too." Margo was on the floor, "Your family should be on the stage they are so funny."

There was noise coming from the front of the condo. It was Max, home with the babies, so we all walked out of the media room together. "What's going on in there?" All of a sudden Sally grabbed Margo's arm and said, "Be still my beating heart" as she looked at Max.

"You like?" asked Margo.

"I have never seen such a handsome man."

"It's Nat's husband."

"It's Nat's husband? Oh, come on, she's not that good looking to land somebody like him."

"Well she did Sally and he is mad about her."

I just loved it when Margo told me what Sally said about Max and the fact that when she and Susan came into the media room she had no idea what was going on as Susan was in the way. The whole episode went over Sally's head. "I hope you are staying for dinner Margo."

"Are you kidding? There is something going down tonight and I am not missing a thing."

"What do you mean something is going down?" I looked at Margo, "You know there is something wrong with your way of thinking sometimes. Sally and Max? Are you nuts? Next you will have Mrs. B. having a nervous breakdown."

"I bet you ten dollars Max and Sally somehow will sit next to each other and Mrs. B. will not take her eye off them, and you are not to keep talking to me so I cannot hear what they are saying. Ok Nat.?"

"It's too near home for me. Anyway, Sally has a steady boyfriend," I said.

Margo just laughed, "So what!"

Guess what, Max and Sally sat side by side at dinner, with Mrs. B. watching them.

"Can you hear what they are saying Margo?"

"What did I say before, if you talk I cannot hear so be quiet please Nat."

I caught Max's eye and gave him 'the look'; that cheeky monkey just winked at me and went on chatting up Sally. As usual, Margo is laughing her head off over this. "Can I be there when you tell Max?"

"No, Margo no, that's it! Please go home now. You are beginning to annoy me."

"Okay Nat, but please have a family dinner party soon and invite me again, as your family amuses me so much. Sometimes I cannot believe my luck that I found you, never have I laughed so much and the sex is the best I have ever known all thanks to the Hawkes family. Goodnight all."

"Look at the time," Sally called out. "What way are you going Margo?"

"Your way Sally let's go."

"You don't live anywhere near her, Margo." I said.

"It's been lovely to meet you all. Bye, bye," still talking as she was running after Margo.

My cell phone rang about an hour later, "What!"

"Can you come over now?"

"Yes, if I can bring Mrs. B. with me because there is no way I could fool her as to where I was going at this time of night. Hang on Margo, Mrs. B. is coming over to me now."

"One of the babies is crying, maybe you should go and see if anything is wrong." said Mrs. B.

"It is ok Mrs. B.," said Max. "It is Bradley, he lost his dummy but he has it now and we are not going to them every time they cry for a few seconds."

"I am getting fed up with you reminding me I have three children Mrs. B. When Margo is here, you never stop watching us. You treat me as if I am cheating on Max. Margo is my friend and only lover. You think because I have three babies to love I should not love her. What kind of person would that make me? My babies would have no idea how to share and when they grow up they will have no idea how to love another, all because I had made them completely responsible for my happiness by showing them I could only love my children. Max left me because I wanted to stay in New York as I had been offered a good job. All Max offered me was the next twenty years not working and raising his kids. I lost half of my life after the accident and it took years for the nightmares to stop. The truth is, I did not want to get married or have children then. I wanted me, now I have my three babies who I love more each day. Max and I had a "Lost Weekend," we were drunk, he wanted sex and I gave in. Max will find a woman that wants his body as much as he wants hers, he does not need a wife that just gives in.

Mrs. B., you carry on as if my feelings for Margo are going to cause emotional or mental developmental problems for my children. I do not have your maturity yet. I am still a young woman and I never thought of myself as a mother. You were not there for your daughter but she turned out well. Liz is liked, kind and giving and a very successful actor. Giving her up was not your fault and you have her now. You have come to accept Liz, as she is, the whole package. Even though she likes the ladies, big deal but that is a big part of her. That's the daughter that you have come to love.

You cannot believe that this beautiful woman has looked for you for years and has come to love you so much because you are her mother and for the first time in her life, she has seen herself in you. She knows now why she does the things she does, because you do it and above all she can feel her mother's love. Please Mrs. B. make your love unconditional for me as you have your daughter. My children will be fine because Max is their father, Susan is their grandmother and you are and always will be my Mrs. B., and in time my children's Mrs. B."

She just stood there looking at me, turned around and made her way to the stairs. Fifteen minutes later she returned with three suitcases and without a word walked to the door to leave. "Mrs. B. please do not go, remember when I first came to Hawkes Manor I loved you as much as Susan and Harry. After a while I heard that the girls used to sleep over with you Fridays nights, talking, watching the ' tellie', talking and cuddling. I wanted you to ask me so much but you never did. Susan always had Harry in bed with her so there was no room, you all asked me to live with you but there was no room. Please Mrs. B., give me the room you gave the girls and Liz, give me the freedom you gave them to be who they are today." At that moment, Mrs. B. broke down crying. Susan was sitting on the couch howling like a dog lost in the desert and Max yelling, "You could have come to me."

I knew I had really hurt Mrs. B. plus the fact that she felt she had let me down.

Mrs. B. Said, "I still think of those times that I wish I was more loving towards you and I wanted you to sleep over but I got in my head that Susan would think I was intruding. Susan just loved you to pieces as soon as she saw you after the accident. Please forgive me Natasha."

"You were the first person I asked for help with the babies, the first member of the family I trusted that would come three thousand miles no matter what. That is how you love, that's a hell of a lot of loving you gave me. I know I said when I phoned why don't you and your sister come for a holiday now because the last one was cancelled. Can you imagine if I had called and said I have just given birth to triplets, I don't know what to do with them. You would have gone into shock thinking I had gone mad and would have no idea what to do with me and where to take me. You would be wondering do they have mental hospitals in America for women that have lost their babies. Would they ever have let me out or would I be doomed to spend the rest of my days at the lulu farm because you had me taken away by the men in white?"

I put my arms around her and said softly, "It was your kind of love I needed then and I always will. It is a love I want for my children. Your love demands respect and trust. As you know or may not know, I am a very wealthy woman. My children will one day inherit a great deal of responsibility. Just because I am their mother they will get away with more than they should as I do not remember my childhood and what was expected of me and my siblings. Thank God for Max he knows not to spoil them. Have you ever heard him chatter to them, "No babies, no, no crying?" You would think he was training a puppy.

Mrs. B. started to laugh. "Max was like that as a child. If a guest sat in Harry's seat Max would tap them on the arm and say, 'Excuse me that is my father's seat, I think you would be more comfortable seating over on that chair.' Do you remember Mary Collins married the chap that owns the hardware store?"

"Yes," I said. "A friend of Max's."

"Well when they were much younger Max did not care for Mary one bit. She and her parents were visiting one day and Mary consistently interrupted one or the other parent when they spoke. Max marched up to her, "Mary, I would like you to know when we get older I will never ask you out on a date or what have you, because of your talking. Why do you think my parents and yours want to listen to your rubbish about yourself all the time? It is boring. What about your future husband? After a while he will have to go back home to live with his parents so he can think how to get rid of you."

"Mrs. B. I told you of my wealth out of concern over the children's future, that they choose the right people to love in life and without trust their love will be wasted, so please never tell your sister my business as the whole village will know. It is about trust."

"I have known from, the age of five years old my sister has a disease."

Oh dear, I thought I have just worded that request wrong.

"It is called ' gossipitist'."

"Good God Mrs. B. I have never heard of that disease before."

"My sister is a good, kind person with a heart of gold. Her human-interest stories, as she calls gossip, most are quite harmless, but for me to tell her how rich you are and she is not to tell anyone would be an act of cruelty. I tell my sister a lot of rubbish that she would find out anyway. Plus, I have known for a long time before you came to Hawkes Manor how Sir Harry and your parents' lawyers made sure your inheritance not only stayed intact but also multiplied."

"Mrs. B, would you like to go home and spend some time with your sister?"

"Yes, I would. She and I are very close and I know she wants me to come home for a while."

"Good. Do not unpack. Go tomorrow, as if you do you may not go and you need a rest." Mrs. B. did go the next day and Susan went with her to the airport, if only to tell her that she was still need and loved and nobody was trying to get rid of her, but she was only to come back if she wanted to.

It was hard managing without Mrs. B. but we got by. A few days after the big bang up, I told Sally in passing the Mrs. B. had gone to England for a rest, that we missed her and the babies did too.

"Oh" Sally said. "I could help."

"Help with what Sally?"

"I will help with the babies."

"Don't be silly, I need you here at the office."

"No, you do not Nat. You are the first to say we have not been that busy, you have found the time some afternoons to go to see..."

Sally turned around and made a run for the office open door. I grabbed her arm. "Sit down Sally," I said, "And close the door. It's very rude to leave in mid-sentence. Please finish what you were saying."

Sally did not speak for a minute, neither did I, then she looked up smiling and said, "Well Nat, you found the time to visit someone close by because you walked. If you went early in the day you came back to work."

"What, what, what am I missing here Sally? Why did you run out of the office in mid-sentence?"

"What I thought was, is it worth losing my job so the answer was no, I am not telling you, and why I am not telling is because then you will realize how smart I am and fear for your job.

Oh! Please," I said. "Let me fear for my job, tell me!"

"Well sometimes when you came back from your outing you looked fantastic, you just glowed." The tears were running down her face from trying to stop laughing.

"Surely you do not think you would lose your job or I would fear for mine over you thinking I might be going to a beauty salon, did you? Why would you think that, Sally please tell me? Am I such a cow that I would fire you over you thinking I go to beauty salons, it that what you are saying? That makes no sense Sally. I am going to box your ears any minute now so you will never hear gossip again, which I think you live for. This job is not for you, you should be a gossip columnist for the daily newspapers." I just sat looking at her but she would not give in. I thought, she knows I never went to a beauty salon so for her to run out the office, she thinks that I think she does not know.

"Ok Sally, we will leave it at that. I am leaving now. I looked at my watch. I will phone you in a few hours here to see if anything is happening." Normally, if I left at this time I would let her to go too. It now appears turning into a battle of wills and for her sake, she has to know when she has gone too far. Others have feelings and her need to win all the time has to be checked and not just because I am her boss. It is because nothing endears you to staff, peers and bosses more than a winner that knows how to lose with grace. That is what true leadership is. "Do you have a list of phone numbers where I could be reached?"

"Yes."

"May I look?"

Sally went to her computer.

"No, I said I want you to let me see the paper copy in your drawer Sally. Why is this last number hand written by you?"

Sally looked up, "It's not in the computer because you never put it in the computer and if all else fails I may need to reach you."

"Then do you know who it is, Sally?"

"Yes."

I was very upset now because I had forced Sally to show her loyalty to me. What the hell can I say now to try to make light of it.

"You will never guess what I thought you were going say Sally, "my you look fantastic, just glowing you must love having sex in the afternoon."

Sally screamed with laughter, "I would never have come out and said that to you Nat." "It's when I saw Margo's phone number handwritten, by you, on a list, in your drawer that I knew I could turn my phone off."

"You never would have had the nerve to sit next to my husband and flirt with him in front of me unless you thought she and I were involved."

I had just left the building when my phone rang.

"I am home packing," she said, "as one of my clients wants me to spend the week-end at her East Hampton house. She is getting a divorce and wants me to help with getting her affairs in order, plus a new will written, now!"

"Oh! Ok," I said.

"Nat that's the buzzer, I have to go I am sorry I will call as soon as I can."

CHAPTER 24

We had spoken only on the phone since the big bang up a few days ago. As Mrs. B. had left, I spent more time at home with the babies, so I had expected to see her today. By the time I arrived home, I had gone into my 'Spoilt heiress' mode and I was mad as hell. She is nuts if she thinks I am going to put up with this. I walked into an empty house. Max, Susan, and the babies had gone to the park. I sat down and cried like the lonely child inside of me without a woman's love to keep the wolves at bay. Margo phoned a few hours later.

"I know you are mad I would be mad too. I have good job and I am paid well. Some women would like to know me better but without you and that nutty family of yours I would have nothing; do you know that Nat?"

"Yes."

"Good because you're the reason I get up every morning and for sure you're the reason I go to bed every night! Goodnight Nat.".

"Was that your girlfriend?" Betty asked

"Yes, she was mad our weekend was postponed, she is mad, mad as the Hatter."

"What is her name?"

"She is called Nat for Natasha she will kick me when I get home."

"Well that's funny because that's what I would do too. There is nothing like good kick for a naughty lover."

Betty said, "Whatever I say now never leaves this room."

"Betty, you have had me checked out, checked over three times by different people so you know as a professional lawyer and person I am trustworthy."

"I had a daughter Natasha, such lovely name; she was the result of a very short affair when I was seventeen years old. Peter was an Englishman over here in the States attending some university. My parents would not let me keep her so she was to be adopted by Peter who was a good few years older than I am. He was outraged that a child of his and the Bennett family would be farmed out to be raised by anyone, unaware of the strict laws of adoption. By the time my baby was born,

Peter had met the woman he was going to marry. His mother came over from England and gave my parents money. My parents were good people never asking for anything, just happy that the child was going to her own father. Peter's mother saw nothing wrong in giving her granddaughter's other grandparents a better and more comfortable way to live. The baby was registered to Peter and his new wife two days after they were married. My parents and I heard from Peter only once and apparently, Natasha and Peter's wife bonded right from the first day. They had a son and another daughter on the way. Peter's mother lived with them and Natasha was the apple of her grandmother's eye. My mother somehow found out Peter's mother died, and not much later, the rest of the family were killed flying over Scotland in a private plane near a house they owned. I read about it in the papers and checked that it was Peter and his family.

I always dreamed my daughter and I would meet one day but that day never came and that dream was never meant to be. At the time, I was married with two little children so after a while I had to put the accident out of my mind only to have it come back time and time again. I have four children now Margo, and have married very well, twice. You think it would be enough, but it appears to be human nature to wonder and worry about the one that got away! Are you feeling ok Margo, you have gone white as a sheet?"

"Well yes, no, I am not having much luck processing what you are saying. You had a daughter, Natasha who as a baby went to England with her father and stepmother to live. Natasha's stepmother was registered as her real mother."

Betty smiled, "Money can speak, if you know the right language."

"That's for sure, said Margo. Well, I am so sorry you kept this all to yourself all these years."

"Yes, but what would have been the point of telling my families. My two children with my first husband would have felt sad and sad for me so would be inclined not to talk about it or share their feelings knowing once there was an older sibling. The second two who grew up in a more open world would never have stopped talking about it. I wonder if she looked like me, was as pretty as me. I hope she was happy living in England. Did she have an English accent? It would never end, each day more stories would be made as they tried so hard to bring her back to life. My parents are still alive. They come here for the summer but we never talk about it. I know if we three could go back we would have kept her; you never get over the loss of a child. They acted out of love for me, not wanting me to be saddled with a child. They did not know. They thought my future would be narrow with fewer opportunities, not realizing we all have to pay the piper some way or another."

"You look so tired Margo, go to bed. We can start early in the morning. I will show you to your room. It is a beautiful room overlooking the sea, and you have all you need. Here is the TV, the bathroom over there and please use the house phone. It has a New York line."

"Thank you, Betty." I called Nat as soon as Betty left the room. "Hi, it's me. I am going to sleep but wanted to call first."

"It's only ten p.m. Margo."

"I know, but I am so tired. My bedroom overlooks the ocean. I wish you were here."

"So, do I."

"Funny thing to ask, but what was your mother's first name?"

"Jane."

"Ok, I was just curious. Good night Nat."

"Good morning Margo, it is a lovely day." Betty put the cup of tea on the bedside table. There was no reply. "Margo, good morning." Still nothing. She walked around to the other side of the bed and looked at Margo who was peeking back at Betty. "You startled me, are you ok Margo?"

"No, I am not. I have no idea what to say and where to go to find out if I can break your trust in me as a lawyer. I just wish you had not told me anything and we could go on with our lives and you could go on with your life. I have not slept all night thinking what to do!"

"Should I go out, come back in maybe ten minutes, and see if you really awake or are you sleepwalking in bed because you are talking nonsense?" Betty was thinking she ' got a right one here', leaving Margo to sleep off what appeared to Betty as some kind of not so happy sleeping pill. Thirty minutes later Margo was dressed and downstairs looking for her host. She found her off the kitchen sitting at a table in a breakfast nook eating an egg with toasted soldiers. The morning sun highlighted her hair, Natasha's hair. You could see were Nat got that way of making people feel they were welcome in her world.

"There you are, what would you like to eat?"

"It's ok Betty, just tell me where the cereal is and you finish your egg and soldiers."

"Oh, you know the British way to eat eggs from your Natasha. What's her full name? Margo was silent." Margo did you hear me."

"Yes. Natasha Taylor Bennett. Her father Peter and mother Jane were both deceased in a flying accident over Scotland with their three children. At first, all were declared dead. Later a child was found. It appears she may have been pushed from the plane before it crashed. The eldest daughter Natasha has no memory of the accident or life before." The egg with her soldiers slipped from the table onto the braided rug, sounding like a sigh.

CHAPTER 25

"**S**he is alive, all these years and I never knew. What is she like? Please tell me Margo, everything you know."

"She is tall, fair like you, and charming. She has no memory of her parents or her life before the accident, which has left its mark."

"In what way and who looked after her when Peter was killed?"

"Peter and a very old friend, Harry, had guardianship papers drawn up for both of their families as they had under-aged children. She was in hospital, then went to live in her new home. They loved her and never gave up on her. Betty, this family is hers, she looks like them, thinks like them and this family loves her as much as if she had been born to them. Their leader, the mother, is as mad as a hatter is. She and she alone rules the roost, the husband is somewhat laid back but if he puts his foot down, Susan (the mother) will listen. At twenty years old Susan gave birth to triplets, identical girls who tormented their mother until they were adults. A few years later Harry and Susan had a son."

"Harry is the husband?" Betty asked.

"Yes. Oops, I also forgot to mention Mrs. B. When the girls were little Mrs. B. came into the family as a live-in, nanny and never left. She is seen as a member of the family just as much as the rest of them. Susan and Mrs. B. are best friends but will fight and row every full moon and all the little moons in between. Max the son was nothing but a joy to Susan, the most handsome man I have ever seen. He has loved Natasha and only Natasha. They married and came to New York to live but Max wanted to go to back to England to live. Nat didn't and in time they found out they were wrong to marry, as she really preferred the ladies. There is a lot more to what I am telling you and what I am telling you could find out very easily. What is not common knowledge is up to others to tell you. Later, Max and Nat became the best of friends as they had always been. Nat still loves Max very much but not as a husband. She and Max spent New Year's together. As a result of what Nat calls their 'Lost Weekend' she later gave birth to triplets. Max was by then in New Zealand."

"Oh, my God," said Betty, "This is too much."

"I know it is a lot and it is only half of it. Just a few more things, Susan and Nat are so much alike. She has a very strong bond with Susan, Harry and Mrs. B. In fact, the whole family is tied together in a way that can never be broken. When they are together, you can feel their love. They are all nuts, every one of them thinks like Susan and none of them know it. You will look, listen, and really wonder if she is for real. She is so powerful and of all the kids, Nat is the only one that can stand beside her. She loves Natasha and if she thinks anyone is going to hurt her, which includes her own son, God help them. Susan has the power of love and she has shared it with family and God can you feel it when they are together. Natasha's IQ is over the top and you know her strength but inside she is still that little girl.

Because of my own personal involvement with Natasha I would like to know what your plans are, if any, that include Natasha after you have a think. As your lawyer, I am bound by oath never to tell what I have learned from you, which puts me in an emotionally difficult situation. You will find very little under her name, Natasha Bennett, if you do a web search. She works for the Government and that is it, as her work is highly confidential. They have bent over backwards to accommodate her. Oh yes, she is one of the wealthiest women in the USA and UK and that's a secret only a very few know."

"Of course, I will release you from your oath as neither one of us knew what we were getting into when I told you of my past. I will write that out and sign it for you. First, I am going to give you your check in case I forget what with all this going on."

"Betty, this is too much. We agreed on a different amount than this."

"I know, but you have told me my daughter is alive and very much loved. That is priceless. Thank you! We are not working this weekend and there are swimsuits here that will fit you. I am having a dinner party tonight, which I forgot to mention. I was not going to put you in the attic working away when we are eating and drinking ourselves silly below. A very good friend and confidante is a guest tonight. He is a lawyer but does not practice. If there is an opportunity to speak to him I will see what concerns he has about Natasha, so I may need you if that's ok. I would love to have gone back to see Nat, but it's not every day you tell someone their daughter is alive."

It was a wonderful dinner party, with a mixture of the strangest people to have together. There was such a mixed match of guests together at the same time, but you know, it worked. Betty sure knew how to entertain and if you knew how, it was very simple, never invite people that live or work in a box. I met a few that I knew I would hear from again when they knew I worked for Faggott, Faggott & Faggott.

The next morning Betty woke me with tea. She was not leaving for New York until the next day. Her neighbor was flying back to New York in about hour and he would have room for me. "Would you like to leave now?"

"Yes, yes please if it's that ok with you Betty."

"Fine, we can talk on the phone Margo. I am thinking of going slow with Natasha. It was such a shock for me that if we meet both knowing we were mother and daughter maybe our expectations would be too high. We will talk about how I can meet her without her knowing who I am. Margo, I am so scared I will disappoint her."

"Betty how could you. You are her mother and I know I would be proud, very proud if I were Nat."

"Thank you so much for allowing me to bully you into coming all the way here to work, which we never did."

Margo ran to the plane as the pilot was starting up. "It is ok" he yelled, "Just warming her up."

"Oh hi," Margo said, "We met last night"

"Yes, we did. Betty always gives the best parties. My name is Colin Myers. I have been Betty's neighbor for twenty odd years, since we were just young kids with younger kids. Both of us have seen our lives change, somewhat like looking at the afternoon soapboxes on TV. The wife and family are staying for a week or so but I want to get back to get an early start at work, leave much later and traffic is too much."

He looked at Margo and she smiled. "My name is Margo Roth, Lawyer, without a plane." Margo didn't phone Betty or Nat from the plane as she thought she might hurt Colin's feelings so she just sat and listened to a nice man talk about his family and how they were too busy talking to listen to him. Anyway, she was not sure if it is ok to use cell phones on these little hop-hops.

Natasha's cell phone rang, it was Margo saying, "I am outside, shall I come up or go home?"

CHAPTER 26

"**Y**ou get up here now." I opened the door to her smiling face. "I did not expect to hear from you until tonight."

"Betty was staying until tomorrow so she got me a ride with her neighbor on his plane. How are the babies?"

"They just left with Max for the park."

"And Susan?"

"She's having a nap."

Margo told me all about Betty and what an interesting woman she was.

"We did not do any of the work that she was in such a hurry to do. Instead, she talked about her past that she has shared with only a few. Last night Betty had a dinner party with the most interesting guests from all walks of life. I may have made some business contacts for Fag, Fag and Fag."

"So, you had a good time without me?"

"Yes, I did Natasha." looked at me funny.

"Don't look at me like that Margo, I get scared. Going to Betty's and meeting those people made you happy, why would I not want you, who I care for so much, not to be happy? Margo, I want for you what you want for yourself, that is found with the power of love. I know sometimes you like to make me feel jealous and I go along with it but that's our little game we play together. I must admit I was disappointed you were going away. I had not seen you for a few days. I think you would have felt the same way, that's part of life, things come up."

"Damn, why did you have to say all that to me now? They are home Nat."

"Hello, we are home," Max calls out, "Home with hungry babies."

We had dinner all together, watched a little TV and Margo decided to stay the night. Susan said she looked too tired to go home. After we watched TV I said, "If it's ok with you Susan I would like to turn in and have an early night. It's too early to feed the babies. Would you help Max with that? Thank you, I think will run a hot tub now."

"I will be up in a while Nat. I want to talk to Susan," said Margo.

"Talk about what Margo?"

"Well, if I wanted to talk to you too about it I would have done it over dinner. Go have your tub."

Susan and Max just loved this, if anyone can get the better of me with one-liners. I looked at them, "Why do you think this is so funny?"

"Because Nat, you are so clever with your knack of keeping the foe at bay so when someone comes along and just gives it back to you it makes life worth living."

"I may have Sun in Libra but my mercury is in Scorpio and I can sting." I left with Susan and Max laughing, and Margo smiling like that cat from Alice.

"No, don't go Max. Stay. It's about my weekend."

"Just a sec. Margo, you do know Nat will be back soon and kick you and this one will be a hard kick. You may have ten or fifteen minutes. She is now lying in that tub getting madder, madder."

"Well I am getting a little scared. I am going in to work later tomorrow so after Nat leaves for work we will talk more. I just do not know what to do. Did you know the Bennett's very well Susan?"

"Nat's parents you mean? Yes. Harry and Peter went to Windermere School so from boyhood they were the best of friends. Of the threesome, Peter, Harry and Lesley Faggott, Harry and Lesley would know more than I would."

"Did you go to the wedding?"

"No, it was all of a sudden. They were married and had a baby two days old, and I had not seen her for a few months before. She did not look pregnant or say she was pregnant." Susan stopped talking for a moment then said, "She was not Nat's mother, was she?"

"It does not appear so."

Susan was very calm about the whole matter, and it was Max that went into high gear drama.

"Oh boy, oh boy, then who's the mother, who is Nat's mother, oh boy, oh boy."

"Oh, for goodness sake shut up Max," Susan said.

"But Mum, Nat's mother could be a criminal, done time in prison for the criminally insane, a psychopath; you never know with these people. They are so charming after they steal all your money your neighbors and friends would say he/she was such a nice person. Look at Nat, she can be the most charming person you have ever met but maybe she is half a psychopath."

"Maybe Max, maybe Nat's mother has done time in prison but if you do not shut up now, you will see your real mother doing time."

"Do you believe what you have just said Max?" Margo asked.

"No, I do not. All this searching for herself. I have been hoping lately that maybe by now she would not have to do that anymore as she has three babies and their future will be Natasha's future. She is ours, we do not stay together as a family because as one we are weak, it's because we all put a penny in the pot and so far, no one has taken anything out. Our love has grown and grown and anyone can join, as nutty as they think we are."

Susan stood up saying, "We will talk about all this tomorrow. I know Nat will be down any minute and one of us is going to be kicked. Good luck, Margo. What are you going to say we were talking about?"

"I will think of something. I know, I will tell her I was asking you if you mind if we get married."

"You are kidding me I hope."

"Yes, I am Susan. Anyway, don't laugh, this will not be a problem tonight, the door will be locked and my bag outside."

"The third bedroom down is empty and the bed is made up. I like you Margo."

"I like you Susan."

The next morning the three of us sat around the little dining table, three babies in cots beside each adult.

Margo told the whole story right from the beginning to the end. "As I said, Betty does not want to meet Nat as mother and daughter right away in case Nat is disappointed. She has never told any of her children. Oh yes, I took the liberty of telling Lesley Faggott, who arranged for DNA testing which proved a mother daughter match. Lesley took care of that so you will have to ask him how. If you are worrying about Nat's money, Betty has no legal claim and neither do her children. It is so tied up and it will be up to Natasha's children and grandchildren to sort out. This is old money going back many generations. Lesley says the Bennett's family were low key but acquired and hired only the best. Everything about them was top quality right down to the cook's helper. All staff were paid well and looked after in old age. Now Natasha has a great deal of personal wealth and as time goes by, more is available if needed from trusts around the world. They are untouchable at the moment. That is all he would tell me and that's all we will ever know, and I personally do not want to know any more at this stage."

"Nat has to be told about her mother, we agree," Max and Susan said, "but out of respect for Betty, we will do it her way." "Now I better change Jack," and Max walked away with Jack under his arm, waving his feet at us.

"Do you trust Max, Susan?"

"No, one day at the most then he will begin to crack he cannot keep secrets."

I picked up the phone and asked, "Betty, what time can you be here today? Betty, I am running this show now not you, what time? Well that's all the better she can come also, we would to like to see her. Susan and Max know who you are and Susan and I know Max can only keep from saying something to Nat one day or two at the most. I will tell Nat that you are in town and are dropping by with some papers for me to look at."

They arrived about 6p.m., Susan stood by the elevator door waiting for Betty and her daughter to appear from behind the sliding gate.

"Hi, I am Susan and you must be Betty."

"Yes, this is my daughter Jennifer, JC we call her."

Susan walked ahead. "We are just down the hall."

"There is a rainstorm coming with very high winds, with a warning not to travel on the highways in coastal areas. We are lucky we made it in time."

"Are you both hungry?"

"Yes," said JC. "We did not stop in case the traffic became worse with the weather."

"I know, midafternoon is crazy. Do you like Italian food?"

"Oh yes," said the daughter.

Susan looked at Betty, "That's fine with me, good."

Susan went ahead opening one door then another and finally the door to the room with a view; the view that took your breath away.

Betty and JC didn't move, transfixed by the view, a live painting of Central Park. "and…. people ask why we love New York," and if I were alone I would cry. Betty almost looked like she could. Then she saw standing nearby Margo holding one baby and Max with two others. All three were squeaking, they loved company, new faces to touch. Betty and JC ran over to them, which made the babies squeak more much to the delight of the adults. JC could not wait to hold Jack.

"Now hold on to him, he is a real kicker."

JC was smart, she held him facing out so Jack was just kicking thin air.

"Now that is clever," Max said laughing.

Betty would not take just one baby to hold saying, "Please put them on the sofa so I can put my arms around both." I stood at the doors looking at this lovely picture. The girl was nearly my height and coloring, holding Jack with his feet facing out just kicking away. Betty holding the other two babies starts screaming," Oh, what a lovely family" Betty said to JC.

Mario's Italian food was delivered so we sat down at the table to enjoy the food.

"So, please tell us about yourself, Betty. "Whereabouts in New York are you from?"

Betty declared "This has been a very pleasant evening, but we ought to leave now, time has run away on us."

"I am sorry Betty, the 475 is closed tonight because of the flooding and high winds as are the rest of the routes. You both will have to spend the night," I said. "I did not want to say anything earlier as we were having such a fun time together, so I decided you might as well spend the night here instead of in your car making that long journey back to the Hamptons." Funny, Betty looked like she was going to cry then.

"That's good," JC said. "Yes, I can help feed the babies and put them to bed."

"You like children JC?"

Betty said, "JC baby sits for a family in the Hamptons but this year they are not coming, family troubles, so she had interview with a family in Manhattan."

"That's nice, why don't we all go on the terrace with a brandy or what have you and sit and look at the stars, babies and all." Well it was too cold and you could not see the stars for the clouds so we sat inside still able to see the park.

"You are getting too thin Margo," I said as we all made our way to bed, Max pushing the sleeping babies up the ramp. "Do you ever cook for yourself?"

"Sometimes, not much. This is the time of year when I go and see my sister in Connecticut. She fattens me up as she cooks all the time for her husband and four kids. I always have a good time there."

I thought, here it comes, this past weekend, and soon she will be off to her sister's for a few weeks. I think my family is too much for her, three babies and a husband still on the scene. She needs her freedom too much, that's part of her soul. I said nothing. What could I say?

Margo also had two brothers and they live not too far from her so every other week she would go to one or the other for dinner. If they are having a party or if one of the brothers and his wife would like to go away for the weekend, she will baby-sit. Margo said she thought one day she would have this contentment of sharing her life like her siblings did. "Well, it never happened and I just accepted what my life was. Remember the first party of yours that I was invited to when you hit on me?"

"I what?"

"Well, you did ask me if I wanted to look around the condo and that included the bedrooms. After that, I had no interest in anyone else and when you said you were too busy for me it was the first time I felt my heart break. At the second party I realized it was not me that was keeping you away, it was Max, the babies and this big family. When you said you liked 'it' in the afternoons, I knew, one day I would be part of this family with you. When Susan said tonight 'I like you Margo' you could kick me a hundred times and I would never leave you because you are my 'happening', that has changed me and my life to come … Nat, I want to tell you about last week-end."

"I knew it, I just knew it."

"Stop it you silly cow, that's not it. When Betty was telling me about her past she spoke of a daughter she had when she was seventeen."

I didn't say a word until Margo mentioned that Lesley Faggott had DNA testing done and confirmed Betty was my real mother. Apparently, American newspapers never corrected the error that all had been killed when in fact I was found alive.

"Yes, that is right," she said.

"And Harry and Susan did not know about Betty?"

"No, neither Susan nor Harry went to the wedding of their good friends Peter Bennet and Jane. Susan had seen her a few months earlier and Jane did not look pregnant or say she was pregnant."

"I cannot believe this Margo, I think it's a joke."

"I know Nat, but I spoke to Lesley Faggott. Peter and his wife married two days after you were born yet no one can remember her being pregnant. You were registered as her child, and at the time why would anyone question it? They were two fine upstanding people and did what they thought at the time to be the right thing. As far as they were concerned, Peter's wife was his daughter's mother. As far as I can understand, they loved you and the other children all the same. I know this a shock Nat, but I have never met someone who has been loved by so many as you have. Three children, the job you wanted, a family that loves you, me, and now another family to love. Oh, I forgot money, tons of money."

The next day no one went anywhere due to the flooding and high winds. I was in such shock I had no idea what to say or do and at ten a.m. the phone rang. I listened and said "Ok, ok. I have to go into work."

"How will you get there?" Max asked.

"They are sending a truck or jeep for me. I have no choice something has come up. I phoned Sally, "It's urgent, I have to go in and I need you with me." "Ok. Hang on." Sally was talking to someone in the background.

"Ok Nat, my brother has a jeep and he thinks he can make it. Bye."

I dressed and packed a bag. "I have no idea how long I will be it could be a few hours or a few days or more. I know, JC, you have been longing for the babies to wake up so you can bring then down here. Maybe you can help Max and Susan care for them as they love to play kick."

"Oh, I would love to," said JC.

I kissed Susan and Max, held Betty's hand for a moment, and left with Margo who saw me to the door. "Margo, I will try to phone, if not it's because I will not be able to use a phone from the site." I now can only think of what lies ahead of me. It took four days and the crisis was over in the field. When I walked back into my office, my staff stood and saluted me. This was when I was at my best. Never once did I take my mind off the problem. I can see so clearly the light at the end of the tunnel and if not, then I will make a fire. The secret is to know your limits. It is so easy to burn out. It's funny how I am not very good at solving my own personal issues. Maybe that's what life is all about. To know yourself, and your limits. I held Sally's hand as we left the building telling her how proud I was of her on the job.

"Thank you. You have no idea what that means to me and never will I think I am anywhere nearly as smart as you Nat."

"I know that Sally, and I am glad you know that now," and we laughed as we went our separate ways. Sally's brother was across the street waving to her from his jeep. I called home about my babies. Susan answered.

"How are my babies?" I was crying for my babies.

"They are fat Nat. JC feeds then as soon as they look at her but they miss you and so do I, we all have missed you."

Then I whispered, "And Margo?"

"Not seen her much as she's out every night."

"Out, out where?"

"I don't know, she does not tell me her business."

"Well, I bet she is sleeping at her own place."

"I don't think so Nat. I have called her a few times and no answer."

"Let me speak with her now. You think you are so funny, Susan."

"How long will you be Nat," Margo asked.

"Ten minutes."

"I will come down to the lobby and meet you. Come on babies, we have ten minutes to get down to the lobby."

As I walked in to the lobby, there were my babies screaming their heads off and nobody else was there, just three screaming babies in a pram. "Hi babies," I said. Suddenly they stopped, saw it was me and screamed louder than before. Then the lobby became alive, Fadil and

Riccardo were hidden behind the desk and a few of the residents were laughing. Then there was Susan, Margo and JC.

"We did not know they would scream like that, my God!" said Susan. "I hope nobody phoned the police." Smiling at Riccardo, I said, "Are you working here now?"

"Yes. My father will only allow me to work part time, as I have to learn his taxi business from bottom to top before he dies."

"Before he dies? Surely you mean retires?"

"No, my father thinks only one way. You work 'till you drop! "

"You must like it here."

"Yes, I do, it is one of my life's lessons to see how others live, which my lifestyle at the moment does not afford me."

Standing beside Riccardo was a smiling Fadil.

"I know Fadil is laughing at me talking about my life-style," said Riccardo, "But in so many years when I come back here to buy my first condo, Fadil will still be here behind the desk."

"I think not. I said when you come back to buy your first condo, Fadil will be right beside you buying his second condo."

"Thank you, thank you Miss Bennet."

"You are welcome Fadil."

"Boy, Nat you really know how to work a room."

"I know Margo."

"What do you mean 'work a room'?" JC asked. "Margo, what does work a room mean?"

Well, if you sleep from eight p.m. to the follow day at two p.m. and are only awakened then by Susan with coffee you have charmed someone indeed.

"You must not sleep so long you will never sleep tonight."

"The babies?"

"Fatter and fatter."

"What is JC feeding them?"

"Toast and jam."

"Is that ok Susan?"

"They are still alive."

I asked Susan, "What do you think of Margo?"

"You have chosen well with her Nat."

"I know. Do you think it's too soon?"

"Yes, give it time when it's time for us to go back to England. What is she going to do?"

"Well Susan, she's hoping we will hate each other by then."

"Sorry Nat, I think she's a 'keepie'. Anyway, I do not believe she said anything like that. It sounds like one of your silly stories."

"I wish I did not love so much sometimes it hurts my heart Susan."

"Please tell me you do not say these melodramatic statements to Margo, she thinks we are all nuts. You saying that will only confirm it."

"Max, how has he been?"

Watching JC feeding the babies toast and jam, "Max would like her to mind the babies for the summer."

"Oh no, Susan. What if I don't like Betty later? What do we do with JC?"

"We are talking about JC looking after the kids for the summer Nat, not a life commitment."

"That's all I think about, and am I being disloyal to you by accepting her as my natural mother?"

"Nat, I am very secure in your love for me. Our bond can never be broken, we are Hawkes. Natasha, you so want Betty to be your mother you are scared to death that in time she will not like you. You are going to reject her in case you do not match up to her other children. Why Nat? We never gave you reason to doubt yourself like this. When you came to us Harry and I swore our love would keep you safe and you would know what love was again. Sometimes the wrong words are said at the wrong time and once it has been said it can never be taken back, only to be embedded in the heart of a child. Sometimes it's your makeup, part of your genes; your ancestors may have acted differently still carrying the same gene. You are so bright and strong in so many ways, this doubt may soften you, taking the edge of your need to be in charge. It may be the reason that you are loved. Hey, what do I know?"

Betty came by to see if it is ok for JC to be here and to make sure JC had not been carried away and talked us into giving her work for the coming summer.

"Oh no" said Max. "The babies love JC and she is so good with them."

"Betty also showed us some family photos of her parents, her oldest daughter and the two youngest children, a boy and a girl. "The oldest daughter's name is Peppy, nineteen years old and is in college. The youngest are staying with their father until school gets out there."

"You think this is all right with JC? I am not sure Susan."

"Honest to God Nat, you are not home in the day. We are, and Max likes her and thinks she will be ok. No one is rushing you to accept Betty and her family, least of all Betty, your mother. Betty has known from the age seventeen she had to give you up and thought you were dead. She has had to live with this in her own private hell, unable to share this pain with anyone else. Natasha, you will show her compassion and kindness if nothing else, do you understand. Not everything is about you and your needs."

Next morning at breakfast, Betty sat down beside me, holding my hand. "This has been such a shock for both of us, and I am going to leave this up to you Natasha. If you wish to contact me, do so, if not, I understand. Thank you all for your hospitality. Come on JC lets go."

"What's going on Mum. Why are you crying?"

Margo gave me a look that said, 'go to her', and I just looked away.

"Why? She gave me up."

Margo picked up her handbag put on her coat and walked out the door.

"Wait up Betty, please."

"Just a second Margo, I am coming too. We will leave you two to look after your babies." Susan turned around and left, leaving Max and I alone.

"Nat, you have everything that anyone would need, and still it is not enough and it never will be. Because Betty gave you up when she was still a child herself you are going to punish her as if this woman has not punished herself enough. Then I see no reason for me not to punish you for marrying me. If you knew when we married that you were not interested in me as a male partner, then why did you? By that way of thinking at your age you should have been fully responsible for your actions. Just as Betty had a choice if she could keep her baby at seventeen. Her parents did not want their child at her age to start out in life looking after another child. As far as I can understand, Betty in no way has ever blamed her parents. When you were less than ten years old the plane you were on crashed and killed your family. Tell me Natasha, what has this got to do with the woman that once again is crying over what she did all those years ago, that just walked out of your life, my life, and our babies lives? There would have had two grandmothers to love them and they would have loved in return. Nothing, but as always you will make it something so you can tell our children what they have missed out on life because your mother gave you away. You have too much Nat and you know what happens to people that have too much?"

"Please Max, tell me this is a joke that you and Susan are playing on me, for always getting the better of you two. I know this is madness to think you would do that to me but I cannot get my head around that I have a mother that's alive that looks at me like she does her own daughter JC, that I was once inside that living person. All this instead of a dream, no a nightmare, of being abandoned by parents and siblings through death. I am so scared that after she knows me and the dark side I have she will walk away too. You are right Max, and I have never been able to get the better of you because you always let me win. As a child, I believed they didn't love me enough because they left me behind to live without them. As an adult, I know that is a silly thought to have, but to a child's mind damage can be done which lasts into adulthood.

I have you Max. We together, you and I, have made the best babies and it's mainly because of your genes, and just think how good-looking they will be. Did you know a young Susan told your father that he is going to be father of her children, because she loved the way Harry's own father showed Harry how much he loved him, and the same with his sister, plus Harry's mother too? With the right upbringing from us and our family, along with our resources, they too will have the power of love to share with others in this new world to come. Susan has said if men and marriage are not in your plans and you would like a child, let it be Max's please. She said, "The older Max gets, well you will see. Remember I know you, my son knows you. Sometimes you would let us in at your darkest hour, we saw nothing that frightened us or made us walk away. We knew when you saw our love your night would turn to day." Now Max is crying.

I hate it when Max cries. I am somewhat concerned that the babies, when older, may want to cry like their father. I personally have never heard several whales calling for their mates but I do think of whales when Max cries. It's an awful noise followed by silence, then a water canon of tears, followed by another noise.

As I have often told Margo, Max chatters to the babies constantly. As we all know multiple birth babies often chatter to each other in a language of their own making. Max seems to understand every oooh and aaah said. I will be left to go slowly insane from hearing constant, never ending chatter that only the four of them understand. In my dreams I hear the call of the male whale, and me praying the female will respond before the night is over.

"I am so sorry I had to say all that to you Nat, but sometimes things fly over your head and you don't get it, then you are so upset because it did not work the way you thought it should or wanted it to."

"You know that is ok Max, you know me better than I do."

"What you are going to do now?"

"Is Margo the only one that has Betty's phone numbers and N.Y. and Hampton addresses?"

"Hang on Nat, I think I saw Betty writing something which she gave to Mum."

Max walked over to the dining table. "Here it is, I bet she has gone to her N.Y. home because Betty said something about JC going for job interview tomorrow."

"You phone Max, see if she is there."

"Betty, yes it's me Max."

Betty replied, "Oh hello Max, your mother and Margo are here. They seem to think we needed an escort home. Did you want to talk to them?"

"No thanks, just checking up on my mother. She is getting on

Betty screamed with laughter and repeated to Susan what Max had said.

"What?" he heard his mother say. Max put his hand over the phone receiver, "Nat she told my mother what I said."

"Good luck to you Max. Now you are the bad child."

"Max are you there, Max?"

"Yes Mum."

"You don't know Betty well enough to abuse your mother by making up your cruel jokes under the guise of a concerned son. Now, in time I will tell Betty my age after I tell her how long it took to housetrain you."

At that point, Max was rolling on the floor. I took phone from his hand. "Hi Susan, he is on the floor laughing. Susan, shall I come there to see my mother or will you bring her back? I do not think Max is up to staying on his own with the babies."

"Are you sure Nat?"

"Yes, I am Susan. I would prefer her to come here for Max to see and hear what is happening for my sake because, as you know, if he does not hear the story himself he will be asking every hour on the hour for the next few months for details. He will nag at me saying, ' please Nat, tell me everything that was said and in the order of who said what and when, were they laughing, did everyone…'

"Oh Nat, you cannot help but love him and he has three children to follow suit."

"Shut up Susan. Where did Margo go?"

"Nowhere, she is here telling Betty to give you time, that you cannot believe all this is going on and are afraid it is one big joke."

"What's happening Nat?" Max asked.

"They are all coming back. Thank you, Max, for loving me when I am unable to love myself. Max, by the way what's with Sally, were you just flirting or…?"

Max went red.

"I have never seen you blush Max."

"Yes, I like her but would never ask her out without your ok because you are her boss."

"Max, here is what you need to know. She does not like to lose; she is very street-wise but too young to run the show. You must earn her respect. Do not make me the brunt of your jokes with her. If I feel I am being discussed, she will go and boy will she be mad at you. With me, she knows she is going places within the job. Sally is so clever she can worm anything from you she wants to know, so be careful."

The buzzer, sounded. "Hi Miss Bennett, Harry Hawkes and his sister are in the lobby."

"Good God send them up please. Max, Max your dad is here." I ran to the door.

"How is my girl?"

"Oh Harry, I am so pleased to see you!" and we kissed and cuddled, the usual thing.

"Terri, I am so happy to see you."

"I have come to see the babies," she said.

"You do not have to give a reason for coming, nobody else does, they just turn up." I gave Terri a big hug. Terri has one big heart. I called out to Max as he may not have heard if the babies were screaming. "Harry, all they do is scream if they are happy, when they see me after work, see a new face or if they have not seen you for one hour. Wait until they see you!"

"Nat," Max yelled down stairs, "warm their milk, I am bringing them down, ok, and make lunch for us please."

"What is going on, our Max giving orders, getting babies?"

"He's the housemother," I told Terri.

Well, Max came down stairs with the babies, and not only did the babies scream when they saw Harry and their great-auntie Terri, Max screamed with them.

Oh, somebody was banging on the door. Max ran to open the door and there stood Fadil and Riccardo, asking, "Are you ok?" "It's those terrible babies. They saw my father and my Aunt and screamed their heads off."

"Ok, then one of the babes sure has a deep voice", they laughed.

As I have mentioned before, Terri is Harry's twin sister and has been here a good few times before. She comes without her family of five children and husband. Their five children did not arrive until Dan and Terri were in their thirties; three of them are working and are not planning to leave home until they have to get married. The last time Terri was here she stated, "I know what they are up to, all three. When they meet their partner to be, they will say ' just overnight Mum, you will never know they're here' or it's best if so and so stays here the week-end. We will both be nearer the friends we are seeing.' Next thing you know they will all be sitting in the front room watching' telly' and one of the kids calls out. "Put the kettle on Mum and did you buy any bickies today?"

"My dream is the working three (that's what I call them) will move out together and take the two young ones with them."

"Why don't you give in and buy a bigger house?"

"We did. This is the biggest house in our neighborhood. Neither Dan nor I wanted to leave the area to find a bigger house."

"Buy land and build one," I said.

"Why would I want to do that Nat? The only time I am alone is the few minutes I am in the bathroom. Then I am not really alone. Someone is always wanting me, hand on the doorknob, are you in there, Mum, Mum is that you? My kids call me Mum, Dan calls me Mum, and when my parents visit, they call me Mum. Even if we build a much bigger house with twice as many bathrooms they would hunt me down. Walking down the road neighbors call out, look there is Freddy's mum, or Alice's mum. Once I wore a T-shirt for a week with 'my name is Terri' printed on the front and back. The first day out wearing it one neighbor asked me who Terri was. It was the same on the street where we lived before. I was always someone's mum so there is no point in moving. If one day I should phone you and ask if the kids and I can come over for a holiday hang up, phone Harry or my parents to have the police come around to the house to see how mentally fit I am to make long distant phone calls wanting to bring the children."

■

This is where Max got his chatter from, Harry and Terri's mum is a chatterer. The chattering missed Harry. I think Bradley and Jack will chatter away and my daughter will have to move out of the house when she is sixteen, unable to handle the chattering any more. Which will make no difference to me, as I will be long gone chattered into insanity."

CHAPTER 27

"Where are they Max? It's been hours since I spoke with Susan." "Where do you think they are? Susan, Margo and Betty are now a team. You can see that all three like one another, so they have gone to lunch and are now drunk. The three musketeers are drawing their swords and pledging undying loyalty to each other."

"Don't talk so silly Max, that's not Margo's nature, running around with little groups of women."

"Maybe not Nat, but Susan and Betty are the kind of women friends Margo likes. It's a silly way to think now days with all this equality between partners. I hope you know Margo is the boss and with her two new teammates, she will easily win them over to her way of thinking so you had better check with Margo about any plans you are thinking of making now."

Max is laughing as he is saying all this. Sometimes a fox is outfoxed by a bigger fox. I stood there smiling at Max when Harry and Terri caught my eye; both were sitting on the couch with their mouths wide open. Suddenly Harry came to.

"What's going on, who is this woman Betty you have been talking about and do I know I her?"

Ok back to me, who is still smiling "I know Margo is the boss but she does not know that I know. You are seeing Margo and me only from a man's point of view. The under currants of how women play together maybe obscure to others only because many said women had to play a role in history dictated to them by society to give them some identity. As most societies can only function in a box, so do most people. Tell me, Max, why you have to comment on Margo being the boss and that I have been outfoxed by a bigger fox, and that she is going to win Susan and Betty over to her side. You would never think or say that if Margo were a man. You would think that is ok. No, no I take that back you would never even give it a thought and saying what you did about Margo and it shows me that you still have a long way to go. I know you mean no harm Max." I came closer to Max so the two sitting with their mouths open would not hear me. "Nothing would make you happier than if Margo and I invited you to join us in bed one night soon." I could not look at him in case I laughed. "I have been reluctant to say anything to you before, because soon would not be soon enough for you, as the anticipation may cause you physical harm."

"No, it will not Nat. I promise you, it will not. Just…say when and I will not think about it anymore. Oh boy, oh boy, was this your idea or was it Margo's? Nat, please say it was Margo."

"You son of a bitch," Max was laughing so much he fell down and I hit him with a cushion.

At this point Terri is looking at Harry like somebody has gone mad and it is not her. "What are they talking about? Who is this Margo, and why are Max and Nat talking this nutty talk? I told you not to marry Susan because as much as I like her, there was something odd about her even as a teenager. The stories she would come up with, and now listening to these two, their conversation makes Susan's stories seem normal."

Well, here they are, thank God.

Three very happy women staggered into the condo, and Susan found her way over to a chair with great difficulty. "Good heavens!" she yells. "I am too old for little drinkies at noon. I am seeing things. This was your idea Betty."

"Excuse me Susan," Betty said. "When we were walking by an ice cream parlor it was a cold drink I wanted. It was you, Susan, that pushed us on to the bar next door. It was you, Susan, that walked through the bar door into that dark hole in the ground and we had to follow you. It was so dark it took us over three hours to find our way out again."

Margo looked at me.

"Nat, I have not stopped laughing for three hours."

I smiled. She knows how happy it makes me when she enjoys my family so much.

"I am seeing things. Does anyone care?" said Susan.

"We do." Harry and Terri said.

Harry and his sister were sitting at a small round table at the far end of the 'room with a view.' Neither Betty nor Margo had seen them but Susan did, as she was the only one to be facing Harry and Terri.

"It's a mirage from England, some people when they drink too much see snakes. What do I see? Harry and his sister. Susan stands up walks to her 'mirage' saying, "Is that you Harry?"

"Yes, it is Susan."

"Oh Harry, I am so glad it's you and Terri and not snakes."

"Bloody wars, Harry, let's leave now while we can, while we still have a semblance of a working brain."

"No Terri, we have to find out what is going on. I have good news Nat, Terri and I will only be here until after the weekend, then the girls, Liz and Mrs. B. are coming over. I know Susan will not come back with me as all the action is here."

"I am sorry, Harry, you are right," Susan said, "All my children under one roof."

Margo looked at Nat and said, "Well is that not funny, that's when I am going to my sister's for a visit."

"After you come back maybe you and I can go away for a few days."

"What about the babies, Nat?"

"We are not taking them Margo. Susan, Max, Mrs. B., the girls and Liz will be here and they can look after them for a few days surely. Good God Margo, when you say 'what about the babies' have I no rights? I look after my family; they are welcome to come over here at no expenses to themselves. I did not want children, I did not want a marriage I just wanted to be 'me'. I stay home every night because I feel so guilty for working and you say, 'what about the babies.' Of course, everyone says how wonderful Max is." By now they are all look-ing at me.

"What are you looking at, what do you want from me? I could pay for a whole team of people to look after my children but no, I have a family. Has any one of you thought to ask if I would like to go out and have some fun some night and not worry about my babies? Look at me Max, this is what you wanted, you carry on like you gave birth to them but do you ever ask how I feel? I am worn out. Every one of you can walk away but me because they are 'my' babies. I feel so trapped and you are right Max, Margo thinks she is the boss. Margo you think I should not be leaving the babies for a few days so you and I can go away together. Have you ever asked me to join you when you go out with your friends clubbing or just on a date, you and me? Never! Well screw you, because that's not happening anymore and another thing Margo Roth, your loyalty is to me first and if it is not then we do not belong together because that is something I demand. Becoming a Musketeer so the three of you can gang up on me when needed is not all right with me. I am going upstairs to shower then I am going out on my own. Please do not follow me upstairs, the door will be locked." I then walked out of the room-with-a -view with Max calling out "It was only a joke Nat, about the three Musketeers. Why are you so upset? It was just silly-talk. Natasha?"

Terri spoke up. "What did I say to you Harry, about Nat and Max and that crazy conversation earlier today, that they were crazier then Susan. For example, Max telling Nat she had been outfoxed by a bigger fox."

"Where are you going Betty?" Margo asked.

"Up to see Nat."

"The doors will be locked," said Susan.

"What kind of lock. If it is a key, I can get in?"

I just got out of the shower when I heard the knock. Whoever was on the other side I so wanted to kick I opened the door my foot already in position to strike.

It was Betty. "May I come in Natasha please?"

"No."

"Please Nat."

"No."

Then she, Betty, my mother kicked me.

The next kick, Nat, will put you on the floor, please let me in."

I sat down on the bed still wet from the shower. Betty took the towel from me and said, "Please let me." She dried my hair and I cried as she whispered, "My baby, my beautiful baby. What would you like to do now Nat?"

"Get into bed and sleep. I am so tired."

"Good idea. You will always be my daughter but it is up to you whether I am your mother."

Betty already knew that by my answer, by her 'power to love', we had already bonded.

Susan later came with cup a tea.

"I am sorry Susan."

"Why? You were right; you are a young woman with a big family and not one of us bothered to ask how you are. We come and go as we like. You have done right by us by giving us three new Hawkes family members. Nobody would have known if you had an abortion. We know how much you love them; we can see it in your eyes when you come home from work. You cannot wait to see and hold them and they know it, they feel your love. We understand now children and marriage were not for you and to be on your own and have triplets was too much."

"You know Max is seeing Sally."

"Is he?" asked Susan. "And you are worried he may have more children with her and leave!"

"Yes!"

Susan sat silent for a minute.

"Well, it's best to have a dead hero as a father than a deserter. We will do away with him. That's our plan and leave Sally penniless."

"That's ok Susan, but that means I will have to go out to find a new father."

"No, we will find him on the internet."

"Then what, he will expect sex."

"Good God no, Nat, we will look for a gay man."

"Well, I feel much better now Susan. If Max leaves us to make more babies, we will do him in and no one will wonder where he is or be any the wiser, and for some reason we will make sure Sally is poor and the next father must be gay. What do you think Harry will say about all this?"

"What do you mean what's Harry going to say, he is the one that is going to do Max in so there is not much he can say!"

"I am getting up now, where is Margo?"

"She is downstairs, mad at herself and us for being so thoughtless. Also, she is not the boss she told Max. She was telling him off for his bad timing and silly chatter. She also said she has more common sense than you do, Nat. She said if she took notice of you all the time you two would always be in trouble. Then the cheeky monkeys started laughing and now are playing cards with Harry and Terri. Give up Nat, you can't win with him, he is 'The Entertainer'. He loves to entertain people and he loves setting you up for his humor because you never see it coming. Betty has gone to her N.Y. house to see what JC is up to and to tell JC that she has a job for summer holidays with the triplets."

Bang, my bedroom door flew open and there stood Harry, Terri and Max.

"Ok, what the hell is going on with this Betty, where did you find her? It appears to me she has just moved right in. She has gone home now but it would not surprise me if she came back with her nightie on and goes up to bed. Is she blackmailing you, have you told one of your daft stories to the wrong person? Max is too frightened to tell me what connection she has with this family."

"Shut up Harry, the past few days has been too much for all of us. I phoned you a few times with some questions but you were not there."

It's only when you have been away from this family for some time that you know the true definition of Anglo-American family disorder.

"Ok Harry," said Susan, "You want to know, here it is briefly. Betty is Natasha's real mother."

Harry's twin sister grabs him by the arm saying, "We are out of here."

"Just a sec, Terri. How do you know this Susan?"

"Margo told us."

"The lawyer, the lawyer downstairs? Nat, you told me ages ago that she, Margo, was going out with a gangster. Did you not tell me Nat that Margo was once a gangster's moll?"

"When was this? Oh boy," said Max, now worrying about a gangster's moll in the house.

"Please, out of my room we can all talk downstairs. Now go and I will dress."

"Susan, will you ask the gangster's moll to come up?"

Margo appeared in the doorway. "When did you tell Harry I was going out with a gangster? "

"The night you hit on me."

"Sometimes Nat, you have such a way with words."

"What I said was, you look like a woman that goes out with men with big necks, white shirt collars too small, never carries credit cards just tons of cash. You know Margo, I love you more each time I see you."

"I know you do Nat, let's go."

We made it easy on ourselves at the small round table at the end of the room with a view. We had one gallon of white wine, one giant pitcher of beer, wine glasses, mugs and nibblies. "Ok, who starts first with this story of the lost mother?" asked Harry.

"Me," said Margo. "It all began when a client of mine asked me to spend the weekend at her Hampton Beach house as she was seeking a divorce and needed a new will made up. By chance, she, Betty, heard me on the phone speaking with Nat. Afterwards, Betty asked if that was my girlfriend, and what was her name? Natasha, what a lovely name she said. After a minute or two, Betty swore me to secrecy on my lawyer's oath. Betty had never told anyone this before, neither to her first husband and children nor second husband and children, only she and her parents knew. When she was seventeen years old she had a daughter, Natasha. Her parents only wanted the best for their young and only daughter Betty, so decided it was best for her not to keep the baby, as they thought at the time it would limit her education then and future opportunities."

"Well," puffed Harry. "Where were these good parents when their teenage daughter was off having sex?"

"The sex, Harry, I was told, and I believe it, was a onetime deal. The man came to see Betty's parents full of shame, as he did not realize Betty was that young. Then by the time Natasha was born he, Peter Bennett, had met the woman he was to marry."

"Why have I never heard this before now? Peter and I were very good friends, sounds like someone is after Nat's money to me."

"Have you finished Harry? You are just like the rest of your family, you want to know the final act before the script has been written."

"Peter would not hear of his child being put up for adoption and he and his to be wife, Jane, wanted to take her. Two days later, they married and became a family of three. Jane Bennett was put on record as the birth mother. Peter's mother came over from England to meet Betty's parents and was well pleased with them. Plus, she had them checked out, including the history of both sides of the family because you never know… what was classified as being criminally insane years ago would not be called that now. If she did find something that would indicate Nat's background was not quite right it would be changed. It appears Peter's mother did have the clout to do this."

"Oh boy, oh boy! I knew, I knew it, I always knew there was something odd about you Nat. Look at you with your high IQ running around looking for Lost Souls. You know what I think…"

Max's chair slipped from under him as he fell to the floor.

"Are you OK Max?" Harry said, trying to help Max up. "Say another word about Nat's job and you are gone. I will see that it is to jail for telling secrets. Get up you arsehole."

All were concerned for Max and his fall, not realizing that it was Harry that kicked Max's chair away.

Susan, Margo and I began laughing. "That was a joke on you Max," said Margo, "like this afternoon when you found it so funny to tell Nat I am her boss and that she has been outfoxed by a bigger fox."

"Peter Bennett's mother did not go around changing records of Betty's family history because there was nothing to change. It's one thing to pay off officials for changing a baby's birth records, which I would think has been done down through history. But to change prison, hospital and government files would be beyond Peter's mother's capacity, do you not agree Max, when you think about it?"

Poor Max, that will teach him not to say an untruth about my Margo again.

Harry got up from the table and walked towards the stairs. "Come Max, lets you and I get the babies so the ladies can feed them."

"No Dad, I am not." Come on Max let's all three of us get the babies." I said. At the top of the stairs, Harry pushed Max all the way down the hall, opened the door to the last bedroom and pushed him inside where no one could hear.

"Max, I am going to leave now and go back down stairs, because I do not care what Harry does to you and I could not stop him anyway."

I put the babies in their big pram and wheeled them down the ramp.

"Nat, where are Harry and Max?" Terri asked.

"Still upstairs, talking." Thirty-five minutes later Harry and Max joined the ladies.

As for Betty being Nat's birth mum, Harry could not quite believe it.

"What did you think at the time, did you think any funny business was going on Susan, about the baby?" Harry asked.

"All I can remember is the last time I saw Jane a few months before they married there was no sign of her being pregnant and she never said anything about a baby. If the baby was Natasha, and I believe it to be so, this would explain why Jane never looked pregnant. Phone Lesley Faggott tomorrow Harry," said Susan.

"Yes, that's a good idea," Harry said.

When we were going up to bed Margo asked, "What was going on with Harry and Max?" For some reason, neither Terri, nor Susan and I could understand what Max was talking about. He talks such rubbish when he gets excited and then no one bothers to listen."

"Well, that's it. He talks rubbish, but why Harry wanted to talk to him upstairs is beyond me. I just went along for the ride so we could bring down the babies."

"Nat, I work for one of the best law firms in New York City. They did not hire me because I have half a brain so I will repeat the question, why was Max scared to go upstairs with Harry, what did Max say that made Harry so angry?"

I closed the bedroom door. "It's none of your business Margo."

"What I can make out from what Max was saying you do not work for Lost Souls and something is odd about you. Lesley Faggot would fire me on the spot if he thought in some way I knew you were involved in shady business."

"Excuse me Margo I work for the US Government Secret Service. That is all you and Lesley need to know. If anything, Lesley should fire you for implying I may be involved in shady affairs. I never discuss my job with anyone not authorized to know, least of all Max. As far as what Harry was angry about, you will have to ask him."

Margo went home that night.

I did not sleep much that night, as I know I had really hurt Margo by showing my lack of trust in her. This was at the core of Margo's soul as a person and a lawyer, that she can be trusted. I told Susan and Harry the next morning what happened.

Susan was upset. "So, that's the rubbish Max was talking about. Go to her now, Nat. When I got to know Margo, I stopped worrying about you. Go."

I arrived at six-thirty a.m.

"Oh, you have been crying," I said. "Please don't, I am so sorry. I do trust you. I thought it was a foregone conclusion that I could never discuss my work. Susan said you are a 'keepie' and if I go back without you she will be so mad and she is thinking about doing Max in."

Margo laughed at that one. "Well, we had better get over there. I have to dress. Come in with me while I get ready." We got back just in time for breakfast, and as we both were due into work today so it was a case of eat and run.

Susan stood up. "I better get upstairs and look at the babies."

Just as Susan was getting up, she saw Max coming down.

"Are they OK, Max?"

"They are fine Mum."

Susan put her arms around her only son and nearly kissed him to death. That's how Max saw it, more than two kisses from his mother meant she was coming in for the kill.

"I hear you are seeing Sally. How fond of her are you?"

Max looked at her smiling with those beautiful white teeth of his.

"If all you are going to do is smile, remember who paid for that smile. Harry and I went out and worked in the fields to pay that crook of a dentist."

"Ok Mum, she is fun, likes to be in charge, very career minded, and does not want children until her mid-thirties. Her wishes and hopes for the future are to follow Natasha up the ladder until she has learned all she can. She has never met anyone as smart on the job as Nat. I asked Nat before I asked Sally out if she would mind me dating her assistant. She said it was ok as long as I did not make her, Nat, the brunt of my jokes. If I did and Sally lost respect for her as boss, Nat would fire her. Well, need I tell you what Nat said Sally would do? Apparently, when Nat first got her new job she was told to get herself an assistant. Nat found Sally in the typing pool on the fourth floor but had to fight tooth and nail for her as the higher ups told Nat Sally had no experience for the job. Nat won."

Susan looked at Harry and made a funny face and that was that.

I decided my first stop would be to see George Johnston, my old boss and good friend. As I have said before, the building I work in is huge with many offices for federal and local governments, plus private shops catering to all the needs of the workers. In fact, you could live in there and never go out for as long as you wanted. Now, I thought George would be the second thing I would do, this morning before arriving at work. The first would be to look at the store fronts for a dress or 'what have you' to buy for Margo. So where do I look first is a bookstore. Why? I will never know as I could never find the time to read a book. Let me just look at the *New York Times* bestsellers list. Something made me look up and step backward so I could see over the rows and rows of books at the back of the store. At first, I thought it was just a look-a-like. But no, it was Max. What the hell was he doing here? Then I went into shock, as standing next to Max who was showing his big white teeth, was Ann Gilbert. Of all people in this world, Ann Gilbert, my first love, and my still first husband Max were in a bookstore and I was looking at them. I dropped to the floor and crawled along on my hands and knees past the bookstore got up and ran, turning at the first passageway to the elevators. Still in shock, I made my way up to George's office. "Hi George."

"Nat. Nat is that you? What on earth are you doing here with the low life?"

"George, I am in such shock I may have to go to the hospital. "

"What happened?" George looked very concerned. "Did some man pat your bottom?"

"Very funny, George. Now listen. I was in the bookstore and you will never guess what, 'who and who' were in there?"

George is now beginning to think. "So, what you are saying is 'who and who' were in the bookstore and you saw them but did 'who and who' see you?"

"No."

"May I ask who ' who and who' are?" George asked.

"Max, my still first husband and Ann Gilbert."

"Tell no one Nat. You never saw her, and she may go away. If you think about her, she may turn up. She is cuckoo, nuts, and this time you may not get away."

"Why is she with Max? She is up to something."

"Both June and I are very fond of Margo. She went far beyond being a lawyer to help June when she was so ill. So, do not mess it up. Thems your orders!"

"Yes sir! Give my love to June. We will be in touch soon for you both to come over. I cannot stay and talk now George, I am in such a tiswas over seeing Max and Ann together. May I go and say hi to the old gang."

"Need you ask."

There was a sign on the door "Door to Nowhere." Sometimes I wish I were back there again opening the door to nowhere, seeing all my old work friends. Some were still here, some had moved on and some never came back to walk through that door to nowhere. I reached out to push the doorbell and stopped. I heard a noise. A man was trying to get by me with a cart. "Move on Lady, please." Yes, I think I will thank you!

CHAPTER 28

I arrived at work late, sat down and had a think. Sally was nowhere to be found, so I had a bigger think. Max's IQ had escaped a lot of people, even his mother, because of his Attention Deficit Disorder (A.D.D.) as a child. It was a lot more noticeable then. Now as an adult he had learned with help how better to manage it. Still when he gets overly excited or frustrated with people and conversations no one understands what he is talking about and he can say the silliest things. The other day when Max's was telling me about Margo's need to be in charge, that she had befriended Susan and Betty and any plans I had should be checked with Margo first, it was clear Margo now had backup. Max was nowhere near being in what I call his 'A.D.D. moment' when he said all that. Had he seen something or felt something about Margo that I have not? Also, Margo did not tell me it was next week she was going to her sister's and I have yet to meet any of her family. Now I think about it she showed no concern about me being upset that we never go out in the evenings. When I phoned home, Max answered. "When you are taking the babies to the park?"

"About two this afternoon" he said.

"I would like just you and I to go, there are a few things I would like to talk to you about alone, so I will be there by two, Max"

"Oh boy, am I in trouble?" said Max.

"No, no it's not about you, I need some advice."

"OK, Nat, you have never asked me for advice before."

I arrived home at one fifty-five. The babies and Max were ready to go with only two prams as a wheel had fallen off the big pram for three. Jack was in one pram, Brad and Alex in another. Max had everything down to a 'T', milk bottles at the bottom of Jack's pram along with napkins and facial swipes. Of course, I blame Max for this but our babies are whoppers. Alex and Brad have to sit opposite one another in a pram because they are too fat to sit side by side. Of course, they have to be in their best clothes when Max takes them to Central Park, as anyone that's someone will stop, look, and talk to the Hawkes kids.

Susan and Terri had gone out for the day to shop and then to meet Betty at East 55st for lunch where she is a member of the core club.

"So, what's up Nat. You rarely ask my opinion on personal matters."

"How do you know its personal Max?"

"Because you don't want anybody in the family to hear you and I are home at two from work, that's personal for you."

"I am not sure if you were trying to give me a message or just being funny. There are the remarks you made about Margo wanting to be in charge by getting on the best side of Susan and Betty, and there are other things I have not noticed before. I would like to hear from you now, that's if you are a little concerned."

"I do not think the word is concern Nat. It was not until much later that I gave thought to what I had said to you. Oh dear, I am trying to find the right words… I see and feel she loves you very much but there is something missing. Has she been in a long-term relationship before you?"

"No."

"Well, that maybe it. She still thinks as one, she may feel differently, Nat, but she thinks as 'one'."

"Please do not say that I asked about Margo to Susan, she thinks Margo is perfect. What you have just said makes sense but I feel there is more to it. When Harry announced the girls, Mrs. B, and Liz were coming next week, Margo announced she is going to her sister's home. I know every year she goes to see her and her family for week or so, but Margo never mentioned it before now that she is going next week. Then I suggested when she gets back we go away for a few days, Margo's first reaction was to say, and she meant it, "what about the babies?" I think going to her sister was the only time she was taking off work so there would be none for us. Max, I have no idea what's going to happen when the family goes back home to England. Months ago, at the beginning, I told Margo the family is moving back home in a year or two. Margo said maybe we would be 'over' by then. I told this to Susan, maybe different wording. Susan said it sounds like one of my stories. Well, it is a little bit more than that. I have three children and would like to know now what her thoughts are and does she want a role with them in the future. Does any of this make sense to you Max? Poor Max." Then I started to cry.

"Please don't cry Nat. Oh my babies' poor mother. Look Nat, the babies are crying too. Stop it Hawkes babies, only mummies can cry today."

Only Max could make me laugh, and we both looked up laughing, then the Hawkes kids started screaming.

"What the hell?" said Max?

There in the little cove we had found for ourselves, looking at us was Betty, Terri and Susan. As it was after five they had come looking for us. Where had the time gone?

"What's going on Nat and Max, and why are you crying and laughing Natasha?" said Susan.

"It's ok Mum, I have taken care of the matter," said Max.

Here we go, Susan and Max are now going to compete with one another about who is my best adviser.

"Is that right Max?" Susan said.

What a wise woman Betty is, she is not going to say one word. I wonder what she thinks of us. She can see this family stays together and still loves even though they are always crossing one another's boundaries. We are like Special Forces trained as a unit. We are of one mind. This family has found the power to love with one mind. We made our way home, crossed the avenue and saw Harry getting out of the cab. Max called out to his father, "HARRY." Max's voice echoed through Central Park and every 'Harry' stopped, looked around on hearing his name, shrugged his shoulders, and then moved on.

Harry knew no more than he did before having lunch with Lesley Faggott. "Peter Bennett's estate, will and trust, had been set up to cover his wife Jane as well as, his children Natasha Taylor, Michael, David, Mary Anne, and any future children. Just one funny thing, there was a vial of his blood along with the will. Lesley also checked Peter's blood with Nat's and Betty's. Both were parents of Natasha. Other trusts and attachments etc. will be made available to Natasha when she is thirty years old. Lesley appears to trust and like Margo and if he knows more than he is telling, he is not telling me."

The phone rang and Susan picked it up.

"Oh, it's so nice to hear your voice, thank God; the only ones that eat properly are the Hawkes kids. Are you sure? Oh, you hear gossip better when you are cooking. Give me the list… Look forward to seeing you tomorrow, bye. That was Mrs. B. Max and Nat would you go to the market now? She only wants fresh food from the market and I have the list here."

"Real food tomorrow, Mrs. B. is going to cook real food," Max sang out. "Are you and Harry ok with the babies? We may stop for a drink. Do you want to come with us Terri?"

"No, you two go off and have some fun."

Max and I decided we would walk to the market, stop about half way, have a drink and then get a cab back home with all the goodies from the market. We just sat down with our drinkiepoos when my phone rang. "It's Margo, Max. Hi, well that's just what Max and I are doing, then we are going clubbing. That's not your concern Margo, and you be careful too. Oh, ok. Goodnight. You heard me Max I told her we were going clubbing Oh! She says we are out drinking too and who is minding the babies, well I told her it was none of her concern. Then she tells me to be careful which is why I said and you be careful too. Then she got huffy and said she was only going out with her sister and brother-in-law. And that was that."

"Max, I feel it's over, she has stopped caring about me. I knew she would after a while. I think she just gets bored not just by me but with all the women she has known. At the moment I do not care, but in time I will, after I stop being mad at her. That's it Max, I am not going to do to myself what I did over Ann, and I have three children now."

"Do you ever think of Ann Gilbert, Nat? I know she meant so much to you at one time."

"Yes, yes, I do. I wish her well, and I hope she is happy. For me Max, it is awful to love someone so much and when they go, I end up disliking them. It does not say much about me as a person and the way I love."

"I am so glad your babies are my babies Nat."

"Thank you, we will do right by them, you, the family and me. Do you like Betty?"

"Yes, I do. The thing is, do you?"

"Very much. Each time I see her I feel her love and I know mine is growing for her. This is still a shock. Sometimes when I look at her I see myself, I look like her. Do you think so Max?"

Max put on his sweet face and smiled when he wants me to know he has big love for me that day.

"Yes, I do."

Max would say yes even if I looked like Batman and Betty looked like Robin.

"Max dear, what were you doing in the bookstore near where I work, talking to Ann Gilbert? The truth please, Max not a story. It will hurt me much more later if I find out you are not telling the truth now."

"I am sorry I cannot make this into a big drama full of intrigue with a deep plot that only a few will ever know the answer to! Last week, the babies and I went to the park on our own, just me by myself."

"I know what you are trying to do Max, you are going to drag this story out, till I am so bored I don't care what you say. Get on with it please."

"OK Nat. I sat down on a bench soon to be shared with this woman and daughter about five or six years old. She did not look at me she spoke as if she was talking to someone standing in front of her and said the funniest thing. 'My God, you are as good looking as I am beautiful.' Then we both burst into laughter. We talked about how this can be such a handicap in some ways. She had been living in Europe the last few years and had been in New York the last few days; she used to live here. She had to go back to Sweden suddenly after her mother was killed. Now her life is back in order, she was wondering if her daughter would have a better life here as she, the mother, was born in USA. Her name is Ann Gilbert."

"Stop, please stop Max, this is too much. Why, why did she not tell me? I would have helped her, whatever was happening. What does she look like now? Is she rich, poor, where does she live, is she with some-one?"

"Nat, I do not know the answer to any of your questions, except she is as beautiful as I am good looking. After a while, I asked her if she would have lunch with me the following week. That's when you saw us. Nat, I was at my best with my witty retort. When I asked her out to lunch she looked down all shy like and said sheepishly 'I don't sleep with men.' Look at me Nat, please, just my face."

I did not want to but I had to know what silly, silly reply he thinks was so funny and clever. He looked down with a daft look on his face and said, 'Neither do I.'

"Nat, she burst in to laugher and said yes to lunch."

"Well, what did she say at lunch, does she know who you are, are you seeing her again? You say she has a daughter, if she is five or six Ann had the child before I met her. She didn't live with Ann then; maybe the daughter lived with Ann's mother. She never once told me she had a child. I cannot believe this Max."

"Yes, she knows my name."

"Did she ask you or did you tell her?"

"No, she did ask me, I remember when we were sitting on the bench. It didn't seem she knew who I was. Did she know your married name?"

"I am not sure, Max. She may have just known me by Natasha T. Bennett. Wait a minute, she stayed at Hawkes Manor once, so yes, she did know. She knew Susan and Harry were my guardians, plus she knew they had a married son. Did she make any reference to me or the Lake District? How could I have forgotten that? It was not the best of times, so maybe I blocked it out. She said nothing of being in England, never mentioned friends or anyone she knew in NY before she left?"

"No, she said nothing about her life here before she left, when her mother was killed. In fact, it appeared she went out of her way to say nothing about the time she lived here in NYC. We had a very nice time we met early in the bookstore, as she needed to buy some books, so I said I would meet her there earlier. I asked if I may phone her some time so we can do this again, and she said yes, and that was that. I was thinking of not telling you, what with Margo in your life and you were happy with her."

"Thank you, Max, for telling me. I would like very much to see her again, but not now, I have to sort out what and where Margo and I are going. For all I know Ann may not want to see me again."

"Mrs. B. did not mean the market back home in England," said Susan as we returned home much later.

"We stopped for a few drinks."

"Well that's ok if that's all that happened…" said Susan.

I asked Susan if she had a good time today.

"Wonderful, just wonderful, I am so glad Betty is in our lives. I feel a whole new world is opening up. The core club is something else."

I spent the rest of the evening thinking, thinking about Margo. What was I to do, break it off now? If she were thinking of coming home with the family and me, she would have said something by now. She never asked about or showed any interest in Hawkes Manor, the Lake District or England. We should not have reached this point. Margo knew from the beginning she could not leave NYC. No love would be strong enough for her to give up living in NY, leave her family, friends and job. She was born here, and I didn't ask her if she would go, it would be too much to ask anybody. However, she has never once asked is there anything we can do to keep our love alive, this love we have found together. A love like she has never known before. She never asked if I could go back and live 12 months a year at Hawkes Manor. The life I want for my children is not the life I want for me. I want for my children the life that the Hawkes gave me. I cannot give them that on my own in NY. Some people are ' tourists', two weeks here, two weeks there, then there are travelers who like to visit and live in other countries.

I have changed my mind about including Susan in my thoughts about Margo. That is not fair to her to just find out Margo is out of my life and not tell her why. "Susan, do you have a few minutes, please?"

"Yes, Nat, what is it?"

I told Susan every thought I had about the relationship with Margo, and why it had to stop, as I can feel the hurt now. "I cannot and will not go through what I did last time with Ann. Susan, both you and I have known people, couples that have made the impossible, possible. The Hawkes family has made raising our children together possible. She knew from the beginning we, the family, were going back to England and because of that I believe I never met her friends, parents or siblings. When I suggested we go away, her response was "what about the babies?" You would think she would only be too happy to go away with me, just the two of us. Susan, I do not want her in our home again. There is something about me, which does not work well in partnerships. There is something missing, I pick the wrong people. There is nothing wrong with them; they are just not the right people for me. Max is a good man and Ann Gilbert a good woman but Margo plays me for a fool, just wanting sex and a good laugh. She knows how much I loved her did she not think or feel at the end how this would hurt?"

Susan sat in silence. Then she said, "I am at a loss for words Nat. Many times, Margo has told me how much she loves you and everything will sort itself out. You will have to talk this out with her. I am so sorry this has happened. Maybe I read her all wrong. What you need is a holiday."

"Funny you should say that. I was thinking of going to California. Do you mind if it's more than few days?"

"My dear, for what you and Max have given the family, you do what you need. I doubt if Jennie will have any more children after this one. They tried so hard to get pregnant and it has been such a rough pregnancy too. Maybe one's enough. Claire's a Doctor, she may never marry. Crewe and Liz, you never know. Lots of single girls ask male friends, if they're nice and respected, to donate. We will see. When were you thinking of going?"

"Sometime the end of next week."

"That soon?"

"If it's ok with you, I was thinking of asking Max, Liz and Crewe. I would ask them only if Betty and JC would come over, stay, and help with the babies and only if that would be OK with you. Would you feel if Crewe and Liz came with me it's taking time that you would of like to spend with them?"

With a big smile, I said "This way you can butter up Betty to take you and company to the best places in town, where only the rich go. Because, you will fit in. You see, I am the only member of this family that knows how damn rich you and Harry are due to one simple act of kindness. You and Harry both showed love for many years to a man you thought was penniless, with no home and asked nothing in return. He in return gave you wealth beyond your dreams. The happiness you gain is up to you. Of course, Ben wanted you to share this with your family, so they would never have to worry about money. If you tell them the amount that was left to you, they would worry continually about the money and who was getting what. I hope to God you have not and never will, for the sake of the family. Lesley Faggott and maybe Harry think I have no idea how much I inherited from the Bennett Estate. I got the lot. Susan, I am telling you this out of respect and love for you and Harry and no one else. When I began to question my inheritance, I called in every favor that was owed to me, to find out where my interests would be best served and who I could trust most. I found a wonderful lawyer of wills and what not, and a private investigator."

"Please Nat," I hear Harry's voice calling me. This is for him to hear too. "Harry, Harry I am in here."

"I tried the door a minute ago and it was locked," Harry said.

"Nat is telling me things you need to hear for me to understand."

I caught Harry up to date, on what I had told Susan, which took him by surprise.

"Harry, Susan, I was quite taken back by Lesley's response to me; to be told I have inherited my father's estate but when I asked how much, they did not know. Since I had no idea if it entailed ten dollars or ten thousand dollars, he still would not tell me. When I asked to see the will, 'in time' was the reply. After all these years, my father's will is still not in order and the beneficiary is not permitted to see the will. It took over a year to find out how much my inheritance was and to see a copy of the will. It appears to me there is and has not been a reason not to show the will or tell me what I have inherited, and the reason is Harry?"

Harry by now was so red in the face, I was unsure if I should continue.

"You and Max were married. It was such an unbelievable amount of money for one person to have and to acquire it so young. I underestimated your ability to handle what you saw as your responsibility to the Bennett's name and how you saw it not as your money but something that would allow you to do good as you did with George Johnston and his wife. I was worried about Max and if he could cope. I begged Lesley to hold off telling you as long as possible. After a while you gave Max money, bought this condo from him, and paid the Johnston's hospital bill, so I thought Lesley had told you how rich you were. I was so proud of you, so very proud that you could cope all on your own."

"Thank you, Harry, I know you meant well. As you know, the money was mine as soon as my father died. It is so involved and complicated. Also, the will was set up in a way that only my father's children, their children would inherit."

"I will reimburse you for the monies you spent on finding out what was going on with your inheritance." Harry said.

"No Harry, please no. I am glad that this is now settled. I am sure Lesley is still feeling very uncomfortable hearing from the lawyer; maybe you can pop in and see Lesley, Harry so he knows there are no hard feelings."

"Thank you for being so gracious about this Nat," Harry said.

"I must tell you and show you both what was found by the Private Investigator I hired. A few years after the plane crash, a book was found in an adjacent field. It was in fair condition as it was in a plastic grocery bag. Anyway, it ended up in an old bookstore in a village nearby. The book was written for my father Peter, by his father. The contents are not that important, but handwritten on the back pages was a letter by Peter's father to Peter:

'My father, like many before him, had a dream, a dream that belonged in children's' books and in old men wishes. All the 'if onlys': I regret to inform you, did I ever tell you, the phone call that's unanswered, the most I regret is I wish I had loved more.

Peter, I am an old man now, and most of what I have written is about regrets that most humans have. Try not having the last one yours. When you were a child, I told you every day how much you were loved by me. I hoped and prayed those words would carry you through to become the man you are today. Do not forget your children so they in turn will not forget theirs. If we were all to live like this one day we may hear the words of love over the sounds of war. Your Dad.'

I said nothing as they both sat reading what my grandfather had written to his son Peter, my father. I could see the tears in their eyes. My father had been given the power of love. When he died, I came to a family that had the power of love, above everything else, the fights, the kicks and yelling, punch ups, nothing was as important as this love the family shared. Then my thoughts became my voice as I told Susan and Harry "It's only when Margo said to me, can you feel it?"

"Feel what?"

"The love, this love embraces you all, when you are together as a family. Now I wonder how many families and people have the power to love, but never talk about it in case others laugh because it's just not done. My three children will have it, so in turn they will give it to their family and friends. The power of love they will learn only through their own self-love and respect that all living things have a right to live with, respect and be free."

"Is this a dream maybe? Some dreams do come true. If this does not, your children will not be around to know! We have much to be grateful for, and it's time we as a family put our words regarding hope for tomorrow into action," Harry said.

"There are a few things I would like to talk about first," Susan said." I believe we have to go back to England to apply for four landed immigration papers with your help. Harry said it would be easy."

"Why, Susan, why? Please tell me what you are thinking?"

"Well, last week Max, out of the blue, said to me 'I think I am going to have trouble going back to Hawkes Manor to live.' He went on to say to me, 'Now just hear me out Mum, nothing I say is written in stone, just some ideas. I love New York, I love everything about it, and I also love Hawkes Manor and want my children to feel it's their home too. What's going to happen to Nat? She will have nothing to keep her mind alive if she goes back.' Max started to cry. I have never seen him so upset before. Nat, he was more upset that you would come back to Hawkes Manor, end up alone and never have a sex life again," Susan finished.

I just sat there looking at Susan wondering how I had survived all these years living under Susan's spell. What a fool I am to think I am normal, how could I be? Every night I will pray that my three children will have a sound mind.

"Max is playing you Susan, and using Nat to do it," said Harry. He is just Max to you both. To the folks back home he is 'Max the Boy' they have known most of their lives. To the Central Park, Manhattan, New York women he is what their own husbands or boyfriends are not.

It is not just his good looks, it is the way he smiles when they stop and look at the babies. Max holds one of the babies up in his arms, looks right into the woman's eyes and says isn't he handsome. Girls I have seen and heard this little act of Max's so many times. She will reply yes, he is, I bet you would love to kiss and cuddle him all day long, and then a piece of paper is tucked into the babies' pram. I was with him one day when some woman ran by saying 'Hi Max' and holding out her hand. He took it smiled at her and asked her how she was doing. Her reply was why don't we go over there and find out (trees). Max asked me not to move saying 'Dad, do not take your eyes off the three babies.' Before he comes home he checks out the pram for odd bits of paper."

"Very funny Harry, you are just as bad as he is with your off-color humour," Susan said.

I chimed in, "The son of a bitch telling you I will have no sex life if I go back to Hawkes Manor, what does Max know? Susan you are as dotty as Max is crafty. At his age, he is in full-blown hormone discomfort. That is why he is happy most days and never minds taking the babies to the park on his own. Well you have to hand it to him, even as a child Max took full advantage of the situation in which he found himself."

Harry at this point was laughing so much at Susan, when she said, "I don't want to go back to Hawkes Manor and live there the rest of my life, I love it here. It is a new world, which is a gift at my age and a new life Harry, for all of us! I would like Christmas at Hawkes Manor. For the summer, I would love to buy a large house near the sea, in the Hamptons maybe. We could get a much bigger condo here in Manhattan for all of us with several floors. All the family can be together but with private spaces for each. The babies will always have a family to look after them. When they are five years old, we will have to think about education, school, home schooling or just give them away. I am not saying we have to move as a block. Meaning, some might like to live at Hawkes Manor in the spring, like Mrs. B. She might want to spend more time with her sister at Hawkes Manor and that is up to her. Natasha, the babies will never be your sole responsibility. As I have said many times before, you have given the Hawkes three hearts to add to our tree, we will give to them the power of love."

I sat there thanking God for this family, now that I did not care about Max setting me up with a sexless life at Hawkes Manor. I now felt I had some control of my future. I am not thinking it will easy. It was many years ago that Susan had to run after three-year old children that were up to no good and thinking only with one mind.

"Harry, what do you think?"

"Go ahead we have a lot of thinking and planning to do. As far as building onto the manor, we can stop now. If in the future we are not using the extra rooms, which we may still do as the family gets bigger, Claire would love to add them on to the clinic, which she already has told me a dozen times."

"Is that what you see Harry, our family getting bigger?"

"Yes, I do Nat, and you will have a partner, so please take no notice of Max."

"Nat, I have no problem with your asking Max, Liz and Crewe to go on holidays with you, but you have to make sure Betty and JC will stay while you all are away. Mrs. B. and I will not be able to cope with all three. In addition, we have to prepare Mrs. B. for Betty coming into our lives, which it is going to be a shocker for her."

"Thank you, Susan. I will phone Betty after I see if Liz and Crewe are interesting in going to California with me, maybe L.A."

"I would call Betty first, Nat, to see if she is free. You know the girls will say yes."

"Maybe you are right Susan." I said.

"Are you not going to ask Claire to go with you?" Harry asked

"Oh Harry, I didn't give it a thought because she would say no thanks, but I should ask. Harry, thank you, for reminding me. Of course, I will ask her, what with Jennie deciding not to come because the doctor wanted to keep an eye on her and her mother-in-law (MIL) would do nothing but worry all the time Jennie was here, that would only upset Jennie as MIL has a bad heart. What does that have to do with not asking Claire if she would like to go to California with me? Nothing I am just looking for an excuse for my thoughtlessness."

"One more thing" said Harry." If it's ok with you Nat, Terri and I would like to stay on longer. I have missed my wife and would like to spend more time with her, and if for some reason Susan needs to go back to be with Jennie, Susan has me or Terri to be with her."

"What are you talking about Harry Jennie is only seven months along? Do you know something I do not know Harry? Out with it now Harry!"

"No, I do not Susan. Mick's mum is watching Jennie like a hawk. If you want to go back now and be with Mick's mum good luck to you. The woman is a worrier. She is the doctor of nothing, thinks the baby may come early. If this is the case, you as the mum will have to go and be with the other grandmother. OK Susan?"

"OK Harry. Mick is such a nice guy, where did he find that mother of his."

Harry laughed. "That's the same as what Mick thinks about Jennie."

I stood up. "Just a second, the cleaners are leaving, and I will be back." The ladies have done such a good job the place looks spotless. The kitchen was extra shiny just for Mrs. B.

"Wonderful job ladies." I gave each one a bonus. One or two ladies arrive every day, but today a crew was here to clean so the girls would see what the place looks like when tidy and clean. Hopefully, then they would leave it like it is, not one big mess.

Buzz, buzz, it was Fadil.

"They are here, Mrs. B., twin women, and, and that…"

"Forget it Fadil, it's just not going to happen," as Fadil was referring to Liz Michaels.

Max was upstairs dozing with the babies. "They are here! They are here." I called out. I heard Max fall out of bed and the babies were screaming. Harry and Susan ran to the front door to be greeted by four Brits. They pushed Harry and Susan aside, saying, "where are the babies? Babies where are you?" Max called out, "We were still napping, and I am changing them. Come up and get them." Claire, Crewe and Liz each carried down a baby. Three happy aunties, three very happy babies.

CHAPTER 29

I am so glad I asked Claire if she would like to go to California. "Yes, I would," she said. Liz and Crewe wanted to go the next day and Max had already packed his bag. Now I have to phone Betty. I was so excited I forgot to phone Betty first "Hi Betty, I will get right to the point."

"Yes dear?"

"Can you and JC come and stay with Susan, Harry and Mrs. B. while Max, Claire, Liz, Crewe and I go to California to have wonderful time without you? We hope one week from today, for a week or more?"

"Yes dear."

"Will we see you tonight?"

"Yes dear."

"OK, see you then. Oh, and Betty, will you have lunch with me, say Tuesday, near where I work?"

"Yes dear, bye."

I needed to talk about Margo again and wanted to know what Betty thought I should do. Margo phoned just before we sat down to dinner that night.

"Hi, Nat, how are you? Are the girls and Mrs. B. there?"

"Yes, we are going to sit down any minute now."

"Ok Nat, I will let you go then."

"I think you have already done that Margo!"

"What the hell does that mean? I love and miss you. I will be home the following weekend and we will talk then. Ok?"

"Yes, I think we need to. I am going to be busy with work and family until then so we will talk then."

"I will not call then. Have fun."

I sat down to dinner as the tears rolled down my face. I felt Betty's hand as she guided me away into the media room.

"It is Margo, right?"

"Yes, no, it is me. She is not interested in me meeting her friends and family, she is going out on our own. She will not invest the time because we are all going back to the UK."

"Well Nat, I do not think Margo quite sees it as an investment of time. Have either of you taken the time to sit down and talk about it, the future, and what it entails? No, you have not. She is an educated woman. Can she practice law over there?"

"I don't no."

"Why not Nat, why do you not know? I would have thought you would have checked into that, just so you would know her options. Margo was born and raised in New York, she knows no other way of life. She cannot talk about it, because she already knows the answer. Margo is terrified of losing you. She has gone to her sister to discuss family matters; families always see the single child of all the siblings as the one responsible for the aging parents. Margo's sister lives out of state but the two brothers live near their parents and they are not going to be too happy about this, they have their own responsibilities now. Their sister cannot up and leave. It's unfair but lots of families appear to see it that way."

"When did Margo tell you all this?"

"She did not," Betty said.

"Well who did?"

"Nobody, I have surmised this, it's common sense. She has gone to see her sister as there will be trouble in the family and the brothers will look to Margo's sister now for help with the parents. Margo told me the sister is the only one that knows of Margo's lifestyle. Nat, it is not that unusual for first and second-generation families from the old country to have passed down the old ways and guilt is number one. I know you have not asked her to leave everything behind to live at Hawkes Manor, but is there another choice for her? Margo will die of guilt. It would be one think to marry a Brit and live in England. Her family may not like it but would understand. However, to go to England and live with a woman and her family when they know nothing of her life style is another matter. It's too late now for them to understand. If you want a happy Margo that loves you, you will have to stay here. You have me now, I am your mother and there is nothing in this world that will part us again, do you hear me Natasha? In addition, as you know Susan and Max are not going anywhere either, they both love it here. Anyway, my dear we should get back now. We can talk more on Tuesday. You should have come to Susan and me much sooner as you have no talents for solving your love problems. I could kick you, Nat you have so many options."

We had a wonderful weekend, and Betty and JC stayed over. I was beginning to think Harry and Terri were growing to like Betty; all three have a very dry sense of humor.

I arrived at work Tuesday early only to find that Sally was there earlier.

"Hi, the Big Boys came by to see you. When you get in they said please go and see them."

"Ok, Sally. I am surprised to see you in this early."

"Well lucky I was, what with the Big Boys turning up."

I walked up to a desk were a young woman was sitting trying to read what was on her computer screen. "It's either a new computer or I need new glasses. May I help you?"

"Yes, it is Natasha Bennett."

"Please go in the door behind me."

"Thank you."

I knocked on the door, the door opened, and a man I had never seen before was just leaving as I entered.

"Come on in Natasha and sit down. Have you given any more thought to where you will be living in the future; your babies, all three of them must need an army to look after them. They must be walking by now. My wife and I have six kids, all born within five years, two sets of twins. My wife said the next one would be a shotgun."

"All that I am saying now has only happened in the past few days. It appears my still husband Max does not want to go back to England to live, just to visit, and neither does his mother. As for myself, this is where I live and work, my partner is a New Yorker and that alone would make me rethink about living in the UK full time. I have a large family and I am sure we can work this out. However, I do have three children and they already know I am their Mummacow."

"Ok, we are the Big Boys as your assistant Sally calls us. We are so pleased with the progress you are making on the job. Nat, you have an exceptionally bright mind, this is where you belong. I must say, you were right about your assistant. You work well together and she understands what you are thinking, you're thought processes. We also know that you are wasted on the level you are working at now, so you are fired. Therefore, now you are an agent without portfolio. For a while there has been talk of creating a new department." He opened a desk drawer and took out a large folder with 'top secret' stamped all over it. "I just heard you are going on vacation. Ok, after you are back, please read this and take your time and let me know any ideas you have no matter how small or significant. Also, how would you set it up to work, as a self-contained program or one of many? I am not going to give it to you now as you may lose it on the way home. You cannot take it on vacation. After you get back and are ready, please contact me and I will have it delivered to you personally. Nat, this is 'for your eyes only' and it is always to be in your safe when not in your hands. It is printed out, so you cannot lose it. Do not copy or put it on your computer etc.

If I may be more personal with you, you know, off the cuff so to speak, you have a full life with family and children. I know and you know they will never be enough for you to be the person you one day hope to be. You have a mind like I have never known before. I am not saying you are perfect or never make mistakes, but that is ok because you have an insight on the job and that in itself is an asset. Nat, we can give you the work that will set your mind free to enjoy other aspects of your life."

"Thank you so much for your trust in me. This is such an honour. I will be in contact as soon as I can. I am going to the west coast at the end of this week with some of my family, no babies and it is the first time away from them. I would like to ask Sally if she would like to come. She is not due her holiday yet! The four days we were in lock down she was outstanding. She knows what I expected of her."

"Of course, take her with you, and she can still have her vacation when due. Before you go tell George Johnston if there is anything he should know. Mummacow, of course you are a Mummacow. I must phone my wife and tell her she is the Mummacow. My wife is always saying why the kids don't come to you with their problems, why is it always me, now I know, it's because she is the Mummacow. You have to leave now Nat. I cannot wait to phone my wife and tell her. Oh, I just love this Mummacow title. See you in about a month Nat. Bye."

"Thank you, Sir."

"Guess where I am going Friday?" I said to Sally when I returned to our offices.

"You are taking a couple of weeks off work."

"But do you know where I am going with Max, his two sisters and Liz the TV star? California. What are you going to do while I am away?"

Sally looked as if she was going to cry.

"You could always come with us to California; an all-expense paid first class plane ticket. Tomorrow we can go out and buy you some clothes for the California sun, my treat."

"You are not kidding me are you Nat?"

"No, I am not kidding Sally. We leave Friday I am going to the travel agent now on the fifth-floor mall now. I booked six plane tickets first class, one hotel with adjoining suites."

Betty was already there when I arrived at the dinky little restaurant she had picked a few blocks from where I work. The tables had bright white and yellow tablecloths, yellow walls with old black and white photographs. At the far end was a big black board, the menu written in white chalk. At the top was printed 'Every meal has been cooked this morning; do not ask for a meal you had last week, because it ain't going to happen'. The place was packed, the food was unbelievable, and the wine came in an unmarked bottle. "Where do they get the wine from?" I asked Betty.

"They will not tell you and they will not sell it to you either to take home, it is the only booze they serve."

"Why have I never heard of this restaurant?"

"It is one of these rare places that nobody tells you about in case you go there. The hours are 11a.m. to 2p.m. from Monday to Friday for lunch, and from six thirty to ten thirty p.m. Tuesday to Saturday for dinner, and closed Sundays and Monday evenings It is packed every night and they never advertise. Now about Margo," Betty said. "Does she know you are going to California with Max and his sisters?"

"There are going to be six of us, Liz, Crewe's girlfriend, and Sally my assistant at work, and Margo does not know anything about California and I am not going to tell her."

"And why not, Nat?"

"Why should I Betty, she will make a fuss. I need to go away to see what's out there. Is all this worth it? How much does she love me, is it enough? A year and never once have I met her family or friends. I must show my children what it is like to be proud of yourself and not let anyone hide you away in shame for what you are. Also, I have not told her our plans have changed. You are right Betty, I should have spoken to Margo before and not left it all up to her, I was afraid of losing her if she felt pushed by me. I am mad at myself for not seeing all this before. You know what Betty, before being with me Margo jumped from one bed to another. When we met, she found what she was looking for and I believed that then, and I believe it now. Before me, there was no one to take home to meet Mum and Dad. Margo never saw any woman long enough to take home. Margo left them before they meant anything to her. She allowed it to go on with me because I was going back to England. Margo is completely unaware she does this. She needs and wants to belong to another like her sister and brothers do. If she came with us and it did not work she would have to come back to nothing, as she thinks her family would have disowned her. I never asked or told Margo she must come and live at Hawkes Manor. When I told her of the family plans all she said was something like we could be over by then. She knew my plans and she has never told me if she had any. Please do not tell me that I am wrong and that my thinking on love matters is that of a dim wit. And one more thing Betty, I am my children's 'Mummacow', that means they will look to me first to see how I feel about myself as a person, then a woman. Let's hope I get it right about being a woman for my sons to know what kind of woman will love them, and who they can trust and be the mother they want for their children. I hope and pray that my daughter will want to be something like me, and that I am the kind of woman my daughter would want for a mother. The kind of mother I see in you.

The tears cascaded down my mother's face as I held her hand.

I have noticed when Betty is talking about herself, what would be a monumental happening in someone else's life, she would just slip it into the conversations in passing like: Betty Windsor and I have ridden

together many times, she has a good stable of horses. Now today's biggie was a real biggie, she just slipped it in with tears still in her eyes
and me holding her hand.

She started. "Well, at the beginning of the year, out of the blue, I
said to myself, don't bother having anyone stay at the house this year.
Well that was good thinking. Now you and your family and friends can
stay there. I have had a crew already go in and clean and make it ready
for six people. There will be two daily maids. In the morning they will
shop for you, they know where to buy the best food. Please tip them
well they are the best help I have found and I like them. They are good
people. There are staples, booze and cocktail foods in the kitchen. There
is one car and pop-pop motorbikes in the garages. About three miles
up the highway is a place that rents cars, good cars. My house is well-
patrolled. I will give all six of you maps of how to get there and back
from LA. I have written my friend Larry's phone number on the maps
in case you need to know something. He will pick you up, as I will give
him your flight number and cell phone numbers, yours and Max's.
Using the motor bikes to tour around the area is a lot of fun. You may
meet some well-known celebrities. Larry can tell you where to go. You
are not to ride the bikes on the highway to LA, as they are only pop-
pop bikes so the police will pick you up, and if you break down at night,
you are asking for trouble. Do not forget to go down to the beach, as it
is beautiful. As I said before, Larry can help he knows where to go to
have fun. He can give you a list of all the best gay and straight bars,
clubs to go to, and where not to go. One more thing Nat, only rent a
couple of cars. Do not travel alone as none of you knows LA or the
area. It is not New York. This I would say to any young women or men
if they were not familiar with the city."

It was Friday and the condo was like a mad house. Betty and JC
had arrived, Mrs. B was cooking, Susan and Harry were in with the babies and Max was still in bed with his bag packed. Three hours later,
we were ready to go and the limo was downstairs waiting. Harry was
looking through my handbag, making sure I had the tickets and money
and credit cards hidden safely in a pocket in my bag plus the cell phone
charged up. "Please Nat, take hundreds of photos of Betty's house via

the iPod inside and out, every room, the view from the house and send some every day, do you hear me, Nat?"

"Yes Susan." We met Sally at JFK airport and flew to sunny California.

CHAPTER 30

We arrived on time to be met by Betty's friend Larry. He was standing there with a board with 'Larry' written on it. Max walked over and introduced himself.

"Good, are you all here? I am parked right out front with the police so let's hurry."

He took one of my bags plus another from Liz and Claire. He dashed across the road and kept on running until we reached a light blue convertible that easily would seat six I hoped. "Betty said you were meeting us in a van."

"Oh, I never drive this car when I am with Betty in case she thinks I have money. It will take us about an hour on the highway to get to Betty's and after a few days you will never want to leave. I live on the property. Betty and I breed horses and have done very well, as we sell only to people that are horse lovers and very rich. Where you are staying is Betty's house, not mine. I never go into her house unless I have been asked to. In your case, Nat or Max, your privacy is guaranteed. When you are in the house it's easy to get out and to get in you must have a code number or ring the bell. Any problems with the house or if you need to know something, I may not answer right away, but I will get back to you. Other than that, I will not see you until you leave. If Betty were here, she would show you the horses and what we do here. I am sorry I do not have the time, but neither do you because you will be too busy reading the e-mail that Betty sent you on what you can do and where you can go; I have printed this out for you. I have also made a list of the fun bars, clubs and restaurants, straight and not so straight. In the kitchen are menus of restaurants that will deliver over a few hundred dollars; with the six of you, you will spend that easily. I am suggesting this for tonight. If you want a meal cooked here ask the two ladies that come daily, anyway it's all in the e-mail. Oh yes, they will buy your groceries, if you ask. That's it, no more talk."

Well, it looks like my mother Betty is a real dark horse so to speak, the traffic was heavy so it took way over an hour. We took a few turns onto different roads, driving by homes that were beyond description.

We arrived, turning into a long tree lined avenue. About half a mile down the road, the trees were replaced by fields with old western wooden fences. Behind the fence, horses were running beside the car, laughing and smiling that Larry was home with company.

The car stopped, Larry went to the trunk and got our luggage and walked towards the house. No one moved, no one said a word as we were all spellbound. Then of course, Max lets out a noise that sounded like he was happy with what he saw. "Nat, take pictures now, get your camera out. Susan is going to be as mad as a hatter, as we are here and she is not, Oh boy, Oh boy!"

I got my laptop out and e-mailed Betty. Boy, are you in trouble now I told her. I just e-mailed Susan pictures of the front of your house and the field with the horses. We have just arrived and are still sitting in the car stunned by what we see.

She replied, "Nat I can hear Susan calling my name, I am going to hide. Betty wrote,

Nat: Susan is getting madder by the moment; she has looked for me in every bedroom and still she has not found me. The way she is calling out to me has changed. At the beginning it was Betty now it's BetTY!

Now Harry is shouting, "Good God Susan, the woman has the right to own a house in California without telling you."

"I must say I bet I am having more fun listening to these two carry on than you are sitting in the car. By the way, I bet it's the blue convertible that Larry tells everyone I know nothing about, in case I think he has money, silly fool."

Of course, Max got a big kick out of Susan hunting Betty.

Larry opened the door to a medium sized foyer. Beyond that was what looked like one huge room and to the left was a sitting area with the most comfortable large colorful furniture. Surrounding the biggest brick fire place, I have ever seen.

Further down was the dining and combination kitchen area with a long wooden table and wooden chairs with big fat blue cushions. There were a couple of large wooden hutches, sideboards, a smaller table which children could sit at plus all that would make a kitchen/dining area look like a work of art. At the far back near where the cooking action took place was a set of stairs going up.

Beside the entrance we came into was another set of stairs. A circular staircase led to the second floor with a balcony where one could look down to the floor below or up to a stained-glass skylight. This is where the bedrooms were.

To the right was a library, next, a pool table then another sitting area. Big wooden carved posts were placed around inside the rooms, I presume to give support to the house. They also gave the impression of where you would find the area of your interest. There were glass windows and sliding doors with posts once again, instead of walls for support. A terrace with all kinds of furniture encircled the entire place outside.

Between the pool table and library was a larger exit to the longest swimming pool with tranquil water. There was wicker furniture at the sides with wild flowers and bushes behind, and at the end of the pool was a backdrop of small valleys, hills and fields with groves of trees. I took more photos saving them for tomorrow to send to Susan. If I sent them now it may be the death of Susan or Betty.

"I am leaving now to go back to work," said Larry. Everything you need is here in the kitchen: maps, lists and Betty's e-mail. Her e-mail, please read tonight. An old car outside will get you up the hill. Make a left out of the driveway and about three miles along is where you could rent a car or two. Have fun."

As Larry turned to leave, he turned back. "I nearly forgot to tell you, after dark, you will see a tall, big man behind the horses' fence. He guards the horses at night. We lost some horses a few years ago as they were stolen. He lives a few miles from here with his wife and eight kids. His wife makes him a night snack so he needs nothing. He leaves only when he sees my people or me. Name's Bert. Very nice man, he never comes to the house or leaves the horses. Oh yes, the front door has a two-way speaker. Bye!"

"Find the menu now so we can order food, then we can look around" Max said. "We will order everything on one menu; what we cannot eat tonight we will eat tomorrow."

"I think we should go up and choose our bedroom now in case we are too tired after we eat," I said. The bedrooms were big and lovely, an ensuite in all rooms, and two had king sized beds. Crewe and Liz took one. "I suppose you want the other Max?"

"Yes please." I looked in the other bedrooms until I found one with four twin beds. "What do you think?" as I showed the other two.

"Oh good" said Claire. "I did not want to sleep in a room on my own."

"Neither did I." said Sally.

"Me too. Look, each room has a double lock door to the next bedroom so we can use that bathroom too."

"These rooms are so big with closets that have rollaway beds in them" said Sally. "Look, we can sit outside on the balcony."

The food came and we ate and ate, what food was left we would have tomorrow. "Sure, we will, Max will be down in the night and finish the lot." We decided we should take it easy tomorrow and lay around the pool having drinks. "We can ask the two ladies if they would get in some groceries for us," so we made a list. We also planned to rent two or three cars. Planning done we went to bed exhausted.

I was the last to wake the next morning. I could hear all five of them in the swimming pool as our bedroom balcony overlooked the pool. Two of the girls were nude coming out of the water. This I had to see. Max was using the steps to get out and all four girls were sitting nearby waiting for Max.

"Throw me a towel please ladies."

No response.

"Please ladies." said Max.

Still, no response.

"Come on now, this water is very cold; I am not getting out so you can have a good laugh at me."

Still not a word from any of the girls.

Max was getting upset and I was already mad. If Max was finding this funny that is Ok, but he was not. The way I saw it, this was no longer a joke. Maybe Sally had, but the rest may not have seen Max nude as a man. Max or any man with five women would see himself as the defender of the pack, not some man to be looked at and laughed at because of his size. All he would see now is that there would be four sets of female eyes all looking in one place. Why they could not understand this was beyond me. Cold water can change the size of men's egos.

Now they are laughing.

I called out to them, "Would one of you silly little girls please throw some towels to my husband and move away from the steps so Max can get out of the pool with some dignity." I waited for Max in his room.

Max I am sorry if I made it worse by saying that to them. I was so mad, you are such a stallion and they would have not known then."

Max laughed, "I know that Nat, but tell me how you would know to compare and where would the personal knowledge of yours come from?"

I knew better than to make a funny or not so funny comment on personally having knowledge of other men.

I gave Max a kiss on the cheek and opened the door to leave.

"Where are you going, Nat!"

"To get dressed."

"No, you are not, you are going back for more blood. Please no, Nat. My time will come."

Well we both laughed about that.

I walked along the landing to our room when I heard the girls talking on the other side of the door. I knew if I went in there would more trouble so downstairs I went for some much-needed coffee.

It appears that the two daily ladies had already been here, Max had given them the list and they were home with the groceries.

"How would you like to be paid? Now, each time you shop or hand, at the end of our visit?" I asked the daily ladies.

"We will keep the receipts for the money we spend plus extra for time, car use, and gas. Then we will give you the bill when you leave, okay? Mrs. Betty says you have big money, very big money and not to worry. Thank you. We'll tidy and clean a little."

Max came in the kitchen and sat down.

The four girls were still in the bedroom when I got back.

"Maybe Nat, you were more upset than Max was. We admit that Max was getting mad with us because he is the man and we were told to give him a towel. If he was that shy, he should have worn trunks."

"Liz, in no way am I going to be as polite to you as you have just been to me. That has to be one of the silliest, stupid, made up excuses. Many women find him very attractive and at his age with his looks he is 'the man' just as you are 'the woman.' How old are you Liz? That was a high school game. This was your game you were playing and these three silly cows just went along with you. You all went skinny-dipping. He did not know the four of you were all going to study him. He asked you for a towel to cover up as he felt uncomfortable with his two sisters and a friend and you said no! Max grew up with three sisters. This was no big deal for him until you made it one. And one more thing Liz, who died and left you in charge? That's his business whether he wears trunks or not. Maybe you do not like men telling you what to do. Well I have news for you, that's men. You do not have to kick them in the balls. You have every right to want equality, but at what cost? Learn to pick your battles. Today you showed a boy you are 'the woman'. I am sure there are a lot of men who make uninvited moves on you that you just hate. Most men are not like that… you say no, they say ok. Liz, the world you work in sells sex. Here we are family. We came here as a family. What happened I think, and understand now, is a nude Max upset you. You must have felt you can never get away from this."

I stopped and Liz walked out the door.

"You had better go to her Crewe."

"I will, thanks Nat."

I sat down on my bed. "Well, that's that" I said.

"I had no idea at the beginning what was going on with the towel, then you called out and I thought why we are doing this too our Max. It's no excuse but the best I can think of. It got ugly and I could not think why?" Tears filled Claire's eyes and I just sat there saying nothing while Max looked so unhappy, shame on me.

Sally went to speak. "It's ok Sally, we are okay." I was not going to have Sally think this was her fault too. She has a good soul. Next time she will know what team to play for or when not to play at all.

There was a knock on the door and Sally got up to open it. "It's Max."

"Well, let him in, Sally," I said.

"She's leaving," said Max.

"Who's leaving"? Claire asked.

Max gave Claire such a look, "Who do you think Claire?"

"What about Crewe" I asked. "Is she leaving too?"

"No, just Liz," Max said.

Liz said, "It's them or me."

"Surely not, how upset is Crewe?"

"She's not at the moment. I am going back now to see what's going on. I'll talk to you after she has gone," said Max.

"I know what he is going to say," I said. He'll say, "It's Ok Liz, I was not upset, let's be friends, and it is all forgotten."

Max opened the door and came back in. "STOP! I am not going to say anything of the kind, not after she said to Crewe, 'it's them or me'."

"How is Liz getting to the airport? Looks like she will have to call a taxi. I am going to check this out. I made my way down to the first bedroom and knocked on the door. No one answered and I did not hear anyone talking or moving around when I put my ear to the door. I went to the kitchen where Max and Crewe were sitting at the table, looking in a dream, drinking coffee.

"What's happening?" I asked. "Where is Liz, did she talk to you?"

"She phoned Larry for a ride," said Max, trying to control his anger.

"She what?"

"Liz phoned Larry and left a message asking him to take her to the airport. He then phones me to ask what's going on. I asked him not to return her call and that I would take care of it, and apologized," said Max.

"Crewe is she always like this?"

"No, never. I have never seen her like this before, and to ask me to choose between family and her, was nuts. I said 'no' thinking she would not go without me. I thought it was just fun at the beginning then I saw Max was getting mad. Wait a minute, I thought of something. Just before you called out, I said to Liz 'this is silly' and I went to get up and throw Max a towel. Liz pulled my arm saying ' no, do not go to him.' That's when you called out to us. I looked around to Liz and it's only now I realized she was trying to wipe away tears from her face. Oh, God she was crying over what! I must go to her!"

Good for Max, now he has tears in his eyes. "No Crewe let me go, you are too close and she still may not be ready for you to know and become very defensive."

"Please, I will go. Max stay with Crewe."

I made my way back to Liz's bedroom and knocked on the door. I was surprised she opened the door.

"What do you want?" Liz said.

"May I come in?"

"Well, you are in aren't you! Well say what you have to say, then please go," Liz said.

"I am sorry Larry is too busy to take you to the airport; you will have to call a taxi if you still want to go. However, we are your family now Liz. You and Crewe will be Godmothers to one of our children. We came together as a family and when we go, we leave together as a family; your mother's heart would break if you left us now. When Margo first met Susan, she thought Susan was as mad as a Hatter and still does. The family follows close behind when we are together. Margo has felt the love we have as a family and so have you. Am I right Liz?… Am I right Liz!"

"YES!"

"What I think happened today… I maybe wrong I think not, and you are not alone as it has happened to both woman and men. You had a memory or flashback from the past that didn't make sense at that moment. This morning for some reason, the image of Max looming out of the water nude took you back to days when you felt you had no control. I too have been to that dark hole were only shadows live and been too frightened to let in another in case they will stop loving you or find out they never did. That's only the dark hole talking back to you trying to stop you from going before it caves in. Stay with us, feel and know what the power of love is. Liz, find someone, a specialist, that knows this subject so well, that can help you open that door. I will always be here for you. We are downstairs having coffee please. Join us then we can go and see what cars there are to rent."

I did not look at Liz just in case she gave me the evil eye. I was not sure I had reached her. I left her sitting on the bed.

I had one foot on the step going down to the kitchen when I felt her behind me. My first thought was to roll when she pushed me down the stairs. Instead, her hand slipped into mine I turned to her, kissed her on the cheek, and whispered, "You do know who is the boss." She laughed and said, "Do I ever!"

CHAPTER 31

Tonight, we decided on The Not So Straight club. We spent the day in the sun, so we would not look too much like tourists. One of the cars we rented was a ninety-eight, big enough for six of us. There were lots of people sitting or standing around drinking and only a few dancing but it was early yet. We found a table and ordered drinks. After a while I said, "Not much doing here." then in walked a group of women who sat near us. Good old Sally gets up, walks by the women to the bar, then walks back by them again and stops to talk.

"We are on vacation and new here, is this place to be for fun?" she asked.

One woman called out to Sally, "Why don't you come over here and find out?"

Sally ran back and sat down. Another woman called out, "Is she straight?" meaning Sally.

"Yes," I said.

"And you?" another asked.

"I am here to have fun."

An hour later, we had joined our tables. "The best times to come here are Thursday, Friday and Saturday nights," the little redhead said. "We are here to meet a couple of friends but it appears they may have got lost."

Lost maybe, but when you saw them they were hard to miss as in walked, no, in strode three tall, not bad looking women that looked like a lot of fun.

"Max what is it, what are you mumbling about? "

"It is a sin, a sin I tell you," Max declared.

"What's a sin?" asked Claire.

"Look, the one in the middle! Girls, please down on your knees with me and let us pray she is not gay!"

Well the closer she got we could see she really was a looker, beautiful milk chocolate-colored skin, hair a little darker, very short with curls, long legs and hands, slim. When she came even closer suddenly you noticed her eyes, her eyes were blue green. What a combination of colors.

"Don't look at us," the girls from the other table said. "It's the other two that are our friends," the redhead said. "We have never seen the dark girl before now."

The tall girls rushed over .One of the three tall girls were full of apologies and introduced their friend, Georgia. "She lives near us, we told her next time we came here we would take her. Well, we had to wait for her to get ready as when we went to her house to pick her it seems we had forgotten to tell her we were coming here and she should be ready for us." Well that was good for a laugh.

Max was at his best; he was in top form. He was not too pushy, giving her time to find her own comfort zone knowing she had just met all these people and knew only two of them. He did not talk all the time, but then very casually said, "That is nice music, do you care to dance?" He had her right then. We never saw his mouth move all the time they were dancing, she just chatted away.

"My God," said Crewe. "He is going to ask her to marry him any minute now." They came back sat for a few minutes, then danced again. After a while they did not come back to our tables but sat over on the other side at a little table for two with a lamp.

The evening was drawing to a close; we all had a lot of fun and hoped to see our new buddies Saturday night.

Georgia was telling Max she has two children, a girl five and a boy three-year-old. They all live with her parents, brother and sister. She said her husband, who was in the army, was killed overseas two years ago, leaving a big hole in all her family's hearts. "David was white like you, fair and tall but nowhere as good looking as you. You are the first man other than my family or very close old friends that I have danced with in nearly three years. David loved his children, he loved me, and I knew it every day." Tears came to Max's eyes and knew then this woman was a keepie. Max wrote his cell phone number on a napkin gave it to her then asked her for her number. "When can I see you again?"

"As I told you, I am a professional photographer and tomorrow I have a few assignments, which will take all day, then I need to be with my children, but Wednesday nothing. Why don't I take you and your sisters and friends to some lovely places that are not on the map?"

"That sounds great. I will have to check with the ladies first. In case you do not know, I am not the boss."

"Who is?" Georgia whispered.

"Oh, that's for you to find out, and when you know, you will not question yourself for one moment," Max whispered back. "What is the best time to call you tomorrow?"

"Anytime Max. I may be too busy to answer. If that's the case just leave a message, I will phone you back."

"Will your friends take you home?"

"They better. Ah, here they come now."

"Are you ready Georgia?"

"Yes, thank you for a nice evening Max."

She held out her hand, Max took it with both his and smiled right into her eyes if one can do this kind of thing.

All three walked away, Georgia's friends on either side of her saying "OOOOoooo!"

All six of us piled into the car and all said at once "Well, do you like her, are you going to see her again?"

"Yes, and yes, on Wednesday, and she asked would we like her to show us some beautiful places that are not on the map. I told her I was not the boss and have to ask, so what do you think? Yes? Good. I will phone her tomorrow. We can use the other car as it will seat more."

Next morning, I noticed one of the daily ladies had around her neck, a silver chain that I admired very much. On their way to visit an Auntie yesterday, they came across a group of local artists selling handmade silver 'what-have-yous' on the side of the road. This is where one of the daily ladies got her silver chain. With directions in hand, Sally and I set off together the rest, finding it rather boring hunting down local artists when you can buy silver anywhere.

Sally knew nearly all about my private life, there no point in not telling her, she was the nosiest cow I have ever met. At work, I didn't go to the personnel Department/human resources when I wanted to know anything about hiring staff who wanted to come to us from another department. What do they know, when I have Sally? She told me gossip before the person that was the cause of the gossip knew.

Anyway, I asked her what she thought about Liz and what happened at the pool.

"Well Nat, you and others have told me the father died when she was 10 years, that's why Liz says she does not remember too much about him or exactly when he died. I think he died much later and she remembers more than she says but to what extent I don't know. As for those six loving Aunties of hers, does she ever talk about them? I bet she got out of that family environment as soon as possible. It must have been a nightmare and it came back to her when she saw Max coming out of that pool knowing he was nude. At first not giving him a towel was a joke then she had a flashback or something, I don't know, suddenly realizing, now after all these years, she had some control by not giving into a man's demands, in this case Max wanting a towel."

"Very good Sally, now Sally...."

"Stop, Nat I known the differences between this horror story and gossip, that is, if we have it right."

"I am sorry Sally of course you do. You know it's really none of my business."

Sally laughed then. "Everything to do with your family and people you love, you go out of your way to make it your business."

"OK, Sally, Liz will be going back to London after our holiday here. I wonder if she would let me find the best doctor that specializes in this field. You know if it was not for Betty, I would still be lost."

"Nat, in times to come, when I am writing poison pen letters to you every day for some reason, your family will always have my loyalty."

We traveled on a two-lane road surrounded by fields and long emerald greens lawns scattered with houses. In the distance, I could see a few cars pulled over and people standing looking at stalls. "We are nearly there Sal, right up ahead." All of a sudden, we heard a bang behind us. I look in the rear-view mirror, the white convertible driven by a woman that had followed us the last few miles had landed in the ditch. I stopped, turned around, drove back and pulled up behind her. "Are you ok?" Sally asked. "Yes, I think so," said the woman getting out of her car. Her rear left wheel tire looked like it had blown out. "You were lucky we both slowed down."

The three of us stood there looking at the rear wheel for few minutes and then decided there was nothing we could do. "Where do you live?" I asked the woman without a working car. "Not far, about a mile back, then a few turns. I was going to see what the local artists were selling up the road."

"So were we. Why don't we three go and look, then we can drop you off at your house on the way back. I am Natasha, this is Sally."

"My name is Nancy."

Nancy sounded and looked like she was from the Boston area, a college graduate. She carried herself well, as though she had done her time at a good school, maybe Wellesley. She had short, thick, straight hair and when she walked her hair bobbed up and down. I knew her story even though I did not know her. She always wore Birkenstock shoes. After graduation she would have headed for the hills, where she would raise her children, in wealthy little towns dotted through the Northeastern area. As time passed, she daydreamed of college days and the girls she had crushes on, waiting until her perfect man came along. I wonder if she thought she was one of the lucky ones that got away. By now, she was sure some of her older friends back home were marking their knickers with big black crosses to know which was front or back. I would guess thirty to thirty-five years old.

Both Sally and I thought the others were fools not to come here. The ' what-have-yous' were made from good silver, beautifully designed, and none were the price you would pay in the city. Susan would love these. The local artists were looking tired and like they were thinking of leaving. "How much for the lot?" I asked a woman, who appeared to be the leader of the gang, "How much for the lot?"

"Three" she said. I stood there just smiling at her.

"Twenty-six, that's it!" Then we both started laughing.

"My name is Joan, and yours?"

"Natasha."

"Nice doing business with you, Natasha. I will pack them and bring them over to you."

"Maybe I should help you Joan," and she laughed at that.

"No flies on you, are there?"

"I hope not," I said.

"Hope to see you again."

"Me too."

It didn't take us long to get to Nancy's home and what a beauty it was. There were two cars parked outside, and a man and two children came running out of the front door.

"Are you ok, where is the car?"

"It's in a ditch about a mile up the road. The rear tire blew out. These ladies were driving in front and came to my rescue, then we went and looked at silver at some stalls…" She looked at me asking "What is it you call them, 'what-have-you'? Remember that Dennis when you forget the name of something—call it a 'what-have-you.'"

"Sure will, Nancy. I am Dennis. Come on in ladies, the least we can do is make you a drink."

Four drinks later and a bit to eat, Dennis phoned the house. Max answered the phone straight away. "Hi, Max?"

"Yes."

"This is Dennis French. We live a few miles from Betty's house, Nat and Sally are here, and nobody is sober enough to drive them home."

"Oh" says Max. "May I speak with Nat, please?"

"Hi Max! We have all had too much to drink to drive. Who is going to tell Max how to get here?"

"I will," said Nancy. "Hi Max, my name is Nancy. Nat and Sally came to my aid this afternoon when my back tire blew out. I will tell you how to get here ok?"

Max, Liz, Crewe and Claire pulled into the driveway. We were all around the swimming pool, sitting and laying on the most comfortable furniture. Dennis jumped up and called out, "We are over here." waving to them over the gate to the pool. Max and company were escorted by three dogs; two very large and a small one, barking their greeting.

"Say hello to them and they will stop." and they did. The usual greetings and introductions took place. "Please sit down, and what would you like to drink?"

Max answered, "Not for me. Ladies? Sally called out "have what we are drinking. It will knock your socks off!"

After the second drink for the ladies, Max said "I think we had better go, we have a busy day tomorrow."

"I am so glad my tire blew out, we have had so much fun. If it's alright with you lot I would like to e-mail Betty and tell her we have met."

Max and the ladies all looked to me.

"That's fine with me as I am the only one that calls or e-mails home, because of the children. Betty will get a kick of how we met."

"Excuse me," Max said.

"Oh! I am so sorry, of course Max phones his mother Susan daily to see if the Hawkes kids have been put up for adoption yet by her, Mrs. B. or Betty."

"We are having friends in Friday evening for drinks, cookout and a swim; we would very much like you all to come," said Dennis.

Max agreed for all of us, "Thank you, we will love to come."

"What a lovely day we had, Sally."

"Yes, we did, Nat."

"Ok, Ok, looks like we should have gone with you. What a nice couple, I am glad they invited us to their party," Max said.

When we arrived back at the ranch, the big man whose name I have forgotten was walking a horse. He stopped, looked over to the wooden fence and stared at the car, wanting to do battle. I jumped out of the car and waved at him. "It is only us, friends of Betty." Max walked around from the other side of the car and waved too. "Hi, remember me we met yesterday. Max."

"Ok, I remember now, good night," he said.

"Oh boy." said Max. Nobody is ever going to steal those horses again."

Within ten minutes, we all were going up to bed.

"Remember, Georgia will be here by ten in the morning, and please be ready, thank you."

"Good night Max."

The following morning, I woke at eight a.m.,'bright eyed and bushy tailed', I went down stairs sat at the table with coffee and opened my e-mail. Already there was mail from Betty:

'My dear Natasha: Funny you running into Nancy. They are good people, I hope you all enjoy the party Friday night. Both Dennis and Nancy are charmers. It appears from Nancy's e-mail that she is quite taken with you Nat. If you feel Nancy is being too charming, watch your step, because before you know it, you will be in her bed. Good luck. Love, Betty.'

Sally had joined me by now for coffee and when I showed her the e-mail, it amused her no end.

"Nat, there is no getting away from it, just think if I didn't know you, I would be going through life not knowing any women who secretly wear lace up shoes."

At ten a.m. five women were standing at the front door with our hands held out for Max to inspect our hands and nails, and fifteen minutes later we all piled into the van, setting off for parts unknown, with Max as Captain and Georgia as first mate sitting in the front.

We arrived back at Betty's house about nine p.m., exhausted from a day to remember.

Our first stop, we were about an hour on the highway before Georgia asked Max to slow down as we were going to make a left turn at the sign ahead that had an arrow and nothing else. We ended up on a dirt road with a house some distance away. Georgia asked Max to stop so she could drive, as it was tricky.

"Are you sure this ok, it looks like private land to me," said Max, looking a little nervous. "I know the owners and it's ok. Stop here Max, and please sit in the back. Nat, would you please come up here in the front," Georgia said.

"Why?" Max asked.

She looked at Max with the biggest smile and said, "Because I asked you to." He, in return, gave a bigger smile and said, "Of course you did," and got out of the car and into the back.

I hopped in the front. Oh, what a clever woman, I thought. She gave him the reins at first, letting him drive on the trip she had planned. Now she wanted the reins back and she let him know that was what she expected from him. She expected the same respect that she gave to him. There will be no "little woman" act with these two.

Georgia put the car into reverse, went back a bit, put it into drive and gunned the vehicle as fast as it could go, moving slightly to the right all the time, then a sharp left. We flew through the air over the ditch and landed sideways on the other side, safe and sound. Georgia turned the van and drove slowly to where all that we could see was the sky meeting the ocean. "Come on," she said, as she stopped the van and ran. The green grass gave way to rocks… we were on top of a cliff. "This is the only spot of land that you can fully see, the entire cove including the caves that are at the end of the north side. It is a cove, an inlet, a sanctuary. It's too dangerous to climb down."

The view was breath taking, and I so wanted to go down there. I could see the waves giving way to other life forms swimming towards the cove until the inlet was alive with the 'what-have-you' that lived in the sea. I felt that we were sitting on the edge of nowhere looking at life as it should be.

"My plans for today," Georgia said, "didn't include coming here. It's only when I got in the car this morning and was overwhelmed by the love that you all share that I felt inspired. Are there more of you?"

"Yes," said Max. "This world was made from chaos, our history marked by battles and wars. Most of humanity has been enslaved by a few, why should anyone expect a fair deal in life when most look the other way. We have the power of love but it is not enough. We believe it does not have to be this way. We do not have the answer, just hope that the power to love will grow and grow and we become one, to take our place in this universe as proud humans we now have become."

"'All it takes for evil to flourish is for good men to do nothing,' Edmund Burke,"

Georgia spoke with tears in her eyes. "A few weeks ago, friends and I went to a fair. "As we were walking around, a fortune-teller dressed up like a gypsy called out to us to come in. She wanted to tell my future, and I had nothing to lose.

She took my hand, looked and then closed it. "You don't need me, soon you will meet strangers that will be family and your life will never be the same. God bless you my dear." Georgia looked down at her watch, "Come on, let's get out of here. Sorry to rush you but we have a lot to see."

Georgia drove along the green grass until she found the opening to the drive up to the house where her friend was waiting on the stone steps.

"This is my friend Sandy he owes me so many favors. He is going to take half of you up now for about half an hour to show you some of southern California from the air then come back and take the other half." Georgia's friend had picked Claire, Crewe, and Max for weight. "Georgia, Liz, Sally and I were the second group. "There is a powder room just inside, if you need it, and I suggest you do before flying." Sandy said. In forty minutes, the helicopter was back, ready for the next lot. "It was fantastic!" all three said. "You will love it! We were up in the air in five minutes. Liz was sitting far too close to me for comfort, my hand found hers and held them, close to my breasts, both knowing we were flying into a danger zone. With each beat of my heart, I was becoming less and less interested in the view of the earth below. All of a sudden, Georgia's voice broke in to our dreams, "What you do think girls?"

"I think we both feel the same way, right Nat? We love it."

We landed and exchanged views with each other and thanked our host/pilot.

"Max, I hope Georgia does not think she has to pay for all this,"

"So, do I Nat, I will speak to her later and settle up."

"Thank you, Max. This holiday I pay for, you understand me, Max? I don't care what you tell her."

"Our last act will be to eat. You can get other dishes, but this place serves the best seafood I have ever had. Is this ok with you?" Georgia asked, smiling. "The restaurant has a lovely view of the sea; you can hear the ocean washing up on the rocks. It's usually packed at night, so if we go now we will be early enough to get two small or one large table." Georgia was so right; the food was out of this world. Afterwards we walked along the beach. Sally found some seashells she liked and stuck them in her bag. Which smelled all way the home? We all thanked Georgia for a truly wonderful day. Us gals made ourselves a drink and sat outside around the pool while Max walked Georgia to her car. She wanted to go home as she had an early appointment the next day. Max asked her if she would be interested in going to the party Friday.

"Well, just look at you. Here a few days and already getting party invites." Georgia replied.

Max told her how we met our Friday night hostess when Sally and I were buying silver from some local artists on the road.

He told her I bought the lot. The design and silver are top quality and a lot cheaper than in the city. Nancy, that's our to-be hostess' name, blew a tire on the same road that Nat and Sally were on. All three went to see the silver then they took her home, met the husband and kids sat around the pool drinking, got too drunk to drive. I, Liz, Crewe and Claire had to go and pick them up. After a few more drinks, I was the only one that arrived home sober. Also, it turned out they were friends of Betty, the lady that owns this house." "Oh," whispered Georgia, "and who may I ask is Betty, and what relationship is she to you and the ladies?"

"Well," Max whispered back, "that's Natasha's long-lost mother, but that's another story for another time," smiling at her with his big white teeth, the teeth his parents had worked in the fields for, so they could pay that crook of a dentist "Ok". She whispered again, "When are you going to kiss me Max!"

"I thought you would never ask." Max said kissing her.

All of a sudden, Sally calls out, "They are kissing, look they are kissing!"

What did I tell you? If there is a story or gossip to be had, Sally is on the spot. Oh, this is too much; they are now going for a walk out of sight. By now, all are looking out at Max and Georgia walking off.

"Nancy is that you?"

"Yes, it is."

"Hi, it's Max here. Would it be okay if I bring a date with me Friday?"

"Need you ask? Wait until I tell Dennis this, just off the plane, and you are coming with a date. Dennis has told all the women looking for fun that the most handsome man he has ever seen is coming Friday without a date. We may have to cancel. Oh no, please, I am only joking Max, and they will still come, just to see your date!"

Friday evening arrived and Max had gone ADD. "Nat, all these women are going to be looking at me."

"Women look at you all the time. Why you are so concerned now?"

"Well, I am with Georgia."

"What does that have to do with it?"

"Well, she may not like it, because she is with me."

"Max, look at me and please do not let your mind wander. Georgia is looking for a man, not one to lean on, but one with whom she can have a family. She will never live with you and you would never ask her. You would have to give her your name. She would like to live above her class, but would never marry just for money, and your background will be very important to her if she is going to have your children. I think when Georgia got in the car Wednesday morning, she knew what she had been looking for… you, Max, with a family that has the power of love. Max, when you and Georgia walk into the party Friday, she will hoist you up, sit you on her shoulders and say, "Look girls, I have found me, The Man." "Georgia is a proud woman, nothing will make her prouder than to be with you, my darling Max. Don't rush her."

Max went to pick up Georgia at her home and the rest of us drove to the party in the other rented car.

When Max and Georgia walked through the patio doors Friday, hand in hand, into the crowded room, the room went silent. Georgia looked stunning, absolutely stunning. She wore a good three-inch high heels which made her about six feet tall, a very simple sleeveless dress, green-blue with beads of many colors necklace which matched her eyes, making them stand out even more. Her makeup was perfect, including big red ruby lips.

Dennis came over to her and held out his hand to her, the room sat silent waiting for Dennis to say words that would court her beauty. "I cannot find the words to express what my eyes see and my heart knows, welcome to our home."

The party was a success and a wonderful time was had by all. Georgia looked so happy with Max. I hoped that this woman was Max's Keepie.

I could not sleep that night as I kept thinking of my babies, and maybe I should go back Monday, as the holiday rush was beginning to wear off now. I have had great time but Mummacow needs to go home to her babies and I need to know were Margo and I are at. Susan has never mentioned that Margo phoned nor has she phoned me directly. There have been no e-mails from her so I have presumed it's over. Our love, my love, was not enough for her. Maybe at the time, she and I loved with such raw passion, then life got in the way and our love was just not worth the trouble for Margo.

I took my IPod downstairs to the kitchen to have some hot milk, which always helps me sleep.

Sitting at the table was Liz.

"Hi, what's up I asked?"

"I was thinking about us on the plane the other day. Nat, if we could have… would you…?"

"Yes."

"If I may ask, would it have bothered you, because of your relationship with Margo?"

"Margo and I are no longer together."

"What? Why?"

"This happened a few weeks ago. I thought you may have heard this by now, but now I think who could have told you and Crewe." Nobody wanted any more trouble. So, I told Liz the whole story including that I had not heard from Margo since and neither had Susan.

"No, that's not true. She did call just before you came over from England, and she was going to stay another week at her sister's. I told her I would be busy that week. I didn't tell Margo we were going to California. "

"Are you sure this is not just in your head? I remember Crewe a few times saying to me Margo looks at Nat like she is best thing since sliced bread."

I sat there in silence trying to make sense of what she said. "Just listen to yourself Liz, who else but the Hawkes family would describe love like sliced bread. We are all nuts. No, I am not sure if it is all in my head and neither are you," repeating what Crewe sees as Margo's love for me as 'sliced bread.' "I question what's in your head. After processing what I have said, your idea of a valued comment is to refer to 'sliced bread'. It's nearly as nutty as the comment made earlier this week. They were not the same words, but the impression was the same 'It's all in my head'. I have not heard or know of you personalizing disagreements with others, as you do with me."

"That's not…."

"I have not finished talking. Up in that plane I was thinking Margo should be with me, she would love this, and I felt my heart was breaking. I needed her with me. When we sat together on the plane I felt the warmth of you so close, like you were inviting me in to your world. Then all I could do was think as I felt your heart racing along with mine. Yes, I would have enjoyed our time. How you felt afterward that's your problem, not mine. I am mine to give, with no promise of tomorrow. That's how I saw you and it had nothing to do with Margo or Crewe, just another to love. The time we shared was not theirs. We didn't pick each other up in bar for sex, we met in friendship and for that one moment wanted more. Margo and I could have made ago of it together but she chose not to try. I never met her friends or family. I really thought our love would never end, what a fool was I. Good night. I am leaving here Monday as I have to see my babies."

I walked out of the house into the darkness, found a rock to sit on, and pondered my fate. What a rotten end to such a nice time. There would be just my babies and me. Max has found his love, oh he will hang around awhile, then he will come out here to California and live. I will end up sending the Hawkes kids to him every summer.

Margo didn't love me enough. I thought she did. I should have seen this a long time ago, how could I have been so dumb? I looked at my e-mail. Oh, one from Liz. 'Hi, still in the kitchen waiting for you, please let's talk.'

'Okay', I wrote back. 'I will come in the front and use the code to get in. We can sit on those comfy chairs.'

Liz was sitting on a sofa and patted it for me to sit there next to her so no one could hear us talk. Liz said, "Crewe likes Margo. When we are all together they were always having chitchats and I like that, all the girls becoming friends with one another and not just as a family group. Sometimes Crewe told me what Margo said about you; that she has never been so happy, she has never loved anyone like this and she has no idea what's going to happen when you go back to England, and she cannot live without you. Margo is the single girl and they all, that is her sister and two brothers, look care to her to take of the parents. Margo thinks she will die of guilt if she left them."

"Let's for the little time we have, leave her in New York." Her lips found my mine; my hands found her breasts, as we slid down the sofa.

Next morning, we were both in the kitchen drinking coffee when the others joined us. Max, Claire, and Crewe, all three pulled out their IPods at the same time and looked and checked e-mail. "It's from Mum. Jennie has had her baby, a girl. Mum has already left New York to go back and see the baby and Jennie, so we should leave today" said Crewe to Claire.

"I will take care of that," I said. "How many are hoping to leave today, Claire? Crewe? When do you have to be back in England to work?" I asked Liz.

"Monday, next week."

"Are you going with Crewe or returning with Sally and me, and stay longer with your mother? I said.

"If I go back to London I will be on my own, which is ok, but why, when I can spend time with my mother," said Liz.

"Why are you not coming with us to see the baby"? Crewe asked.

"You have your mother, two sisters, brother-law and his mother. You don't need me, when I can stay and visit with my mother, which is rare due to my work. Crewe, I am not with you to meet the needs of your family and you constantly. At one time, I had a free life now all I do is answer to you. You know what's going to happen once the two mothers get together? There will be trouble, nothing but trouble, all standing around in the hospital ward wondering what to say. Ok, so I am not coming. I have heard about Mick's mum and she will run the show, telling us when to wear masks not to blow your nose near the baby, when we can visit and for how long. She will have us wearing hospital smocks and silly soft slippers, which we will have to buy ourselves."

Why did I have to say anything? Poor Max looks like he is going to run any minute.

Then and there, I decided the adult triplets would drive me up the wall if I had to live with them. When I first came to live at Hawkes Manor the girls were away at school, the holidays were so busy for us kids, I didn't feel like we were living on top of each other. But this week for some reason, they plain annoyed me. No wonder Susan needed help with them.

Then Claire jumped in the ring. You know, Crewe, you go on your own. I am not going there to listen to the two mums fight about which side of the family does the baby look like, or what if baby's first or second name are names from the wrong side. What if the baby's second name is Susan or Mick's mum's name? God help us all."

I could see Crewe's mind just ticking away. What next, she thinks!

"Well Max, it looks like just you and I are going to represent the family" Crewe said.

I never knew Max was in the picture. No one had mentioned his name. No one for one moment thought Max would go, least of all Max. Oh she's a crafty one, our Crewe is, if he does not go he will be the next to be set up us a heavy. Crewe will not say anything to me, I am going home to see my babies.

Max laughed. "Crewe, I am not going with you. After today's rejections you will be looking for trouble. I've got myself a woman and I ain't going to any warzone, cause after you lot have gone they will have closed the ward down."

"That settles that" I said. "I will book two seats to New York. The daily ladies will not be in today, so I will see them tomorrow. I want to make sure this place is left the way we found it, plus I need to pay them."

"Just a second" Crewe said. "I think I will come back with Liz to New York and leave when she does."

"What about going to see the baby, Crewe?"

"Well, maybe Liz and I will go up some other time or leave the next day after she sees her mother."

Sally had joined us a while ago, never saying a word in case she broke the concentrated effort of the group and would stop the war that she saw was going to erupt any moment.

I looked at Max. He was not going anywhere either. He hated it when his mother was on the warpath or someone was out to get her, but this was different with the sisters. It was about time someone brought them down to the place were other mortals lived. One of their 'sins' as he called it was their refusal to learn how to cook for their partners. Their attitude was if they wanted to eat let them cook for themselves. Now he had heard this story years and years ago, so the cooking story may have changed but he still hung onto it. As much as he loved them, and he truly did, he never forgot how they treated his mother when they were young. Sometimes when he is mad at them, for some silly reason that only he knows, he reminds them when he was a little boy how he had to console his mother when their father was away fighting for freedom. Their mother believed she would never see Harry again and cried every night. Their mother and little brother looked at Harry's photo, but the triplets never helped, not once. All they cared about was themselves. Of course, Max made the whole story up. They never sat there looking at Harry's photo crying, if anything Susan would stick pins in his picture. When they were little girls they only had one mind, they did everything together, and they answered each other's emotional needs. Susan told me, "As they grew older and made different friends and met new people, their needs changed. They no longer looked to each other, but one by one, they wanted to know what I or Mrs. B. thought and would we help them and why do we love them. Not do you love me but why? It was as if they came with one soul and soul said one day this is just too much and turned into three. In addition," Susan said, "That is when they became my three daughters."

Ok, back to real life. Liz stood up, looking at what Sally thought at the time was Liz's ex-girlfriend, and said very slowly "What did you not understand Crewe, about me going to see my mother and spending time with her until I have to be back at work? I need to be on my own with my mother to get to know her and for her to know me. For all I care, you can stay here until Christmas."

"What do you want to do Claire?"

"Crewe and I will fly to London and we can decide from there what we do."

Well, if looks could kill. "Why are you looking at me like that Crewe, this is not my doing, this is your lack of understanding about Liz needing to spend time with her mother. For the first time in her life Liz can say I have a mother that loves me. If you can't understand what is happening here…" I stopped then… enough said.

Claire said "Maybe we can leave today Nat."

"I will try."

Claire and Crewe left that day.

"Max, go back to New York when you want to. I will settle with the daily ladies and have them clean the house so it looks just the way we found it. If you use the ladies please tip them well and pay them up to your departure."

"You know Nat, it was that haircut that did Crewe in."

"Shut up Max."

I phoned home. Mrs. B. Answered. "Oh, it's so nice to hear your voice Nat! The babies are just fine, they look fatter each day. I have asked JC not to feed them anymore, but as soon as they see her, they scream their heads off. I am off to the market to buy good carrots and she can give them to the Hawkes kids. Other than that, JC, she is fantastic. She can do in one day what takes us old birds a week to do. When you get back and settled, the three of us, Betty, Susan and I, are going away on a little honeymoon together. I never knew three old girls could get on so well running a home. You know it's Betty. She has a peacefulness about her and I love it when she tells Susan to shut up, I've heard enough. You know Susan has gone to see Jennie, the baby, and the mother-in-law."

"I know," I said. "We will leave here Tuesday, that's Liz and me. All I know is Crewe and Claire left today for London, under very unpleasant circumstances. Max is staying on. Mrs. B., Max has met someone. She has two young children; her husband was killed about two-three years ago overseas in the army. Max is the first man she has gone out since. She lives with her parents, brother and sister, and we all like her."

"Here comes Betty, shall I tell her to pick up the other phone and she can listen, saves me repeating it all?"

"Please do Mrs. B."

"Betty, Betty. It's Nat on the phone. Pick up."

"Hi, Nat. How are you, have you had a good time?"

"Yes and no, I was just going to tell Mrs. B. about yesterday. I decided I was coming home as I miss my babies too much and I need to see Margo."

"So, you have not heard from her then"? Betty said.

"No, nothing, and what with all the 'hoo-haw' here yesterday with who was going to see the baby and the mother-in-law and who wasn't… well, looks like nobody is going. Crewe wanted Liz to go with her and Claire. And Liz, she was not going to listen to the mother-in-law quibbling and she wanted to spend time with her mother, as she does not have to return to London for work until Monday. Then Claire was not up to listening to the mother-in-law either. Max would not go with her, and he said Crewe is looking for trouble, and that after they visit Jennie's baby and the mother-in-law the hospital will have closed down the ward because it turned into a warzone. Anyway, he is staying on if that is ok with you Betty. As I said, Max has got himself a woman and he ain't going anywhere. This one is a keepie. Crewe was not going to go. She was returning with Liz, but Liz is staying in New York so she can see her mother. Then they can fly home the next day, and both see the baby."

Liz said "Crewe, I am not with you to constantly meet the needs of your family and you. I once had a life of freedom, now all I do now it answer to you. You are not coming back with me to see my mother. Why can you not understand she and I need to know one another more? Then Crewe gave me the evil eye. It's all my fault now. I need to know now who's flying where so I can book the seats on the planes. The daily ladies are not here today so tomorrow I will settle up with them. I want to be the last to leave here, knowing the house is as tidy and clean as we found it. Max needs the ladies to know that he pays and tips well. I know Crewe thinks because I asked Liz if she was going to see the baby or her mother, I must have put the idea in Liz's head. Well, it ended with me more or less telling Crewe where to go. Claire and Crewe left today, poor Claire. I am telling just the basic story now. I know it sounds bad but it was at the end. We had a great time, which I will tell you about when we get home. Betty, will you need to go home when I get back?"

"Oh no, but I am going to have to tell my children about you soon and I so want to. They kept asking why I am here looking after babies and do I need the money? They asked why JC is not leaving here until the babies are in high school and I am not sure what she thinks. Whatever she knows, no way is she going to rock the boat when it comes to the Hawkes kids. My elder daughter is phoning me twice a day, which is unheard of, to see if I still sound the same as yesterday and have not gone bonkers overnight. My other two are still at their father's and both phone every day, demanding that they both come home.

"I am happy Nat. With you, this family, Susan and Mrs. B., I have found more people to love. I just may tell JC tonight and see what happens."

"Mrs. B., Liz needs you now more than ever. "I know it's none of my business but it's never stopped any of us before. While she's here give her all your attention, make her talk. You do not have to have the answers."

"Come here Liz, I am talking to your mum; Hi Mrs. B., Liz is here" I said.

"Hi, Mum I will see you Tuesday ok?"

"Hi sweetheart, it is nice hear your voice, I am so pleased you are coming here" Mrs. B. said.

At that point, I left Liz talking with her mum. I found my way to the kitchen where Max and Sally were talking.

"Hi Nat, would it be ok if I invited Georgia and her family over now for a swim and then order some food?"

"What a lovely idea Max, it will take our minds off the drama of the day. What do you think Sally?"

"Well you do know, Nat, there are thirty-five of them."

"Don't be so silly Max, you will walk off and leave me to look after them all."

"Sally is joking Nat. There are Ma and Pa, brother and sister, Georgia and two little kids. "

I said "Ok, you both help."

One hour later Ma, Pa and the kids arrived, carrying home cooked food for the masses.

Pushing or carrying all kinds of bottles and crates of beer, at first there was only Ma, Pa, with Georgia walking a few feet ahead.

"Where are the rest of the kids?" asked Max.

"They are coming." said Pa.

For some reason we, that is Liz, Sally and I, expected to see four children, Georgia's siblings and her own two. Well, one was way over six feet tall the other maybe five feet ten both. Her siblings had lighter skin then Georgia, although neither had Georgia's eye coloring. They sure did have the looks, and Georgia's children made you cry they were so beautiful.

"Phone Dennis and Nancy, Max."

"Hi, it is Max. Georgia's family is here and we are wondering if you and the kids would care to come over, call back when you get this message."

Ten minutes later, they answered, "You bet! We will be over in half an hour."

By the end of the evening we had bonded, a friendship that could be picked up next time we see each other. They all knew they would be welcome in New York anytime.

Liz looked like she was having a good time and didn't appear to be upset by Crewe and her doing battle. Sally said she was going up to bed. I wanted to see if Liz was okay.

Liz and Max were in the kitchen talking about the nice time they had. I gave Max the buzz off look and sat down with Liz. "How do you feel?"

"Not bad. I think Crewe and I need a break from each other at the moment. Sometimes I work fourteen hours a day and when I get home, I feel like I have to entertain Crewe. I don't know if it is because she is one of three and she had to fight all time for others' attention. I am an actor, we are self-centered, and we want the attention, that's why I act. I love her dearly but there is only so much of me that I can give to somebody else, and sometimes it's hard to walk off stage and find yourself. You may be suddenly aware the part that you are working on would be better served if played differently. I wish sometimes I were the type of person who would scream shut up, just shut up damn you."

I laughed, "You could act the part, and you may have to for a while if you and Crewe want to stay together. When you first got together, Crewe told you she was not one to mess with. By saying if I don't like you, I will not sell the painting. That's the Crewe I know good, kind and very much to the point and I bet she gave you the painting. She knows no other way to be than direct, more so than the other two, like Susan in some ways. She does not mean to hurt anyone. That is just her. You are much more complex, more interesting and more giving than most. There are so many parts to Liz Michaels it would be hard for me to describe you. You hide behind your sweet smile and nature until you see something you want when a sweet smile is not going to cut it."

Smiling at me, Liz said "And what was that Nat?"

"Me," I laughed. "You crazy cow, I was yours from day one of this trip!"

"Will Sally say anything if you sleep with me tonight?"

"To her, this would the biggest gossip story she has ever known, because she lives for gossip. If I want to know about someone, I ask Sally. But alas, this story will never be told by Sally, because in the telling she will meet her untimely end."

"Surely, she does not believe you will do her in," said Liz.

"I am joking Liz, Sally would never betray me. I will be about thirty minutes," I said.

Sally was already in bed, reading. "I am going to have a shower Sally will you be ok on your own?"

"Nat, they call this a holiday romance. "Please don't take it back with you."

"Goodnight Sally. "

"My brother is meeting the plane, and my mum told him to meet me so I get home safe and sound. She does not want to lose me at the last minute to one of those crazy cab drivers."

"Ahhh, that's nice," said Liz.

We were taking off now. In some ways sad to leave, in other ways glad as I was longing to see my babies and the whole family. I know Max will not stay that long, now I am going back, he will feel guilty. Now he has got himself woman, I hope he can cope.

Liz was thinking that she and her mum would go away for a few days, and we thought it was is a good idea for all of us.

We sat in silence for the longest time, then suddenly I felt compelled to say to Sally, "If I think you are getting a fat head because you know Liz and I have a little secret, I will box you ears and then box them again, then again." The three of us laughed as we said goodbye to L.A.

CHAPTER 32

Sally's brother was waving, looking very pleased to see her. "Don't come in to work until next Monday. I will call you if we have to."

"Are you sure Nat?" Sally called out, smiling away.

"You are very fond of her, Nat."

"Yes, I am. She is a good worker and I like her heart, though she thinks one day she will be writing poison pen letters to me for some reason," I said laughing.

Taxi! We are on our way home to our mums.

I phoned home. "Hi Betty, we are nearly there, are there three of you at home? Good, maybe you can be outside pushing the Hawkes kids and I will surprise them. Half an hour, ok."

There they are now in strollers so they can sit up. "Oh, look Liz they are so noisy just like their father."

I walked by them to see what they would do. Nothing, too busy looking around, then suddenly Jack started screaming, trying to look back to see if it was me. Betty, Mrs. B. and JC turned the Hawkes kids around and they looked at me standing there in front of them. The three screamed, so loud traffic stopped and people looked. Someone took a video and posted it on YouTube as I am yelling, "I am home babies, I am home! Three babies were screaming to get out of their strollers… a happy 'day-one' on Central Park West. I e-mailed Susan and Max about the video on YouTube, also Dennis and Nancy, Margo, Sally and all friends and work mates, plus Harry, Terri, Claire and of course Crewe, Jenny. Oh yes, half of England.

Max phoned as soon as he got my e-mail and looked at YouTube. "I have to come home soon in case they forget me. I will call you when I am coming."

It was like a mad house as soon as we got in, the kids were running around, showing off, laughing, screaming and squeaking. In twenty minutes, they were fast asleep. "Guess they were pleased to see you" Mrs. B. said.

"So, Betty, what happened with you and JC?"

"Well," I said to her, "We should have a little talk. "No Mum, I dislike your little talks with me. It's always about stuff I don't want to know, like we should go home now. "Nat, JC look liked she was going to cry. "Oh, it's nothing like that, it may make you happy."

"Oh, I know that Nat is my sister, if that is what it is."

"How the hell did you know that? "I asked.

"We all look alike. It's in the eyes, not so much the color, but we all have that intensity."

"Hell's bells, when did you start seeing and understanding people that way JC, you based Nat being your sister on eye intensity?" asked Betty.

"No," said JC. "Peppy told me a few years ago we had an older sister."

"She what… you two knew, why you didn't say something?"

"Peppy said we must never tell you we knew. She said you had to give her up as you were too young to look after her, and Grandma and Granddad didn't have enough money to buy her food and clothes. Then you were told the little baby was killed in a plane crash when she was older. Peppy said it would break your heart to talk about it to us, and we would think you were a mean mother. I told Peppy that I had found you again and that you were grown up with three babies of your own." Peppy said it was wishful thinking on JC's part, because JC so loved the Hawkes kids she wanted them to be part of the family too.

Just as Betty finished telling this unbelievable saga, Susan walked into the room with a view. I could barely say Susan's name so I had to wave her over to us. "Please JC tell Susan what you had told me, I am in shock, Susan."

At the end of hearing all this, Susan said "And how did Peppy know all this?"

"It was a deathbed confession," JC told me.

"Who died? Susan said.

"I know," said Betty. "A few years ago, it looked like my mother was going to die. Peppy and her Grandma were very close; my mother may have found a need to tell Peppy, so Natasha could live on in the family."

"Well that's something to cry about" I said, with tears running down my face.

"Betty, you still have not told your parents about me, why?"

"They are going to the Hamptons next week and Peppy will be up there. I have been waiting to see if you and I … if my parents could feel the love that we have for each other, and also the love I shared with your family. The family that loved, cared, and helped you become the beautiful woman you are today. If I had told them before and it didn't work out, my parents would have blamed themselves even more than they already have."

Betty sobbed and sobbed and sobbed, "I am so happy now."

"You are happy? I cannot image my life or my babies' lives without you now. I see myself in you and JC and it's ok. What has made me really happy is the friendship that has formed with you, Susan and Mrs. B. Now you know you can fight and like us, get mad with each other, and that's the way the Hawkes play."

"Is that right? Betty said. as in Susan's mind Margo was a keepie. Susan also told me because of Margo and I she does not have worry anymore, because now you and Margo can both listen to me.

I have asked Peppy to bring my parents here. The Hawkes kids will be a bit needy for you at the moment what with you being away and going back to work. Would this be ok with you?"

"Yes of course Betty. Just tell me something, what if I had said no?" Nat asked.

"But you would not have said no."

"Are you sure Betty?"

"Yes, you see I am your Mummacow."

I laughed. "Don't be silly, only babies and little children have Mummacows."

"Don't you be silly, you are my baby, and always will be."

"I thank the day that you forced Margo to go with you to the Hamptons for the weekend," I said.

"That's what she said, that I forced her? That cheeky monkey, you know Nat when I told her about having to give you up, and how I thought you were dead, Margo realized that evening that you were my Natasha. She was so white and upset I sent her to bed she looked so awful. Next morning when I took her up a cup of tea, she was hiding under the bed covers, and when I did get to see her face she looked nuts and talked nuts so I thought she was nuts. I left her bedroom and ran down the stairs in case she came after me. After a while I made myself eggs and toasted soldiers. Just as I sat down to enjoy my eggs Margo came into the kitchen. She looked normal so I made small talk, and then asked her what your full name was. She didn't answer me but I knew she heard me. Last night she went white, this morning she was 'nuts', now what was she going to do? Maybe this was not such a good idea her coming here to work. I wish she had told me she was potty before now. Well, this is my house and I will show her who is in charge. Did you hear me Margo? Yes Betty, her name is…By the time, I had heard the story and that you were alive. My eggs and toasted soldiers, which I was so looking forward to eating, had fallen from the table onto the rug, never to be eaten."

All the way through Betty's rendition of Margo and that weekend, I sat there laughing. I know Margo when it comes to her being a lawyer, nobody is going to call Margo a lawyer that does not keep her word. She is so proud, and honest about her profession that when on the job or finding herself in an unfavorable position, her intensity level is frightening. If I had been Betty, I would have run downstairs, gone right by the kitchen and found comfort in a neighbor's home.

"I went to see my husband when you were in California, and told him about you etc., and I wanted to know his feelings about me telling our children. He asked me not to tell them yet. He said he had been phoning me and e-mailing for two weeks now. He never had been looking for a divorce, he still loves me and was so sorry 'the other woman' she was a mistake; she went back to her own country about a week ago. He said, "I know I have no right to ask you to take me back, I have never been unfaithful to you before and I will never be again, please forgive me, I am so sorry Betty. I made a fool of you and myself. I mean it, Betty please. We have always enjoyed one another. I don't think I was a rotten husband before but how much this must have hurt you, just out of the blue. You trusted me and I am asking you to forgive me, which is something I am unable to do for myself."

"I told him, I would think about it, but if he ever hurt me or the children again like this I would take every penny he has, then I will hang his balls outside my bedroom window.""

I also said to him 'If I do, it will not because I need you as I did before, it will be because I know you are good man and maybe I should have thought of your needs more instead of making our marriage all about the children. You know why? I have found an inner peace knowing my first child did not die, and her destiny was not mine to make. The guilt that I carried around all these years has finely been lifted. I would like you to really think about us, is this really what you want? If so and you come back and you do this again, I will forget all about the inner peace I have found and do all the things I said before plus more and smiled at him."

"My God, I said, no wonder I have a dark side, I thought it was Susan's influence now it's in my DNA."

"Now you know, my darling daughter, we are so alike it's frightening. The only thing is, we never do anything about it, thank God, and we have charm that can make the birds sing at night, and love like no other."

"I love you Betty."

"While you are still loving me do you mind if Peppy comes over tomorrow for dinner?"

All three of us got an e-mail from Susan: 'Enough is enough. I will be home tomorrow, leaving Harry, Crewe and Claire here at the mother-in-law's home. Jennie is good, and the baby is lovely. I know Harry and Mick would like to make a run for it, too bad I beat them to it. The woman should be strung up. Love, Susan.'

If Margo were here, she would find this funny. Where is she? I went and got my e-mail from the last ten days, it was never ending. I sat with Mrs. B., Liz and Betty in the room with a view.

"So where are you two going tomorrow, Mrs. B. and Liz?"

"Nowhere, I was just showing my mother the e-mail from London that I just received from the Big Boys at GTV. There is a big meeting Friday and all must attend. I e-mailed back that I could not leave New York USA until Friday morning. That will be okay as the meeting is at four p.m., I can catch the 'red eye.' I want to have two full days with Mum. I hope they are closing down production."

Mrs. B., Betty and I looked at Liz in shock.

"It is too much. Do you know I am in nearly every scene of an episode and it is getting to be too much. The lines are getting longer and longer and the truth be told, I never have enough time for Crewe and it's not fair to either of us. Plus, I am getting bored with the part, there is only so much you can do with a two-dimensional character. My contract is up soon and I do not need the money; my father left me well off, plus, I am paid well by GTV. Anyway, I will talk to Crewe, that's if she is talking to me. In addition, I can spend more time with my mum."

"Oh dear, what am I going to tell people I meet now? Oh dear, you will really have to think about this dear. You were going to be the calling card for Susan and me so we would be invited to the top New York society galas and parties. We thought we would meet the cream of the crop of Manhattan and would be photographed with "who's who" of class and wealth" Mrs. B. said. And most of all to chit chat with Betty Windsor, about Molly Rafferty, A TV show about an American detective, working for New Scotland Yard in London

We all laughed as Liz and her mum got up and sat at the other end of the room with a view, so they could look once again at the maps of New York City, planning where to go for the next two days together.

"Tell me what to do Betty."

"About what, my dear, you have so many sins?"

"I know," I said. "But what one should I work on first?"

"Do you love her?"

"Yes, with all my heart. After the hoo-haw about who was going to see the new baby and all the trouble everyone saw happening with mothers-in-law I just wanted to come home to Margo."

"Well one thing you are not going to tell Margo is whom you slept with while you were away" Betty said. "And it was not Nancy."

The glass of wine I was holding dropped down the front of my top and rolled down my pants onto the floor. "Well, it looks like I have just given myself away," I said.

"Was it worth it?" Betty asked.

"At the time, I thought so but now I am not so sure."

"All I can say is you better see her soon, she's a good catch. I have had lunch with her twice since you have been away."

"You have had lunch with her twice, why?"

"She's my lawyer and I like her very much."

"Who said Margo is a good catch, Margo I bet?"

"When we were out to lunch a woman came over to our table to say hello to Margo, she had just joined the law firm. Sometimes Margo can be as dopey as you are. Margo missed the signals. This woman wanted to know who I was, not that she was interested in me. What she wanted to know if I was a friend, client or lover. All this was lost on Margo, she just told the woman my name and that was that. Anyway, when she turned to go I hand signaled for Margo to ask her to join us, which she was so happy to do."

"Betty, you are just trying to cause trouble, and why have you not asked with whom I slept? "

"Because, I already know."

"No, you do not."

"Go and change your clothes and I will clean up the wine as best I can. Then I will tell you what this woman is like and what she wants."

"What woman, the one at lunch? You know, you are like the rest of them, love to beat me up. I will change and look in on JC and the Hawkes kids."

"All is well, all four are fast asleep," I said.

Betty carried on. "She is tall, fair, very nice looking with a beautiful smile, in her late twenties. She is new at Faggot Law firm, new in town from Texas. She and her longtime partner had broken up and she wanted to start anew, too many memories. I know Margo could not resist any longer, so I said, I am sorry is HE a lawyer too. Guess what the woman said Nat?"

Oh, I just love this. Betty thinks I am running back to Margo and begging forgiveness for all my sins. "I don't know, Betty, what the woman said to Margo, I was not there. You know Betty you are as nutty as Susan. You are telling me you and Margo are eating lunch and a woman that you have never met before, and Margo hardly knows comes over to your table and makes a play for Margo. Margo, the She wolf of Wall Street who can spot another woman who wears secret lace-up shoes a mile away, but she didn't know this tall beauty from Texas was making a play for her? That's Margo's hobby. She calls it train spotting. She likes to see how many 'trains' she can spot on the street on a given day at lunchtime."

I pressed the secret button for faking phone calls on my cell phone given to me by the department. Just then, the phone started ringing; I picked it up and said to Betty "It's Margo. Well, I am not going to answer it for her to tell me she has met another," and put the phone away. I looked down very sad and said to Betty, who by now was looking worried, "Knowing Margo, the Texan is already in Margo's bed." I got up and walked away slowly looking down.

"Please Nat, come here. Maybe I got a bit carried way, maybe the woman was not making such a big play for Margo after all," Betty said.

I looked at Betty, smiling and said, "Maybe there was not another woman at all, Betty dear. I am worried Betty, I feel I have lost her."

You know Nat, I did phone her home a few times and left a message, asking her to call me and she never did," Betty said.

"I played games to hurt her and I ended up losing her and hurting myself. Well, that was that. Betty, they say time heals everything but it's the time that you have to put in that nearly kills you. Hang on a sec. Betty I want to show you something." I ran upstairs to my bedroom and came back with some folders. "Betty, if something ever happened to me, please give these to her, as I want her to know I loved her."

Betty looked shocked. There were three condo deeds in Margo's name, all rental payments to be made to an account in Margo's name only; plus so many millions of dollars in ' so and so' funds payable to Margo only. If she lost me, I never want her to feel that I did not love her enough not to look after her.

"When your father took you, he cried, he was so sorry to take you from me. I will give her the best life possible. Thank you so much. Your kindness comes from him my dear Nat."

"I have no idea what monies you have Betty but I will always look after you, and your family."

"Thank you, Nat, I have plenty."

I was just getting out of the shower and Betty was in my bedroom calling me. "Natasha, Natasha, she is in hospital! Margo is in hospital, but she is recovering now and coming home tomorrow."

"How do you know this?"

"After you left to go to bed, I thought I would phone one more time, her mother answered the phone.

She asked me if I was friend of Margo's and I said yes. "Oh dear" she said. "I have just dropped one of Margo china dolls. Boy am I in big trouble! Oh dear, here is my other daughter. She will talk to you."

"Hi, I am Margo's sister and you are, Betty, Natasha's mother? Oh, oh now that's nice news."

"Please tell me what happened so I can tell Nat. She has been away."

"Margo was hit by a car when she was at a stop light on her scooter. When she was hit, she went flying and landed on the side of her head and injured her neck. She has been in and out of it most of the time the past few weeks but the doctors said she would make a full recovery."

I asked when she would be leaving the hospital.

Betty replied, "She, the sister, thinks tomorrow. "

"Where is she going?"

"Well, this is it, she wants to come home here" her sister said.

"Who is going to look after her?"

"My mother and I."

"But, you have four children I believe."

"Yes," she said.

"Listen "I said. "What time will you be at the hospital tomorrow?"

"Ten in the morning "

We will be there. There will be a fight on your hands as far as where Margo will recuperate.

The sister laughed, "See you tomorrow."

Oh, Betty thank God she will be ok and did not leave me, I hope."

We both went downstairs to tell Mrs. B. and Liz what happened to Margo. Betty told them about the accident and that Margo had been in hospital over two weeks and was hoping to come home to her apartment tomorrow.

"Who is going to look after her," Mrs. B. said.

"Betty asked the sister and she said that she and their mother would, which makes no sense since the sister has four children and the mother has a husband, and he will not stay there and the sister lives out of state."

"Well it looks like we will be stuck with her," said Mrs. B.

"Looks that way," said Betty. "We may have to put an extra bed in your room so you can keep an eye on Margo Mrs. B."

"Humph! It won't be me that wants to keep an eye on her," said Mrs. B.

"I have an idea Mrs. B. that Margo's mother would want to be here until she feels Margo is ok, so if it is ok with you maybe we can put the mother in with you!" I said.

"All these years Betty, and I still cannot get the better of Nat. No matter what I come up with her next line always tops mine. The only one that wins sometimes is Max," Mrs. B. said.

The next morning Betty and I arrived at the hospital at nine forty-five. Sitting on a bench outside was Margo looking so thin, and what looked like her mum sitting next to her. On the other side of Margo was a look alike Margo. The sister moved up so I could sit by Margo, she looked at me with tears in her eyes unable to move her neck very much. I put my arm around her and said how much I loved her and the tears rolled down her face. The mother and the sister cried and my mother, Betty, cried.

"I will look after her now." Looking at the mother, I asked, "Would you like to come and stay too, and maybe your other daughter would like to stay until her four children demand she come home?"

I bet they were dying to see where Margo's girlfriend lived. We arrived home to find Mrs., B. and Liz already had gone out for the day. Susan was home from the wars and JC was playing with the Hawkes kids. As soon as they saw Margo, they started to scream.

"Be good children, Margo has been sick and crying, a car hit her." Well that was not the thing to say in front of Jack, I turned to Margo's sister and said, "Margo is Jack's girlfriend, soon they will be holding hands," and they were. "Would you like to stay a few days, just to see how well we will look after Margo?"

"Oh, forget Margo, the mother said, we are just here for the view."

It looks like the mother is going to fit right in.

"We would love to. Thank you" said Margo's sister. "I will have to tell my husband Margo fell down and hit her head again. That should do it for a couple more days of freedom. He does not mind me being away, it's when his mother comes to stay she makes him wash dishes, do the laundry and clean, just like his father was made to do."

Things had changed in the family dynamics since I had been away. JC had a helper now. She called the kids to come to the kitchen for their lunch and both Bradley and Alex waddled after JC. Jack was still sitting next to Margo holding hands.

"You had better go now Jack." Margo said. Suddenly out from the kitchen area came my daughter wandering along up to Jack saying something like 'now' and points to the kitchen. Susan and Betty had seen this before but the rest of us just sat there with mouths open. The doctor was right, she is going to run the show. We will have to keep an eye on her!

The house phone rang beside me. "Hello. No, you cannot, there's no room, call next week. Are things going well out there, or have you already said the wrong thing? Good, are you sure? OK, I will phone Lesley this afternoon. Does she know your plans? No. That's ok we will still go ahead, of course they will know who you are. You're the only man that lives here."

By now, everybody had stopped talking and all were listening intently to me.

"Are you having a good time? Good. No, you cannot talk to her, we are going to have lunch. I will have her call you afterwards. Oh! How could I forget Margo has been in hospital the past two weeks! I am sorry, I am happy to say that she is going to be ok and staying here, I forgot. No, she cannot speak to you her jaw is wired shut. No, you cannot come home. Susan will phone you after lunch and tell you all about it."

"Why me"? Susan asked.

"I will be on the phone for hours repeating and repeating details about Margo's accident. He will ask: " What time of day did this happen; was she sitting or standing at the lights; how long had the lights been red; was she hit from behind; from the side or the front; where is the scooter now; was it man or a woman that hit Margo; did Margo cry; is she all there; if not, should Nat keep her; do her parents know; what are they like; does Nat like them; what about the brothers and sister were they at the hospital, if not why not?

Please don't think I told Margo's mum and sister that our Max is a timid little man that we all bully, he is not. Max is still in California and has found himself a woman, we are playing this game at the moment. This woman is a keepie, and Max wants her to know this. He also loves his children very much and worries they will forget him. He phones to say he misses them and has to come home. I tell him he cannot, as there is no room. Now Max knows it's ok to stay and not feel guilty, which Max would feel, and it's all my fault. Max is the best father these kids could ever have.

"What woman is a keepie?" asked Susan. "Max met a woman that he wants to keep."

"You mean marriage keep? Where did he meet her? I bet in a gay bar."

"Funny you should say that Susan, it was called 'The Not So Straight Club'" I said.

"What does she look like Nat?"

"Brown hair very, very short, late twenties, husband dead, two children, lives with her parents and siblings."

JC called out that she was taking the kids up for a nap. "I will help" called out Susan.

"I can manage thank you" said JC.

"Moreover, you know she can. We old women sit here watching JC run after these kids and we get tired just watching her as she has so much energy" Susan said.

"She has always been like that since she was a baby. My 'then' husband built her a big wheel in the garden, like for a hamster, in which she could run around. We took her to doctors, but nothing was wrong with her. He said make sure she gets the right food and eats well. We never leave her alone with the babies as she is only sixteen years old." Betty said.

"Mum," JC called out, "Don't forget Peppy is coming for dinner tonight."

I said to Margo's mum and sister, "Do you like Italian food? Good, that's what we will have for dinner. Peppy is Betty's daughter."

Betty told her six o'clock and Peppy arrived at six thirty p.m. I know she doesn't want to come, Peppy thought. All this business about her mum's first daughter being alive after all these years was made up by JC and their mother just wanted to believe it for JC's sake. Peppy was already in the 'room with a view' before I came in and saw her by the window looking out.

"Hello Peppy, I am Natasha."

She turned around and I saw myself, younger, but it was me. She looked stunned as she stood there looking back then a tear appeared, followed by another then a sound of a sob.

"On my dresser, I have a photo of my mother and me when I was about two years old I would not have known the difference from that photo of my mother and you. When my grandmother told me all about you afterwards I cried and cried, as I so wanted you to be alive. When JC came home with that story you and the babies were alive I was mad at her thinking it was all in her head and just wishful thinking."

I took her face into my hands and looked. "We are so much alike, all three of us. Where are the father's genes, what about the other two? "I asked. Just the same, we all look like our mother. "You would never know we had different fathers. "

Oh, boy I am dying to meet them.

Peppy said "They know nothing of you; they were far too young for me to tell them. They are so going to love it as they both love to tell stories and this will be their biggest story ever."

A bell rang two times.

"That means dinner in five minutes."

We all sat down.

"Where is JC?"

"I will get her," I said and I ran upstairs.

"Come on JC, dinner is ready."

"No. Peppy will make a scene."

"No, she will not, she already knows we are sisters, come you will see." The babies were nearly asleep so we crept out of the room. Mrs. B. Had already phoned to say Liz had rented a car so they were going to stay overnight at an Inn outside of the City and would be home to-morrow evening.

Well that worked out well. Susan and I changed the sheets on the two double beds in the last bedroom for the mum and sister. We tidied up and got the third room ready for Betty. Another one was for JC and the babies. Then there was our room. Where to put Margo? I was thinking of getting out the roll away beds and putting her in the hall-way. Maybe the mum and sister would not care for that. I know, I will give our room to Margo and I can sleep in the other beds in Susan or Betty's rooms. I decided on Susan's room. If Susan snored or made a lot of noise, I would yell at her, I was not sure I could do that with Betty. She may kick me.

Well that went down well, like a ton of bricks, with Margo. Our room had one queen-sized bed and, at the moment, I was not going to share it with Margo. What if I hit her on the head in my sleep with my arm and opened up where she had surgery on her head, then she would be back in the hospital again. Margo had no choice.

Next morning, I asked Betty, "Did you fall asleep straight away last night?"

"Yes, I did as soon as my head hit the pillow. Why?"

"Ask me how long it took me to fall asleep. Forget it, sixty minutes. Susan never stopped talking, I have heard it all before and last night I had to hear it again. I am not going to hear it tonight so I will be coming in with you. If I find out you have been lying to me and make as much noise as Susan, I will suggest you leave then, instead of going home tomorrow."

Margo was looking better already, she looked cute with a crew cut. I made her eggs and toast and watched her eat them in bed. I gave her the TV paddle. "I will leave the door open, I am next door with the kids and JC and then I am going to eat. Then sister and I can get you in a bath." My daughter was standing up in her crib making silly sounds and noisy just like Max. I kissed and cuddled her and said, "I hear you are a bossy girl, is that right Alex?" She nodded her head as if to say yes. JC and I got the three Hawkes kids dressed and took them downstairs.

"So, what are your plans now Betty?"

"Peppy has gone back to our house in the Hamptons with friends and my parents should be joining them any day, as they do every year. I asked Peppy not to say anything about you Nat, as JC and I would like to see how they react and to make sure it's not too much of a shock for my mum and dad. You know I talk like they are in their eighties, but as old age goes they are still young in their mid-sixties. Since we nearly lost my mum a few years ago, I worry about her more. She had double pneumonia but she made it through. She gets shots now and is in good health. Not only is she my mother but also, she is my friend. She has guided me with the upbringing of my daughters. She forbade me from ever saying to my two older girls, ' I hope you don't think you are going out dressed like that.' She never takes sides in front of the children or criticizes me. To my two husbands she has only shown respect. Nat, for me to take you to my parents will be the biggest gift I can ever give them, and maybe the biggest shock! Let's say next week. I can only ask Peppy not to say anything about Nat for a short time. She is young, she and her grandmother love to gossip. My mother has four sisters who have nothing better to do than dig up the dirt on each other, including my mother. Peppy loves hearing the gossip but after a while she will want to one up her grandmother with a story so big and so shocking that she will let the cat out of bag and tell about Natasha."

"I have grandparents," I said out loud. "I will wait for your phone call then and you are coming here right?"

"Yes."

I looked at the sister, "Can you help with Margo's bath, I am a little scared on my own in case she falls and I fall with her."

Margo said it would have to be a quick bath because reruns of "Sex and the City" was on the tv next.

"Damn I saw this episode last week on another channel, just a sec. Nat, I found this folder under your pillow while you were downstairs this morning When did you do this?"

. Three months ago. I did it in case anything happened to me. I wanted you to have it now, even though I may not die for a long time. The monetary value means nothing to me, but the love I have for you does. This will give you a good life with or without me. I wish you had not found this, because it may influence you about you and me. What would you like to do now with your life, and please be honest?"

"I will only say this once Nat, I cannot be without you, and I love you and your children so much."

"Stop," I said. "I am not being fair, will you be my partner through life, and would you help raise my kids?"

"Yes, yes!"

"No one is going back to the UK to live, just holidays and visits to Hawkes Manor. Betty and Max very much want to make N.Y. their base, as does Harry, and maybe Mrs. B. I was left a great deal of money by my father and generations of the Bennett family Holdings, as you may know. I found a lawyer of wills to find out why the amount was never disclosed to me by Lesley. There was no problem. Harry asked Lesley not to show me since I was married, as he was very worried how Max and I would handle the money because we were so young. I am not saying we are not going to use some of the money for a good life for the kids, and us but I do see the Bennett estate as a responsibility to be used for the benefit of humanity, anyway. This lawyer of wills feels that a lot of the assets were hidden. He has no proof of this, just a feeling he said, and that I should call him one day if I need him. This may take me years to find out the truth. I will tell you more of my dreams later you tell me yours. Do you want to stay on with Fag?"

"Yes, for now, I know Lesley likes and respects my work and is willing to help me. He said if I keep up this kind of work, I could make associate one day. I am not doing well at thinking these days and now I have everything I want. We nearly lost each other because of what we thought we saw as our future. We didn't know what to do so we did nothing, as I waited for you to tell me you were leaving to go back home. All I could think of was going to my sister's so I could cry for you and you would never know."

"You will never have to do that again, well until we kick the bucket!"

CHAPTER 33

It appears the mum and sister are having a good time, which I think is helping Margo in making great strides in recovering her heath. Mrs. B. and I went with Liz to JFK International Airport for company. Liz still didn't care if her show ended. She was looking forward to seeing Crewe at Heathrow Airport as they are all lovey-dovey now. Liz and I will always be friends now and in times to come.

On the way back I asked, "Everything ok with you and Liz, Mrs. B.?"

"Yes, it is. I am so glad we had that time together. I wish it had been longer but Liz said we would try for four days next time. There are matters she would like to talk over with me, nothing big time but, now she is worrying about what to with her career. She made a funny kind of remark about Crewe, saying, "You and I have a lot of catching up to do and Crewe has to come to terms with this. I need to be with you to know you and for you to be proud of me as a person, not what I do but what I am." In time I am sure we will become old hat at being mum and daughter" said Mrs. B.

"Oh boy" I said. I sounded just like Max then.

"Liz in the past has had many blessings because of her good looks and personality. Now, I am guessing at this, she has never been sure why people cared about her. She questions is it because of her looks, her body. She is never sure and I bet she's not sure about Crewe. Now you are in her life and she knows why you love her. You are her mother and she is your daughter. For the first time in her life she feels from you what she has been looking for all these years, her mother's love. For some people this love is not so important, for others, it is everything. It all depends how the cards are dealt. Just in case you are wondering, I personally do not think for one moment you not being in her young life was the reason for her sexual preference."

Then Mrs. B. said the funniest of things. "I am glad you two care about each other beyond the family love."

I was just going to say what do you mean, then I thought better of it. People think what they want to think.

All was quiet when we arrived home. Mrs. B. and I ran to the kitchen for a cup of tea so we could face the day. Susan was pouring boiling water from a kettle into a teapot, the only right way to make tea. She must have heard us come in and was making a much-needed cuppa for us.

"Did you hear us come in?"

"Yes, I heard the bell."

"What bell" I said?

"The bell that rings when the front door opens."

"Neither Mrs. B. nor I pressed any bell."

"No, because there is not a bell for you to press."

"So, if there is not a bell to press how come you heard a bell?"

"Because you opened the front door."

"Ok, that's it Susan, you have been away far too long with the mother-in-law, now you are back with your normal family!"

I checked in on JC, the kids and Margo, and all were still asleep.

The three of us sat by the windows in the 'room with a view,' with our second cup of tea, and fell asleep. My phone rang.

"Where were you?"

"I was asleep Max. Mrs. B. and I saw Liz off. She flew to London for a meeting at GTV. You are up early, anything wrong Max?"

"No. Are you ready for this?"

"No Max no, you are coming home today?"

"Tuesday! Georgia has a photo assignment in New York, and she has never been to New York before."

"That's nice. Are you and Georgia staying anywhere close by?"

"Very funny, Nat. I am so nervous about this please be nice."

"I am sorry Max, I have so much on my plate. Liz left today, and Margo's mum and sister are here for a few days with Margo. Betty left yesterday. Margo has our room. So for the first night I slept in Susan's room but never, never again. The noise and talking that went on. I only had a few hours sleep last night also because we had to get up so early to see Liz off. I hope Margo's mum and sister leave Sunday. I will get the cleaners Monday, you will be here Tuesday, and my grandparents will be coming sometime in the week. They have no idea who I am.

Max, when you get here you are to wait on me hand and foot okay? Since Betty has gone home how many rooms do you wish to book sir?"

"One please. I really care about her Nat, but I am not sure what to do. Should we just visit each other for now? I would like her to come to New York for a while to see if she likes it, but she has two children to uproot and there is no way I would move to California and leave my kids, you and the family. That's what I am asking her to do, move across the country with her kids on a 'maybe' she will like New York. Moreover, what about Hawkes Manor, what's happening about that? Well, all I can say to her is I have a lot of sorting out to do as to where I am living. In one year of running back and forth we should know if we would marry. Just one more question, remember when you said I will always have a home with you, just me, no wife no kids, is that still true?"

"Oh Max, my dear Max. That was yesterday before I knew what today would bring. You are my children's daddy and always will be. There will always be room in my heart and my home for you, and for whomever you love. I will love them too... Max I truly love you for the man that you are today and the man you will be tomorrow. I am so proud that I had your children and that will bond us together for life. Goodbye, Max we will talk more when you are home. Let me know what time."

Now, everyone was up except Margo.

"Did anyone notice if Margo was awake?"

"Yes, she is, said her sister, "and she is waiting for you to take her up a cup of tea."

When I walked in through the open-door way where she was, the door closed behind me. Without turning around, I said "Come on now, you are sick."

"I never would be that sick."

Margo took the cup from me, drank the tea and pushed me onto the bed.

"Knock knock, it's me Margo, your mother."

Who was going to die from embarrassment first, Margo or me, not sure because in walks mum.

"Sorry girls, I am leaving now. I wanted to tell you now before I leave

"Your dad misses me so much he went out and got tickets for the best show in town. He will not tell me which one but that's okay, so I'm going now to get ready."

"Mum, it is only ten in the morning."

"So, I bet you he has not washed a dish, picked up after himself or made the bed. If I don't go home now and clean he will be in such a bad mood this evening I will not enjoy the show." She walks over to the bed, kisses Margo then me. "Please never hurt each other again, you belong together, I can feel your love for each other. I will phone tomorrow."

Guess what Margo and I did? We cried and talked, then went to sleep.

Susan told JC to go home this morning and not come back until Monday. Good. At dinner that evening, there was Margo, sister, Susan, Mrs. B. and 'moi'. I found myself wanting to have a bitch about my life as I saw it then. Where is Harry, we need him.

"Harry, Max and you, Susan need to take the Hawkes kids home to England so Harry's parents can at least see the kids. It is too much to ask them to fly here. I am sorry it's too late for your parents Susan."

"How do you feel about you and Harry going half-and-half with me to buy a plane and helicopter? I know this a big thing to do. We will ask Harry. We could buy it for the family to fly back and forth to England. Family would have to bring their own gas, BYOG." At the moment, I have not included Max in on the buy in case we never see the plane again. This is something where we would really need to know what we are getting into.

JC will be leaving to go back to school soon, and as far as I know, Max is going to spend the year going back and forth to California with the idea Georgia and he may get together. Max needs to know if she would like it in New York, because this is where he wants to live. I cannot expect Max to be here always for the children but Max needs a wife. I feel this is the woman for Max; we all like her and her family. As far as I am concerned, Max has all the freedom he needs to make what he thinks is the right decision.

"As for our living arrangement, what are we going to do? I cannot expect you two to stay home all the time and look after my children. I really think Max is out of the picture now, and after a while you both will want your lives back again, so please let us know what you would like to do. Susan and Mrs. B., you have already raised a family. I am not sure you would want to do it again, at your stage in life now with your 'best before date' long past, with thoughts of Max having another family, I must look at myself as having sole responsibility for my children for now. It appears from my own personal observation the second family of a husband takes on more importance than the first. The reasons maybe he now knows what he wants from life. He is now older and more interested in his new family and has a bond with the new wife to raise their children together. If Georgia were a New Yorker, she and Max would move in and out of each other's lives and see what fits and what does not. If she moves three thousand miles to live here, Max will have to devote most of his time to her and her children to help them establish themselves. You cannot expect a new wife and children to be on their own. I told Max I was happy for them him, however, my children will not have a daddy anymore, just a man that brings gifts twice a week and stays for an hour or so." I looked at Margo and asked if she was sure this was what she wanted. "Margo, it will be another twenty years before I can dump them out on the streets. Then they will leave me penniless, never to visit on Mother's Day and just to add more guilt to this I will have quit my job."

Susan piped up, "I wish you had not said all this in front of Margo, we are used to your nutty talk about the sky falling down all the time, but Margo has not been around all the years, we have. Harry, Mrs. B., Max and I have heard every dramatic, over the top -idea of yours over the years. Like that school play when you played the lead actor part. That art and drama department was run by the mad 'Gone With the Wind ' was never a play; it was a book and then a film that lasted nearly four hours? What child or parent could sit that long, with you playing Vivian Leigh's part you tortured the audience with your overly dramatic version of Scarlett O'Hara, and that poor boy that played Ashley had to go to therapy for a year because you were so mean to him. We, the family, had to listen to you rehearsing that part for a year. We knew then, with the exception of Max who at the time was thrilled that he knew somebody in show business, that your chance of finding a partner would be a million to one shot and we would have to keep you for life. Now you have let the cat out of the bag in front of Margo. I will give her six months, and then she will be gone. Also, Margo's sister is here she will bear witness to how cuckoo you really are, in court when Margo sues you for sending her nuts."

"That may be Susan," I said, "but have you thought that Margo may ask the Judge to have you appear to show the court that you are the main reason why I am the way that I am?"

At that point, Mrs. B. laughs out loud saying, "ain't that truth."

Poor Margo so wanted to laugh aloud but could not due to her injured neck and head. Her face was red and tears were rolling down her cheeks. Sister was given a box of tissues by Mrs. B., which she held to her nose all through dinner. Margo was still laughing when we went to bed. She said she hated sleeping in our bed alone.

"Ok, but if I hurt you in the night go in with the kids." Later I felt her hand on my face. "About you being cuckoo, I do not care, I have never been as happy as I am with you, though the truth be told both you and Susan should be locked up."

By the time I left for work Monday morning the cleaners were already there and Susan was giving them instructions. Mrs. B. had heard from Liz about the meeting at GTV. The Molly Rafferty police show had been one of the longest running series on GTV and the Big Bosses want to go out with a bang. They did not want to go on and on until nobody watched it anymore and it had to be cancelled suddenly midseason. The spokesman for GTV had said he was sure this was not a big shock to most. He said that if all went well all would receive a good bonus at the end of the season.

Sally was already in the office. We had been away for quite a few weeks. "Did you make plans for lunch Sally? Good, we can go together," I said, "Let's go now."

"It's only eleven twenty," said Sally.

"That's ok, we have a lot to talk about."

We went to a cafe around the corner.

"Two coffees please. Now Sally, I have a lot to say, so just hear me out before you start crying ok.?"

"I already know what you are going to say."

"And what's that miss Smarty Pants," I said.

"You are leaving."

"How did you know?"

"My Mum told me not to bank on you too much with three babies all under the age of two years. She said you might not have any choice, as guilt will make you leave so you can stay at home with them for now."

"Sally have you ever had an IQ test?"

"Yes, after I left high school. It was just joking around, I think 150."

"I am sure it's higher now."

"I am not looking to leave Homeland forever, but I do need time for my children and Margo and the Family. I would like to move to a big condo with a big private office. I think my talents and yours will be served better by working for the Government and private corporations as consultants. Sally, I have no idea what will happen to you when I leave. The ' Big Boys' may offer you a position that you would like or they may offer nothing. If you decide to stay, I wish you well. If what they offer is not for you, I will pay for you to go to university full term plus ' keep' and pocket money. How do you feel about international law? I would like you to go Harvard. Yale, Columbia N.Y. or George-town as they all have very good law programs. It would be better to graduate from Harvard etc. with a law degree, than Mary Pinks school of doll making. If you are not interested in the law we will discuss this another time, as now your mind is all in a muddle with what I just have said. Next time we talk about this, I will explain more about what my long-term plans are and whether you want me to include you. One thing we must get clear, I will pay for your education no matter what. You can go Mary Pinks school of doll making and I will still pay for it but will not offer you a job."

"Why?" Sally said.

"Why not," I said. "I am very fond of you and I would like to keep you in my life as a friend. In the future if you should be looking for good job, I never want you to have to feel you need to justify to anyone by saying 'I am bright you know' or feel you have to impress with how clever you are. When you tell them, you are a Harvard or Yale grad that alone will speak for you. I will try to move things along, you are so bright and you can get further with degrees, is that ok?"

"Oh yes!"

"And you can tell your mother this too, I will not be asking you to take classes in how to be a lesbian ok? I am sure your mother is wondering why I am doing all this for you."

Sally's mouth dropped open, then she screamed, "How did you know this?"

"Because I know you. You go home with little tales of lesbian love about whomever and me. If I ever tell you I know Ms. so and so, you fit her in your stories of lesbian 'what have you'. The more horror you add the more your family is intrigued by the dark side of humanity. Just one more thing, Sally, if I invited you and your family to dinner and a party here your mum would go out and buy herself the most expensive dress she could find, new shoes to match and a handbag, have her hair done and her face professionally made up. Just so we lesbians would think what glamour woman she was!"

"Oh! My God, she would too, also she would have her teeth cleaned at the dentist and she would make sure I did not tell my dad about the dinner and party. Oh Nat, I don't want to be just your friend I want to be your best friend."

"Come here you silly cow and give me a hug. Max will be back with Georgia tomorrow. She has a photo stint this week in New York. After work, why don't you come back with me and have dinner with the family tomorrow. I will tell Margo what we talked about today, and how I am not going to make you take lesbian classes, which was Margo's idea, and how you and I are going to become best friends."

I phoned Max that evening to find out what time he and Georgia would be arriving.

"Just in time for dinner," Max said, "about six oks? Nat, have you told my mum about Georgia?"

"Of course, she's known Georgia is coming with you. Also, I told Susan to dress up."

"Does she know, 'you know'?" said Max.

"No, forgot to tell her," I said laughing.

"Oh boy, oh boy, are we going to have fun with this."

"I am going to bring Sally back with me tomorrow after work. She can have dinner with us and see Georgia again."

"That's right," Margo said. "She knows Georgia from your trip. Did Sally like her?"

"Yes, I think so. Sally the spy was the first to know when they kissed. She was watching from our bedroom window. Max thinks he is going to have a good old laugh tomorrow when Susan sees Georgia."

"Oh, is she ugly? Susan will have a bird, you never told me that. In fact, you never told me what she looks like." I know," said Margo laughing, "she does not speak a word of English."

The next day at work, I could not wait for the workday to be over, to see what Susan and Georgia thought of one another.

"What did you think of her Sally?"

"Well Nat, if those lesbian classes you were thinking of sending me to had worked, Georgia would have been first on my list."

"Oh my, did you tell your mother that?"

"No, I did not in case my dad found out. If he had met Georgia, he would have been first in line to take the course."

When Max and Georgia arrived, we were all sitting in the 'room with a view'

Susan with her Sunday best clothes on, Mrs. B., Margo, Betty, JC, Sally and the Hawkes kids who were told they had to be good babies and no screaming, or they would have to go to bed now.

"We are here, we are here, where are you?"

Jack looked at Bradley and both looked at Alex who by now was screaming and waddling out of the 'room with a view' followed by her two brothers, also screaming. "Leave them JC. Let their father cope with them. They will soon stop."

"Be quiet, babies, and come here for kisses and cuddles." Silence.

"Oh Max, two little Max's and one little Natasha Maxine. Oh, Max they are adorable!"

The Hawkes kids waddled in front of Max through the archway, Max stopped and turned around.

"Come on Georgia, you know they are going to eat you alive, no good you prolonging it."

There was no getting away from it; her beauty was magnified by her self-pride, as she stood there with the setting sun shining through the windows. I know Susan went into shock she just sat there looking,

"Mum, Mum, Mum. Are you alright?" Max said.

"Of course, I am, just a second."

I knew it; Susan was heading for me. I got up and ran out the room laughing, with her calling out to me.

"I've had nightmares over this. Please excuse my rudeness Georgia. Natasha, without saying the words, led me to believe you were short, fat and ugly and could not speak a word of English, and I am sure she was encouraged by my son. Where did my son find you? We will have another party soon just to show you off. He must be so proud of you. Now I would like you to meet everyone else. This is Sally, Nat's assistant and friend at Homeland 'what have you'."

"Sally and I know one another."

"Of course, you do, Sally went out west with the gang. This is Betty, Nat's new mother, this Mrs. B. who has been a member of our family for many years and without her, our children would not be the adults they are today. JC is Betty's daughter and this is Margo, Nat's partner, who was struck by a car on her scooter while at a red light. I see my son waving at me. I am just going to give him a hug."

"Georgia, they are all nuts, every one of them, and in time if you stay, which you will, you will love them as much I do," Margo said smiling.

Georgia laughed, "You think I don't know that just by listening to Max's chatter?"

Susan told Max he and Georgia had the end bedroom. "Maybe you can take your luggage up and Georgia may want to clean up and rest, dinner is in an hour."

What a happy dinner, Susan was in love again, and Georgia was her victim. Susan loves to woo new people, at parties she will flirt with men or women, regardless of gender, it's just her way. I personally attribute this to Susan's moon, in Libra, which has a given sense of harmony and balance. She can make you feel you are the most interesting person she has ever met. Just remember the next person Susan meets up with and likes she will give them the same importance. Because the moon waxes and wanes, woe betide you if you are near Susan when that moon tips and is out of balance.

We all had our brandy and coffee in the 'room with a view' when Betty's daughter Peppy phoned.

"Nat, that must be Peppy phoning about when my parents are coming to the city on Thursday," said Betty reaching for the phone. "What did you tell them Peppy? Oh, you said that you met and became good friends with some very important people and that you will not take 'no' for an answer and you have to come Thursday for dinner. We will leave early afternoon. Now Peppy, why did you feel you needed to say, 'important people' How important are they? What if your grandmother phones me and asks who they are? You have already told her! Told her what, who they are…" The rest of the family was now beginning to smile then laugh at what Betty was saying. "Yes Peppy, you have only been here to Nat's home once, and you are beginning to sound like Susan."

"Ok Mum, I told them it was Elizabeth Michaels's mother. "

"That's nice dear and who may that be?"

"You know Mum, Mrs. B.," Peppy said.

At this point Betty looked like she was going to die from laughing.

"But, dear, that is only one person."

"I know," said Peppy. "I thought if I told them the daughter would be there too they would want to come more."

"Have they heard of the daughter?"

"No, so why would they want to come then?" Betty said.

"Because it would make me happy, I think."

"Ok dear, if Granny phones I will say the same. Love you Peppy."

"Me too."

We were all looking at Betty waiting for her to speak. "Peppy told my parents that Elizabeth Michaels's mother would be here and seeing they did not know who Elizabeth Michaels is, they are quite happy just meeting her mother."

Of course, Max has to add to the story. "I always thought that Nat was as nutty as my mother because they were so close when Nat was growing up, now I realize it's in her DNA from Betty. The second daughter is another nutty storyteller like the first."

Thursday arrived and I had to be at a meeting at four p.m. with the Big Boys. Oh, what should I do? The answer is not go, leave at four and go home. Maybe I should check what the meeting is about. I phoned up and spoke with the personnel that sat outside the Big Boys' offices. Hi this is Natasha Bennett, I am very sorry I will be unable to attend the four-p.m. meeting this afternoon, what am I missing?" Whomever I was speaking to knew nothing of the meeting. "Fine," I said. "I have a previous appointment at three thirty. Thank you." I looked at the e-mail again, oh dear, it was addressed to me only. I phoned home and Max answered.

"Are they there yet?"

Max laughed. "They stopped at a mall to get a bite to eat and then lost the father. It was a big mall so it took them over an hour to find him. He was sitting on a bench talking to a gang of retirees, having himself a grand time."

"How are the babies and how is Georgia?"

"The babies are in bed, and Georgia just loves it here so far," Max said.

"Goodbye Max."

Sally handed me a copy of an e-mail she just received: ' To Sally from the Big Boys, please tell Natasha the four-p.m. meeting is cancelled. Will reschedule later.'

"I am leaving now Sally, you can go too."

I arrived to find the 'room with a view ' with everyone in it Max, Georgia, Margo, Susan, Mrs. B., Betty her two daughters, Peppy and JC. Common sense would have told me sitting next to Betty were her parents, but at first glance, I had no idea who they were. For one thing, they looked nothing like old grandparents with jogging pants, sneakers that had seen better days, white socks, and big sweaters on because they were always cold. Holding hands not because they had great affection for one another, but if one dies the other wanted to be the first to know. This is not to say they would not dress for dinner, they had with them grandparents dress up clothes.

I hear Betty say, "These are my parents." I looked again and saw two well-dressed and very well-groomed people sitting there, with their own teeth, smiling at me. For a couple in their mid-sixties they looked fifty. He stood up to shake my hand. Betty's mother sat there looking. She said, "You know, you look like my youngest sister's daughter. Come here, you are standing in my light. Yes, come here and sit next to me. My God, Betty she has your eyes and the kids' look." I know

By now, she was holding my hand and Betty was going to burst into tears any minute.

"What is your birthday dear?" she asked. I told her.

"And what is your name?"

"Natasha Taylor Bennett" I said.

"Betty, what's going on, who is this girl?"

Betty moved next to her mother. "I know this going to be such a shock for both of you. Besides you two, I have never told anyone about our secret, my first daughter." By now the room was almost empty, just Betty's family. "One week-end my lawyer Margo Roth came to the Hamptons to work, her partner's name was Natasha, so I told her about our Natasha. There are over three hundred million people living in the U.S. and it just happened my lawyer's partner is my first daughter. Anyway, it is a long story I will tell another time," Betty said. "It's ok Mum, the British and USA papers printed the first day that all were killed in the plane, the next day only the British press printed that the elder child was found alive. It looked like she had been pushed from the plane as it was going down. DNA testing was done on both of us, we are mother and daughter."

My grandmother grabbed her husband's hand, saying, "You have given us the rest of our lives to live without guilt." My grandmother put her arm around me. Betty had moved over to be with her father who had been quietly crying. There was JC and Peppy. I knew JC was going to drive me up the wall if she did not get to show off her baby nephews' and their sister.

"Ok JC, get them. I am sorry we have years to talk. JC has to show you her pride and joy." In waddle three fat kids not making any noise. They nearly reached us when Alex yells out "Stop!" Jack and Bradley stopped, Alex waddled ahead looked at her great grandparents and screamed, and then the two boys start screaming too.

Max marches in, "What did I tell you, no screaming. If you do not stop, you go to bed, not one more sound. Come on, let's go."

"No," said Alex.

I look up at Max we both knew she was going to give us more trouble than the three of them together. We all sat there wanting to know what Max was going to do.

"Are you coming boys?" "Yes Daddy," both trying to run after Max. "I will be back," said Max." If we do not stop her now she will run the boys lives and ours. The doctor said when she was born that she was knocking the boys out of the way to get out first. The boys in time will have to learn stand up for themselves but Alex has to know now she is not the boss in the family. I hope over the years to show and guide her about how to express her leadership qualities in a positive way without trying to break her spirit. The boys, thank God, are more like Max, dopey. Of course, there is always the possibility we may sell her." Max came back with a baby pram. "Alex, you can be a baby and I push you or walk with Daddy like a big girl." She turned around to look at us, smiled and said, 'big girl', took her daddy's hand and waddled out. What Max did with them, I did not ask. We sat around for hours talking. It must have been so hard for my grandparents to take in all that was happening. Then Betty said, "I am taking them home now, it's getting to be too much. I will phone you tomorrow Nat."

CHAPTER 34

"**D**o you think, Mum, I should go back with Georgia?" Max said. "Why can't she stay here for a while?"

"Come on, Mum, Georgia has two children."

"Did she ask you to go back with her Max?"

"No, she did not."

"OK Max, Georgia is not a young girl of twenty like Nat was. Georgia knows now what she wants from life for herself and her children. I do believe she cares for you, in fact, she will grow to love you very much and she seems to understand your silly chatter that's never ending. She loves the boy in you, and does not care one bit, just like Margo, that we are all nuts. She likes our lifestyle and she would never have to worry about money, that is not the reason she is with you, but it helps. Georgia is looking for a partner with whom to share her life, so she is not interested in a man telling her what to do. You appear to like very strong women. If you are looking to be the boss, look elsewhere. She has it, her late husband had it and you must have it too, that is a sense of duty. You have not known each other very long, and the way she thinks, your first duty is to your current children and family. In time, she knows this will change. If you go back with her now after being with your children for a few days only, she will wonder if you know where your priorities are. You would be showing her you do not understand the consequences of flying in and out of your children's lives. She will feel you have no sense of what she sees as right or wrong and she will be gone. Georgia is not a young silly girl, giddy with love for the first time. She needs to feel she is making the right decision for her and her kids. As far as Nat's sense of duty, 'who would have thought', she now knows and sees that her duty lies with her children and family. I know Nat loves you and looks after you now and will in the future and says nothing will come between you both again. Remember Nat's dark side she always talks about. You hurt them or stop being her children's wonderful daddy that Nat believes you are, you will be out of their lives and she will cut you off without a penny. That does not mean you have to be perfect or have to agree with her all the time or be right in everything you do with the

Hawkes kids. However, never forget Nat is the Mummacow and they are her babies too. Because Nat does not remember her childhood, she looks to you for guidance. Max, you always were and still are, so easy to be with, kind and loving. When your dad was off fighting in some war, you looked after me, as you still do. To you, family is everything. That's what Nat saw in you and that's what Georgia sees in you. Georgia will love the man that you are and needs the boy that makes her laugh. Your destiny is a path of love, the power of love to give to your children, Georgia's children, and maybe more kids to come."

One more thing Max, and I will say no more. When the babies were new, Nat gave them to you to raise because she knew coming home to them in the evening would not be enough for you. She knew you had to have a lot more input into raising them and being with the children. She thought you would find fault with the way she looked after them. Nat trusted you enough to be their main nurturer. She knew her short-comings. Know yours, with Georgia. Max, you are the best son I have ever had. I love you," said Susan, smiling at her only son.

Where is Harry, Susan? Are you not worried? Have you heard from him since you returned from the mother-in-law's (MIL's)?" I said.

"Now that I think about it, no, but I have spoken to Jennie a good few times since I have been back, and she said Harry is still there and will phone me when he has found freedom from the MIL. She has taken a liking to Harry and his ways and thinks Harry is far too good looking and smart for me. Jenny says Harry does not appears to be making any motion to leave yet, and as long as MIL keeps making him cups of tea, washing his shirts, he sees no reason to leave."

Susan said, "Please let me know, Jennie, when MIL has Harry in her bed. Then I can send him more shirts for her to wash and also a letter from my lawyer. Ok Jennie dear, and how are the baby and MIL or is Mick not living there anymore?"

"Mum, yes," said Jennie. "Mick joined the Navy."

"Jennie you silly cow, I was only joking," Susan said.

"Harry told him too."

"Told him what?"

"Harry said if Mick wants to outlive his mother the only chance he has is to sail the seven seas. One evening Mick went around the corner to get himself some fish and chips, as he didn't like the food his mother was cooking. On the wall was this big poster of fish swimming in the sea underneath in big words was written 'If you want to live longer Eat Fish and Sail the Seven Seas.' Mick ate his fish and chips and got on the number 210 bus that was going down to the naval yard where he signed up."

"Jennie does not live anywhere near a Naval Yard," I said.

"I know that, but it appears Jennie does not; she always was the dopiest of the three," Susan said.

"Well, I think being with MIL is sending them nuts. What about the baby, maybe Harry can bring her back here for safety and stay with us" (well maybe that's not such a good idea as Susan is looking at me like I have gone nuts). "Ok, maybe not."

"Well Susan, I am going to phone them to see what's happening." I picked up the house phone and Susan sat down beside the phone. "Oh no Susan, you are not sitting there listening. There will be nothing but trouble as I will be holding the phone and you will be interfering."

"I am not moving."

"Yes, you are," I said, then I kicked her and she moved. "Hi Jennie, it is Nat, how are you and the baby?"

"Hi Nat, it's nice to hear from you."

"Is everything ok over there, and how is Mick?"

"Fine thanks, but Mick shipped out to sea yesterday."

"That's nice," I said. "May I speak with Harry?"

"Well, Mick's mother and Harry are having a lie down now."

I hung up the phone without saying a word in case the madness could be sent down the phone lines from England. I found Margo having a nap on the bed. "Margo wake up, Margo now, wake up." I know I will kiss her. Nothing. I kissed her again, I felt her lips smiling. "Wake up, I have madness to tell you." She sat up. "What?"

Margo was just as bad as Sally loving gossip. I told Margo the whole story and that I had to kick Susan to make her move.

"Oh Nat, I think I may have to go and stay with my sister. This constant laughing is going to make me ill. I would ask you to come with me but I think my sister would be too frightened to have you in the house." Then Margo said, "The MIL and Harry are having a lie down?"

Margo then lost control and laughed until she cried. "Please Nat, do not kiss me any more until you have a shower just in case your lips touched the phone. Please leave now Nat. I want to call my sister, about Mick the baby's father joining the Navy, and you telling Susan that Harry has to bring the baby here for safety, because Harry and MIL were having a lie down together."

Somewhere in the middle of the bedrooms was a little sitting room that nobody used with comfy armchairs, a fireplace and TV. I opened the door, good nobody here, turned the lights on, good still, nobody here and locked the door. I wanted to have a big think about what was going on. After my big think, I had come up with nothing. I sat there flipping through old magazines and a bookmark fell out. I picked it up to return it to the page. The article read The Practicability of a Practical Joke. That's it, this was a setup, revenge on me for all the jokes I had played on the family. I laughed. I just love this, I am an agent, I do, I see, I know, I win, I am. This is the side of me, the dark side of me, which my family and you the reader know nothing about! Now I will have another big think… So far Susan and Jenny are the only ones who have told me this tale, and Margo appeared not to be part of this joke, that is if it's a joke. I am going to phone Claire now.

"Hi Claire, how are you?"

"Is that you Nat? How are you?"

"Good, thanks. I have grandparents now."

"Oh yes. Betty's parents. Did you like them? It must have been such a shock for them."

"I am ok, is everything ok with you. I was wondering if you have been to see the baby recently? "Yes. Last weekend, I did not stay long as I was on my way to see a friend and was running late."

"Did you see Harry?"

"Yes, I did, he looks good. I asked him when he was going back to the States, but he was not sure as he is still a bit concerned about Mick joining the Navy and leaving Jennie and MIL's."

"Who told you he has joined the Navy, Claire?" I asked.

"Mick did, He came by one day to say good-bye, and he was going to sail the seven seas."

"Did you find this odd Claire?"

"Well I did at first Nat, but we all 'got to do what we got to do'."

"And what's that Claire?" I asked.

"In Mick's case, he wants to outlive his mum."

"You know what Claire, you are as nutty as the rest of them, and how you got to practice Medicine is beyond me. Bye."

As I was saying 'beyond me, Bye', I swear I heard Claire trying to muffle a laugh.

I quickly phoned Jennie, line busy, phoned back Claire line busy. Ha! Har!

"Where have you been Natasha? Mrs. B. and I have combed every room looking for you."

"Well I have been here. Don't get angry with me Susan because you didn't find me."

"Betty is coming over for dinner and bringing the younger kids. She will be here soon, so go and brush your hair and wash your face now Natasha please, and please do not give me any trouble because she is bringing the little ones, who I am sure feel left out by now. Oh, yes, Peppy and JC too, and grandparents. You are getting too bossy Nat, all of us feel we have check with you before we can do anything. This has to stop now."

"Who is all of us Susan? As far as I know, I am no bossier than the rest of you. Susan, I cannot make you do something you do not want to do. Maybe I was rude when I asked you to move away when I phoned Jennie to find out what the hell was going on with Harry and MIL and Mick sailing the seven seas. I am sorry I upset you, I too was upset with this 'cock and bull story' you were asking me to believe. Susan, there are degrees of normality as there are degrees of pure nuttiness. On the spectrum of the latter, you are ninety and I am five degrees. I am having trouble coping with constant emotional changes in my live, while you stand there on the sidelines watching. Susan, you know so little about me. When I walk out this door on my own you have no idea where I go or what I do or whom I see. I am an agent, which you have never given me credit for, with all the responsibility and worry being an agent brings. When I was a child you loved me so much. Why do you find a need, now that I am grown up, to tell Margo and Betty that they can worry about me like that's all you did, was worry about me? Through me, you have a new lease on life. You may have the money, but I gave you New York, three grandchildren, Betty and through Betty, you will meet whomever you want to meet.

The buzzer buzzed.

"Miss Bennett, your mother is here plus grandparents, 3 young ones and a young adult."

"Thank you Fadil. Five people, please send them up."

"If I may be so bold Miss Bennett, so many people like you."

"Thanks, Fadil, that was said just at the right time, thank you."

"I am so sorry Betty but I have to go in to work for few hours. There's nothing I can do." I gave my mother a hug and kiss. "I will phone in two hours, ok? "I am sure it will not be any longer. I will be home just as you finish dinner."

Just after I left, Margo arrived home from a shopping spree. My sweet Margo had gone out and bought gifts for the children. "Where is Nat, Mrs. B.?" The smiling face Margo saw a minute ago when greeting Mrs. B. and talking with Betty and the gang had gone. As Mrs. B. turned her back to face the oven, suddenly Margo and Mrs. B. were alone. Margo turned Mrs. B. around as tears rolled down the face. "Where is she?"

"I have no idea. Nat told Betty she had to go in to work. I do not think so, and Nat just could not stay and put on a show."

"What happened earlier?"

"Susan thought Nat was rude to her. Maybe she was, but there was no need to speak to Nat the way she did. Then when we could not find her, Susan got madder and madder, thinking Nat was hiding from her."

"Even as a child …." They both turned around to see Susan standing on the other side of the kitchen isle trying to speak while sobbing. "Even as a child I never spoke to her like that. She shared so much with me and I knew how much she loved me. She does not need or love me anymore; there are too many others that she finds easier to love. My husband is bored with me; my daughters think the worst of me. I wanted to punish her for rejecting me again when she told me not to listen when she phoned Jennie. When Nat accepted Betty as her real mother, I felt so jealous as I did all the loving and work. Betty comes along and everyone loves her and thinks what nice mum Nat has. Betty was just like Nat, so easy to love."

"Susan," Betty was calling out. "Susan there is someone here to see you."

"Hi, how is my gal?"

"Harry is it you?"

"Come here. I have missed you so much," said Harry. "Jennie, Mick and the baby are fine. MIL, well she's alive. I spent the last few days with my parents. They look good and I told them we would bring the Hawkes kids over to see them."

"Funny you should say that. Nat was wondering if you would be interested in going half-and-half in buying a family plane and helicopter. She is not asking Max yet in case we never see the plane again, what with his girlfriend living in California."

Harry hugged and kissed Margo and Mrs. B. "I would love a cuppa, Mrs. B."

"Coming up," she said.

Betty came back out of the room with a view. "Nat just phoned and is on her way home. She will be here in about fifteen minutes. She met up with Max and he knew nothing of me coming over tonight with the gang."

"Hi, we are here," Max called out. "Where are the kids, and where is my dinner please?" Max walked into the room with a view to the delight of all the children. Max's kids were having the time of their lives. Betty's two younger children were playing little kids' game with them. "What is this," Max said, "a father? Hi Harry," giving his father a big hug. "Natasha, where are you?"

"I am here Harry, where are you? Oh, it is so nice to see you Harry!" I said.

"I hear you want Susan and I to buy a family plane with you"

"Good God, Harry! You are just in the door two minutes and you already let the cat out of bag."

"Hey, nobody told me we are buying a plane," said Max. "Anyway, who is going to fly it?

"I will," I said. "Homeland is sending me to flying school."

"Oh, come on Nat, that is not fair. You never told me." Max was nearly crying now.

"You know why Max. We would have never seen the plane again, just a report that it landed somewhere in California." Poor Max, everyone was laughing but Max.

"Susan, would you mind if I introduce them or better still will you introduce Harry to my parents?"

"Oh, I am so sorry, of course I will. Harry, come here please. We forgot about Betty's parents! This is my husband Harry and this is Betty's mum and dad."

"Pleased to meet you Harry, and this is Peppy, Betty's other daughter."

Harry was shocked. "How old are you Peppy, if I may ask?"

She replied that she was nineteen. Harry looked at Susan, then Peppy's parents. He reached into his jacket inner pocket and took out of his wallet a picture of Nat when she was nineteen.

"That is me," Peppy said.

Harry then showed the photo to the Grandparents and Susan, saying, "It is unbelievable how your side of the family has dominated all Betty's daughters."

"Where is Natasha by the way?" asked Grandmother.

"She just got home from work," said Harry.

"Then, said Grandmother, you watch as soon as Nat comes in here, she and Peppy will greet each other first."

I walked into the room with a view, Peppy stood up and we walked toward each other.

"Lunch, Friday, about one?" I asked.

"Yes," Peppy said.

"I will phone before Friday, ok?"

"Well I'll be, said Harry, another happy family dinner."

I sat between my grandparents, trying to answer their questions about my past life and hoping they knew I was including them in my future. I wanted them to know how happy I was, knowing I have grandparents and meeting and getting to know them.

"Oh, you are so like Betty. She had a story to tell everyone too. She also could woo anyone into thinking that her (Betty's) life would be meaningless unless the other person was in it. That is how she got stuck with those two foolish husbands of hers."

"Natasha, it is ok for you to woo us the rest of our lives. Betty is now free from guilt. We believed at the beginning that giving you up was the best thing for you and that you would have a good live with your father. When we thought you were killed, Betty believed if you had stayed with us, that would not have happened and after a while we believed it too. The children just love the idea of you and your babies, and if you believe in love at first sight, we love you already my dear Nat.

"Sounds like wooing is in our genes," I said laughing. "What is Betty's husband like?"

"A silly man, who was too good for Betty. It was her fault he ran off with a girl from one of those Lapland countries. He wants to come back. Betty is thinking about it, and if he does her wrong again she told him she will take all his money and hang his balls from her bedroom window."

"Do you know, that is what she would too," said Grandma. On hearing this, I felt like breaking into the song "At Last". Someone else at last has dreamed my dreams of exacting revenge and it is my mother Betty. In future when the need comes up I can look to Betty for pointers.

"Just a word Nat," as Betty and family were leaving, "I am so glad you and Peppy are going out for lunch but I want you to think, Natasha, and I mean this, do not lead her on with your charming ways and make out she is the most important person in your life. My mother told me how like me you are with the wooing, which amused her no end. She is a wise old bird, she knows most people mean what they say when they are saying it, but barely remember your name when you next meet. Peppy has a young heart and is easily hurt, like her sister. The other two kids of mine appear to roll with the punches and do not take life so seriously, different fathers I guess."

As Margo and I were going up to bed I could hear Mrs. B. telling Susan she had no intention of giving up their 'bedroom with a view' for Susan and Harry. If Susan wanted to sleep with Harry the next bedroom was free. "Mrs. B. you know, you can be so cruel sometimes," said Susan.

"I know I can," said Mrs. B., and that was the end of that.

"Margo," I said, as we entered our bedroom, "Susan and I had an awful fight today. I have to go down stairs and speak to her now."

"Hi Susan, we need to talk about what happened today."

"Yes, I know Nat. It started out as a silly joke as payback for nearly always getting the better of us. The last straw was when you went to phone Jennie, as I already felt dismissed by you and then realized the love we had was gone. There are so many more people in your life now, you don't need me as much as I need you. Harry and I are going back home together."

"Susan, you have just made all this up so I will feel guilty. You were a jealous possessive woman who conquered her demons and became one of the few that really knows what unconditional love is. You have shared and given what you hold most dear. You shared with me the most treasured of all your possessions, Harry and Max, Mrs. B. and the girls, treasures, that you wanted only for yourself. When I came along so sad and alone, you loved me so much you knew your love alone maybe not be enough and gave me your family. You saw how Harry 's love gave me what I needed, a sense of security and belonging, Max's made me laugh and shared his friends.

My first mother, I don't remember; my third mother I have just met. When we were kids Max would say to others and me, 'my Mum this, my Mum that.' I so wanted him to say 'our Mum this, our Mum that'. I wanted you to tell me to call you Mum, because then and now these years are mum years for daughters. I am not saying the old Susan died; she is still around, but nobody would ever say life with Susan is boring.

Mum, all this is too much for me and I am finding it hard to cope with all this new family to love. You are and always will be my Mum-macow and so loved by me. Please do not leave me now. I do not think I can cope, and you would be so unhappy without me."

"Well, what are you looking at you big lump, it was your idea for me to go back home with you Harry. Please leave us now. You have caused enough trouble for one day. I need to be with my daughter."

It was getting late when Susan said, "I want you to stay with me tonight. It's all that big lump's fault there never was enough room for you to sleep with us when you were a child. We can sleep in my bed."

Mrs. B. had made Harry move to the next bedroom, as she would not give up what she thought was her room. As I lay there listening to Susan snoring, I was not crazy about this idea one bit. What one wants as a child is one thing. As an adult, our society has not programmed us to sleep in the same bed with our parents. Then it slowly crossed my mind. Will I, or you, the reader, really know the motive behind Susan's need to be with me. It is because she has a big love for me now and thinks this will make up for the big lump taking up nearly all the bed years ago. Or better still is Susan so cunning, so devious this is her way in keeping this room, 'the bedroom with a view', from Mrs. B. Susan will share it but never let Mrs. B. have it all to herself. What's going to happen tomorrow, what if Harry is still here, who is she going to trick; she needs her bed in with Harry's to be occupied by some else. Max! Max of course is the only one that could sleep there. What will she do, flood Max's room or set his bed on fire? Sometimes I think I am so clever I can out think Susan, other times I think I am so crazy I make Susan look clever.

CHAPTER 35

Harry took Susan home that day. "I am so sorry Nat, Susan is in no state to help you or anyone else, most of all the kids. A joke is a joke but that was too much. What the joke meant to be was nothing, it was the idea that she would go to such lengths to make you believe that nonsense about mother-in-law and I and Mick joining the Navy. I do not think for one moment my daughters realized how cruel it was at this time in your life with three two-year-old kids, a father that any minute may go to California, several new family members, which is emotionally pulling you apart, and your partner who is recovering from a car accident. You also have no idea what to do about the sun and moon that was offered to you at Homeland."

"How do you know about that Harry? I have told no one."

I know, but they told me," said Harry. "We will talk about that later. I have spoken with Mrs. B. and she wanted nothing to do with the joke and told Susan that." Harry smiled. "You know what she said: 'The world is so small now I can be home in a few hours to see my sister and daughter etc., and then be back here again. My heart is here with the children and Nat, who I love, and I am very fond of Nat's new family.'"

Oh, thank God! Without Mrs. B., what would I do?

"You know Nat, for you and Max to have a life outside of this condo you have to give the reins to Mrs. B. She cannot do what she did when you were kids, but she can tell other people what she needs from them. Make her your housekeeper and give her the books and the money to run this home for you. If you have problems with the staff, all you do is, tell Mrs. B. If you want what Homeland has handed you on a gold plate, move to a bigger condo and set up your own office plus staff. Never forget Nat, it was not Peter's wife or Betty, it was Susan that made you the woman you are today. Without Susan and my son, you would not be who you are. Natasha, show the world what Susan's daughter can do."

That evening, JC was playing with the children while the four of us sat down to talk about our future. My phone rang, it was Betty.

"Hi, it is Betty, Harry phoned me earlier today, do you need my help? I would have phoned sooner but I had to make sure my kids were in agreement with us helping you and answer was, yes."

"We were just sitting down to talk about our plans," I said.

"Good. I will be over now," Betty said.

"Betty should be here by now," Mrs. B. said. On the word 'now', my phone rang. "Did you know Mrs. Fowler died?"

"No, I did not know that Mrs. Fowler died, and where are you Betty?"

"In the lobby. It is a quick sale, four floors."

"Get up here now Betty. Shall I tell Fadil to make more enquiries?"

"Yes, please yes!"

"Betty is in the lobby. Mrs. Fowler died. She says it is a quick sale and it has four floors. Open the door for Betty please, Max."

Betty marches in as proud as a peacock with herself. "It probably needs renovation from top to bottom. Fadil will call when he hears more." The house phone rang. It's Fadil. Betty said, "The five of us are coming."

I told JC where we were and to call if she needed us. Mrs. Fowler's grandson was there looking around. The entrance to Mrs.' Fowler condo was the same lobby as ours but with different elevators to the Penthouse. At one time, years ago, there had been two condos of two floors. It was then converted into one condo with four floors. The last couple of years Mrs. Fowler had lived there alone with her memories, much to the upset of her family, even though part of the summer she spent at the family estate. The door was open. Max called out 'hello' but there was no answer. We walked in and found the room with much smaller windows, but still a room with a view.

"Hello, lovely view, one could stand there looking out for hours." Max walked over to the young man and said, "I am Max Hawkes."

"Hi, I am Mrs. Fowler's grandson, David Andrews." "Daddy, Daddy!" two little boys came running into the room. "Mummy, Daddy is in here!"

"These are my sons Colin and Keith Andrews, and my wife Nicky."

"Pleased to meet you." Max was about to introduce his family when Nicky said, "Natasha Taylor Bennett, our all-time best friend who we lost contact with as we lost your home address and never heard from you! I have so regretted that."

As Nicky was saying my name, the three of us were walking to each other holding our arms out.

"What do we do next?" I said.

"Well, in fairness to my family, let's look around quickly, then please come back with us for a drink. Is that ok with you Nicky?" David asked.

"Yes, yes, and please be quick. I am dying to know why Nat is here in N.Y. The three of us were at university together back home in England, and for all that time, Nat was my roommate." We looked for twenty minutes and Max took photos. As we were leaving David asked if I was an agent. I was taken aback for minute.

"How do you know that?" I asked.

"Well you are looking at this condo and that is what an agent does, checks out the place first to set if the clients would be interested in buying. Let us hope they have lots of money."

"Well how much would lots of money be David? "

"For here, about xxx million dollars. Then on top of all that it will need a complete reno that would cost a good amount."

"I would like to come back tomorrow and have a good look if I may."

"Nicky will be here tomorrow so you may speak with her."" It's not far to our place, just the next building."

Max opened the door and called out that we were home. There was lots of noise as the Hawkes kids came running to greet us, then they stopped and saw two little boys looking at them. "Oh, David look," said Nicky. "They are triplets, three beautiful children! Are they yours Max?"

"Yes, they are." At that point, Alex stepped forward and said, "I am girl Hawkes." "What did she say Max?" Alex asked.

"She is the boss and a big girl."

"May I pick you up?" Alex looked at me and when I said, yes, she stood still with arms up. "Oh Nat, she has your eyes and she is a boss like you, Nicky." She put Alex down saying, "I have to look at your brothers now. Come and see me." Jack and Brad would not move until Max told them to go and say hello.

Max said nothing, Alex walked over to the boys and pointed her finger at Nicky and said, "Now!"

"Good God Nat, she has you down to a Tee!" David and Nicky did not stay long after one drink. As I was coming down the stairs from looking in at the kids Margo was saying, "I am so sorry, I have to go bed. I have to be up so early tomorrow morning." As we crossed paths on the stairs, I held Margo's face in my hands and gave her a kiss, and whispered, "Nicky will have a bird over this, good night sweetie," and returned to my guests.

Nicky jumped up. "That's it David, get the kids, I have to go home and sleep. I have to be wide awake tomorrow so I will hear and understand everything Nat tells me about her personal life, because she is not going to tell me anything tonight, not one little bit of dirt, not anything about her sordid past with you lot sitting around listening. Now David!"

"Lovely to meet you all, I hope very much to see you all again soon, like tomorrow morning!" "You love setting up people. You kissed Margo like that because you knew how Nicky would react."

"I know Max, I am so wicked," which everyone present agreed with.

"Are you awake?" I asked as I crawled into bed. "Max said I was wicked to Nicky because I set her up."

"Nat, you do the wickedest things disguised as humor."

"Oh, are you tired Margo?" "I am never that tired as long as you are that wicked." We both rolled over to face each other laughing, Margo full of new found energy and me never so wicked.

That morning over breakfast Mrs. B. said, "Betty will be here in the late afternoon. She will call first to check. So, what do you think about the condo Nat?"

'The possibilities depend on how long the reno will take and what the asking price is. The quote David gave me was silly, far too much money if it's a fair price and the reno does not take forever. I like it just for the room with a view. I know so little about buying and selling real estate I will have to take in other people's advice, that know a lot more then I know. It will be interesting to hear what Betty has to say, being a New Yorker most of her life. She appears to have knowledge of people in the know."

Nicky phoned about ten am asking if eleven would be too early and I said, "No, that's ok, and I shall meet you in the lobby at eleven then."

Nicky let me know she wanted to come up for coffee first and asked if Max would be there. I told her I thought so, asking why.

"Nat, he is film-star good looking, I want to see him in day light. He dumped you, didn't he? He found another woman and you never got over it so you turned to women."

"You silly cow, you have not changed one bit. I will see you at eleven."

I told Max what Nicky said about him being film-star good looking and that she was coming at eleven for coffee to see him in day light. Usually Max, if not going out, will wear running pants, old white sneakers and an old jumper around the condo. He does not shave and sometimes forgets to comb his hair that stands on end, giving him six more inches of height. Well, not today. Max wore a pair of expensive grey pants, light navy shoes, medium navy jacket to match his shoes and the shirt was the color of his eyes. He was shaved, with just enough aftershave to take your breath away, or should I say take Nicky's breathe away, and his was hair well groomed.

"You have a nerve Max, to call me wicked. What you are doing is just cruel, plain cruel."

She was on the dot of time. Max was at the door ready to open it. Nicky came through the door and they locked eyes on each other. I nearly had to help them to the table. There were the four of us, sitting at the table but the only ones talking to each other were Nicky and Max. After listening to their chitchat for half an hour over coffee and cake made by Mrs. B., which Nicky raved about, I said, "Let's get going." "Are you coming Max?" asked Nicky.

"Nicky, I thought you wanted to hear about my wicked past."

"I can hear that another time."

I looked at Max and shook my head. He was trying to pretend he did not know what I was talking about. When we arrived, Nicky told me to have a good look around the first floor so I would know what to say to the interior designer.

"Max and I will look around the top floor. Maybe Max will have to push a door open."

Words cannot describe how mad I was with Nicky and Max. Maybe it was my fault for telling Max that Nicky was hoping to see him in full sun light. I should have known better. It would be hard for him to resist. I felt like child kept from the adults' bedroom. I decided there and then I did not like it here and 'screw Nicky'. I know I am wicked but she is so self-oriented and she would not make a friend for me now. I didn't trust her, so I left the condo of ill repute.

"Well, that didn't take long," Mrs. B. said. I told her what I thought was happening, that Nicky and Max were having sex on the top floor. Nicky and Max returned about an hour later.

"What happened to you," Nicky asked.

"I changed my mind."

"Why? A client may have liked it."

"Well, I can speak for this one."

"Ok. Well I am sure there are plenty of other agents that would love to list it. I will talk to you soon, Nat, bye."

"I like it Nat, I really like it."

"Will you excuse us Mrs. B.?" I pushed Max into the small sitting room. "Max, that was business and you had sex with Nicky. Don't lie to me Max."

Max went red. "Yes, I did."

"Max, I know she handed it to you on a platter. Do you know how foolish and silly I felt being dismissed by that woman? I am still not sure how committed you are to Georgia. Let's face it Max, it is too soon to tell. Three thousand miles distance is very difficult for a romance when both of you have children. You have not known her that long to become a sexual hermit. If one day you both decide you are a couple, I feel Georgia only has to catch you once and it is over. She is not the type you fool with. You mess her up, you mess her kids up, and the way that she thinks is, you mess up her, you mess her late husband kids up. Max, you have a great deal to live up to with Georgia. I am not judging you for wanting to have sex with Nicky, but no matter what she thought, I was there to talk business, involving millions of dollars of security for our children's future and me. She may not have known I was the buyer. I was only the agent in her mind but you knew. Nicky was using my business time to fuck you. As I was doing business for us, you were just 'doing' her. Sometimes Max your looks do not help you, they attract but they do not keep. You knew why she wanted just you to go with her to the fourth floor. You were hoping all along, that's why you were all dressed up."

I phoned Margo up and left a message saying that 'with all the tales I have told you, this one takes the biscuit. I will have to save it until you get home'. I went looking for Mrs. B. There she was feet up sleeping in the room with a view. That seemed to be a good idea to me. "I will have a lie down." So, I checked in with JC and the kids all were doing the same.

I lay down, phoned Betty and told her what happened. Silence. "Betty." Nothing. "Betty, did you hear me?"

"Yes, dear. All I can say is, thank God you have lots of money, you know he is your fourth child."

"Betty, it is not because he had sex with the silly cow, it was because I was there thinking about how many millions this will cost… and those two! I will call you back Betty, someone is knocking on my door." It was Max. He looked awful. His eyes were blood shot and he had been drinking.

"She meant nothing to me. Those three little kids are my world and I never gave it a thought that you were there to find out if this condo was suitable for our family. I have no idea what to do about Georgia. I think I love her, but can I cope with my children, her children and her? Where do I live, do I tell her I am still a boy? I know once we are together I would never cheat on her but I don't think I can be the man she wants."

By marrying Max, I had promised to make a home for him and raise a family together. I promised to love him as a man, yet I had done none of those things. What harm I did, I do not know. All I know is that I love the boy I grew up with, who helped me see the light and showed me how to laugh. He will always be the children's father and to me there could not have been any man better. When I see them laugh and play with joy in their eyes, so happy to be alive, I see Max. He has given me happy babies, two dopey boys and a boss girl and without Max, I would never have known the joy they have given me. Max has such a high IQ but ADD has plagued him all his life.

"Max, I too am overwhelmed about what to do. Several new family members and with Harry and Susan gone I worry all time if you and

Georgia marry, leaving me to look after three children. I have been offered a job at Homeland that only a fool would turn down and I can work from home with help, that's why I need a much bigger place. Thank God, I have Margo but she has a job she loves and she is ambitious. What if you have more kids with Georgia and you forget ours?" I said crying. "I need you to help me and to share your ideas on our kids' futures. You wanted children so much Max. If you walk away and leave me with all the responsibility I swear I will shoot you."

"Nat, I can't believe you would think that of me! I would give my life for these kids. Please, never think that again!"

"Max, the only difference between you and me is I can make things happen, you dream what may happen. Max, share your dreams about our children with me, and together we can build a foundation for our children's future. The rest you share with Georgia if she is what you want. Does she know about your ADD? I asked.

"No," Max said.

"Tell her. Have her read about and understand the good and bad of it. These are facts, not excuses. You have a gift with children. When my grandparents first came here and Alex would not leave the room with the boys, instead of picking her up and carrying her out of the room screaming, you came back with a pram. You asked Alex what she wanted to do, get in the pram and be pushed out like a baby or walk out with Daddy, like a big girl. You and I have always said we should treat them all the same. I feel now if we do we will end up with a rebel that rebels against nothing and an unhappy child. She already knows in her young mind that she can outfox her brothers; they are no threat to her. That she is a girl makes her special, because there is only one of her and two of them. She has a stronger need to win then they do. Time will tell. Max, when they grow up I want to give myself the freedom to let them go, and for them to know although we have money there are no short cuts in life. The world owes them nothing and things you do in life preface with self-respect. These are some of the ways to inner peace and contentment and never be so stupid as to think you do not have to pay the piper before it's your time to go.

You cannot go on like this Max. You are going to have to go out there and talk to her, ask her what her needs are, what she is looking for in life for her and her children. But first, you share yourself with her. She needs to know you have ADD, and how it affects the self-esteem, that sometimes you feel lost, and that you need to be praised. It is not to feed your ego, it just keeps your head above water, always looking and never finding the things you have hidden to keep safe so you will find them the next day. Your constant chattering about nothing may drive her up the wall when in your ADD mode, because she will not understand one word you said, and she never would be stupid enough to ask you to repeat again. Don't forget to tell her all your good points. I cannot bring any to mind at the moment, but you will remember. Just one more thing Max, see if she is open to different life styles."

"What does that mean Nat?"

"Well would she want her home to be just for you, her and the kids, or a private apartment within a family condo. Does she mind living with parents and siblings."

"Georgia would love it, she knows no other way. The more the merrier. What do you have in mind Nat?"

"If I bought a bigger condo and you and she had a self-contained apartment or floor within the family condo, would she like it?"

"Oh Nat, forget her. I would love it!"

"Ok Max, just feel her out. Remember, you are just finding out about each other, and is it worth all the trips back and forth and still no guarantees."

CHAPTER 36

I phoned Nicky. Hi, David its Nat, I did not get a good look at your grandmother's condo, I was wondering if I may have another look now please.

Nicky told me you were not interested.

"Let me speak with her please."

"Nicky," David called out, "The phone is for you."

"Hello, who is this?"

"It is Natasha, I am sorry about the mix up today. I would like to look at the condo now please if you do not mind."

"Nat thank you, I am sorry too. I knew why you left and I do not blame you one bit. It was stupid and rude, please forgive me. My only excuse is David is not interested in me anymore and I saw that Max was at that moment."

"Oh Nicky, that is ok, just forget about it."

Nicky said, "I will see you in forty-five minutes. I will ring you when I get there, bye."

Mrs. B., Betty, Max, Margo and I were sitting around the small round table at the end of the room with a view when I hung up the phone. "Nicky will ring when she gets here in about forty-five minutes. I would like to go alone at first, just to smooth things out with her, and tell Nicky I am the buyer and not a real estate agent." My phone rang.

"I am here."

"Ok, I'll be up." I turned and said, "I should be an hour, then I will ring you Max for all of you to come and look."

"I am so sorry," Nicky said again. "I have never picked up a stranger like that before."

"Well," I said, if this is any consolation, Max is far from a stranger now," laughed and gave her a hug. "Max had said he liked it and I liked it. After we looked around, now my family has to see it."

"Why? Nat, what has it got to do with your family?"

"Well Nicky, we are not going to live here with just the children. It's too big."

"What? What is going on here Nat? You told David you were a real estate agent."

"I am sorry, Nicky, that was a misunderstanding. When David said 'an agent' I did not think he meant real estate. I am a government agent and that's all you need to know. I am interested in this property but the price David mentioned was rather high. We would have to get it appraised. If we agree on the price we can go on from there, ok?"

"Where are you getting the money or a mortgage from Nat? I hope this is not one of your daft jokes from university," said Nicky. "I know, it is one of those funny deals where you are in cahoots with secret partners that live abroad. You never did have much money sense, always giving your money to churches and the poor, telling me we need a ticket to get in to heaven. When I told my parents we must start buying tickets to get in to heaven, they stopped sending me money."

I put my arms around and held her. "Nicky, I was so fond of you because you had to be the silliest person I knew at that time. I had no idea why or how you got into university. They were such fun times, few worries and then you met David and his best friend John. We would make a foursome on the weekends. What happened to him?"

"John died a few years ago, David was so upset I still don't think he is over it."

"How?" I asked.

"He killed himself," Nicky said.

All I could think to say was, "Oh dear. I am sorry."

"Tell me something Nat, if it was women you were interested in why did you not pursue anyone at university?"

"I did!"

"I looked everywhere for your address and never found it, I could not remember your family name and there was no phone listing under N. Bennett."

"By the way, I did send you an invitation to our wedding, it was returned, as you had moved," I said. "Might I call the family now to come up and look?"

"Of course, Nat."

"Hi Max. Ask the ladies to come up."

"Nat, should I stay here?" Max asked.

I put my hand over the phone, "Max wants to come too."

"That is ok Nat."

"Nicky said you come too, Max."

We all agreed it was a go. "Nicky, we will try to get the appraiser here tomorrow. I will phone my lawyer in the morning, Lesley Faggot. Maybe we can have lunch, just the two of us, tomorrow or the day after."

"I would like that Nat."

"I will phone you in the morning Nicky." The kids were still up when I decided to go to bed. "Are you ok without me tonight JC?"

"When you help with the kids Nat, they fool around. When I say 'bed', all three run to their beds."

"Sure, they do JC," I said laughing, "Good night everyone."

"Well, that is strange," said Betty. "She's up to something."

"You had better watch yourself Margo. Nat will be lying in wait for you," said Max.

"Well in that case Max, I better be going up soon don't you think?"

Max's face went all red, "I did not mean it like that Margo."

"Oh yes you did Max. Goodnight all." leaving Max chattering away.

"What are you up to Nat?"

I lit candles and put them around. "Sit on the bed please Margo."

"What is wrong, you want me to leave?"

"Please Margo, do not spoil the moment." I took out of a box two silver chains. Both had two silver ' what have yous' in the shape of two doves together with 'Forever Margo and Natasha' engraved on the back.

"You will never know how much I love you," Margo said.

"Yes, I do Margo, but not now. There is more I have to say, and I do not want any trouble when we see Lesley about the condo and the names on the deed. There are only two names on it, yours and mine. Do you agree?"

"No, Nat no! Why Nat, you have already given me so much."

"I have been given so much, should I keep it just for myself? I know how much you love me. I have three and half children that are mine to look after. Max is a wonderful father but he is no longer going to my partner. I just pray that he will always be here for the children. I realize this condo is my home and you live with me. I like this lifestyle, family and friends coming and going. You know that Homeland has offered me to head up a new department and I can set up my office at home in the new condo. You and I can move next door and make it our home. We can plan together what it will be like. It will be ours to love, bring up the kids and it will be called Margo and Natasha's home.

In addition, you say' no, Nat no' I am too proud. What did you think was going to happen? After you got out of hospital, you said you and I were partners for life, that you would help me with the children and you could not be without me. I am not 'keeping' you and Margo you are not living off my love for you. If something goes wrong with us, you can just walk away. If the roof caves in you can see that as my responsibility to get it fixed. You should be proud that I love you as I do and want you up here with me. Anybody else would think to themselves, boy have I struck gold, she loves me and has tons of money. Not you, you act as if you are doing me a favor. Show me we are partners and help me. You are not going to control me with my own money or trap me with my love for you Margo. You are my best friend, lover and partner and because you are all these things to me, I will look after us financially. What I want from you is emotional loyalty and to be there when I need you. Some areas of my life are none of your business. Never again, put your ego in front of my need as a human being to share with you. It's a crazy way for you to control. I hope it is not what I am doing to you. I have been given a great deal in life. If I told you the size of my financial power, you would think it was one of my silly little stories like I tell the family. I will need your help as a lawyer, but that is for us to discuss at another time.

Sally was accepted at Yale and if all goes well she will come and work for me. If not, it pleases me that with a Yale degree she will always find her way. I paid for her education, hoping she will do better in life with or without me, and that makes me feel good about myself. I was given a second change in life. I ended up living with a mad woman and her family who taught me how to share. In fact, that's why we had so many energetic discussions. We shared too much and learned how to love unconditionally."

Margo was silent for few moments. "I would die of boredom without you, each day. I would awake and if you were not there I would think oh God another boring day. Then you leave me messages at work to phone you back now. My stomach turns over and I think my world, as I know it, is slipping away, and my knees give way as I fall to the ground praying it will be not much longer before they take you away."

Margo smiled at me a smile that told me how much I was loved.

"You rotten cow Margo, tell me I am right, yes?"

"I will, but I will have to whisper it to you."

"No Margo, I am not moving from this chair."

"Ok Nat. I like this way of living, never having to worry about money. Then I worry that you and your family will think I am in it for the money. I feel somewhat guilty I am going to own property, worth a lot of money, when my parents are living in the same old way, when they did so much for me to become a lawyer. As far as me being responsible as a lawyer, I would not be at Fag if I were not a responsible person. My responsibility to my parents and brothers and sister goes without saying. You and I are from two different worlds and I am trying so hard to fit into your world. I do nothing in case I fail and lose you. Of course, it will be our home. I want to be known as your partner, not a live-in girlfriend."

"Thank you, Margo. I know it is not the money, but it does help. It'd put more of a buzz in our relationship if we know how to handle it and what good we can do." I walked over to the dresser with a big mirror on and started brushing my hair.

"Now what are you doing Nat?"

"Oh, just brushing my hair back,"

Margo turned the light down low.

"Leave it up for just a second." I sat down on the bed opened my bedside table, took out a pen and paper and wrote down an amount and gave it to Margo. "That is the amount as of yesterday." and gave it to Margo." Margo said nothing and just sat there with her lawyer's face on. "Margo, I will be just as happy with you being a life partner, but if you would be interested in helping me with my dreams that would surpass every ambitious dream you have had for yourself!"

CHAPTER 37

"**M**ay I leave you to handle all the affairs of buying Mrs. Flower's condo, Margo? David is asking too much money for the condo. Please remind him he has no real estate agent fees. Do you know anything about real estate and the law Margo?"

"No, but I have a very good friend at Fag's that specializes in real estate, so I will ask him to work with me if he has time. Also, I will look at what's out there in the way of interior designers and companies that handle large renovations as to cost and time."

"Thank you, thank you, Margo! I am so worried about Susan and Harry, as we all are, I am going see George Johnston today before or after my lunch with Nicky. Susan as you know has always been a funny duck, but to do this… they have never just taken off like this telling no one."

"I am off now," said Margo. "See you tonight."

I phoned Nicky and we met at cafe near where she lives. "So, what's happening about the condo Nat?"

"Well, Margo has a very good friend at work that deals in real estate. They are both lawyers at Faggott, Faggott and Faggott. Lesley Faggott is the last of the Faggott's line. He, my father and my guardian Harry Hawkes, were boyhood friends at Windermere in the Lake District."

"Does he have any children?" asked Nicky.

"With a name like Faggott, what you think Nicky?" We both sat there laughing like schoolgirls. "Now what I have been dying to know, who were the girls you were far too friendly with at University?"

"Julie Parker."

"The Rugby captain's girlfriend, oh boy did you live dangerously."

"No not really, he had a boyfriend."

"David will just flip over this."

"The last, but not the least was Grace Dumas."

"Grace Dumas, who the hell was she? Grace. The only Dumas I knew was Mrs. Dumas, the deacon's wife. She thought she was the cat's meow, tall about thirty-five, not bad looking. I only saw her a few times at parties and graduations. Oh, Nat, say it is not so! You could have

made me so happy back then, if only you had told me. Nat, it would
have given me such self-confidence to be the only one amongst those
stuck up girls at University that knew you and old Gracie were having
it away. This news is so big I am going to make David pay me money
before I tell him this. What was she like?"

"Very nice," I said.

"How long and when?"

"For about the last six months before we graduated."

"So that is why you were hardly ever around the last few months. I
asked you what you were up to, now I cannot remember your answer."

"Grace had a stable of mares you know. I did not know this when
we first got together. When I found out, I told her 'me only'."

"What did she say?"

"Grace laughed her head off and said fine, you have already won
the Triple Crown. From then on, it was just her and I until I left."

"Were you upset?"

"Yes, both of us, but we knew it had to end. I was starting my new
adult life and Grace I am sure still had a stable of mares waiting for
her return."

"You are right when you said I am the silliest person you knew at
that time, because I never knew about any of your bed hop, hop, hopping."

"Do you think David is seeing anybody else?"

"No," said Nicky. "David is overworked, too tired and worried all
the time. I know he loves me but I would like some fun."

"What does he do? "

"He is a lawyer. We came over to the US three or four years ago. It
was good job, then his boss, the old man, up and died. Then his son cut
back on staff. Now there appears to be fewer jobs. Anyway, he is now
working in a pool. The company he works for handles workers' com-
pensation claims and they only hire part time lawyers to work with the
claimants. He could see two or three clients a day, long hours and not
much pay, and he dislikes the job as he specialized in international law."

"Are you sure, there is not another woman?" I asked.

"No, David is a worker/family man. When we first married, he was
always saying I want you, kids and a job I like. Why, I have no idea, but

he loves to call being a lawyer 'a job' like when cops would say they are on the job. Anyway, I went to a PI and had David checked out, no other woman. The PI said David is all work and no play. Also, he loves our boys so much and would love to have a baby girl. Our green cards are due next year. There should not be any problem getting our citizenship, we will have money from his grandmother's condo. However, David would like to think he has made it in America by having a good job when we go for our citizenship, as neither of his grandparents became Americans."

"Have you ever seen the Faggott building? It is very impressive."

"No. David has applied for a job there a few times but nothing happened."

"Well, it's not far from here, we can walk over. There is a nice bar next to Fag's and we can have a drink. Do you have the time Nicky?"

"Are you kidding?"

Lesley Faggott was walking out as Nicky and I were walking into the Fag building. "Hi Lesley," I called out. Kisses and cuddles were in order as we greeted each other. I introduced Nicky as the wife of the grandson of the owner of the condo that Margo and I were interested in. I told also told him that Nicky and I roomed together for three years at university back home. We chatted for a few minutes about nothing.

"Please Natasha, there is a matter I have to discuss with you right now."

"Yes Lesley, what is it?"

"Has Margo phoned you today?"

"No. What is going on Lesley?"

"Listen Nat, I will call you tomorrow," said Nicky. "It is ok."

Lesley's office was on the ground floor for his many older clients' convenience. "Margo told me about the condo you both are thinking of buying and the deed will be in both your names. She hoped I would still see her in a favorable light and that she is not after your money. It's Nat's idea and she will not have it any other way."

"Anyway Nat, I told Margo when two young people meet and love and have much in common and decide they would like a live together, and one is very, very rich and the other has little money.... Well Nat that was the wrong thing to say to Margo. As the Brits say, Margo got her knickers in a right twist." Picture Margo getting so mad with Lesley and having to control what she says to her boss.

"You know Lesley, Margo has a wonderful sense of humor, she can laugh at herself and she is so proud of being a lawyer at Fag, Fag, and Fag. But to describe her as lawyer at Fag with very little money, I can see the look on her face. You were scared, were you not?"

"Nat, there have been very few times I have been stuck for words and this was one of them. I managed to pull myself together, saying 'Please Margo, let me finish my fable. The richer of the two had a house and as long as the sun shone, it was beautiful. But when the sun went down, the house was always in darkness. Then she noticed that when her newfound love stayed overnight the house was always bright and sunny.'"

"How lovely, Lesley," I said.

"Thank you. Margo was beginning to lose that pinched look she has sometimes when she is annoyed, then I added more to my fable."

"No, you did not Lesley, let's leave it at that." Lesley was being to look worried.

"But I did Nat. I said to Margo…"

"Please Lesley oh please do not say the words that would make me frightened to go home!"

"Nat, all I said to Margo was they lived happily ever after, the rich and the poor one."

"Say it is not so, please say it is not so! Oh God, why did you have to say more? What did she do or say, Lesley?"

"She told me to stick her job were the sun don't shine. I said,"What does that mean Margo?"

"It means, you silly old fool, stick it up your…." He could not get the last word out he wanted to laugh so much. Lesley grabbed a box of Kleenex and blew his nose as if he was nearly crying over what Margo had said.

"She said what? My Margo told you to stick it up your arse! She called you, Lesley Faggott number one gun at Fag, Fag, and Fag, a silly old fool, and that's what you are if you think I would fall for this silly story."

"Oh come on Nat, please say it is not so! You did fall for it right up until the end when I laughed."

I sat there smiling at Lesley. "Margo will never learn she cannot outfox me; I will give you fifty points for that. Lesley, I am surprised you went along with Margo. Did she blackmail you in anyway?"

"You better watch that one. Margo is not one to be crossed."

"Oh, shut up Lesley. You are like the rest of them, just love to see me in trouble."

"You are both very lucky to have found one another."

I smiled. "I know that, very lucky."

"By the way, Nat, if I may suggest, have a real estate lawyer from Fag handle your real estate dealings with the buying of the condo. Margo is not into real estate also she is on the deed. Do you understand Natasha?"

"Yes, I do. That was my idea, thank you Lesley. May I leave that with you, and have your lawyer call me? Now Lesley, I believe a favor is in order. His name is David Flowers. There are a few resumes on file I think, so please do not mention my name. Thank you very much Lesley."

After I left Lesley's office, I went up to see Margo. A lawyer was coming out of Margo's Office. "Hi, Nat, she has just left for the day."

"No, she has not," and I pushed the door open to see Margo sitting at her desk on the phone laughing.

"I am sorry Nat, Margo made me say that."

"OK Lesley she is here," Margo said. "Nat has pushed her way into my office and is sitting here looking at me, and I am scared."

"What are you going to do now Margo?"

"I don't know, it is early yet."

"Do you want to get a room?"

Margo picked up her phone and announced, "I am leaving for the day. Bye."

"Does that mean yes Margo? There was chic little hotel not far from us where you could rent a very nice room for day or week."

There was cute gay person behind the desk. "How long would you ladies be staying with us?"

"What do you think Nat, fifteen minutes?" Margo looks at the cutie behind the desk and says, "What the hell, let's make it an overnight booking."

We left a few hours later. The desk was now turning away people, full house. We gave our key to a young couple. "There twenty hours left on this room, give the desk clerk thirty dollars and it is yours."

We passed papers for the condo and took full possession within two weeks. Because we foresaw no problems with acquisition of the property, we went ahead. We already had the keys and were next door making plans.

CHAPTER 38

I decided today, this very morning, I was going to dress up, head south, look around the stores with my daughter, and show her how to shop and what the best stores downtown are. Alex, my daughter and I, need to have a strong bond, a relationship based on trust, with mutual respect and an understanding that I am the Mummacow. She is always sizing people up and she is only two and a half. Alex, at her age, has no idea why she watches people and of course, you would have to be as clever as I am to understand why she loves other people's idiosyncrasies.

It's because that's what Max did when we were young and to some degree still does. He would say things like, "Why is that man's eye bigger than the other Nat? Fancy wearing big woolly socks with a good suit on…" And of course, there was the day when we were teens, Max and I were walking down our village High Street, across the road, looking in the shop windows, was a woman that had forgotten to put on her skirt. I prayed then and there that Max would not see this poor woman's folly. Well alas I was wrong. At first, Max could not understand what he was seeing. Suddenly the woman saw Max's reflection in the store window. It was then that she realized that she did not have her skirt on and saw Max's face of concern. As he started to come over to her, she let out such a scream of terror, she ran down the street and over the bridge with Max in hot pursuit, why only Max knew! Of course, the police came and Max was taken to the police station before I able to tell the arresting officers that Max was only trying to tell the woman she had no skirt on, and that he was only fourteen and looked older because he was so tall. Susan and Mrs. B. went to the police station and threatened to have the police arrested for cruelty to children, and to this day I have never seen such a performance. Max was crying, Susan was banging her big stick on the floor and dragging it across the cell bars. Mrs. B. was threatening the police with no more free dinners to be given to the police station in future. Well that did it. The woman without a skirt on was given a ticket for indecent exposure; Max was driven home in the front seat of a police car, wearing a policeman's helmet.

Back to me, taking Alex to the stores, Mrs. B., JC and the boys came down to the lobby to wave us off. Alex and I decided against going to the big stores as our feet hurt, and we would go to a store that just sold shoes. I took Alex out of her stroller and sat her next to me as we chose the shoes together. A woman walked by looking at Alex, said hello. Her finger touched Alex's head. Then and there, Alex decided to scream like she had never screamed before. I grabbed my beautiful baby girl, pinched her ear and whispered, "I will pull your ear off if you scream again."

"Ok Mummy."

At home, Alex loved to sit on grown up chairs. She would sit there thinking she was a grown up and look around nodding and smiling at other chairs. If she was moved so a grown up could sit there, she would get so mad and scream. You know what she thought, that the woman in the store was going to move her so she could sit down. The woman was so upset she kept saying that she was sorry, she only touched the top of her head.

"It is ok, it's ok, my daughter is two years old and mean as hell." She was still shaking ten minutes later. "You know what would make you feel better? A nice cup of tea," I said.

"Oh yes, indeed it would," said the shaking woman.

We had tea and a sandwich. She was from Boston, Mass. and was in New York on business, going back tomorrow, and was staying just up the street on Central Park with friends who had left today for a vacation in France. "You know," she said, "I fancy a drink."

"That's just what I was thinking," I said.

She ordered a martini and I had a Beefeater Tom Collins, sweet. Her name was Sara, about my age, with a lovely shaped mouth with big white teeth.

"I have never tasted a Tom Collins," she said.

"Please try mine." She put her mouth over the straw I had been drinking from, looked up saying, "I like that, yes I would like that very much."

"How far are you up on Central Park?" I asked.

"Just at El Dorado Apartments."

"You're kidding. I have always wanted to look around those apartments." Sara's eyes looked right into mine and said, "Just in case I am reading us wrong, do you wear lace up shoes?"

I laughed, "Yes I do, and I am wearing them right now."

As we neared my condo, as luck would have it, we saw Mrs. B. JC and Betty. "Look Alex, there are the boys, this is good timing," I said. "Sara this is part of my family, Betty, JC, Mrs. B. and my sons, Jack and Brad. Ladies, would you mind please taking Alex to the park with you. Sara is staying, at the moment, at El Dorado apartments and she is leaving and going back to Boston tomorrow so I have the opportunity to look around the apartments?"

"Oh, I would love to look around El Dorado," Betty said. "That's nice, maybe one day in the future you will be given the opportunity to visit the El Dorado again."

"That was mean," Sara said, laughing.

"No it was not. Betty lived in one of those apartments years ago, she was just trying to be cute in case we are going to have fun." It was so easy to get in her bed and the hardest thing to get out. She was asleep, I got up and dressed, wrote her a note and left. I walked home after spending the afternoon loving a stranger.

"I was beginning to worry," said Betty. "You have been gone a long time."

"I am sorry Betty. I did not want to leave her."

If Max comes home before Nat, do not tell him JC. I cannot listen to his chatter nonstop for hours." It will be all Natasha's fault because Betty never told anyone about the serial killers in her family history.

"Hi, Betty it's…"

"I know who it is," said Betty.

"Are you ready for this?" said Mrs. B.

"I am always ready for something when I get a phone call from the Hawkes household." Nat is all dressed up and has taken Alex downtown shopping on her own. Nat thinks it is a long time coming. The kids need time on their own with each parent. Alex may need more time as she is the only girl, very strong willed and very clever; much more than the boys but that may change in time. Nat wants a strong bond and for Alex to know Nat is the Mummacow, and as long as she lives under Nat's roof, as she grows up Alex can think she is the Queen Bee all she wants, but her mother will always reign supreme."

Betty laughs…:" only Natasha would see herself as a supreme mother only thing wrong is she does not have a church."

"Anyway Betty, what do the boys do?"

"Smile and wave Nat and Alex goodbye from the lobby, then set about pulling the heads off her dollies. Max of course, will blame you as you never told him of the serial killers that are part of your family history," said Mrs. B.

"Sometimes I think he is nuttier than his mother" said Betty.

"It was not always that way Betty," said Mrs. B. After he and Nat broke up he never was the same boy as before, and Nat will never forgive herself for not loving him as she promised. She realizes now how she hurt him. No matter what she says when she gets mad with him and sends him on his way, she will always look after him because…"

"Because what?" said Betty.

"Because… they have a love like no other," said Mrs. B. "They had only been married a short while when out of the blue Nat turned to me and said 'You know what Mrs. B.? The only thing wrong with my life is that Max is a man! Other than that, I love him to pieces.'

■

I went upstairs the kids were already asleep. I phoned Margo at her sister's. "Oh, hi Nat, we are playing cards and I have lost all my money."

"Don't tell me that Margo, how will we eat?"

"Nat, my sister and husband want to take me to the bank to take out some more money, but I am beginning to be bored now, so I will be home tomorrow. Ok Nat?"

I went downstairs to say goodnight to all that were still up. Betty was making tea for Mrs. B. and herself.

"Night Betty."

"I am staying the night Nat. Peppy is at home with my younger kids. Come here Nat, give me a cuddle. It happens to so many people. They meet a stranger, time stands still and it's magic."

"Margo is coming home tomorrow."

"Thank God for that," Betty said. "It was all her fault anyway we will blame her she has no right to go and see her sister more than once a year. It appears to me, Betty said, when Margo goes to her sister you go looking for her in other women's beds."

"Betty, no Betty! You may think that all you want, but never put it into words. It sounds like I am such a silly sausage that knows nothing about myself, or life. By the way, where is Max?"

"He is still in the little sitting room trying to fix the heads."

"Fix what heads?"

"We forgot to tell you the boys pulled the heads off Alex's dollies."

"What did she do?"

"Max told her they were having a bath and would not be dry until tomorrow." She was so tired from her day out and did not care too much and went to sleep.

Margo was home by three. Max fixed the dollies' heads. Peppy and the young kids were coming over for one of Mrs. B.'s best dinners. Later Mrs. B., Betty, Max, Margo and I would sit around worrying again, where the hell were Susan and Harry.

Max and I phoned Hawkes Manor several times. Claire had not seen them and neither had Jennie. Crewe, being in London, had not heard from them. What about contacting Interpol, FBI or the New Scotland Yard. I know, what about Molly Rafferty. We decide to wait until Monday, then I would go into work and see what I can do.

CHAPTER 39

Since being back from L.A., I had contacted Headquarters and the secret papers were delivered to me in person ... don't laugh... by three armed guards. I personally thought this was a joke and maybe George Johnston was behind it. I read it, put it away in the safe, took it out and read it, then put it away again. At dinner that night, I informed everyone that I would be locked up in the little sitting room upstairs, and no one would be let in for the next fourteen to twenty-four hours. Betty and Mrs. B. looked at one another and laughed.

"What job?" Betty asked.

Well that remark just ticked me off. "I do work Betty."

"I am sorry Nat I thought you were fired."

Margo stood up. "Excuse me, I see trouble, big trouble for you Betty. Nat is now going to put you in your place, and she does it so well. Now Betty, you are thinking let her try, I am her mother and older just let her try. If I were you, I would run for the door now while Nat is thinking of the right words to tip your windmill."

Mrs. B. was going to the kitchen very quickly, "The kettle is boiling," she calls out. I looked at my mother, Betty, with two tears on her left cheek, hands shaking, knees knocking. "I am so sorry. Come here baby come to your mummacow." I thought to myself I must try this one-day, false tears, hands shaking, knees knocking. This way she still saves face and gets nothing but sympathy from all four of us, and in her mind, one up on me. Oh, she is so my mother. Mrs. B. poked her head out of the kitchen," Cup of tea anyone?" and within five minutes, Margo, Max, Betty, Mrs. B. and myself sitting at the kitchen table drinking tea and eating Mrs. B's Apple pie made in heaven. Playing in the background was Max. If he had said it once, he said it a dozen times, "What little sitting room upstairs? I have never seen a little sitting room upstairs. Nat, you are making this up, you have met someone else and going off for little slap and tickle!"

"What the hell is a little slap and tickle?" asked Margo.

Mrs. B. laughed her head off. "Max, only you could think up such a story about Nat."

"Ok, let's start again. I have to work and it will take about three hours to twenty-four hours. I can go into work and sit at a desk on a wooden chair, then come home as mean as hell or work from here. What I am doing is for my eyes only. I am sorry, what I should have said is, I need complete privacy. You hurt me Betty and the funny thing is you may have no idea why. I am now going up to see my children maybe I sounded a bit too dramatic before. When I said no one would be let in, what I should. Good night, I will see you in the morning."

I opened the door to the kid's room, and then rushed back to my bedroom to get a camera. All three kids were lined up with JC facing them. "Now, the first lesson today will be a slow one to warm up." JC turned on her what have you and soft music played. "Remember kids, one-boy, and one-girl. Brad, you dance with me, Jack with Alex."

"NO!"

"Why not, Alex?"

"I dance with you, ok, but that makes you boss, no me" "Come on boys, hold hands and dance."

Well, whatever the boys did it was not dancing; one hit the other then they were rolling on the floor. I had forgotten about JC's high energy level. Boy was she strong. She picked up both boys holding each under her arms, and then she said very softly, "If one of you boys hits me, there will be hell to pay." JC put them down. "Sit." They sat.

"Alex, get over here now, do you hear me, now."

Alex did not say no or why, she waddled over sat down and said, "Yes JC." All four were now sitting on the floor. JC made a fist of her hands, gently tapped her chest and said "I am boss. You know why, because I have the ball?" She takes out of her pocket a small ball and bounces it very quickly. "I have the ball. I am boss. Now, can you do what I am doing?" JC threw the ball across the room, it bounced off the back wall and came back. JC caught it and for the next five minutes JC did tricks with that little ball that were amazing. The kids were yelling "Me, me, me!" Each one tried. "Why can you not do this?" The boys had no idea what to say. "And you Alex," she looked and thought.

"Show me now."

"Very good, that is the answer, not just me but others that know how to bounce the ball. That's how you become the boss. You listen,"

JC touched their ears, "You learn," touched their head, "Then you keep doing it until you know you are good."

"Me still boss," said Alex.

"Why is that…?"

"I am girl. Brad and Jack play without me, so me boss." JC did not know what to say to that, so said nothing.

"Thank you for listening to me kids, maybe we can play ball tomorrow evening. Yes, yes, please get ready for bed and I will get you juice." "Grown up beds, me grown up beds," Bradley said.

"Yes, where are they? I will ask your daddy." JC poked her head in the room with a view. "Hi Max, are you here?"

"Yes, I am, JC."

"Max, if I was not here nobody else could lift the kids into their baby cribs, where are their grown-up beds? Bradley would like to know."

"Oh yes, I will phone tomorrow," said Max. I was coming down the stairs because I wanted some juice too, to take back to the kid's room to be with them and drink our juice together. I could hear JC's raised voice in the room with a view. "No, you will not Max, if I had ordered them we would have had them weeks ago."

"Hey, watch it JC!"

"Watch what Max? You promised the kids weeks ago they were getting grown up beds. Well, where are they?"

"It's none of your damn business JC," Max said.

I could not believe what I was hearing or seeing, suddenly Mrs. B. jumps up, gets a pillow and hits Max on the head. "Shut up Max," and then she hits him again. Betty joins in with another pillow. I grabbed JC and said, "Let's go." We ran to the kitchen, got mugs and a bottle of juice and ran upstairs where Margo was sitting with the Hawkes kids.

"Thank God. What's happening down there? I went into the kitchen to put the kettle on then all of a sudden bang@!%>"* coming from the room with a view. I came up to tell you when all I found was the kids, so I stayed, thinking you were down there causing all the trouble."

"No, not me this time. Margo, take my camera please and look at what I filmed, and we can talk about it later. I am going to have chitchat with JC."

"I was coming to see the kids when I saw you showing them how to dance, but I was not spying on you. I stood and watched, as any mother would have. I am so proud of you JC, at sixteen, you have such insight, and you showed me how lonely my daughter is, thank you. We hugged. Well I have to go down stairs and save Max from the pillow women."

"Please don't be mad at me Nat, I did not mean to kill them." Both Mrs. B. and Betty were lying on the floor with pillow covers pulled over their heads. "I have killed them Nat."

"No Max, you have not killed them dead." Then I screamed and screamed. "No Max, say it is not so! Oh please say it is not so!" Margo and JC came running, knocking each other out of the way, coming down the stairs; the Hawkes kids rolling down all the way, trying to enter the room with a view at the same time.

"What's wrong, oh my God what's happened?" Not realizing the kids were so close I yelled out, "Max has gone and done them in!"

As soon as Margo saw the kids, she pulled them back and closed the doors. JC stayed with the children. "I have to... No, stay with the children now," and pushed JC out of the room. Well it just got too much for Betty and Mrs. B. They tried to pull the pillow hats off to little avail. Trying to stand up, then walking around with arms outstretched Margo opened the door so the kids and JC could see all of us were ok. The lobby desk buzzed. "Oh, I knew they must have heard us in the lobby," said Max. "I will get it," said Margo. "Hi. Who? Yes, yes, send them up of course you silly person, send them up now."

"Who is it?"

"It's a parcel. I think I will go. Come on kids." I opened the door. "Oh, how we have missed you!" The kids did not scream and they ran into the arms of their grandparents. Margo closed the inner door and walked away back in to the room with a view. No one took any notice of Margo they were all talking at once. Max was holding JC, he was so sorry he spoke that way to her. He just did not want to talk about the beds now as he was so worried about his parents. It was only when he was being beaten up by the pillow women that he saw the funny side of two women way past their prime ganging up on a young man way over six feet tall. To save pride he would have to do away with them.

At the end of the pillow fight, Max said, "Let's get Nat. Lay down and play dead." By now there was nothing left of the pillows but the covers. "Put the covers on your heads and lie down. No, not side by side, dead people do not lie like that. Loosen your shoes, pull your skirt up a bit Mrs. B., and you Betty, lay across her and I will put jam running from your lips."

"Nat's not going to believe this silly setup," said Mrs. B.

"Maybe not," said Max. "But just for those few moments, she will not be sure and be so scared.

"You two, honestly. We could be here hours on the floor with pillow over heads feeling very foolish," said Mrs. B.

"No, I saw Margo running at top speed up the stairs."

Max was right. For a moment, I was scared, but on the second scream a body moved and scratched. Then I went into full drama. And oh, how we all laughed at just a bit of innocent fun. The kids had no idea why they were laughing but that's what kids do. Sometime later I was wondering where the kids were. Margo, I noticed, had returned from seeing why the lobby had buzzed and now had left again. Suddenly the lights went out. Some whispering and noise, then back on again, nobody said a word. We were all

looking at the same spot and nobody said a word, then Max screamed, I cried, and Mrs. B. Said, "About time. Our leaders were home and 'we are family'."

CHAPTER 40

"**G**ood morning, Mrs. B., are you the only one up? It is early."

"Yes. I want to make some of Susan and Harry's favorite muffins for breakfast. Thank God they are home. It has been such a worry."

"What time do you get to bed last night Mrs. B.?"

"About four this morning, as Susan, Betty and myself sat around this table talking. They stayed in France and she is feeling so much better. I told her how worried we were and glad she was home."

"Morning ladies, where is my cup of tea?"

I ran over to Susan and held her close. "Never think Betty and her family will ever replace you and Harry as you cannot replace the past with the future. It's not human nature to stop loving one child when you have another so the same goes for mothers too. I have grown to love Betty and her children. You said it was ok to do that. I loved you and trusted that our love was so strong it would survive and Susan, if anything it has doubled for me."

Mrs. B. made the best family brunch for this family day with Susan, Harry, Betty, JC, Peppy, the two youngest of Betty children, Hawkes kids, Max, Mrs. B., Margo and myself.

After brunch, we all went next door for Susan and Harry to see and pick what floor, and how many rooms they would like to have. Susan looked so happy.

"Now it's going to take time. We are interviewing contractors in a few days to see what they can offer. First thing I need is a large office, then we can go from there. I will catch you up to date on what's what later Harry. One thing is, we must know now what we all need and want now."

It was raining, so any thought of us taking the kids to Central Park did not happen. I was so glad Betty's younger kids were here as they were so good with the Hawkes kids, playing games with them. JC gave up her prize ball so the older kids could show my kids what to do with a ball. What I did notice was Betty's youngest daughter Debbie was showing more interest in Alex. I sat down by Betty. "Oh, look Betty." Alex had brought out her Dollies to show Betty. I held Betty's hand.

"I am so sorry," Betty said, "about what I said about your job. You know I think I was jealous that it would keep me from talking or seeing you for twenty-four hours. "

"You are such a silly mummacow," I said laughing.

Debbie had taken Alex's dollies, "Thank you, are they mine to keep?"

"No, mine!" Alex started to cry. Debbie looked at her mother for help. "You had better fix this Grandma or Alex will never share anything again," I said as I pushed Betty up off the sofa.

I was up at six a.m. the next morning. I bid my farewell to Margo. "Oh, you silly cow, how long do you think you will be? See you tonight." With coffee and a 'yesterday' muffin in hand, by six thirty a.m., I was locked in the little sitting room (that Max still could not find). By twelve thirty p.m., I had completed my assignment and by one forty-five p.m., I was up in the Big Boys' offices. "I need to give these papers to General Big Boy in person," I said to the person behind the desk. She picked up the phone, "Natasha Bennett here to see you sir." "Go in please." Fancy that, she remembered my name.

"Good afternoon General." I handed back the 'top secret' folder. "Enclosed is a draft of what you need for the new department."

"Oh good Natasha, and how long did it take?"

From six thirty a.m. to twelve thirty p.m."

"Ok, I have to write the time it took for the other Big Boys to know. What day did you start at six thirty?"

"What do you mean what day, Sir?"

"The date Nat, the date."

"Whatever day today is, I started at six thirty this morning and finished at twelve thirty this afternoon." The General just sat there looking at me as if I was the daft one.

"Maybe you misunderstood what I wanted from you?"

Silly old fool, why does he not read what I have written and then get someone else to show how the program works, then he can decide if I am daft or not. I stood up and looked down on him, "Good day General. If you wish to see me again you may leave a message on my phone."

"Good afternoon, Natasha," the person behind the desk said. I turned and smiled at her and your name?"

"Kathy Collins."

"Well Kathy, see you again."

I think I will go down, see George Johnston in the same building, and have a bit of a natter. "Hi George, it's me."

"Come on in Nat, you do not look very happy. Have two men touched your bottom today?"

"General Big Boy asked me to do something, and just because it only took me a few hours he looked at me as if my elevator does not reach the top floor, and maybe I do not understand what he was talking about."

"That's why he is a General; he is a brave man to take you on. What did you say?"

"If he wants to see me again, leave a message."

"That's the way to go Nat. I bet he was sitting down and you stood over him."

"Oh, George you know me so well."

"I am so glad you are here; a mutual friend of ours will be here any minute." As soon as George said that in walks a well-dressed, nice look-ing man, slightly on the short side. I turned to George and whispered, "Who the hell is this?"

"Natasha, Natasha. You look beautiful." I was in shock. It cannot be Dolly. "Is that you, you too look beautiful. When did this happen?"

"Couple of years ago I went on a diet. It took me about a year and half to get down to this size."

"Oh Dolly, you look wonderful, just wonderful!"

George got three glasses out and we sat back enjoying our Southern Comfort. George always had a bottle in his desk drawer. We sat at George's desk on the worst chairs I have ever sat on and talked and talked for two hours. Dolly had flown in yesterday on business, had dinner with George last night and was flying off tomorrow.

"Next time you come you will have dinner with me and stay."

I told him early in the evening about the new condo and that we were looking for contractors, which I knew, was going to take too long for me. Where do you start and how do you know if they are good or not? It's no good being good if it takes forever. After a few more minutes of me going on and on, Dolly changed the subject.

"Will you excuse me Natasha? I have to make a very important phone call. I will be back within ten minutes and, true to his word, Dolly was back in ten minutes.

"I have heard from George what a wonderful friend you and your partner are to George, his wife and children. It is George's opinion you never told him the true cost of the medical bills for his wife. Uh oh! Georgie, I have just said the wrong thing, please forgive me Georgie! He swore me to secrecy not to tell anyone about what a good human being you are. Will you forgive him for telling me?"

"Only if I can call him 'Georgie' too" I said.

"Yes, you can" said Dolly. "He knows he can never repay you with money only his un-dying friendship. However, for what he has done for me, maybe I can be of help to you."

He took out of his brief case one of his business cards and wrote on the back 'Edward Bigwig Esq. Tel: #^^^'. "Please may I have your business cards too, Natasha?"

"Yes of course, Dolly."

"Edward will phone you tomorrow at nine a.m. He would like to come around and look at your new condo. He will give a fair deal and what is being said now stays here. He can bring workmen from all over the world, artists and materials."

I touched his hand. "Dolly, I want nothing coming back on me in twenty years do you understand?"

"Yes," Dolly said. "There will be nothing too come back on, you will pay a fair price, not an inflated price. All you are doing is jumping the queue."

"Thank you, thank you Dolly, please give me two of your cards. Can I phone you anywhere in the world with this number?"

"Yes."

I looked at my watch, my God the time, where has it gone? I have to go home now, it's so late, and I kissed both goodbye. "I will phone you tomorrow Georgie. Once again, thank you Dolly." I rang the house phone. "Hi, I am just getting into a cab, I am so sorry, twenty minutes."

Of course, Harry had to meet Mr. Bigwig and be at my side through the whole process. He arrived at nine a.m. with another man, carrying a camera and other work-related tools.

"If I may, I would like to look around your home now, so I can get a feel of where you are coming from if I maybe so personal."

"Yes, please do."

When we arrived at the room with a view, the doors were closed.

"Do you always keep the doors closed?"

"Never," I said, and whispered, "It's closed because all my family are in there hiding from you."

Mr. Bigwig whispered back "Let's surprise them."

Mr. Bigwig opened both doors and walked through to screaming kids and smiling women's faces. Oh yes, I liked Mr. Bigwig, he is one of those men who just loved women, loved everything about them. Old or young, fat or thin, tall or short, women felt comfortable with him and he showed nothing but respect, and he loved what came with women …children.

Now Mr. Bigwig sets about wooing Mrs. B., Betty, Susan, Margo and JC and when he reached Max he said, "You sir, have the most beautiful babies I have ever seen, may I pick them up?"

"You have to ask their mother, Natasha," said Max smiling. As he was coming over to Harry and me I whispered to Harry, "Oh Harry, I just love him so."

"I bet you do," Harry laughed. "Yes, he does have away about him."

"Natasha, you are smiling. You think I am going to woo you with words you have heard so many times before about your babies. No." Mr. Bigwig whistled at the kids, "Come here please and sit down like me, legs crossed." Neither Bradley nor Jack looked to Alex, they came over first. Alex was the last to sit.

Your daughter will stop being so bossy as she grows to know herself and gain self-confidence. She will understand there is so much she has to offer the world and will turn her ego around into more inner strength with her belief in humanity and God, and she always be your daughter, Natasha and Max. Bradley has the foresight to lead your family into the New World. He will be a leader and much loved. As for Jack, he will see the world as his playground, he will never stay away too long as he sees his duty to his family and his family to come. They will always be each other's friend. Because you all have the power of love, every one of you. I felt it as I walked in and if you come to my home, you will feel the same. Ok Natasha, stop crying and let's have a quick look upstairs." Harry, the kids and I followed Mr. Bigwig upstairs, leaving behind in the room with a view a family in somewhat delighted shock. By the time Mr. Bigwig had looked around upstairs the kettle was boiling, coffee was made and a cake and muffins baked this morning were on the table.

"Now if you would just let my man and I into the new condo, we maybe a few hours looking around taking pictures and checking the structure. You know, just looking for trouble. It's best to find the trouble now than later."

"I am sorry Mr. Bigwig, we are all going to sit down with you and have cake, muffins, coffee and tea."

Half an hour later, I showed Mr. Bigwig and his man into the other condo. "You have my phone number with you."

"Yes I do."

"Call if you need me."

Well, the General had left me a message. "Natasha when I was told how smart you were, I had no idea how smart you really are! Please excuse my abrupt manner when I last saw you. I would very much like to meet with you again, as soon as possible."

"Hi Kathy. Yes, it's Nat Bennett."

"Hi, what can I do for you?"

"The General and I need to meet, the day after tomorrow in the morning, for me. Will you call me back and confirm the time? Thank you. "

My phone buzzed. "Hi, it's Ed Bigwig. I will be at your front door in five, ok?"

I found Harry in the room with a view nodding off. "Harry, Harry! Mr. Bigwig will be here in a few minutes."

No sooner had I said that when Susan was yelling from the hall, "Mr. Bigwig is here." Within no time Max, Mrs. B., Susan, the kids and JC were in the room with a view.

"Cup of tea men?" asked Mrs. B., referring to Mr. Bigwig and his man.

"Yes please."

Mrs. B. walked towards the kitchen calling out, "I am not getting anybody else anything." Mrs. B. was back in no time with hot mugs of tea and muffins for the men. "Thank you everyone for turning out to hear what I have to say. As far as could be seen, we foresaw no major structural problems. An architect and I will be here Friday morning bright an early. Would you, Nat, notify the front lobby that we are coming and would like to go straight to the new condo. After the architect has looked around and taken notes, we will come here and see you about nine a.m. I will phone ahead, so please have ideas of what you are thinking in the way of design, and what kind of living arrangements you want. Please call Nat if you think there is something I need to know or you need know."

Over dinner that night, I reminded the family about what Ed Bigwig said about our ideas and plans for our New York home. "I need an office and room next door, separate on the first floor. The rest will be for family living, kitchen, dining room, room with a view, plus other smaller areas. I would like the kids to have separate bedrooms when we move in, as they will be over three years old. I have spoken to the powers that be on multiples, separations and this would a good time. That is not to say we may not still have problems. We could leave the boys together, but I have no idea how this would affect Alex by her leaving the nest knowing the two boys were still together, so that's three bedrooms. Including our bedsitter, that's four. I am thinking about… and this is open for discussion…, a mother's helper, not a nanny, but a young woman to live in, maybe from the UK, that's looking to come to America."

"I have a headache so I may lie down for a while." It was not a headache that sent me from the room, it was a feeling of wanting to yell at all of them 'I cannot cope anymore, it's too much, it's just too much with three children and worrying if Max is doing 'the right thing.' Now I wish I had not had gone into to see General Big Boy, and why did I have to return his call and make appointment for tomorrow? I know, I will make out I am dopey, and the Top Secret draft I wrote for the new department was just a flash in the pan. On Friday when Ed and the architect arrived, I bet not one member of the family will have one idea between them: I don't know, what do you think Nat? The rest of the meeting will be about me wanting a mother's helper. Oh dear, it is so going to upset JC, like Ed and the architect care. Nobody remembered that JC is still in high school and the summer holidays will be over soon.

The last thing I remember was opening the glass door to the shower.

Meanwhile back at the ranch, the excitement of the day had caused Harry to fall asleep. Susan and Mrs. B. had gone to the kitchen to make tea and serve cake made by Mrs. B. earlier. Max had asked Margo to dance and she had declined, due to the fact there was no music.

In the middle of the tea party Max jumped up. "Oh no, I forgot to remove my, to quote Nat, 'foul smelling sneakers' from the window sill in my room. Nat said the cleaners complained to the point they refused to go in to clean and will not go back until the sneakers have been removed for two weeks, with the window left open. Now I have to move my clothes etc., to the next bedroom, which has been set up for Georgia and me."

"Have you been in his room? The smell coming from his sneakers is foul," said Susan.

"Now why would I want to do that Susan?" said Mrs. B. "It's something like a passage of time, or like the young brave going out along in to the desert or forest to become a man."

"I know," said Susan. "It's like a Bar Mitzvah. To become a man, as a boy you must have had foul smelling sneakers. Well, it's time Max grew up."

Harry and Margo were asleep in chairs in the room with a view. As Mrs. B. and Susan were leaving to go and watch the telly, an awful screaming and yelling echoed through the condo. Max was yelling for his father. "Harry, Harry, help! It's Nat!" Margo was first up the stairs followed by Harry, then Susan and Mrs. B.

Max found me laid over the shower drain, my body blocking the water from draining out, my hair wet with blood and water with my face underwater. Max carried me out and was doing CPR, crying, "Please, come back Nat, please Nat, please!"

"Now me, Max. Rest," said Margo, who was there in one move.

I spat out water and coughed.

After a couple of minutes, I knew I was ok. "My children, I can hear them. Please let them see me, Margo."

"Already there," said Susan. She is trying to comfort them, as they heard Max yelling for Harry. She will bring them in when she feels they are ok.

"JC is not so good. She had to say with the kids while we were here saving you. Thank God Max and Margo both knew what to do. There she is, waiting to see you and make sure you really are alive."

JC was sobbing. "Come here." She laid next to me on the bed as I held her, telling her she was only sixteen and she was my hero to stay with the kids, when the world outside her and the kids' room was falling apart.

"Mrs. B. is phoning your mother," Susan said.

JC said, "I am not going home. I have to stay with the kids and you Nat."

"Of course you do. JC, maybe Max can bring in a roll-away bed so Margo, the kids, you and I can all sleep in here tonight."

"Just a sec Nat, I think Harry wants to take you to the hospital soon."

"NO, Susan, NO! I am not leaving my children tonight. They will never get over this. "

Susan went and looked for Harry who was on the phone talking to Nat's doctor. Susan whispers to Harry, "Nat won't go."

"I know that," Harry said. The doctor is coming over now."

"The doctor is coming here Nat," Susan said.

"Good."

"You look such a mess Nat."

"Well that's why the doctor is coming here to see me, silly."

Guess what, the doctor gave me no choice. "To the hospital you go, you must be checked out."

I was home in ten hours and in bed with the kids, toys, dolls and silly cartoons on the telly. Betty did not arrive until after I left for the hospital, something about the taxicab running out of gas. Harry phoned General Big Boy, explained what happened, and that I would be in contact with him when I felt better.

I told only Harry how I was finding it hard to cope with everything. "You know Harry, the night of the accident I felt like dying just so I would not have to worry any more. It was a mistake buying the condo next door, as it's too much for one person to take on; nobody else is showing interest in it. I have three two half year old children that need their mother, me. I know now, it's me that is the one that will have to take my children to see your parents. What happened to this great love your parents, you and sister shared as a family? England is a hop skip and a jump away. I know it would be a nightmare to fly with three kids. Hire a plane and bring your parents over here."

"Of course, it's too much for you, and I will go and get them."

"It's not that I do not think about them. I thought it would too much for them, too many people and kids and they may not be able to cope. But really, I now think it's me that could not cope with bringing them over and worrying all time if they were happy. I will ask them how they would like to fly."

"You never know Harry, they may love first class with the airline looking after them."

"Nat we nearly lost you. From now on when you have a shower, I will have one with you ok?"

"Yes, Harry."

"Nat, another thing until next door is running smoothly, you and I are partners. You and I will discuss what you want then, I will talk with Ed and the architect. The first thing you want done, if possible, is the first floor with your office. Plus, a door into the family area and a private door from the office into another room, the only way in and out. The rest of the first floor will be an all-family area kitchen, dining room, room with a view, media room, a smaller sitting room and storage, very similar to what we have here."

CHAPTER 41

Max did not go to the airport to pick Georgia up today. He had not slept, he was in such a tiswas after I nearly died. Georgia is getting a taxicab and coming right here. I found Max in the room with a view. "What are you doing out of bed Nat? The doctor said bed rest."

"I know. I am going back, I just wanted to thank you Max for saving my life and being there for me. You are very fond of Margo."

"Yes, I love her. Is that ok Nat?"

I had to laugh. "Of course it is ok Max. Because of what happened to me, nearly dying, I am now worrying about what would happens to the kids if something did happen to me before they were grown. Margo and the kids see themselves as a family now. Please never take them away from her. Max, please don't think I am trying to take your rights as a father away, please share our children with her. But they should live with her."

"You have my word Nat. What if Georgia says 'no' to me? What I would do with myself, ask you if I could have one room here, and take the kids to the park every day looking to get it up with some woman I hardly know? I so need to belong."

"Max, your need for a perfect world full of love clouds your judgment, your thoughts lose their meaning and anxiety takes over, then you start doubting yourself. You have no idea what a catch you are. Max, we did not work out. It had nothing to do with you. Because of our background, you were and are the only man with whom I have been intimate. Because I loved you, I hoped when we married, I would fix what I have always known as a teenager and woman. I have never been interested in having sex with men, but because I love and trusted you I thought I would change. You so wanted to get married I thought if I didn't you would stop loving me. The truth be told Max, I was not sure since I had nothing to compare it to. Though I had slept with a few women before we married. Because of all my family deaths and me nearly dying I have had many demons to fight, but I can assure you loving women is not one of them. And I rejoice in who I am. We know Max, you and I, what happens to people that judge and turn their anger on others and feel they have the right to tell others how to love and live."

"What's that Nat, what do we know?"

"Well I do know one thing Max, nobody makes me laugh as you do; I am going to kick you. You do know of whom I speak; Nemesis, Goddess of Divine Retribution. I have never told you this before in case you made me repeat it and repeat it, but Georgia once told me she could not believe that you, a Greek God, could care for her. She is frightened to come to New York City in case she gets beaten up by gangs of woman that roam Central Park looking for you. As far as Georgia is concerned, she is a wise owl that does not miss a trick, she knows on what side her bread is buttered, she has found you and she is not going to let you go. I feel when her husband was killed she nearly died. She has that kind of love and she is ready now to share it with you Max, on an emotional level. She may need you as much as you need her. Just one more thought, there are many men with your sensitivity, they find women who love the man they are and nurture the boy within. Stop replacing one worry with another. I love you Max. I am getting tired now."

CHAPTER 42

Betty took JC home to rest, and for her not to feel she had to watch the children and me all day. Margo stayed home from work to be with the kids and me. Georgia arrived about seven thirty p.m., and came running up the stairs with flowers, chocolates and sexy magazines to see me. It was about eleven before I saw Margo as she had fallen asleep in a chair. Nobody woke her because they thought she would not get any sleep once she came up to bed, as every time the family came to see me I would talk their ear off and was still talking as they left and ran downstairs. She looked so tired as she walked over to the bed and sat down.

"I am going to have a shower then get into bed."

"Thank God for that. I have been waiting all this time for you."

"You are kidding me, you were dead yesterday."

"That was yesterday and today is your lucky day." Just as Margo was getting up, she saw the magazines that Georgia gave me, and laughed her head off.

"Good old Georgia, I will be back to read them."

"Hold on, I am coming in with you. Harry said I must not have a shower on my own and he has to be with me. So if I tell him you were with me, he will be ok with that." We showered and got back into bed.

"I have been thinking Margo."

"Not now Nat, think later."

I told Margo later what I had said to Max about the kids. "If anything happened to me, he is not to take the kids from you if they are still young, although I do not think anything is going to happen to me. He knows how much you love them and he never would. I believe him, but just in case, it will be in my will."

Now Margo was crying. "Oh, I love you and the kids so much. If you had died last night, my life would have been over too."

"Max told me he is very fond of you, in fact he loves you and asked is that ok with me. Of course, Max, I said." Margo laughed at that story. "Nat, if you know how he loved me you would mind."

"That son of a bitch," I laughed. "Always hoping, that's our Max. Has he said anything?"

"No, he has too much respect for you and he would be frightened to death and what you would do to him. He is such a chicken."

"You know Margo, once I told Max as a joke that you and I would like him to join us in bed one night. Max replied, wanting to know whose idea it was, and please say it was Margo. The night you hit on me was the luckiest night of my life. Come here Margo. "

"Only if you let me read those magazines."

We lay there exhausted. "Margo, do you think there is something wrong with us?"

"What do you mean is something wrong with us? In what way Nat?"

"Well, as soon as we are out of bed, you and I want back in."

"Nat, we are two very lustful women. I only hope and pray when we are old and, in our fifties, that we are just as full of lust as we are now. If not, our love will carry us through until the end. The lust and sex we have together works, because our love completes us."

CHAPTER 43

We both walked back into the office feeling a bit tiddly from the bottle of bubbly we had finished. "Are you happy Margo?"

"I have never been this content. I know life has its ups and downs, but at this moment I am so happy with us. I never thought I would meet you and have what my family has. My parents, sister and brothers have told me how lucky they have been in marriage; they found the right person for then. Some of my brother's friends have not done so well. This one friend said he comes home from work but she is not there. He may see her but she's not there for him, she is feeding the kids, taking them to sports practice, the mall, at friends or what have you. She will cook his dinner but half her mind is on the TV, the rest is asleep. He is seeing another woman but it's not the sex so much, it's having a woman that's interested in listening to him.

You know what Nat; my sister went to church every day praying for THE man to come into my life. After a while any man would have done, she didn't care. She prayed our local church would burn down and the parish priest would come and live with me, as he had no place to stay. Then he would leave the church and marry me. Anyway, I had to tell my sister something in the end, so I said I did not like sex.

She answered, "Well Margo, you will just have to put up with it. You know your trouble Margo? You do not like being inconvenienced."

"That's it," I said. "You have to be the dopiest sister I have ever had. I sleep with women."

She just stood there with her month open. "Well, no wonder you cannot find a man, you're too busy sleeping all the time."

"Please tell me you are joking," I said to my sister, "please tell me you have half a brain."

She started to laugh. "Years ago, Dad told me you liked the girls."

"How the hell did he know?"

"Just a feeling." He was quite adamant about it. I told him not to be so silly. Dad said, "You think what you think, and I know what I know." My sister asked him if he was upset. He thought about it and he said, "No. If it had been one of the boys, yes. Margo, she is a good-looking woman who likes to have a laugh at the world and be proud. She has not told us because we are from the old country and we are her parents, and we know nothing about life, feelings, sex, and love! When Margo went to Law school she did not only go for herself she went for us, her mother and father. She is good daughter; she is also a good sister to you and your brothers. What has her sexuality got to do with her being a fine human being, and off course it helps when you have lots of grandchildren from your other children? Your mother and I are very proud of all our children."

"I cried as I am going to cry now, it was then I knew how much he loved me. I never knew if he told my mum so I never talk about it, and my sister said she never believed him, but she wishes I had told her before now, as she had wasted all those prayers on me. I would a like to have all my family over for dinner Saturday week. My sister will have to stay the night. Her husband's mum will house sit with the kids."

"Well, we better start wooing Mrs. B. Now," I said.

"No, we will have it catered with staff. We will eat here, not next door. The luxury may overwhelm them too much."

The first and second floors of our new home were finished but the only rooms that were furnished were my office and our secret room love nest. In a couple more months and it should be ready to move in, as Ed Bigwig was here a lot making sure his men and the building were moving along at a good speed, because we all know when the cat is away the mice will play.

"Come on Nat I am not going back in there again, I have things to do."

"So, do I!"

Later in the evening, Max gave me Ann Gilbert's phone number. "I have removed it from my computer in case Georgia sees it."

"Does that matter Max?"

"Well, it may upset her. She may think I was interested in her."

"Max, you are never, never to tell anyone in the future that I was once married to you. I never want anyone to know how stupid I was. I cannot imagine what stories you have told Georgia. I am sure one is that the three kids were virgin births. Max, when you and Georgia are out together she struts like a peacock beside you and everyone turns to look at this unbelievable good-looking couple. Georgia loves it, just loves it. She is telling all who look, he is mine and I am his. Because she has not been with a man since her husband, who was killed, and you are the first, this endeared her to you and you felt special. Why would you Max make out you are a monk saving yourself for your next wife? Has she ever asked about me or other women?"

"No."

"Then how do you know she will be upset about past women?"

"Because, she has never asked me."

"You are nuts, Max. Knowing Margo, she spends half the day looking at other woman, that's her hobby. I would not dream of asking her how many she fancied. She loves me but I do not own her. As Margo does not take herself seriously, why should I?"

I had long given up the idea of contacting Ann Gilbert, if Ann wanted to see me she would find it quite easy to do so. Margo was all in a tiswas on the Saturday that her family was coming to dinner. That included her mother and father, sister and husband, two brothers and two sisters-in-law. I bet the sisters-in-law could not wait to get here and check the place and me out. Our gang consisted of Harry, Susan, Mrs. B., Georgia, Max and Betty. Guess who was Betty's escort, her still husband, so what do you think of that! Mrs. B. was told under no circumstances was she allowed in the kitchen tonight.

Margo's parents, two brothers and wives came together in a taxicab. As they came in to the room with a view, Margo's mum saw Max stand up to greet them. She turned around and said, "Oh my God, Dad, look at him. Can you see him girls, have you ever seen such a beautiful man? One of Margo brothers was telling his mum to shut up."

"Hi, my name is Max you must be Margo's family." Max took mum's hand and held it with both his hands. "Come on in, let's get you setup with a drink," guiding mum over to the bar with a gentle touch of his hand on her back. Both Margo and Georgia were standing at the entrance to the room with view laughing at what was going on. The rest of the family had gone over to the windows, spellbound by the view as mum had already seen it before, what did she care, she was in love.

"Margo, you better put Mum next to Max at the dining table. If another woman sits where Mum thinks she should be, Mum would give her the evil eye all night."

JC came with Betty to look after the Hawkes kids. Everyone was in the room with a view, waiting to go in and eat when JC and I brought the Hawkes kids in to say goodnight. Max had spoken to them about screaming if they did straight to bed and lights out. They walked in like little angels, one behind the other. Alex just stood there looking, Jack ran over to Margo and held her hand. Bradley sat down with crossed legs.

Alex could not believe what the boys did. "Bradley up, Jack here, now."

Margo gave Jack a little push. Alex looked at the guests and pointed at Bradley. "Bradley boy, Jack boy, me Alex girl… boss." Then she curtsied with a smile, turned to the boys, nodded her head, and they both bowed. The whole of the room with a view went into an uproar of laughter over Alex's speech and the boys.

"Now you follow Alex around the room, say hello, and then get up to bed and watch TV with JC." The sisters-in-law never gave me a second look as they were too busy looking and listing to Max and Georgia.

There were three persons to serve; the several main courses served were the usual roast beef, chicken, pork chops and lamb ribs. The meats were at the suggestion of the restaurant after Margo remarked there would be six men way over six feet tall, as guests. There were also different types of seafood, and fish, pasta and ratatouille. As an accompaniment for roast or grilled meats, onion tart, mussels in cider, a French styled dish with butter, cream, apple and mustard, red orzo risotto with goat's cheese, plus other dishes from other lands.

There were several red and white wines. I am only going to mention two of the desserts: chocolate peanut butter cheesecake in very small slices in case you had a stroke, and espresso and hazelnut cake.

"Margo, there's enough food here to feed a hundred guests." I knew as soon as I said it. I was in big trouble. Her back was to me as I spoke. Margo's shoulders appeared to double in size, her neck grew thicker and every hair on her head stood on end. Then I heard this awful noise, a hisssssssssing, then a long red tongue flew up in the air and came to rest across Margo's shoulders, hissing and appearing to look at me with a two-pronged tongue. It was then I knew what fear was, true fear, as Margo swung around to face me.

She looked sad. "Oh Margo, please forgive me. What I should have said was, my what a variety of dishes you have."

"You know Nat, some cultures have dinner parties that last several hours with food served at all times. All you Brits do is serve beer and you would be lucky if you got one slice of toast and a boiled egg. This is a family party, so when my family leaves my mother and father will take home food. My two brothers and sisters-in-law will also take home some food to share with their children tomorrow. My sister and husband, they have four children and they like good food too. Then I thought to myself, Margo you will appreciate the meal more tomorrow when you are not so anxious, and you know what Nat, you are damn lucky you have me."

"I know Margo, and every day I thank God for you putting up with me."

This time was like no other for Margo. Her parents, two brothers and sister were here in her home, accepting Margo for the woman she is. My Margo was so happy how the dinner party went. We all ate too much and drank too much. Did we care? No.

Stop. I nearly forgot to tell you dear reader what happened during the evening. The oldest of the three servers was at the table clearing the rest of the dishes. It was getting late, all the cutlery was to be taken back to the restaurant and washed. Max said with that cheeky smile of his, "Now don't you be taking any of that wonderful food back with you."

"Good, so you enjoyed your meal," the server said.

"My compliments to you sir, for serving one of the best meals we have ever had."

"Good for you Max," someone said. Then we all started clapping, the men were banging the table and yelling 'HEAR HEAR' (from the phrase 'HEAR HIM, HEAR HIM') first heard in sixteen century British parliament?).

"Then I must tell you I am here under false pretenses. The third server that was to come this evening broke his toe today, so I the owner-manager, and one of the cooks had to replace him. I was surprised to find in your kitchen several fridges /freezers, like we use. I, as a restaurateur, am always looking for new and different recipes. I found several half-portions of dishes. I tasted everyone, some I tasted twice. Never before have I enjoyed a treasure trove of delight I found hidden in a small fridge at the far end of the kitchen in a corner. An apple pie is an apple pie, but your apple pie, with each bit I tasted different kinds of apple and there were spices in the pie that I, as a good pastry chef, would have never have dreamed to mix in with apple. The pastry has a very, very slight taste of cider. I must know who created this dish and all the others. Whoever created those dishes is an artist. Would the real artist please stand up?" Nobody moved.

"Would the real cook please stand up," Harry said once again. Mrs. B. Stood up. "Mrs. B. may I ask your first name?"

"No, and the reason is I have forgotten. It's been so long since I have answered to any name other than Mrs. B., I cannot remember the name I was given at birth."

"Oh, and your husband?"

"I am a widow. Will you excuse us, I believe this man is after my pies?" said Mrs. B.

Georgia, Betty, Susan, Harry, Max, Margo and I all looked at one another and laughed, then only to hear Susan saying, "He is after more than Mrs. B.'s pies."

"She's drunk," said Max, looking a bit concerned. "I have never known Mrs. B. pick up men like that. I thought that was a bit cheeky of him asking for her first name."

"Come on Max," said Harry. "When have you been around to see how Mrs. B. gives the come on to a man? For all you know, Mrs. B. could have her knickers off before he thinks about it." Well, that was met with loud laughter from all.

After a very enjoyable dinner food, wine, and company, we sat out outside on the terrace with coffee and brandy. Mrs. B. sent Mr. Eric Simmons, our third server and owner of a new restaurant 'Tongue and Cheek' a frozen apple pie to share with his staff to say what they thought. The next evening Eric phoned his apple pie new partner and ordered twelve fresh large apple pies. As it was such a late night, JC stayed over so we could sleep in the next morning. I must say Betty's husband appeared to be very nice and Betty seemed quite pleased with herself. I did not get a chance to talk with her last night but knowing Betty she will phone to today or come by. The house phone rang. Mrs. B. answered and said, "Six thirty, bye. Betty and Peppy will be here at six thirty in time for dinner."

As soon as I saw Betty, I asked, "What is happening?"

"I just want to get the house cleaned up before he moves back in. The kids and I will go to the Hamptons, then the cleaners can spend a good few days doing what they have to do," said Betty.

"Oh Mum, Freddie does not care, he just wants to come home," said Peppy.

'Freddie', what happened to Fred or Frederic? It is only JC, Peppy and I that call him Freddie; he does not like it but puts up with it. Everyone else calls him Frederic. I told Peppy about that wonderful meal we had last night so we are here to eat. That's if that Margo has not given it all way to her family."

"Are you kidding? They all left with plenty of food and still lots left over, let's eat."

The wonderful meal we had last night was even more so. Harry told Betty that Eric went home with a frozen apple pie he was going to share with his staff to see if they liked it.

"Oh really," said Betty and burst into laughter.

"What's so funny in that?" said Mrs. B.

"Nothing, nothing."

Betty is still laughing at what Susan said last night.

Susan piped up, "Say something Harry, ask Nat if she is interested."

"Ok Susan. Nat, what do you think if we all took the Hawkes kids to Hawkes Manor for my parents to meet them?"

"For how long?"

"I can only speak for myself Nat, a week. It appears Ed Bigwig has everything under control for the next few weeks. If all goes well, we will be moving next door a lot sooner than you think. After that, we will be busy getting the new condo ready, furnishing it and having a house warming. If my mum and dad feel they can make it over here to New York and then California for the wedding, then there will be that too. Georgia is going home tomorrow. So is Max, Mrs. B. (to visit her

sister), Susan, you and I, and of course the kids. Margo, I have not mentioned you, you are as much part of this, the family, as we all are. My
sister would have already told my mother about Nat's new lifestyle and
for you to come with Nat would be the icing on the cake. Wherever
you two go, they with follow, hoping one of you will make overt sexual
touches and praying before the week is out you both will kiss. At first,
Terri and my mum will never stay in the same room with you alone
until they know you, in case you grab and kiss them, because the truth
be told they believe that is all 'them there lesbians' want to do! Then
there's the story about Nat's birth mother who was not Nat's birth
mother. She has been replaced by another who gave birth to Natasha.
They will never stop asking questions; why did Max have to go California to find a beautiful black woman, are there none living in New
York? And is that the reason Nat 'turned' because Max left her for another? These questions will be repeated and repeated until the day we
leave. So, you are you coming Margo?"

"I think not," said Margo laughing.

"I think I should go, as I would love to see them and be with the
kids." Nat replied.

"Would you like me stay, Margo?"

"Good God. No."

"It is such a large place for me to be on my own. I am thinking
I may ask a friend to come a stay with me."

"Who."

"It's ok Nat, nobody you know."

And where will she sleep!"

"With me, silly."

"You think you are so funny Margo."

Margo let me think all day that was what she was going to do. Have
a friend stay over. She now thinks she will like to stay at her parents'
home. You know it's your moon in Pisces Margo. Pisces are known to
be sweet, kind and giving. But those of us in the know, know that there
is a dark side, especially with the moon in that sign, like the Cheshire
cat when putting out her paw to play as the mouse runs away.

■

The phone rang at five am Wednesday morning I knew then I was not going on a plane anywhere. I had forty-five minutes to be downstairs where a jeep would be waiting for me. Sally and I arrived at the same time neither knowing how long we would be saving the world. Well there was nothing to save this time. The same jeep took me home at four in the morning, I phoned ahead just in case Margo was there, Hi I am nearly home."Tell her to leave."Then I heard Margo's voice, "quick you better leave now, Buttercup quick quick, run as fast as you can, she has a gun. Bang the bedroom door went. "Is that you Nat! I am so glad you are coming home".

We flew to London England on the Friday as a good friend of mine from British Intelligence (B.I.) e-mailed, reminding me of one the biggest women's bashes; straight, not so straight and damn right crooked on Saturday night. This was Margo's first visit to London. We booked into one of London's posh hotels, dined out and took a couple of bus trips around London's West End.

I spoke to Max earlier in the day and the kids were doing fine. "Last night," Max said, "We all sat down for dinner, including the kids, when Bradley demanded to know where Mummacow and Margo were. Guess what Alex said."

"What did she say Max, 'in bed together'?"

"Nat, she was smiling and she is only three years old."

"Shut up Max, you have just made that up."

"Well, you ask Harry. He laughed so much he put his head under the table. Thank God, it went over my mother and sister's heads."

"Are the kids there, Max?"

"They are outside with their Great Grandfather, whom they have taken a shine to."

"Oh good, how do they look?"

"Fine. They look just great and are so pleased we are here and they cannot wait to see you again."

"Oh, oh dear. I will phone you tomorrow, bye Max." I told Margo what Brad and Alex had said.

"She always smiles when she thinks she has an audience," Margo said laughing.

The next day, Saturday, we were to meet my British Intelligence (B.I.) friend and her friends for dinner, then go on to the party, about which I was now having my doubts. I was recalling the last women's bash that I went to. It was ok if you were single or had been together for donkey's years and were open to a one-night stand, or as some of the of bashes were known for, maybe two or three one-night stands. For some of the straight women it was one of the best nights of the year! Anyway, I will ask my B.I. friend Judy what she thinks.

By the time I asked Judy what she thought or heard about the bash, she and I were nearly pie-eyed and we were having too much fun at the restaurant. Our waiter was beginning to have that 'worried waiter' look about him as he was starting to see a fair size group of happy women settling in for the evening until closing, then getting out pen and paper and each adding up their dinner and how many drinks they had. They were hoping the individual amounts added up to the bill, and then change purses would be emptied onto the table. British coins would be pushed into the middle along with change that came back after paying the bill. As some still like to pay with cash, this was his tip. Women still are not paid the same wages as men so why expect them to tip the same.

I excused myself and walked by our waiter on the way to the ladies' room and gave him xxx pound notes and told him to give me the bill at the end of the evening, and that I would also adjust his tip. Now he had that waiter's look, which was only for other waiters to know, you know, that 'up yours' kind of look!

We woke the next morning to find a text message on my phone from Max. 'If you phone and I do not answer, do not worry, I am busy planning a big cricket match for tomorrow—long week here followed by an outdoor picnic. The girls, Liz and Mick are coming, Auntie Terri and her gang and partners, not sure about Mum's sister. Mum thinks she may be still away visiting her daughter in Skye, who has a B & B for the summer there; she goes to help setup for the season. Mum and Harry went up there one year and they really liked it. Listen to this Nat. You will never guess what, not in a million years would you guess. Claire is coming with a boyfriend, a real man.

Susan is beside herself about what to wear and whether the village hairdresser will have time in the morning to do Susan's hair, as she and husband are coming. He is top cricket player. Mrs. B. is already cooking away with help from Mrs. Lovelock her sister. Mrs. B. has told everyone that is coming to bring food to share and if you are a heavy drinker to bring your own beer or bottle and then you have to walk home. About half the village will be here and all will ask about you. Don't bother phoning Susan, she has decided she is mad with you for not coming. We all wish you both were here, it's family, Nat.'

A tear ran down my cheek as I showed Margo the text message.

"How long does it take to get home?" she said.

"By car, about five to six hours and that's stopping for cup of tea and a bun," I said.

"Well, we have the rest of the day to sightsee more of London, and I would love to see where you grew up."

"Ok, we will ask at the hotel desk where to rent a car. Maybe they take care of that for us. They can tell us, what is the best way for us to sightsee for a few hours today," I told Margo. "I don't think we should leave much before eight-thirty, as we didn't want to arrive too early. I have no intention of working in the kitchen serving up food. We will walk in sit down as guests; in fact, we will sneak in."

We drove off in a red two-seater sports car with the top down. The sun was shining, the wind was blowing and we were moving, how happy can you be.

Then there is always someone or something that wants to steal your happiness away. The traffic almost came to a stop about a dozen cars up from us. An old car with about six passengers had run out of petrol. Some silly man was sitting on top of the car with a sign that read 'Need petrol please help'. The people in the cars driving by were so mad at the broken-down car someone had thrown eggs at the sign, one had hit the silly man in the face, another got out of his car and kicked the old car's wheel. The driver then punched the wheel kicker.

It only goes to show you happiness is a fleeting moment. We soon stopped for petrol and tea. As we were parking, two women walked out of the cafe. We found a table by the window and we both watch them, never saying a word to each other. Their car made a left turn going north, and within one minute the car come flying back and squealed to a stop. Liz Michaels and Crewe came running in. "We were driving for about twenty seconds then we both looked at each another and said, 'That was Nat and Margo!'

"That was funny, we both saw you coming out of the cafe, found a table by the window, watched you drive off, a minute later flying back and never said a word to each other." We were so happy to see each other carrying on like schoolgirls that had been thrown out of knitting class for good.

"So," said Liz. "I presume we are all going to the cricket match."

"What sandwiches did you make?" said Margo.

"What do you mean sandwiches?" said Crewe.

"Mrs. B. said bring food to share and if you are a heavy drinker bring your own bottle. We hear half the village will be there and more, and she cannot cook for everyone."

"Well, you will have to give us half of yours," Crewe said.

"Half of what? We don't have any food and nobody knows we are coming. The story is," I said, "last week Susan, Harry, Mrs. B. and Max took the Hawkes kids to Hawkes Manor for their great grandparents to see them for the first time. Margo decided not to go as Harry's sister Terri has told the mother all about my new life with Margo. Harry said the mother and daughter would follow Margo and me everywhere hoping we will kiss and carry on and did I 'turn' because Max has found another to talk to 24/7. Susan is now mad with me because Harry's parents are upset, because we are not there. I was going home but was called in to work at five in the morning. On Thursday I received an e-mail from a good friend reminding me of one of biggest women's bashes held in London. Come over have dinner here with a group of friends then we would go to the bash. We never went as we were having such a good time with the group at the restaurant. That was Saturday night. Meanwhile, Max left a message on the phone telling us about the cricket match on Monday, and he may be too busy to talk to me from now until after the match. He said that we should be here with family. Well it was Harry that put Margo off from going in the first place. All this time Max and family thought we are in New York. Nobody knows we are coming and we do not want to arrive too early as I do not want to get roped in to the kitchen and serving food to half the village. So when you both get there and start your kitchen duty, please do not say you saw us."

"I have a better idea," said Liz. "We will all arrive together later with donuts." We all agreed. We turned into the manor driveway. Crewe stop got out of her car "My God.". "The whole village plus some are here! Look at the cars!"

We parked near the end and took the shortcut across the field.

"Oh my," Crewe said. "I had forgotten all about this path. We used to come and go and Mum never knew."

"Just a second Crewe, do Harry's parents and Terri know about you two?"

"I hope not. The times I went to see the Grannies, Liz was working on the show, so I never said anything. This will keep Granny alive another twenty years just thinking about it. Two in the family and I bet there are more, she will be telling Auntie Terri as they get out family records and bibles that have never seen the light of day before, checking if old family members had never married and making a list.

CHAPTER 44

Margo and I sat down on the sofa in a small sitting room off the kitchen. We could see Mrs. B., Susan, Max, Harry's mum and a few of the village people standing at the sink counters looking out of the window at the cricket match. The Hawkes kids were standing on top of one side of the counters watching. When Max made a noise at a missed ball, the kids also would make the same noise. I sat there staring at the back of Bradley's head. There's my boy. It took him two minutes to turn around and looked at us smiling. He then turned back, got himself down and slowly walked over trying not to make a sound. Now that took thinking at three years old. Then he ran into our arms.

"Mummacow, good."

The other two turned and started screaming.

"Stop it kids. Grandpa (Harry's dad) is going to hit the ball any minute now."

I put my finger to my lips so they would stop. Bradley went back to the counter and showed them how to get down. My God, I thought, the Hawkes kids could be kidnapped and not one adult would know. Max only looked around when the kids yelled, "Mummacow's here!"

At the moment, they all looked around to see us, Grandpa hit the ball out of the field.

Kisses and cuddles were in order, as they all decided Margo and I had brought Grandpa good luck. When it came to Harry's mum, we both expected her to run out of the kitchen.

"Come here and give us a cuddle," she said, and then looked at Margo saying, "and you too." Then Grandma did run out to find her daughter Terri no doubt. The sun was setting, people were leaving, the cricket match was over and as always when people have had good time, they said, "We will do it again next year", and we did.

Harry and I found part of a chocolate cake. Just as we were cutting it in half we heard, "Oh no Harry, that is ours."

"Oh no Mum, that will be your third piece of cake today, no more."

Grandma was telling Harry and me later that evening that Crewe introduced her to a friend that came with her to see the cricket match.

"She was a very beautiful woman and I am sure I have seen her somewhere before."

"Maybe she's plays Molly Rafferty on the telly."

"No," said Grandma, "and she is a friend of Crewe."

"Yes," said Harry, "They have lived together a couple of years, isn't that so Nat?" Good old Harry, dragging me into this.

"Crewe and Liz are living together."

"Why, surely Molly does not need the money to have to share a flat." Grandma's mouth was moving but she was unable to speak, her mind was racing trying to think. She looked at Harry, and he gave a couple of little nods. "Thank God you had Max, though your father and I thought he was a bit of a fruitcake."

CHAPTER 45

All of us New Yorkers thought we would stay on an extra week at Hawkes Manor. We had met Claire's new beau… "Hi, nice to meet you " exchanges… that kind of thing. He is coming for dinner Wednesday evening. Susan is all in 'tiswas' about him coming here. All she knows about him is that he is a doctor, a specialist, an anesthetist at the same hospital where Claire's patients who need hospital care are. He is thirty years old with dark hair and brown eyes. As we are a very tall family, he looks short at a little under six feet.

The four of us, Crewe, Liz, Margo and I, decided to stay on just to entertain the grannies and Terri while the rest of the family stayed on to watch us entertain. Harry was so pleased as he could see how happy his parents were with all the family together once more. Mrs. B. stayed most of the time with her sister but if we had special dinners or get-togethers, Mrs. B. would come to the Manor to help cook and eat.

"What is keeping you here Mum," asked Harry. "You and Dad can come over to the States, stay with us in New York for part of the year, then come back here when you want to. I know you and Terri are close, so she can come with you."

"Let us come over and see if we like New York and how we would live and take it from there Harry," said his mum. "Max was telling me that he and the black woman from California would like to marry in New York."

"He and the 'black woman'. Her name is Georgia, not 'black woman', Mum."

"And that has upset you Harry, because I called her black? I have lived in this village all my life and I have known maybe three or four black people. Do not… and I will say this to you only once …do not ever speak to me like this again. I asked Max what she is like. He told me, she a proud black woman, she is my black beauty and that's the way I see her because she will not let me see her any other way. Max only hopes that one day he can be as proud of himself as she is of herself, and by the way Harry, her nickname for Max is Pinkie Now run along Harry."

I will be glad when it's Thursday and the family dinner is over with, then Claire and her boyfriend can go home. Claire lives here where her medical practice is and I am sure Ray does too, just that Claire has forgotten to tell her parents. Now Ray is working long hours and does a little sleeping at the hospital. This sounds like a silly Claire story to me. If any doctor needs a good night sleep, it's an anesthetist. We are all going to be uptight in case Susan says the wrong thing to Claire and makes fun of her Ray as he was the first boy Claire brought home for dinner. She tells her mother, "There is a good reason Mum, because Ray does not believe me when I tell him how nutty you are."

The four of us, that is Liz, Crewe, Margo and I, our friendship was on solid ground again, about which we all were very happy. We took the Hawkes kids to the seaside. Grandpa still has the same van he had many years ago, he had put windows in it, and to this day I still remember as a child the trips in Grandpa's van. He had looked after it and it is just as safe as it had ever been. The color now is Daffodil yellow. We drove on country lanes, past old churches, and farmhouses. We stopped so the kids could see the cows, horses, and sheep that were all new to them. Alex, who loved anything with four legs, was jumping up and down with excitement.

"Now kids, if you scream they will run away."

Poor Alex, it just got too much for her when one horse came near the wire and stopped.

"Come here horse, come here!" she screamed. The horse took off. Alex cried and Jack tried to cuddle her. "No!" she said. Then Jack, who always knows the right thing to say and will in the future, said, "Maybe daddy get you a horse that will let you scream at it." "Yeah," said Alex, and stopped crying.

At last, we reached the sea. It was off-season and all you could see was the sea, the Irish Sea. The beach was a never-ending line of sand and stones, and not a soul in sight. The only kind of 'land water' the kids had seen was in Central Park. I think they were a little frightened and could not understand what they were seeing. On the way back, we stopped at a cafe for tea, scones and 'what have you's'.

I suddenly realized I consistently lie to my children, as I said to them "What does that say?" looking at the menu written on a blackboard outside the cafe. "Well it says any child or kid that screams while in the cafe will be made to leave to stand outside with no food." Liz walked over to the blackboard and started to read the menu. After reading, rereading and reading it again she asked, "Where does it say that?"

"Say what?" Margo asked.

"If your kids scream, they will be asked leave with no food and stand outside!"

Wednesday morning came and went, Wednesday afternoon arrived, then it was Wednesday evening and the whole family sat down together to eat. All was going well until after the main course when Ray had a phone call. There was an emergency operation and he had to leave for the hospital.

Claire began tapping her glass with a spoon. It took a few minutes before everyone realized she had something to say and the table went silent as Claire stood up.

"I believe you all have met Ray. I love everything about this man. There is nothing I do not love about him. He is good to his parents, he is good to me, he is just a good man and I have never been this happy. He wants us to marry, now, today and have babies. And this 'now', I cannot do without much needed help and advice from my mum and family."

Good God I went in to shock as never, ever have I heard Claire talk about or show her feelings, and now in front of the whole family. I looked at Crewe who had put her hands to her face. Then I looked at Jennie. She had her head on Mick's shoulder, holding the baby with one arm and wiping a tear from her cheek with the other.

Claire continued, "My childhood is so different from his. He is an only child and from the day he was born, he was programmed to be a doctor. Why, because his father is a doctor, his grandfather was a doctor and two uncles were doctors. A regular MD was not good enough Ray had to specialize. Ray as a child growing up was given goals to meet and schedules to keep. He always felt his parents loved him. Ray sees nothing wrong with the way he was brought up and it worked for him. But, you see that's not the way I grew up. I had a brother and sisters and we were given all the freedom in the world to be whoever we wanted to be. I did not have to carry all my parents' dreams for them on my shoulders. If one of as failed we had siblings to stand in our place and share the load. Now when I look back, I realize we had parents who asked so little of us and gave love unconditionally. They never took the love away when we were bad, which I remember was all the time. We were so naughty and stupid, I am now having to go for cooking lessons because I knew it all and would not let dear Mrs. B. show me how to cook. I had no idea how to boil an egg, with or without water. I am scared. I am not a goody two shoes like Ray, I am a Hawkes and proud to be. I have a picture of our future with children where Ray will be walking out the door with his suitcase leaving me now with father-less children. I worry my husband will yell, "you never told me they were this nuts, and you never told me you were nuttier then the rest of your family." Maybe I am the nuttiest of us all. For me, my children with my genes, I would see this like being in prison and I would be made to be a guard. So, the way I see it and this is where I need advice should we wait a couple of years with exposing Ray to the utter mad-ness of our family? I know one should not speak for others but in this case, I will say my sisters and I had a wonderful childhood. The only thing is Mum, Dad and Mrs. B. did not know what a great time we were having. We know now what we did not know then, how much we loved our mother and how safe she made us feel. When you have three minds that think the same thoughts at the same time, we thought we knew it all back then.

Just a few more words, I would love to thank Max and Nat for lov-ing our mother so much and giving her the joy of motherhood as we girls were nothing but trouble from day one. Our Dad was away for a long time in a war we knew nothing about and came home a shell of man. It was our little brother, Max, that saw our mum through these dark days. It was Nat that loved our father so much and needed him. Her love gave him the reason to get well and return to all of us. The umbrella of love that covered us all was our Mrs. B. Who allowed us to live with her all these years?"

The sobbing and crying had now been replaced by laughter, banging the table with our hands cheering and calling out I love you Claire. My Susan sat at the table crying "I am so happy!"

CHAPTER 46

Every day I phoned my assistant Sally at our new office in the condo to see how things were going. Due to my family's needs, working for General Big Boy and any other commitments at this moment is more than I hope to accomplish.

Sally will be graduating soon due to her high I. Q. and soon to be a lawyer. She still had a lot to learn on the job. Because she works for me and I am a Government Agent with secrets, Sally has to go off to some silly boot camp to be an agent too. Not only is she very bright and knows it she also thinks she is queen bee with her government badge.

General Big Boy is now telling me I can only work for him and will not let me work for anyone else within the government or elsewhere, as it is against the Big Boy Law-act 27.

"What is against the law General Big Boy?" I asked, smiling at him, daring him to tell me another silly story.

"Nat, I know where you are going and what you hope to be. I hope I am still around to see it happen. I am going to retire in a few years stay with me until then. You may have the money but I have the connections with people that may help you in the future and I also know people coming up in the world. When I go down to Washington sometimes, you can come with me and for that trip when I need you, I need you at that moment 100 %. You will have a lot of freedom as long as your assistant is your stand-in and knows how to get a hold of you in seconds. Of course, there will be other things to sort out, we must keep Sally busy or we will lose her due to boredom. What are a few years? Five at the most, it's an offer you would be foolish to turn down. For all we know we may be busy most of the time, if not then you have time for the kids."

Both Sally and I agreed the opportunities would be fabulous with a two-year review. My family agreed that the Hawkes kids would be cared for which goes without saying. What I did tell General Big Boy was that I am prepared to teach, show, and tell all that my job entails to Sally. "I have a great amount of faith in her and she is so bright, so there will be no need to send her extra work like the crosswords you cannot do and the words you cannot spell."

"Thank you, I will remember that."

That morning, on the Thursday, Sally phoned me saying, 'There is big trouble Nat. You have one hour to be ready and a helicopter will pick you up at Hawkes Manor, and fly you to Blackpool Airport. There, a jet will bring you to JFK where you will be met. See you then Nat."

I woke Margo up. "Help me pack. I have to go back. There is a helicopter landing here and flying me to Blackpool airport, where there is a jet waiting for me to take me back home to see Big Boy."

"Good God Nat, a helicopter and jet coming for just you. Your head is going to get so fat you will not be able to wear the cap of the chief of armed forces, and there will be no talking to you."

"Do you think it will upset the kids to see me flying off in the big bird?"

"Yes," said Margo. We said our goodbyes. Margo went to tell the family who were mostly still in bed. It was still early but I wanted to say goodbye to my children. All three were fast asleep. I could not wake them so I gave all three each a kiss and left. The family were all waiting to say goodbye.

"Susan, tell the kids that I had to go back to clean the house because we left it in such a mess."

CHAPTER 47

General Big Boy stood at the door, as Sally and I were leaving. He came to attention and saluted us both, which we saw as an honor.

"Good day, Sir."

I stood at the front door of my home knowing my family was just behind the door. I was nearly crying with happiness as it had been almost two weeks since I boarded the jet that flew me to an international, internet crisis of monumental proportions.

I rang the doorbell, Margo opened it.

"Welcome home baby."

I heard Max yelling. "She's home, it's Nat, she's home!"

Then I heard the screaming as the three kids came running to the front door. I had to sit down on the floor while the kids ran around me jumping on me and kissing me. Alex stood still all of a sudden. "Me missed you Mummacow."

Everybody was talking at once. I was so pleased to hear their voices but I did not understand one word that was said.

I said, "I need coffee, a bath, and sleep. Then I will listen to you all day tomorrow." All three kids were trying to sit on my lap together. Then they would fight because one of them would push another off.

"Stop it kids," Margo spoke, looking at them with the evil eye. What made me laugh, the kids stopped fighting and said nothing. "I have come up with good idea. Jack, Bradley, Alex and I will go upstairs with Mummacow. You three can wash Mummacow in the bathtub, put her in bed and sit with her for five minutes then she goes to sleep, ok kids?

"Yes! Yes!"

I started to say I was not too keen on this when Margo stopped me. "You may not like it but they will, for a few minutes, so you can all play together and wash if only so they can feel and touch their mother. Let them help you get into bed, sit and lay with you for a few minutes while you fall off to sleep. The pictures in their minds will change, as they will know you are safe instead of worrying if you will find your way back from England. They think you must be lost there."

Half an hour later Margo was back downstairs. "All are fast asleep" said Margo, Nat has no room to move as Alex has to somehow managed get right in the bed next to Nat and the boys are lying on the bed with their hands touching her legs. I think

subconsciously they are holding on so she will not run away. Anyway, it makes a beautiful picture I took a few shots with my camera. Of course, Max cried, and why not, it was picture in a million. I made copies for the rest of the family."

"It's funny you know," said Susan, Nat has not spent 24/7 with the kids and yet all three know they belong to her, and they are here because she, Nat, is the leader of the pack. Whoever their mother loves, they love because the 'whoever' loves their mother. Every time Nat goes away, with your help my dear Margo, they will be ok. However, I have a feeling she will be talking to General Big Boy that she, Natasha, will be running the show from now on.

I woke early the next morning, well at nine a.m. which was early, if anyone had been with me in the night, they had long gone. I phoned General Bigboy's office. "Hi Kathy, it's Nat Bennett, is he in yet?"

What do you think? No, he was here very late last night. I did not leave until after nine p.m. and I could hear him singing your praises."

"We'll wait until I tell him what he does not want to know."

"He already knows that."

"How do you know that?"

Oh, I cannot tell you that don't be silly."

"Please tell me or I will come over there now and make you tell me."

"And how will you do that Nat?"

"Well, I walked right into that. I have my ways."

"I bet you do," she laughed. "Ok, he was telling some high-up on the phone and I quote 'It's alright you saying that. She has three kids, triplets, the kids' father is still around and the girlfriend and they all want a piece of her. Nat does not care about that. You do not know who she is, do you. Bennett Foundation, Bennett Ltd. (UK) Bennett Company, Bennett Holding, the list goes on and on, and she is the only Bennett. Sir, you have every right to go over my head if you do she will walk, good night Sir.'

"Oh," I said,"This is fun. Ok, does he have any appointments today? Good. We will be there at two p.m. will you tell him Kathy, please."

"Yes. Nat, please don't mention what I said about what he said on the phone."

"I am very good with secrets, are you?"

"Yes."

Margo, Max, the kids and I arrived at General Big Boy's office at two p.m. to be greeted by Kathy the General's ' what have you', who was sitting there with her month open. "Kathy, I would like you to meet our children, Max Hawkes, their father and Margo Roth, my partner, Kathy's mouth began to close trying to form words that only could turn into laughter. The buzzer buzzed. "Yes, Sir," said Kathy, trying to maintain some composure. We are here to see General Big Boy."

"Is Nat here yet?"

"Yes."

"Well, stop talking to each other and send her in."

Oh, this is going to be such fun. Kathy opened the door to the General's office and looked at Big Boy's face, as the family marched in. Her laughter was covered by pretending to cough.

"Good afternoon General, these are our children, Max Hawkes, their father and Margo Roth my partner."

General Big Boy sat silent for a minute. "What are you up to Nat?"

"You and I know it's very hard to change the game play half way through."

"It was nobody's fault, it just happened that way. I left the children in a very dramatic way, and I was not able to say goodbye, as they were asleep. I was gone for two weeks. They were worried that I was still in England, lost. They lost weight, which upset their father, my partner and their grandparents etc. What I am trying to say General, two weeks is too long for me to be away. I am their mummacow, they know it, and I am the most important person in their world at the moment. As they grow they may need their father more, but the stage these children are at, their needs are for the mother and thank God they are very close to my partner. General, I know now what I didn't know when we last spoke. You may think I am nutty and mad for thinking it, but I see the kids as triplets. They do not. To them we are a pack of four as they feel they are here to look after me not the other way around. Why? Maybe when I was carrying them they felt the pain of my loss as a child and the deep sadness I carried. Anyway, that's the way I see it. I said I would work two years, review it, then work with you if all is ok until you retired all told five years. Well the review is a little early."

Would you excuse us please?" I said, looking at Margo and Max. "I will be out in a few minutes." I sat back down.

Big Boy said, "When should I leave Nat? Or shall we just change chairs for now? Four adults, three children and you are the only one that knows what is going on."

"Well now, you will. I believe in time that I can set up a program so that when we are in crisis mode I can be in my office, at home doing what I would do if I were at work here. It would be a gradual progress, at the beginning 75%. There will be two copies of the program that will be impossible to copy, yours and mine. It will be costly, new rewiring of my office, top-of-the-line CPU and programmers etc., it's a lot of work if it works, you will be the golden boy. As for now, in a crisis I will stay away from home only one night, maybe two at the most. I will come into work every day until I feel it's ok not to. Just think what this will do for the US. It could knock us out of the ball game and we can play ball all on our own."

"You are nuts Nat, but that is often the case. The cleverer you are, the crazier you are. Barring a new crisis, I will get back to you."

"Am I being dismissed Sir?"

"Natasha, I would never make the mistake of dismissing you."

"Ok, let's go. Bye, Kathy."

"Bye, Nat. Bye family," Kathy called out.

As we made our way to the elevator, Max remarked, "What a nice woman that Kathy is."

"Yes, very friendly," said Margo.

"Yes, I like her," I said.

"Oh, should I feel a little jealous?" Margo said. "Well, maybe more than a little jealous?"

"Ouch, that hurt Margo."

"It was meant to," laughing as we caught up with Max and the kids.

CHAPTER 48

Just as we got into the cab to come home from meeting with General Big Boy, Susan phoned. "Where the hell are you? We had no idea that two thirds of the family had left for the day, leaving Mrs. B. and I to cope. No shopping had been done so I had to run to the market because Mrs. B. has to have market food only."

"Susan, I asked Max to tell you where we were going early this morning. I had to tell General Big Boy no more ' just two weeks' and that I planned to work from my office. I am sorry. Would you like me to hit Max for you or shall we wait until he gets home and you can beat him up."

"Don't be so silly, Nat. You hit him."

"We will be there in twenty minutes."

"You never told me to say anything to Mum about going to see the General," said Max. "Nat, you just lied."

"Don't you be so silly. I was not going to let her hit me Max." I said.

Before we left to see General Big Boy, I received an e-mail from Ed Bigwig. He would like to see all the family that is moving to the beautiful condo this coming Friday at three p.m. in the room with a view. Betty and her gang were coming for a big family dinner tonight. I wonder if Betty or the girls would look after the Hawkes' kids while Ed is here? It must be about the condo and 'business' does not want the kids running around, screaming.

"Where has all the wine gone?" Susan called out to anyone that could hear.

"Max, Max… did Harry drank it all?"

"Harry did you drink all those bottles of wine?"

"All those bottles of wine, what wine Susan?" asked Harry.

"The wine that you bought not too long ago, two dozen bottles."

"Susan, that was a few months ago and the way you drink and the size of this family it does not last long."

"Well Harry, you and Max better go and buy some more so I will have more to drink. Have you seen, Betty? The way she knocks them back, she puts me to shame."

"I am going to tell her just what you said Susan."

Harry and Max just got back when Betty and her gang arrived.

Harry asked Betty, "Whatcha got there?"

"Couple bottles of wine," said Betty.

"What happened, did Susan speak to you about how much wine you knock back when you were here?" Harry asked.

"How would she know, when I am still knocking them back, Susan is laid out flat on the floor."

Of course, nobody finds this funnier than Margo. The jokes and funnies were just flying over dinner that night.

"Betty where is your husband Ray?" asked Mrs. B.

"He is at home."

"What the hell is he doing there," said Susan. "Why is he not here?"

"Oh. No... no...no. it's too soon, he has just moved back home. If I bring him here every time I come before you know it, he will be dropping by here all the time on his own and soon he will be running the show instead of me."

Betty decided to take her grandchildren back to her place Friday so her children could show all their toys to the Hawkes kids. Going to England and flying on a plane was nothing compared to all the toys that were at their grandmother's house for her own children to play with.

Alex was quite happy playing with the toys, until she saw a real live cat sitting in the doorway.

Alex screamed with sheer joy and the cat took off with Alex following in hot pursuit. Every now and then, you could hear Alex calling "Cat come here, cat, where are you?" Betty told Alex if she comes back and plays with the toys he would come to see her.

"Yeah," Alex said sitting down. "Cat a boy?" she asked.

"Yes," said Betty. His name is Marguerite."

The cat came back.

"Hello."

"Hi, it's me, how are you doing Betty?" I asked.

"Oh, Nat. Alex is crying and laughing with happiness, the cat has let Alex touch him."

"Oh, no, Betty I did not know you had a cat and you let Alex touch him? I might as well kiss Alex goodbye, she will never leave your house now. She thinks her father is going to buy her horse to live here because she saw one in England. Alex screamed at it "Come here horse. "It soon took off and she cried. Jack told her Max will buy her a horse to scream at. She just loves animals, bugs, snakes, rodents and birds, and she so wants a cat. Your life is over now she knows what buttons to press on the phone. She will phone you and bug you all day long about the cat. Mrs. B. will not let Alex have one until she is older."

"What the hell has she got to do with it?" Betty said.

"Because, she will be the one looking after it."

"Now what am I going to do," said Betty.

"I don't know, but Ed is here so I have to go, bye Betty."

"I will be back in a minute Peppy."

"Ok Mum."

"Come on put the toys away, now please, we are going over to Nat's."

"NO!" said Alex.

The doorbell rang. It was Gladys from next door.

"Hi Betty, I have come for my cat. Where is he? Marguerite where are you? There he is, come to Mama baby." Gladys picks up the cat and starts to walk out the door. "NO!" screams Alex. "Grandma's cat."

"No dear it's my cat. Grandma, your grandma was only looking after him for the day while we all pack. The family and the cat are going away on holiday."

"Thank you, Gladys," Betty said as she was pushing Gladys and the cat out of the door, whispering, "after we have gone put him in the back door, you have a key right? Thank you."

"OK, Betty."

"Come here Alex, don't cry. Cat is going on holiday he will be happy with his own family."

"Will you call a cab Peppy? I will not drive in case Susan forces a drink down me."

When Alex tries to butter me up or talk business, my name is Mummacow.

"Mummacow," she said in such a sweet voice, "Grandma next-door woman has a cat, it goes on holiday. Grandma's sad, she wants cat for her now."

Well, well, well, looks like Betty told Alex it is her neighbor Gladys's cat. Now Betty 2 (Alex) at three years has come up with a story to beat Betty's first story. I am to get Betty a cat because Grandma is so lonely and sad.

"I will live with Grandma and help look after cat," said Alex smiling and kissing my hand.

"Ok Alex, I am not buying Grandma a cat. She is far too old and you are not moving in with her, because Grandma once again is far too old to look after you all the time."

Betty did not smile but Susan laughed her head at what I said to Alex. "By the time Alex is six, Betty, she will run rings around you and your stories."

"Guess what Betty, we are moving in one month. Ed said get out there and start buying furniture. We all went over there this afternoon it is so big. Margo is going to do most of the decor downstairs in the family area, with your help. Margo does not think my decorating skills are any good. Please suggest to Margo that she ask Mrs. B. what she needs to make the kitchen comfortable for her."

"Good thinking, Nat. What are you going to do about this condo?" asked Betty.

"Not sure. Leave the furniture here and sell maybe, but Margo said as soon as the 'to be' buyers see the furniture they will run out the door screaming. Anyway, it is not a worry at the moment."

"Well, when you think about it and would like to sell, let me know."

"Ok, Betty. Hey, what are you saying Betty?"

"You heard Nat."

"Are you thinking of buying? If it is with the furniture it will be more money you know, Betty."

"No Natasha. You will have to arrange for Goodwill to come and get it. I am kidding you, dear there is nothing wrong with it; Margo has different taste from us. If I were you, ask Margo to show you what she is buying first. I am going to help her but I cannot watch everything she buys."

"Has she ever told you she is colorblind?"

"No, she has not Betty and I hope you are joking! "

"The first time she came to the Hamptons I asked her about something to do with colors in the dress I was thinking of wearing the night of the party. The colors she saw were a lot different from what I could see, so I asked if she was color blind, she went all red in the face and said, yes."

"Silly me. Well thank God you told me."

"If I may ask, and I know it's none of my business, I hope you are not carrying the load for the new condo."

I gently steered my mother into the room with a view and we sat in a corner by the window.

"No, I am not; next door has been registered as three separate apartments all under Margo and my names. The condo maintenance, utilities bills, taxes etc. Apartment two will be paid by Harry, Susan, and the same for Max's apartment Three, plus extra for food and house cleaning."

Extra for food and house cleaning, Betty screamed with laughter. "And you are going to run around asking them how many cups of tea and cakes and dinners they have eaten this month."

"No, Mrs. B. is," I said.

"Mrs. B., Mrs. B. is," now Betty is nearly cracking up with laughter. "What is she going to do, give them a piece cake with the amount written on a check under the plate? Oh Nat, I cannot sit here any longer with you, you have to be nuttiest of them all. Even Susan would not think to do this."

As soon as Betty stood up to leave, Margo walks in to the room with a view. When Betty saw Margo, she, for some reason started laughing some more and had to sit back down again.

"Why is Betty laughing like that Nat?" Margo asked.

"She has heard half a story and made up the other half and then is telling me I am the nuttiest of them all, including Susan."

"Let me tell Margo the story. Nat is going to charge Susan and Harry etc. and Max and family, extra for food downstairs in the family area next door. So when homemade cake is served by Mrs. B., under the plate will be a bill with the amount written on it."

"Oh, come on Nat, that's too much. Why she is doing that, is Mrs. B. also going to charge Betty and her family too! "Oh! I never thought of that, I will ask Mrs. B. what she thinks. as she is the boss. Also, if Mrs. B. says Alex is too young to have a cat, she is too young." What if I bring my own cake will Mrs. B. charge me for service?" You ask her Betty, what's the point of having Mrs. B. as the boss, so stop asking me all these silly questions."

Both Margo and Betty are looking at each other now. Margo is beginning to show her teeth and I know both will be laughing their heads off any second now.

"Now listen to me Betty, a few months ago Harry told me to get a housekeeper when I was offered a good job at Homeland and Mrs. B. is the right ticket. When the girls were little Mrs. B. ran our house for years, we never worry about hiring, paying wages looking after the accounts. She did everything. She is not as young as she was but she does not have to be. She will run everything for you if you pay her well and her give a big budget to work with.

Betty, before you laugh and ask is Mrs. B. sleeping in the kitchen? She is not, she has her own apartment next to us, which Ed Bigwig made separate from us and the kids, and she pays nothing and gets free cake." Then I stuck my tongue out at Betty.

"You are so my daughter Nat. Letting me think I am winning all along, then at the end going in for the kill." Betty starts walking out of the room with a view. "Come on girls, let's find Susan so we can have a good laugh."

CHAPTER 49

Susan and Mrs. B., we're having none of Margo and Betty being the only ones to furnish the downstairs family area. The four of them would sit at one computer fighting over which store and what floor they would go to on-line. Should all the walls be the same color? What color and feel should the carpet have on the two sets of stairs from the very top near Susan and Harry's apartment to the bottom family room? The stairs were made with the children's safety in mind. For them the carpeting, size of steps and landing spots if a child should fall had to be planned while still looking like they fit in with the rest of the decor. Elevators were installed on either side of the stairs; with buttons placed too high for the children to press at their age.

Georgia came, stayed a few weeks, so she and Max could get their apartment ready, and to check out the schools for Georgia's kids. Now, it was somewhere to put them until they all were settled in their new home, which is a far cry from California.

We were all very ready to move in, when Ed Bigwig said sorry, another four to five weeks are needed to finish everything. I had been working on my Homeland project so it didn't bother me, but the family members were at a loss as what to do with themselves. A few hours after the family heard the unhappy news; I was on the phone telling Betty all the family had fallen apart.

"Really, Betty said, "and I have just the ticket to fix that. Ray, that's my husband…"

"What a silly thing to say Betty. I know Ray is your husband. "

"Well, my husband is out in California opening up my house; please note I said my house. Maybe in the middle of the week we all could fly out to sunny California for a few weeks."

"This not a joke is it Betty? Because if I tell Susan and you are kidding it will kill her, and who is 'we'."

"Well, my tribe, your kids, Margo, Susan, Harry, Max, Mrs. B, and your friend Sally could come. This is up to you, if you wanted to ask the girls plus partners, all three. Would you be ok with that Nat?"

"Why wouldn't I Betty!"

"No reason Lamb Chops. I will phone you back, ok?"

Ok how did she know!

"Hi Max," I said as he was walking out the front door. Betty wants us, the family, to all go out to California next week for a few weeks. Are you interested?"

"Are you joking? This better not be one of your stories, Nat."

"I was just on the phone with Betty. Her husband Ray is in California, opening up her house. Betty would like all us to go out together next week, and it was up to us if we wanted the girls and partners to come too."

Well forget that Nat."

"I agree Max. It's too much and the truth be told, I will end up with all the responsibility; they will be coming in to N.Y. on different flights. Where will they sleep? The baby will cry all the time and they will bring the mother-in-law."

"That's it. They are not coming and mum's the word," said Max.

Max ran back to the room with a view and started doing cartwheels in front of the family, with the kids screaming. "We are going to California next week," he was singing, out of breath. If Susan was dozing off, she was not now.

"Who's going to California?"

"We are."

"Who's 'we'?" said Susan, getting annoyed with Max.

"Nat, Margo, Mrs. B., Harry, you Susan, Sally, the kids and Betty's tribe are all invited."

The mood in the room with a view changed from a rainy night to a sunny day.

I e-mailed General Big Boy to tell him where Sally and I would be for the next couple of weeks starting the following Wednesday, California. Enclosed was a close up and aerial view of the area and a red mark where we would be staying, also the address.

'General, this is a courtesy e-mail, please do not send helicopters for us as this is a horse farm and Rome must be burning before contact is made.'

Also, I phoned Nicky, my university roommate, to cancel our lunch date until after we got back and she then could come of over any time to help with the move. If not, we would see each other at the open house party. I asked about David.

"He is a new man now, thanks to you; he loves his job at Fag, Fag and Fag."

"I have no idea what you are talking about Nicky, David got the job on his own merit and I hope you have not said anything differently to him."

"No, thank you. Bye Nat."

We had the best of all times. We went in to LA and did sightseeing along the coast. As Susan, Harry and Margo had not been to California before. Mostly it was lying around the pool, or lying around Dennis and Nancy's pool, visiting, Betty and Ray's friends in their big ranch style homes, eating and drinking. It was like one big continuous party and we loved every minute of it. When we arrived, as they had before the horses ran along beside the fence trying keep up with the cars. We were all thankful Alex was fast asleep. As more horses began to join the chase, Alex suddenly awoke, she looked, she screamed and she yelled, "Max, Max!" She had decided about a month ago only babies called their daddies, 'daddy', so for now it was 'Max'."

"You buy two horse now dear Max."

This was the first time Bradley, Jack and Alex had seen a swimming pool. The end close to the house was little kid friendly as it was built when Betty's kids were small. Brad and Jack loved everything about playing in the pool. Alex was ok with it, but what she loved most was her brown bag full of cut up carrots for the horses.

Betty was adamant that all three kids learn to swim now. Each Hawkes kid, if in the adult side of the pool, had to have an adult with them in the pool and not her children. Betty's children could teach the kids to swim, but they must have an adult with them. She had seen or heard of too many near drownings because the responsibility of a small child was given to a preteen or a teenager who was not trained to be a lifeguard. Usually, what goes along with private swimming pool is family, friends, food and booze, and it is asking too much for of a teenager to give 100% attention to watching little kids in the water.

Max and Georgia went away for two days and came back married.

"Thank God," said Susan, "as I think it would have been too much for me and for others too, to have the moving, the wedding, and then a big open house party all within weeks of each other."

I think we all agreed on that. We were very happy for Max and Georgia and they were pleased that we were ok with them going off on their own and marrying. When it was time to leave, we were a little sad but we had a lot to look forward to.

Betty and her tribe also returned with us. Her kids loved California, but they were New Yorkers and missed their friends and all that was going on.

I was so glad Sally came with us. The third day after our arrival we were invited to good friends of Betty and Ray. Their son took a shine to Sally and they spent most of their time together. Sally's old boyfriend had long gone. Dennis and Harry spent a few good evenings and weekends playing golf. They really appeared to enjoy one another. Everyone we met we invited to the open house as that is what happens when you meet new friends, at the best of times, on holidays. You hate to leave them so you make plans to see each other again, even if it's three thousand miles away in New York.

Within six weeks of our return home, we had all moved in to our home and settled in. At the moment, the Hawkes kids did not mind being in separate rooms as we had decided on bunk beds for future sleepovers with new friends. Georgia, Max and Harry had already returned to get her children and her parents who had never been to the east coast. The truth is Harry had gone to play golf with Dennis, his new best friend and for years to come. Dennis and Harry would be the best of friends.

It was time for the Open House. People started arriving about eight thirty. The Tongue and Cheek Restaurant catered the party along with Mrs. B.'s now famous apple pie. Later, Margo told me such a funny tale about Mrs. B's new friend, the Restaurant owner, Eric. He whispered to Margo that evening he was forever in her debt for when she chose the Tongue and Cheek Restaurant that few had heard of to cater a dinner for our family, and now this. He said to her if you ever need of a job, you just call him!

Well, well, well, look who just walked in, Sally hand in hand with the young man from California, the son of friends of Betty and Ray. Sally saw me and came running over.

"I am so happy Nat and I owe you so much, just look at him standing over there waiting for me. You are not to worry I already told him I am a New Yorker and that California is very nice but I am going places with you Nat and New York are my home "

"I love you Nat and we will always be best friends along with half of New York." Sally turned to wave her California boy over, where was he? He was dancing with a woman, with another woman, and boy was Sally dancing too, with handbag swinging right over to him. Well it turned out the woman was Margo, she had asked him to dance.

Oh, look there is Margo waving her hand at me. The trouble with Margo is every time we go to a big event she has to tell me every bit of gossip she hears then and there. Not like me who saves all the gossip up that I hear in the course of the evening and then tell her later on.

Peppy and JC shared the time needed to look after the kids. There was plenty of food, drinks, and a band playing all kinds of music for dancing. Earlier in the day a company that rents out and installs dance floors for parties, special occasions and ' what have you' laid down a floor on part of the living room and extended outside onto the patio. Armchairs, small tables with chairs were placed around the dance floor made to look like a café. People love to watch others dancing to old swing, jive music and old-time rock and roll. Margo was still waving at me, no she was not, she was pointing to the band. Up on the stage was a very handsome young man with a black bowtie and suit. It was my Fadil. Ladies and Gentlemen, I would like to introduce to you to my friend Riccardo and his dance partner Lucy who will show you what Latin dancing is. Fadil introduced each dance and told the history as they were well known in the old country for their rendition of Latin music and dance.

Riccardo and Lucy danced the Tango, Samba, Rumba. Next Fadil stepped down from the stage and walked over to were Liz was standing, already knowing Liz was a very good dancer. He asked her to dance.

"I can't dance like that " Liz said.

"No but I can." Riccardo and Lucy joined Fadil and Liz on the dance floor. My God I never know Liz could dance like that, next the Mambo followed by the Charleston then my all-time fav old time rock n roll. Before each dance Fadil would show Liz the steps to the next dance. The house came down, people just went wild. Never have I felt, heard or known the passion of the art of the dance as I, as we all saw that night. Our open house was Manhattan society's news for the next few days.

Later Margo and I sat in the room with a view #2, watching the night sky turning into day. I turned to look at Margo.

"Please do not look at me Natasha."

"But why? WE HAVE ONLY JUST BEGUN."

"Because I need to rest before you tell me, we are going where no woman has gone before."

The End

Cc Sumner

P S. Well dear readers I hope you have enjoyed reading about some of the stories of my family. At this writing, Margo and I are in Greece at a beach hotel waiting for our seafood lunch, enjoying our gin and tonics. This was Margo's idea. She gave me an airline ticket the day after the open house announcing we would be leaving in two days. "Max already knows, the kids will stay with him. We can Skype with the kids every day from the hotel. The rest of the family may or may not go away for a few days."

"Oh No, Margo I can't leave in two days, maybe later on we can get away but not now.". "Natasha, I am leaving for a two-week holiday in two days with you or without you, I need a rest and so do you. If I go alone when I get back I will not be visiting, you at the mental hospital because that's where you will be. Wondering each day that I am away what I am doing and whom am I doing it with!"

She just stood there smiling, no, grinning at me. Max was right she is the boss.

Love Nat xxx.